A BIASED JUDGEMENT

The Sherlock Holmes Diaries: 1897

by

Geri Schear

© Copyright 2014
Geri Schear

The right of Geri Schear to be identified as the author of this work has been asserted by them in accordance with the Copyright, Designs and Patents Act 1998.

All rights reserved. No reproduction, copy or transmission of this publication may be made without express prior written permission. No paragraph of this publication may be reproduced, copied or transmitted except with express prior written permission or in accordance with the provisions of the Copyright Act 1956 (as amended). Any person who commits any unauthorised act in relation to this publication may be liable to criminal prosecution and civil claims for damage.

All characters appearing in this work are fictitious or used fictitiously. Except for certain historical personages, any resemblance to real persons, living or dead, is purely coincidental. The opinions expressed herein are those of the authors and not of MX Publishing.

Paperback ISBN 9781780926742
ePub ISBN 978-1-78092-675-9
PDF ISBN 978-1-78092-676-6

Published in the UK by MX Publishing
335 Princess Park Manor, Royal Drive,
London, N11 3GX
www.mxpublishing.co.uk
Cover design by www.staunch.com

Love is an emotional thing, and whatever is emotional is opposed to that true cold reason which I place above all things. I should never marry myself, lest I bias my judgment.

(Sherlock Holmes: The Sign of Four)

A BIASED JUDGEMENT

PROLOGUE

For his one hundred and tenth birthday, Lucy gave John a cardigan and his family legacy. The cardigan took six months of knitting, swearing and dropped stitches. The legacy took eighty-four minutes.

"Arthur wants us to come to Sussex," John said one day over breakfast.

"For your birthday?" Lucy said. "What a good idea. I'd love to see the cottage."

John made a face. "It's ancient. Dull. Miles from anywhere."

"You mean it isn't London."

"Well, it isn't."

As she handed him his pills and checked his pulse, Lucy said, "Not to put too fine a point on it, but how many more annual visits do you think you'll be able to make down there? Ten? Twenty?"

He laughed and patted her hand. "Oh you are good for me, Luce. Best idea I ever had was hiring you."

So they went to Sussex.

By the time they pulled up outside the cottage it was already dark and she could see nothing of the Downs. The air tasted of sea and promised snow.

They were all there. John's brother, Arthur, one hundred and eight year's old and still walking two miles a day. Harry, John's son, who did something hush-hush for the government but who seemed too jolly to be a spy or a bureaucrat. And John's grandson, Jack. Dear Jack. Newly home from Afghanistan and the camera still attached to him like a papoose.

"Lucy," Harry said, kissing her cheek. "Thank you for persuading my dad to come."

"And thank you for driving," Jack said. "I would have been happy to pick you up, but we thought Gramps would prefer it this way."

"I did," John said. He shook his head at Lucy in a long-suffering manner, and she laughed. He refused the wheelchair and the cane, but readily took her proffered arm. They slowly climbed the haphazard steps and went into the cottage. The sitting room was small but cosy. A generous fire burned in the hearth and the armchairs were soft and well-cushioned. Lucy stared at the pock-marked wooden beams that crossed the ceiling. "Are those bullet holes?" she said.

"Of course," Arthur said as if she'd asked if they'd have kippers for breakfast. "My father liked to use them for target practice. Alas, one day the report shattered a gift from Queen Victoria. Mother made him stop after that."

"Dinner will be at eight o'clock," Harry said, pouring tea. "You don't mind waiting?"

"Not at all," John said. "Well, Lucy. Does it measure up to all your expectations?"

"It's bigger than I expected," she said. "You hear 'cottage' and you think tiny."

"A family joke," Arthur said. "Elizabeth the First slept here, so did Walter Raleigh. Not at the same time."

"And Churchill," John added. "He was a friend of father's, you know. And he adored mother."

"Speaking of mother," Harry said. "We put you in 'Parliament', Lucy."

"I'm sorry, Parliament?"

"My mother's bedroom," John said.

Arthur said, "When John and I were boys, whenever there was a family disagreement or a major decision to be made, we'd discuss it in mother's bedchamber. Hence, 'Parliament'."

"Best room in the house, Lucy."

A BIASED JUDGEMENT

"I'll say," Jack said with a comically tragic sigh. "I've never been allowed to sleep there."

"I consider myself privileged," Lucy said.

"I have such fond memories of that room. Of mother and father..." John said, and fell suddenly silent.

Lucy squeezed his hand. "You okay?"

His smile was unconvincing. "There are so many things I want to know. We have the stories, of course, but it's not the same."

"Was your father really like that, the way he is in the books?"

"Oh no," Arthur said. "He was much worse."

"And better." John added, laughing.

"Tell us about him," Jack said. "Like, how did he end up married? Come on, Gramps. I want a story."

"I honestly don't know," John said. "Every time I asked, Mother said I was too young for such a lurid tale - her idea of a joke, I have no doubt - and that she'd tell me one day. That story, all their stories, were to be our legacy, you see. Mine and Arthur's. Only as with so much else about my father, it was all shrouded in mystery."

"It was all going to be told us one day but it never happened," Arthur said. "All we got was a cryptic hint from father that the owls were guarding the tales."

"Owls?" Lucy said. "What owls?"

"Well, if we knew that we wouldn't be sat here seventy years later still wondering. Silly beggar took the truth to the grave."

"He was mourning our mother," John said. "I wish you could have known him, Lucy. You'd have liked him. Women did, for some reason. Does that surprise you? Of all of us, Jack is the most like him. They look so much alike: that strong profile and especially the hands."

"He'd be very proud of you," Harry said. "Of the work you're doing in Afghanistan."

This was all very sweet, but Lucy was dying to know about the owls.

"I'm afraid we know no more, Luce," John said. "Arthur and I searched from rafters to cellar looking for the rotten things."

"The nearest we came," Arthur said. "Was when we found a nest out by the stables. We came tearing in, all excited, and father laughed so hard he cried."

"Mother too," John said. "The pair of them, chortling right here in this room. I was, how old, about fourteen, so it must have been nineteen eighteen. Yes, the war had just ended and father wasn't long home from Europe."

"We begged them for years to tell us more, to give us another clue, but they wouldn't budge," Arthur said.

"So what happened?" Jack asked. Now and then he focused his camera and clicked the button.

"We forgot about it, more or less," Arthur said. "We grew up, went to university, went to war… I suppose it started to feel a bit like a fairy tale, a story to entertain us children when we got too noisy."

"I don't think it was, though. One of the very last things father said to me was, 'Don't forget to look for the owls, John.' That was at mother's funeral. He died the next day. I should like to know the answer before I pass on. I'd hate to be embarrassed when I face the old beggar in whatever afterlife there may be."

The sat by the fire and Harry poured brandy to toast John's big day. "A hundred and ten tomorrow," the birthday boy said. "I shall soon have to start behaving like a grown-up."

Lucy sipped her brandy and felt hypnotised by the fire's flickering and sparking. She was half-asleep when she heard herself say, "Isn't 'parliament' the collective noun for owls?"

One hour and twenty-four minutes later they found it.

Jack took photographs of every inch of his great-grandmother's bedroom and they all studied them closely on his laptop.

Lucy spotted the carving, very faded, at the back of the big, dark closet. "There," she cried. "That's an owl. No wonder you couldn't spot it. It's so faded. We'd never have seen it without Jack's pictures."

A BIASED JUDGEMENT

They went upstairs to Lucy's bedroom and, yes! There was a false wall at the back of the closet. They slid it back with some effort and found a room, some eight feet by ten. There was a trunk filled with photographs, cameras, a woman's shawl, letters in a man's hand to 'B'. But the real excitement was in the file cabinets. Hundreds of documents, accounts of the cases, the true stories. And at the bottom of the last drawer was the real gold: His journals.

They all sat in silence John on the big bed. Lucy and Jack on the floor. Arthur and Harry on the armchairs. Jack opened the first diary at random and began to read out loud.

A BIASED JUDGEMENT

1

22nd February, 1897

I am home at last in Baker Street. For the first time in more than a week I find myself well enough to take pen in hand, though my thoughts, I fear, lack the coherence Watson has convinced a gullible public is my unalterable habit. I have persuaded the good man to take advantage of the mild weather and go out for the evening. I believe the break will be beneficial to us both. Worthy soul though he is, his solicitude becomes trying after a time, and I am fatigued with continually pretending myself better than I feel.

Now I have a few hours alone I must try to put my thoughts in order. Alas, I can think of no better way of proceeding than to begin the tale at the beginning, or as near to it as I can get. It is at just such moments my respect for Watson is elevated. He has an extraordinary talent for making the recitation of events seem compelling and for knowing what details are extraneous to the narrative.

As an aide-memoire I shall review the weeks before my assault. Why is it so hard to think? Damnation! This state of addled wits must be how other people feel all the time, poor beggars.

Well, I recall that the beginning of the year was filled with a myriad of cases, great and small, primarily the latter. On February 15th I was consulted on the curious death of Sir Eustace Brackenstall at Abbey Grange which I resolved to my own satisfaction, at least. Then there was the mystery of the Appleby burglar, the bizarre matter of the screaming nun, and the recovery of Lady Stanthorpe's diamonds: For the most part, these were cases that seemed interesting initially but

A BIASED JUDGEMENT

whose explanations were ultimately revealed as banal. Too much of such trivia had made me restive and, I must own, quarrelsome.

So, just a week ago, recognising my need for the quiet of the syringe, from which I had only recently, and most reluctantly, been weaned, Watson suggested a walk in the 'good fresh air' might be more conducive to my health and my mood. I attempted to remonstrate. The weather that evening was hardly congenial and, more to the point, I resented being managed.

"Go to the Diogenes Club," my friend suggested. "Go visit your brother. Do please, Holmes. It's been some time since you saw him."

It was obvious remaining at home would not be tranquil and so I agreed.

I took a hansom from Baker Street and within a moment observed another vehicle follow. The cab maintained a discreet distance, however, and turned left towards Haymarket where we turned right towards the club. I paid the driver and stood on the steps of the Diogenes for a moment, but my shadow had vanished. It was bitterly cold and I did not linger. Did I feel uneasy? I cannot recall.

As is so often the case, despite my initial misgivings, I found the evening to be most enjoyable. Mycroft was pleased to see me and entertained me with his conversation and his table. We enjoyed an excellent bottle of claret and a dish of oysters. It was a welcome respite and I was forced to admit Watson's suggestion had been an excellent one.

It was almost midnight when I left and despite the inclement weather I decided to walk back to Baker Street. I had eaten and drunk rather more than is my custom and I determined the walk would clear my head. The entire length of Pall Mall was deserted as far as I could see, and I decided that anyone foolhardy enough to wait for me to finish my most excellent meal would be frozen solid by now.

As I have done so many times, I walked through St James's Square. The paths were deserted in respect of the hour and the frigid temperature. I was within sight of Duke of York Street when a bald, tattooed creature sprang out from behind the trees and leapt upon me.

I felt the knife before I saw it. It entered between my ribs and the sharp pain made me cry out. I hit hard with my cane and caught the villain just beneath the right jaw. He screamed and fell backwards. I gasped, trying to catch my breath. The man raised his blade to strike again. There was a sudden cry and a youth flung himself upon my assailant.

I sank to my knees and fought the pain and nausea. If the villain decided to fight, the boy would stand no chance. Fortunately, however, he turned and ran. My rescuer came at once to my side.

"Are you 'urt, Mr 'olmes?" he asked.

I shook my head and struggled to speak. "Knife—" I gasped. "Chest."

"I'll get you to 'ospital—"

"No," I said. "Too risky."

"Baker Street?"

"No, I cannot risk bringing harm to my friends." I gave him instead an address on Jermyn Street.

"All right. Can you walk?"

I nodded, though to tell the truth, I was not confident of my abilities. However, the boy took much of my weight on his shoulder and we staggered out onto the road. Fortune smiled and moments later he was able to flag down a hansom. I told the boy to pay with the loose change in my pocket. He hesitated, then with the punctilious honesty of his caste showed me exactly how much he had withdrawn.

What next? What next? Think! If only I could think.

I do not remember the rest of the journey. When I awoke I was being half carried up the stairs to a room I use for emergencies. The boy had the presence of mind to pay the cabby for his assistance. It was fortunate for I could not have managed on my own, not even with the boy's help.

Alas, the subsequent hours, indeed days, are a blur. I remember pain, blood, gasping for breath. Despite all that, somehow I felt safe. The

A BIASED JUDGEMENT

little room in Jermyn Street is a place where I am utterly anonymous. I am known to the landlord as 'Mr Sykes', an itinerant merchant of bric-a-brac. The boy was by my side every time my eyes fluttered open. He tended me competently, even gently and I felt – feel – that maudlin gratitude one does when one has fallen upon the mercy of a stranger and has found kindness there.

At one point I awoke to find a stranger leaning over me.

"Calm yourself, sir," he said in that unctuous tone one associates with professional care givers. "My name is Moore Agar. I am a physician and I can assure you that you are in no danger."

"How…?" I began, but a fit of coughing prevented me finishing the question.

"Calm yourself, my good fellow," said the doctor. "It would not do to have you tearing apart all my stitches."

"How did you come here?" I managed to ask.

"I received a letter requiring my immediate attention. I do not often make house calls," he added, giving a look of exquisite misgiving at his environment. "But we need not discuss such details now. You must take your rest and I will give instructions to the boy."

He injected me with something and I fell back into a blessedly pain-free haze.

When at last I regained any degree of awareness the room was dark, lit only by the oil lamp beside my cot. The boy was changing the dressing over my wound with a competence Watson would undoubtedly approve.

"Ah, you're awake," he said. "Fink you might manage ter eat summat?"

"Yes," I said. "I think so."

"Right-o," he said, pinning the bandage. "You lie still. I won't be long."

Left alone in the gloom I lay back and tried to focus my thoughts. It occurred to me I knew nothing at all about my rescuer, not even his name. Where had the doctor come from? How had he been engaged?

A BIASED JUDGEMENT

There were mysteries here and I cursed my drugged and injured state that I could not piece the puzzle together.

About half an hour later a light footstep on the stairs and the smell of chicken heralded the return of the boy.

"Right," he said. "Sorry it took a while; I had ter run t'Piccadilly. Didn't fink yer'd care for winkles or oysters, not after what you've been through."

I shuddered at the thought. The idea of eating something cooked at the side of the street made my stomach heave. I can only surmise my features betrayed my opinion for the boy grinned at me. "There now, guessed right, I did. This'll set you to rights."

He handed me a dish of soup, some bread and a block of good Cheddar. While I ate he busied himself making coffee. He handed me a steaming cup as soon as it was ready.

I sank back upon the pillows. While the food had done me undoubted good, the very act of eating had exhausted me.

The boy fixed my pillows and shook out the bedclothes so I was quite comfortable, or as much as was possible in my condition.

"You've had some experience in the medical arts," I said. "But you're not a practitioner."

He cocked his head on one side. "What makes you say that, then?" he said.

"You understand the need for food; you've done an excellent job of dressing my wound; but this bed does not have the regimented appearance so approved by Miss Nightingale."

"Spot on, sir," he said. "My dad died a few years ago and I looked after 'im for a bit before the good Lord took 'im, Gawd rest 'is soul."

"And your mother, is she still alive?"

"Ain't got no one," he said. "Might say I'm an orphan," and he laughed as if it was a joke. For reasons I cannot explain, I laughed too. That was not wise, for it sparked a spasm of coughing and I was exhausted when I finally stopped.

A BIASED JUDGEMENT

"That fancy doctor left you some linctus," the boy said. "Will stop you coughing and help you sleep."

"I feel I've slept for days," I said.

"You must need it."

I settled back in the bed and closed my eyes. "I don't even know your name," I said as I dozed off.

"Jack," he said. "Call me Jack."

2

February 23rd, 1897

I rather over-tired myself yesterday writing up my notes and have received a thorough scolding from Watson. At present I am supposed to be taking a nap. I confess I am fatigued, but my mind races. I shall instead try to continue my narrative of my assault. Focus will avail me far more than sleep, I think.

After several days I felt sufficiently recovered to return home to Baker Street. Having Watson on hand to tend to my medical needs seemed an excellent idea. Then.

Jack brought a hansom to the door, helped me down the stairs, and escorted me home. Mrs Hudson gave a cry when she saw me. At her wail, Watson came down and between the two of them, with much tutting and expressions of concern, aided me into the landlady's front living room.

It wasn't until I was safely, and breathlessly, seated upon her divan that I realised Jack was missing.

"Where is the boy?" I said. "Where did he go?"

"Boy?" Watson asked. "What boy, old chap? There is no one else here."

At my insistence, the good man went and searched the street up and down, but Jack was gone. I cursed myself for a fool that I had not troubled myself to get his full name or any of his particulars.

"You cannot blame yourself, Holmes," Watson said. "You have been very seriously injured and it's a wonder you are even conscious."

A BIASED JUDGEMENT

"That I am, that I'm not dead in St James's Park, is entirely because of that boy. I owe him my life, Watson. I must repay him."

March 3rd 1897

The Irregulars have nothing to report. Billy, looking as crestfallen as I feel, said, "We did try, Mr 'olmes, but 'Jack from Whitechapel' ain't much to go on with. If you could tell us something else…"

"I know there was something else," I said. "Something not quite right… Damnation, if I could only remember!"

I paid them for their efforts and sent them away with instructions to keep trying.

Lestrade stopped by this evening with his report but he knows no more than the Irregulars. "Not much to go on, is it? Sorry, Mr Holmes. We've had slightly better luck with your attacker, though."

"You mean you've caught him?"

"Well, no… But we have identified him. Take a look at this picture, Mr Holmes. That's the fellow, is it not?"

"Yes," I said. "A sailor then, as I thought? Those tattoos are Andalusian, make no mistake; very popular with the mariner classes."

"A sailor, yes, indeed. Got this picture from the shipping line. Gilberto Calvini is the fellow. An Italian national who came in just a few days ago on a ship from La Havre."

"And where is he now?"

"Gone back to sea, I'm afraid."

"He'll be back," I said. "You know he must return and when he does I shall have him."

"I don't understand, Holmes," Watson said. "What could this Calvini person have against you?"

"I cannot answer that until I have questioned him." I sank back onto my cushions. Watson did not need to tell me I was becoming overly excited.

"We're keeping an eye on the docks," Lestrade said. "The ruffian must return and we'll catch him when he does."

A BIASED JUDGEMENT

There is nothing to be done and I am forced into that unnatural state called 'patience'. I can only pray the wait will not be of long duration.

March 6th, 1897

At my insistence, Watson called upon Dr Moore Agar. My friend is somewhat in awe of the good doctor's reputation: "A Harley Street man, Holmes. Highly prestigious. However did you get him to make a house call?"

"I had nothing to do with the matter, Watson. I did no more than lie there like the idlest man in England. I beg you, go see this illustrious physician, and see who retained him on my behalf."

A few hours later Watson returned and the mystery, rather than being solved, was rather deepened.

"Dr Moore Agar says he received a letter requesting he attend a most important patient in Jermyn Street. The letter contained a ten pound note."

I whistled. Even for a Harley Street physician, that was an extravagant sum for one visit. The man did not know who sent him the letter; it was not signed. Unfortunately, he had not kept the document so I remain as uninformed as before. Whoever arranged for me to receive medical care from Dr Moore Agar not only possesses a deep wallet, but they knew I was in Jermyn Street.

I have since reflected upon the curious fact that when we have ample time to ask questions, we do not avail ourselves of it. Rather we squander those precious moments. Watson cites my weakened condition as an excuse, but I am not appeased. There are too many mysteries here and they make a knot in my brain. Why this sudden assault? There are a great many men in London who would gladly carve my name into a tombstone, but I would, I think, recognise them. This sailor is unknown to me. A man for hire, perhaps? Or – and I am reluctant to even voice this thought – has that notorious organisation of Moriarty's sprung up under new leadership? Ah, there are too many

A BIASED JUDGEMENT

questions and insufficient data to form an answer. And the most pressing question of all: where is Jack?

Other than the boy's first name, assuming he did not lie, and his apparent Whitechapel accent, I know nothing. He is an urchin like so many thousands of others, with nothing to distinguish him. His clothes were obviously second-hand, and therefore a camouflage to my scrutiny. He wore a cap at all times so I cannot even be certain of his hair colour. And the room was always dark with the curtains drawn. Was that concern for my rest or was there another reason? Bah, there is nothing…

No, there is one oddity I remember: the boy's hands. When I close my eyes I can picture them. They were clean and the nails well groomed: These were not the hands of a working lad. Nor did the boy seem to have any occupation, or if he did, he neglected it entirely while I was in his care. And there was something about his accent that was… off.

Another thing I remember: a peculiar odour, something that reminded me of bleach. It may not signify; the boy's clothes may have needed some strong agent to clean them, though I would have thought bleach was an odd choice when simple lye or carbolic would do the job. Another part of the puzzle.

I have thought about it; indeed, I have thought of little else, but I still have not come to any satisfactory conclusion. But I shall. Of that, I am determined.

March 12th 1897. Cornwall.

I am on holiday.

Is there a more detestable phrase in the English language?

Villains are prowling the streets of London; it is possible the most dangerous organisation in the world has regrouped; the youth to whom I owe my life has vanished… and I am forbidden to work. Indeed, I have been forced to refuse a very promising case: the theft of Lady

Dalrymple's rose diamond. I have been dispatched to the 'charming' south for the sake of my health.

Bad enough to have Watson wagging his finger at me, but allied with his new friend Dr Moore Agar, what hope do I have?

I am bored.

Watson is making every effort to keep the locals at bay so I may have "complete rest and solitude." Ghastly notion. You'd think after all these years, he would realise I am not a man who does well with enforced indolence.

I am amusing myself by encouraging the doctor to befriend the local vicar, a worthy fellow called Roundhay who is more interested in Cornish archaeology than theology. I've paid for my sins by having to take dinner at the vicarage. I there made the acquaintance of a morose young man by the name of Treggenis.

Encouraged by my apparent improvement, Watson was persuaded to spend the evening at the nearby pub where he made the acquaintance of some fishermen. "Local colour, Holmes," he tells me. I can see his eyes sparkle as he writes notes in his fat journal. I wish I could find pleasure in such things. How is a man to find pleasure when there is are wicked men walking about?

If I do not find something to occupy my mind soon I shall not be responsible for my actions.

March 18th 1897. Cornwall

Ah, what a relief the last couple of days have been! No doubt friend Watson would chastise me for taking pleasure in a case that did, after all, cause the deaths of two people and the insanity of two others, but I may surely, in these pages, admit my pleasure without reproach. It is not that I was gleeful of the deaths, of course, but of the puzzle it afforded me to solve.

Watson is in a filthy mood this morning. He is cross, justly so, because yesterday I subjected us to an experiment that was very unpleasant and could have proved fatal without his quick thinking. For

A BIASED JUDGEMENT

myself, the nightmares and terrors I faced because of the 'devil's foot' are too hideous to relate. Despite this, I feel much more like myself today and have regained most of my former energy. I had a splendid walk to clear my head and have written up my notes of the case for my files. A very successful holiday, really.

March 20th 1897. Baker Street
I have been pondering this business of love. It is surely monstrous. The terrible things it leads some men to do. Not that I blame Dr Sterndale for the violent revenge he took upon his lover's murderer. As I told Watson, I myself have never loved nor am likely to do so. Such passions must surely bias the judgement and that cannot be countenanced in a profession such as mine. He thinks I'm lonely. "A good woman would make a new man of you, Holmes. There's someone for everyone, I believe. Even you."

Undoubtedly, this conversation and our holiday adventure will appear in one of his tales. I suspect he will opt for some outlandish title involving the Cornish Devil. I, myself, would prefer 'An investigation into the *radix pedis diabolic* and its properties as an instrument of murder.' A vain hope, alas. We never agree about titles and his good friend and editor, Dr Doyle, always takes his side.

As we took the train home to London this afternoon Watson fell asleep and it occurred to me that he, no less than Sterndale, is willing to risk much for love and loyalty. How else to explain why a man of good sense would willingly stay with me while we tested the effects of that deadly root? I really ought to be horse-whipped for taking advantage of his friendship in that manner.

May 15th, 1897
I received a telegram mid-morning from an Inspector Tavistock Hill requesting I repair at all haste to Notting Hill and assist with a murder investigation.

A BIASED JUDGEMENT

Watson and I set off in pretty good spirits. It's been a while since I had a case worth my attention. This double homicide seemed promising. Watson was merry because he won some money from Stanford last night (he did not tell me but his jacket breast pocket was eloquent. He kept waiting for me to say something and so, naturally, I kept silent.) In addition to these little jewels, the weather this week is very mild and pleasant and we can smell the coming of spring at last.

Colville Gardens sits in the shadow of All Saints church. The buildings are, architecturally, sound enough but their beauty is diminished by the squalor that rests upon this entire neighbourhood. A long-necked crowd had gathered and were avid for details, the gorier the better. Is there another country in the world where murder is so relished?

We were met at the door by Tavistock Hill. "Inspector Lestrade said if I needed a hand I should give you a call, Mr Holmes. This is my first murder case so I'd appreciate any advice you can give me. Nothing has been touched."

He spoke with a curious authority for one so young. His demeanour managed to convey calm and confidence, and yet his freckled nose and smooth chin were thoroughly youthful and gauche.

I examined the steps leading up to the house – a terraced building recently converted into flats – and picked up a cigarette. "A Woodbine," I said. "With a very wet tip. This may not have been worth the trip after all. Still, since we're here…"

We went into the building where the victims shared a flat on the ground floor. Hill followed behind me at a careful distance, being exceedingly watchful where he stood. He had two uniformed officers ready to do my bidding in an instant.

The dead bodies were Mortimer Granger and his young wife, Elsie. He was, or aspired to be, an artist in oil colours. His works were scattered all around the dingy kitchen and bedroom, leaning upon shelves, stacked up in piles on the kitchen table. So much had his work dominated, there was almost no room left for domesticity. Indeed, the only domestic element was a once-green apple that sat upon the table. It had several bites taken out of it and was now a brown stump fit only to feed the flies that buzzed unpleasantly around the room.

"The man who bit into this is missing his left incisor," I said to the Inspector. "His lower teeth have a peculiarly misshapen appearance. It was not the victim; he has all his teeth, and the bite is too big for a woman. Therefore, this belongs to one of the intruders."

"There are no other apples in the flat," Hill said. "I thought one of the killers brought it with him."

"Well done, Inspector," I said. "I believe you are quite correct.

"I see the artist used this flat as his studio. What a peculiar style of painting. I would not have thought it possible for the impressionist style to be so muddy. He seems to have a fondness for depicting waifs and other unappealing creatures."

"Well, he was certainly prolific," Watson said, looking around. "And not very accomplished, if I'm any judge."

"Prolific, perhaps. But how selfish of the man to use every inch of living space for his own purposes. I cannot imagine his wife was pleased. But perhaps she was the very indulgent sort."

"Yes," Watson said, smiling. "These driven individuals are the devil to live with." He thumbed through the canvases. "The fellow seems to have – or, rather, had – some radical views regarding politics."

"Radical?" I was following two pairs of bloody footprints through the room.

"Of a socialist nature. These are posters calling for death to the nobility, an end to tyranny, and equal wages for all."

"Is that radical, Watson? It seems to me you have made similar comments any number of times, particularly when you've been working in your clinic at Euston."

"That's looking for our current system to be applied equably, Holmes, not for its eradication. I have no problem with the ruling classes… for the most part."

"Spoken like a true Scot," I said, laughing.

A BIASED JUDGEMENT

Watson laughed too then stopped abruptly. "It is not seemly to chortle when two people are lying dead, Holmes."

Two people were dead, all right; murdered in the most savage manner possible.

The male, wearing only a nightshirt, was lying prone on the kitchen floor. A pool of blood had congealed for several feet around him and the air was heavy with the slightly metallic stench. Granger had lost control of his bladder at the moment of death and the lower half of his nightshirt was still damp.

"A fearful sight this," said Hill. "Throat cut from ear to ear. Almost took his head clean off."

"And multiple stab wounds too, I see." I used my glass to examine these. "The point of impact is slightly curved, you see here, Inspector."

"Oh, I hadn't noticed that. Yes, I see what you mean, Mr Holmes. Only… what does it mean?"

"It means the murderer used what is generally called a Bowie knife. You see some of the skin has actually been removed from the jaw? That is because the curved top bevel of the blade was designed to skin animals."

"Good Lord. What a lot you do see, Mr Holmes. I thought a knife was just a knife."

"Not so, Inspector," I said. "You would do well to always examine the wound. The point of entry can tell you a great deal about the weapon. Sometimes, too, it is not a knife that is used. I have seen screwdrivers, broken bottles, and even hot pokers used to stab the victim. I have a monograph on the subject. I think you might find it useful."

"Thank you, Mr Holmes," the boy-officer said. "I have no doubt I shall." He wrote my comments and my monograph's title in his notebook.

"Where is the other victim?" I said.

"In here."

A BIASED JUDGEMENT

The woman was lying diagonally across the bed with her head towards the bottom. From her position, I surmised she was attempting to flee when she was struck down.

Her nightgown lay in tatters and she was almost entirely naked. The killer had stabbed her repeatedly in the breasts, belly and buttocks. He had then cut her throat, but I suspected she was dead from the first blow which had almost certainly punctured her heart. There was a strand of red hair in her right hand.

The footprints on the floor showed two pairs of boots: a square-toed size nine, and a round-toed size eight. The larger shoe wearer was pigeon-toed.

"Write this down," I said to the Inspector. "You are looking for two men. One is five foot nine and weighs approximately ten stone. He is right handed, has red hair and is a Roman Catholic. He has a permanently slack lower jaw and an unfortunate over-production of saliva. These in combination cause him to drool and make sucking noises. He's also slightly pigeon-toed. This fine gentleman carries a Bowie knife which he stole from an American tourist. He then stabbed that gentleman to death with his own blade. It was about two years ago; Lestrade's case. He can fill you in on the particulars. This beauty is the knife-man and if you act swiftly you may find him on the Portabello Road.

"His companion is five-foot-seven, weighs nine stone, and is missing his front left tooth. His lower teeth are very uneven. He carries a gun but has never been known to use it. Indeed, he generally just keep watch while his companion does his filthy work. You'll recognise him at once because his features are permanently fixed in a grotesque smile."

"Good Lord," said Hill. "You are everything I was told, Mr Holmes. No wonder they call you the Elder Statesman down at the Yard."

"Elder Statesman?"

"You have been an enormous help, Mr Holmes. Would you mind telling me how you knew all that?"

"Well, the cigarette on the front doorstep was my first clue. That wet tip shows the smoker has an over-secretion of saliva over which he has no control.

"There was a red hair in the dead woman's hand, plucked from the head of her killer. I have already explained about the blade and the bite mark on the apple which you were clever enough to realise was brought here by one of the killers… What else? Ah, the footprints reveal height and weight – it's a simple calculation based on shoe size and length of the stride. They also show the killer's pigeon-toed walk."

"But Catholic? The grotesque smile?"

Watson said, "You really ought to tell him, Holmes."

"Well, I did mention Lestrade's case from two years ago… The truth is, Inspector, I know both of these gentlemen. They are called Hacker and Smiley."

"I beg your pardon, Mr Holmes?"

"Herbert Hacker and Harold Smiley: they are your killers. Well, Hacker is the killer; Smiley only comes along to rob. I suspected it was them before I even set foot in here, Inspector. When you see a Woodbine with a wet tip you can be fairly sure that Hacker has been around.

"The type of knife was the next clue. Hacker has a fondness for that particular blade. You might call it his trademark. Then there's the murder of the woman: there is a deviance to it, wouldn't you agree? Particularly in the way the breasts were almost slashed off. Hacker has a pronounced hatred of women and he seldom changes his pattern of attack."

"He's well-named," said Hill.

"Oh, Hacker isn't his real name. It's Ryan. But everyone knows him as 'Hacker' for his style of assault. Likewise, 'Smiley' is really Harold Jones, but he earned his nickname because he has never been seen without that smile on his face. Smiley is a safe-cracker by trade, but he won't let Hacker go out alone. Perhaps he considers it a matter of friendship.

A BIASED JUDGEMENT

"They're well-known, Inspector. If you act swiftly enough you may catch them before they flee the country. They're very good at lying low. It's the only reason they haven't yet faced the noose. Send your men to Portobello Road and you may catch them."

I glanced around the room again. The pale sunlight filtering in through the windows seemed to make the scene even more terrible.

With a mere nod of his head, Hill sent his two uniformed men off to do as I suggested. A man with easy command, then. I think we shall hear more from young Tavistock Hill. But at that moment my thoughts were busy elsewhere.

"Something's puzzling you, Holmes," Watson said.

"Yes. This pair kill only for profit, either by way of burglary or because they've been hired. I cannot imagine an unsuccessful artist would have much worth stealing."

"How do you know he was unsuccessful?" Watson said.

"Look at the number of paintings, Watson. Some of them have a film of dust on them. No, our artist was not earning much of a living from his work."

"I did canvass the area when I arrived, Mr Holmes. There have been no burglaries or break-ins reported on the rest of the street."

"Indeed?" I said. "That is excellent work, Inspector, well done. But if burglary was not the motive it can only have been a paid killing. So who would want an impoverished artist and his wife dead?"

Watson said, "How about this, Holmes?" He indicated a box that had been hidden beneath a stack of canvases.

"Passports," I said, looking through them. "So, our friend was a forger, and not a bad one at that. Well, well… Yes, I surmise he made passports for the wrong man and was murdered so he would not speak of it."

We left shortly afterwards. The family of the victims had arrived and I dislike these scenes of grief. As we prepared to climb into the cab I shook the inspector's hand.

A BIASED JUDGEMENT

"You have made an excellent start, Inspector. I expect great things from you."

"Thank you, Mr Holmes. I shall be sure to mention your assistance to the press and in my report."

"You may certainly mention me in your official report, Hill, but there's no need to mention me to the press. Goodbye for now. I hope you soon find the pair who committed these vicious murders. Lestrade's looking for them too; perhaps you might combine your efforts."

Elder Statesman.

Ha!

May 31st, 1897

Young Inspector Hill stopped by to tell me Hacker and Smiley have vanished. Given the speed with which they fled I suspect they have been aided by someone. There is something singular about this entire affair. Hill feels responsible that he has not been able to make an arrest but I have assured him it is hardly his fault. In any case, that pair will show up again. They are drawn to London as irresistibly as the moth is drawn to the flame.

Hill has read my monograph on stabbings and asked for more recommendations. I have loaned him several volumes.

June 22nd, 1897

The entire country has gone mad. Bunting and fireworks and the streets filled with gullible well-wishers and greedy pickpockets in honour of the queen's diamond jubilee. Somewhere in this madness is my rescuer Jack, still missing despite all my efforts.

Watson has gone out to watch the parade and then meet with Stanford.

"Do come with us, old man," he said. "The entire world is celebrating. Surely even you must feel the excitement."

A BIASED JUDGEMENT

"Feel it? Certainly. But it does not necessarily follow that I should wish to participate in it. Go out, Watson, enjoy the festivities. I have a very delicate experiment to entertain me."

Midnight:
Watson finally stumbled in, much in his cups. It seems most unfair that he may consume several pints of alcohol with impunity while I am deprived a mere seven-and-a-half percent solution of my own stimulant.

The street is still noisy. I fear these festivities are likely to continue for some time. Damn.

August 1st, 1897
I was followed to Simpsons by an asthmatic man with a florid complexion. He is not known to me, but there is no doubt he was keeping a close eye on my movements. He did not approach nor make any attempt to accost me. Indeed, he slithered away towards the Embankment as soon as he realised I had spotted him. Another of that old gang? Or is this something new and different?

Isaiah Collins, Simpsons' inestimable head waiter, was kind enough to let me use the rear entrance just in case the asthmatic had an unpleasant surprise in store for me.

There's no point in alarming Watson, but I have taken the precaution of keeping my Tranter revolver with me whenever I go out.

August 9th, 1897
The mountain has come to Mohammed: Mycroft has called upon us.

Watson offered to leave, but was persuaded to stay. "My brother always behaves better in your presence, Doctor," Mycroft said.

"Heaven help the world the rest of the time then," was my friend's reply.

A smirk flickered across Mycroft's face. Then, somberly, he explained the reason for his visit.

A BIASED JUDGEMENT

"It is a very worrying event, Sherlock," he concluded. "The assassination of the Spanish prime minister could have serious repercussions."

"What do you expect me to do about it?" I demanded. "The Spanish have a police force, do they not? To be sure, they're probably no better than our own Metropolitan, but even they must be able to investigate an assassination." It occurred to me that the timing was curious: only a few days ago I was followed. Was someone checking that I was still in London and therefore unlikely to interfere with their perfidious plans? Or do I give myself more credit than I deserve? It is curious that my shadow has not been back though.

"It's not this assassination alone that worries me, Sherlock. I believe it is part of a much larger sequence of anarchy that is spreading across Europe."

Mycroft sipped his tea and bit down on one of Mrs Hudson's biscuits, sparkling his topcoat with sugar and looking very much like the schoolboy he once was.

"There have been too many assassinations of world leaders in the past few years, Sherlock. A few near-misses too. There was the French president in '94 and the former Bulgarian Prime Minister a year later. Now this."

I know my brother of old and I could see what was coming. He did not keep me waiting but came right to the point. "Sherlock, I suspect the Professor's old gang have regrouped. I believe they have found a new leader."

And though I have thought the same thing for several months, I felt my heart sink at his words.

"Yes," I said.

3

September 14th, 1897

So many times over the past several weeks I have longed for nothing more than the comfort of my own bed. Now I am home at last in Baker Street, in that very bed, and... I cannot sleep. I will write a little of my journal and in hope it may help my mind to rest.

Perhaps I am overly-cautious, but I was relieved when Watson agreed to visit his family in Scotland during my absence. While there is no evidence that he has attracted the attentions of the men who have followed me, I would prefer to err on the side of caution. A difficult thing to do whilst managing not to alarm the good doctor.

"If you are quite certain I cannot be of assistance to you in Europe?" he said as he packed his suitcase.

"I shall travel incognito," I said. "The alias of wealthy Robert Bathgate provided by Mycroft will suit me very well. Really, my dear fellow, I think visiting your brother and his family is a much better idea."

He wasn't fooled, of course. He never is, no matter what his readers like to believe. However, he agreed to my plan without demur. His brother's recent illness coupled with that unfailing sense of duty made up his mind.

I will admit, however, that there have been times over the past few weeks when I truly missed his company. Having someone who will remain silent or speak intelligently as the circumstances demand is a rare thing. Heaven knows what I shall do if he decides to marry again. It was irritating enough last time, for all his late wife's indulgence of our adventures. But I am rambling. It is an odious thing to be too tired for coherent thought and yet unable to sleep. It is a vexing state, like some sort of intellectual purgatory, and holds one captive. Ah, let me try to focus.

Let me see… Well, this morning, duties for the government concluded, I returned home via Scotland. Oh, what great pleasure it was to reunite with my old, and much-missed friend Watson in Edinburgh. He, I think, was equally pleased to see me and we instantly fell into that easy informality which so defines our friendship.

"You've lost too much weight, Holmes," he said over breakfast. "Using yourself far too liberally, I have no doubt. I hope it was worth it?"

I glanced around the busy tea room and said softly, "In the end I believe it was. I shall tell you all on the train, my dear fellow. But how are you? Your brother is well, I trust?"

"As well as anyone can reasonably expect," he said. "I really wish you had let me come with you. Even hiking around the Continent would have been preferable than these past weeks with my family."

"I missed your company too, my dear fellow," I said. "But it was for the best, I think. And here we are, together again, with a long train journey and plenty of tobacco to share." I lowered my voice and added, "As it happened, the assassin was already arrested before I even set foot in Spain. Sentenced to death by garrotte. Uncivilized brutes."

"You cannot think hanging is much better, Holmes," he said, nonchalantly buttering his scone.

"I suppose not… But tell me about you. I see your sister in law continues her Calvinist ways."

"Confound it!" he exclaimed. "All right, give me a moment, I can reason it out…" His brow furrowed as he thought but after several minutes of concentrated effort, he at last he gave it up. "Well, then?" he demanded.

"Your scarf," I said, amused.

"My scarf?"

A BIASED JUDGEMENT

"Your time in Afghanistan has made you very susceptible to the cold. When the weather is inclement you are in the habit of wearing the heavy woollen scarf your late wife made for you. I have often remarked upon its bright blue and how cheery a sight it is. Yet here we are on a cold Scottish morning and you are clad entirely in black. A silk scarf is hardly much protection against the Highland winds. Conclusion, your sister-in-law insisted you wear all black as befits a good Calvinist. There, how did I do?"

"Edinburgh is in the lowlands, Holmes. Not the Highlands..."

"I should have thought about the scarf. You're perfectly right, of course. I packed my dear Mary's blue one on top of my suitcase so I could retrieve it easily enough, but I forgot... I may have been a little distracted." He gave me a quick smile and I laughed.

"Poor Watson," I said. "I have no doubt my dalliance around Europe must have seemed a grand adventured compared to your own experience. Was it very dreadful?"

"Very," he said. "No tobacco, no whisky, no laughter and far too many prayers. By God, I'm glad you're back!"

I laughed again. "Even my dearest friends could hardly accuse me of religious zeal," I said. "We shall be reprobates together. Ah, I am really very pleased to see you again."

"I had thought to return to London a week ago," he said, laughing. "But once I got your telegram announcing your imminent return I decided to wait for you. It's such a long train journey; much better to share it with a friend."

The train journey was indeed long. Eight and a quarter hours from Edinburgh to King's Cross. Precisely at ten o'clock the train pulled out of Waverly Station heading south.

Once we were underway I quietly updated Watson on my adventures.

"My sojourn in Spain was far too brief," I said. "I greatly enjoyed my time in Seville and later in Barcelona. You haven't been, have you? You would enjoy it, I think. The orange trees fill the air with such fragrance and the air is dry and hot. Sadly, I had little enough time to enjoy the local colour. I met with the *Guardia Civil*, as they call their police, and found they had already made an arrest in the assassination of Prime Minister Antonio Canovas del Castillo. The dead man took a hard line against terror, as you know, Watson. There are those who think his brutality was at least as bad as those he opposed. Indeed, the local authorities believe that brutality is why he was murdered. I was surprised to see how much sympathy even the officials had for the assassin."

"Hardly surprising," Watson said. "I remember last year's bombing in Barcelona. There were any number of arrests. And weren't there rumours of torture being used on the suspects?"

"So it was said. Oh, there is no doubt many were pleased about the death of del Castillo, including the Americans. Mycroft says President McKinley is threatening war with Spain over Cuba."

"The Americans?" he exclaimed. "Do you really think they're involved?"

"No..." I lit my own cigarette and inhaled deeply before adding: "But the Spanish assassination cannot be viewed on its own. Mycroft believes, and I agree, that there are those working behind the scenes to try to create a new Europe, one with a very different face from the one we know."

Watson opened the window a few inches and lit a cigarette. "What about the assassin, Angelo, or whatever his name was? Did he tell you anything of use?"

"Michele Angiolillo," I replied. "An Italian by birth with ties to anarchists both in England and on the Continent. I met with him – not alone, alas. Mycroft's influence is not as robust in Spain as it is here. In any event, the fellow would say very little..."

"Come, Holmes. I know that look. You learned something."

"It was what he did not say. He travelled to Spain from France... via London. Does that not seem peculiar to you?"

A BIASED JUDGEMENT

"You think there was someone in here, that is, in England that he met with?"

"It seems exceedingly likely, does it not? Something else, too: Angiolillo claimed he killed del Castillo as a strike against tyranny, and yet there were documents found in his possession that suggest he had originally planned to kill members of the Spanish royal family but outside influences persuaded him the Prime Minister would make a better target."

"How very odd. The papers said he acted alone. You don't think that's true, Holmes?"

"His act may have been his own but I am convinced others were involved in the planning. I have discovered that membership in anarchist organisations in Spain alone runs to tens of thousands. It does not take much to rouse a man's rebellious tendencies. An unscrupulous individual can manage it easily enough. Learn where a man keeps his passions: a thirst for justice or a sense of being unfairly treated can become tools to persuade anyone that violence is not only justified but is for the greater good. Then you show him a target and simply wait. I believe that's what happened to Angiolillo."

Watson shivered and pulled down his overnight bag. With a look of annoyance he ripped off his black scarf and replaced it with the wool. He then shut the window. "Cold," he said, by way of explanation.

We sat in silence enjoying our cigarettes. After some moments Watson said, "It's a pretty alarming thought, Holmes, this idea of an international conspiracy designed to topple some of the great governments of Europe."

For a moment I weighed telling him everything. But it is unkind, surely, to alarm him about a risk I cannot even be sure is real? Time enough for full disclosure once I have proof.

"Yes," I replied. "But we need much more information before we can be sure."

"So what did you do after you left Spain?"

A BIASED JUDGEMENT

"I will not weary you with all the details. Indeed, little of it is worth telling. I travelled around Europe purporting to be a wealthy businessman looking for investments. From Spain I went to Italy: they have many peculiar ideas about government in that country. I blame the Romans.

"However, Italy proved dull indeed, except for a charming afternoon when I had luncheon with His Holiness, the Pope. At his suggestion I headed to Naples where I learned of a thriving anarchist group in France, and so I went to Paris. There, I learned of an organisation who would stop at nothing to create a new world order, one in which Germany, not England, must be prominent. Only whispers, though. No one would speak aloud. All I could find was that they were located in Bavaria.

"In Munich I heard of a certain dealer in art and antiquities who has an interest in politics and I endeavoured to meet him, a man by the name of Porlock. He is an Englishman of German and Italian extraction and he divides his time between Germany and England.

"This man interests me exceedingly, Watson. I wrote to Mycroft and had him conduct some additional research. Between his efforts and my own, I learned that Porlock has been on hand whenever any political scandal has occurred. He was in France in '94 when Marie Francois Sadi Carnot was assassinated, and a year later he was in Bulgaria when the former Prime Minister, Stefan Stambolov was murdered. He was also in Spain the day of del Castillo's shooting..."

I did not add that he had been in London in February during the week of my assault and that he left the city the day Lady Dalrymple's Rose Diamond was stolen. Nor that he was in London on the day I was followed to Simpsons by the asthmatic gentleman.

"Did you get to meet him?" Watson said.

I leaned forward and said, "Yes, I met him at the *Nationaltheater München* where so many of Wagner's works premiered.

"I had heard from a very reliable source that Porlock was taking his family to the opera. Oh yes, Watson. He is a family man, a husband and

A BIASED JUDGEMENT

father to two little girls. Quite the charming group they made as they sat together in the best seats. All of them with hair so pale as to be almost white. Even the wife. They presented a very model of the Aryan family.

"I had arranged for someone to introduce me and though I was presented as 'Mr Bathgate' I have no doubt at all the man recognised me."

I managed to suppress a shudder but Watson knows me too well. "Is he as monstrous as all that, Holmes?" he asked me. "He had a profound effect upon you, I can see."

"On the surface, no, he is perfectly affable. He bowed to me in that precise Germanic manner and said, 'Mr Bathgate, is it? I am delighted to make your acquaintance.' He affected a slightly Teutonic accent, but there is no denying his English origins. From the malice in his eyes I have no doubt my life would not have been worth a moment's purchase if I'd been alone."

"Good heaven! You must be careful, Holmes. If this man is as dangerous as you say, you could be at grave risk. A man who thinks nothing of striking down heads of state will hardly shrink from killing you."

"I have no doubt you are right, my dear Watson."

I said no more and after he finished his cigarette, Watson fell asleep. I found my mind too restless. It is still.

Porlock's gaze was like gazing into the depths of a glacial lake. He stared into me, rather than at me. It felt as if my mind was being probed by a shard of ice. "I hope you are enjoying Munich, Mr... Bathgate," he said. "True, our weather is not as congenial as it is in Italy, but we have, as you see, splendid music."

Was that comment about Italy a guess, or does he know my movements? Almost certainly the latter.

"I do enjoy the opera," I replied. "But Munich is certainly very chilly."

A BIASED JUDGEMENT

"You must be careful where you go, my dear sir. Bavaria can be very dangerous. Just one misstep and you could fall off a cliff. Or down a waterfall."

His pale, almost colourless eyes, sparked malevolently.

I replied, "I am always careful, Mr Porlock. It is why I am still here and others are not."

For an instant, his face contorted into a vision of pure fury. He did not like the reminder that I walked away from Reichenbach while Moriarty did not. So, there is a link, then.

Later, when I returned to my hotel, I discovered my room had been turned out, my belongings slashed and on the wall, written in red paint, the words, "Go home, Mr Holmes."

Since then I have felt his presence like a shadow on my mind. I hoped that shadow would fade when I returned to Britain, but it has not.

I must try to sleep. I will not let this loathsome creature distract me from my purpose.

September 15th, 1897

It was considerably after midnight before I finally fell asleep. By the time I woke, the fire was brightly lit and a second pot of coffee being poured. Watson had already dressed and dined. Indeed, he was on his second lot of kidneys when I came into the living room.

Mrs Hudson was humming and periodically stopped to make sure my friend had a full plate or to pat his shoulder.

"Oh, there you are, Mr Holmes," said she. "What a pleasure it is to have my gentleman back home again. Now, sit you down and I shall get your breakfast."

I winced at this demonstration of bright spirits. Still, I know it will only last until I leave a pile of newspapers on the floor, or conduct one of my more noxious experiments. Really, it is too bad people cannot understand I do not do these things merely for my own pleasure.

After a late breakfast I went to visit Mycroft in his Whitehall office, but first I stopped to talk to Billy.

A BIASED JUDGEMENT

"We was missing you and the doc, like, Mr 'olmes," said he. "Rough old time of it we 'ad an' all."

"Well, I'm back now, Billy, and I have a job for you and the other lads, if you're interested?"

"Cor, a job? You can count on us. Whatcher need doin'?"

I gave him specific instructions then took a cab to Whitehall.

Gillespie, Mycroft's aide, greeted me warmly. I refused his offer of coffee and went straight up to Mycroft's office.

He was pleased to see me, I think, but we spent no time on social niceties and instead got right down to the business at hand.

"You did a splendid job, brother, in Europe. I have done some searching and there is no doubt in my mind this Porlock fellow is worth further investigation.

"He has a house here in London, in Finsbury Park, where he stays for several months at a time, sometimes with his family, sometimes alone. Do you really think he recognised you in Munich?"

"I have not the slightest doubt of it," I replied. "His malice was alive. I am not a fanciful man, but I vow my flesh crawled in his presence."

"Hmm. Now he knows you suspect him, I think it may be some time until he returns to England. In the meantime, my agents on the Continent have him under surveillance and I have alerted the governments of France, Italy, Spain and Germany since they seem to be where he has the firmest foothold."

"Is that enough?" I asked. "Can your agents not find something with which to charge him?"

He shook his head. "He's far too clever for that. He hires underlings to do his dirty work and, I believe, he pays them well, when they succeed."

"And when they fail?"

Mycroft drew his finger across his throat in a graphic representation of murder. "His sort does not allow for failure. Unfortunately, we have nothing to charge him with, and I do not believe the Continent will be any more successful than we. We must be patient and learn as much as we can. I cannot say whether the late professor's organisation has reformed, but I would urge extreme caution, Sherlock. If he recognised you, if the people who have twice attacked you are in his employ… I need hardly say more."

"I take my revolver with me everywhere I go, and I am being careful."

"Do. Please do. I am quite fond of you, you know." He gave me a quick smile and that, combined with his uncustomary kindness, filled me with alarm as little has ever done.

"By the way," he said, handing me a photograph. "This may interest you."

It was a picture of a group of young men standing on the lawn of one of our most prestigious universities. On the far right of the back row stood my old friend the late Professor, and standing beside him the pale and malevolent Albrecht Porlock.

4

September 16th, 1897

For a man who is a very epitome of the English gentleman: honourable, loyal, brave, John Watson is remarkably fond of a little housebreaking.

As soon as I told him of my plans his eyes lit up. Oh, he made the usual admonishments, an Englishman's home is his castle sort of thing, but I knew it was merely a sop for his conscience. "If this man is as dangerous as you believe, Holmes," he concluded. "You know you can count on me."

"Always, my dear fellow. Always."

"What is it you hope to find?"

"If we are very fortunate, I hope we shall uncover documents that will put a noose around his neck. Something so incriminating that nothing will save him. That is my hope. It is not my expectation."

"Then why bother?"

"Because at a minimum I can expect to learn something of the man: his nature, his habits. Perhaps, even, his weaknesses."

A little after midnight we made our way to Finsbury Park. This is a leafy suburb, more country than city, and very popular with the professional classes. It has neither the elegance of Knightsbridge nor the squalor of Whitechapel. It is pleasant, unobtrusive, and, to my mind, a peculiar place to find a lord of the criminal underworld.

Watson and I left the cab on the Seven Sisters Road and walked to the address Mycroft had given me.

A BIASED JUDGEMENT

"Are you sure the fellow isn't home?" Watson whispered.

"Mycroft says he is still in Munich and won't be back for a week. We should be able to work undisturbed. Relax, Watson. We shall be in and out in less than half an hour."

"I hope so. One of these days we'll be caught and that'll be a fine how do you do. I can picture the headlines: *Respected physician and renowned consulting detective convicted of burglary.* Not how I would choose to end my career."

"Hmph," I replied. "At least in your scenario you get top billing. Ah, there's the house."

The home of Albrecht Porlock is ordinary, even elegant and faces the park. It is a three story building with a white stone exterior, a bay window at ground level with a rather savage looking holly bush all around the base of the building. I glanced up and offered a silent prayer that I wouldn't have to climb the drainpipe. Who'd plant holly all around a building so even the drainpipe was protected by its thorns? A man who was anxious to keep out intruders.

We went up the steps and I pointed at the three locks set into the door. I took out my set of picks and began to work.

The first two unlocked easily enough but the third took a little longer. I jiggled it for several minutes and was at last rewarded by a satisfying click as the tumblers fell. I pushed the door open and stepped into the dark hallway. I was instantly on my alert. The house did not smell unoccupied. There was an odour of meat and, beneath it, something else. Something animal and dangerous. At almost the same instant I heard a low growl.

"Back, Watson! Back!" I cried as one of the two Dobermans leaped at me. I struck at the beast with my cane. It fell back with a snarl and his twin took up the attack.

The gaslight came on at the top of the stairs and a man's voice demanded, "Who's there? I have a pistol…"

A shot rang out and the dogs roared.

A BIASED JUDGEMENT

Watson half-pulled, half-dragged me from the building and between us we managed to get the front door closed against the beasts and their savage owner.

Several minutes later we sat on a soggy bench in the park trying to catch our breath.

"My heart is still racing," Watson said. "Good God, Holmes, that was as unpleasant an experience as I've ever known. I thought the house was unoccupied?"

"So Mycroft said."

"Well, it seems he was misinformed."

"Indeed."

Misinformed? Mycroft? I've never known such a thing to happen and the possible explanations alarmed me. Still, this was not the time to think of such things.

"We should not linger, Watson. If you have caught your breath, let us try to find a cab and return to Baker Street."

"You're sure you're not hurt. I really thought that animal had taken hold of you."

"I was fortunate that my cane protected me. My coat and gloves took the worst of it, I think. It would have been a lot worse if you had not pulled me to safety so quickly. You're a good man to have in a crisis, John Watson."

I couldn't see his features properly in the darkness, but I think he smiled. "All the same," he said, "I'll have a look when we get home."

We walked swiftly and quietly to the Seven Sisters Road and there we found a cab. Watson said, "Holmes?"

"Yes... Yes, Watson, just wondering..."

"Wondering?"

"What it is that Porlock is hiding in his house that he protects it in such a savage manner."

It was almost two o'clock by the time we got back to Baker Street. I have a few scratches on my arm from the teeth of the beast but my

A BIASED JUDGEMENT

clothes protected me from serious harm. I shudder to think what might have happened.

Watson cleaned the wound with antiseptic and poured me a brandy. Then, suddenly, he burst into laughter. "Oh, the look on your face when you saw those dogs, Holmes," he said, tears spilling down his cheeks.

"I never thought to end my days as a meal for a pair of savage hounds," I said, laughing just as loudly. Then, as the laughter subsided, "We have been very lucky. I do not mind telling you, Watson, it could have been exceedingly unpleasant. Those dogs can rip a man's throat apart in seconds."

"Do you mind?" Watson said. "I'd like my sleep without a serving of nightmares."

For a medical man he can be surprisingly squeamish.

Watson went to bed but I sat up a long time. Several questions vexed me:

How had Mycroft's information been so wrong? Why had Porlock returned to England? What secrets was he keeping? And how was I going to gain access to that house?

At length I gave it up and went to bed. The temptation to theorise is great but there are too few facts and I am in danger of manufacturing clever answers with nothing to sustain them. Something here is most unpleasant and makes me uneasy. Well, who knows what tomorrow will bring.

I am going to bed.

September 17th

Two men are lurking across the street. I do not recognise them, but there is little doubt they are watching 221B.

I left Watson sleeping and walked to Mycroft's office in Whitehall. The pair followed me the whole way, always keeping a considerable distance, but they made no secret of the fact that they were dogging my heels.

Dogging. Unfortunate choice of words.

A BIASED JUDGEMENT

They made no attempt to accost me and I made no attempt to lose them. I have other, more pressing matters to occupy me this morning.

Mycroft was alarmed at my report.

"It's not like Frobisher to get it so badly wrong," he said. "It might be an honest error, Sherlock. Or perhaps Porlock had a last minute change of plans…"

"Or perhaps your agent is less reliable than you suppose. Watson and I barely made it out of there without serious injury, Mycroft. I have other business of my own to occupy me, you know. I do not need to be your lapdog."

Dog. There's that word again.

"I really am sorry, Sherlock. I understand your anger. I am angry too. I can bring Frobisher in and question him—"

"No," I said. "Do not alert him that you have any suspicions. Just keep a close eye on him."

We sat in silence for several minutes, lost in our thoughts.

"We still need that information, Sherlock," Mycroft said at last. "I do not suppose you'll be able to gain access to the house for some time. Porlock will be on his guard. But in a few weeks, you need to try again. At least this time you can go in knowing what awaits you."

"And why do you not send in one of your own men?"

"You know why. You're the only one with the skill. The only man in the country I truly trust."

I felt mollified even though I realised he was being particularly gentle for his own ends. Few men can manipulate so well as an older, much-respected brother.

"Well, I shall give it some thought. If I go back – mark my words, Mycroft: *If* I go back – it shall not be for several weeks or more. In the meantime, see if you can get any more reliable information on our friend."

"And what will you do in the meantime?"

"I shall hope for a case. Something to wash away the stench of treason and politics. A decent murder, for preference."

A BIASED JUDGEMENT

I left the building by the front entrance and my two shadows waited till I reached the end of the road before they followed me. And they followed me all the way back to Baker Street.

5

September 18th 1897 - Bitterne

Well, well, all my wishes have been granted.

I have a case. And a nice little murder it is too.

In response to a plea from Sir Christopher Summerville, Watson and I have come to investigate the death by strangling of the upper-housemaid, Liz Derby. It is not often I am engaged when the victim is a servant, though the circumstances here are peculiar and the nature of the crime particularly heinous.

Rillington Manor is one of the smallest estates in the kingdom and Sir Christopher has never attracted my attention. His younger brother, however, has excited my interest on more than one occasion, being a reprobate of the first order.

My two shadows followed us all the way to Waterloo. Watson and I managed to elude them, however, and they were still searching the crowd on the drizzling platform as we pulled out on the Southampton train.

Watson seemed preoccupied with the details of tickets and money so there was no need to trouble him about the pair. I must say, for once I am pleased to be getting out of the city. I have felt claustrophobic of late, particularly with my every move being watched. Indeed, this entire year thus far has been a disappointment. All these months and still no word of Jack. I doubt I shall ever find him now and the thought that he lives in squalor while I owe him so great a debt rankles.

In any event, the journey to Bitterne is short enough. The train took us past Windsor Castle squatting most inelegantly on a hill. It really is

A BIASED JUDGEMENT

a very ugly building. Watson was, predictably, appalled at my observation.

"It's hardly unpatriotic to express a dislike of the architecture, Watson," I said mildly.

He humphed and returned his attention to his newspaper.

We arrived at Bitterne station a little after eleven and from there engaged a cab to take us to the manor.

The estate's park is neither large nor impressive. The drive curves to the door in a manner intended to be majestic, but, because of its brevity, succeeds only in appearing foolish. The park itself is pretty enough and though it is September, the roses are still in bloom and their scent sweetened the damp air.

Watson and I were met by the butler and led at once to the library to meet with our client.

Sir Christopher Summerville is a short, stout, snide individual who greeted us as if we brought in a foul odour from the city upon our clothing.

"Mr Holmes," he said in a disapproving manner. "I'm afraid this matter is beneath your notice, but the local constabulary insisted."

"Who is the officer in charge of the case?" I asked.

"A man called Greer. Competent enough, by all accounts, but he insists this case is beyond his sphere of expertise. Don't know why we employ the man if he is of such little worth."

"It is surely worthy of the man to ask for help when he needs it," Watson observed, bristling at the slight paid to the unfortunate policeman.

I asked if we might see where the crime had occurred and a footman was sent to escort us. Sir Christopher, dismissing us like more distasteful members of the serving classes, was glad to be rid of his unpleasant task. *Soto voce*, Watson said, "You'd think this unfortunate woman was murdered simply to inconvenience him." I confess, the same thought had crossed my own mind.

A BIASED JUDGEMENT

The footman, around twenty years old with, I perceived, an ailing parent, led us through a warren of cold and inelegant rooms in the highest reaches of the house: the servants' quarters.

The dead woman had shared a room with the kitchen maid, but the unfortunate skivvy had been sacked a few days before for theft. Until a replacement for her could be found, the victim had the room to herself. It was a luxury she had not enjoyed for long.

"Is the body still in situ?" Watson asked.

"Ah, no, sir, I'm afraid not," the footman replied. "The master felt it was too upsetting…"

We reached the dead woman's room and stood appalled in the doorway.

"Good God," Watson cried. "Did the killer create this chaos?"

Chaos was, indeed, the word for it. Every item the woman possessed had been pulled out and strewn about the room. The washbasin in the corner had been upended and the stain of water across the bare floorboards was still damp. Only the bed linen was untouched and the imprint of the dead woman remained clear upon it. She had been in a kneeling position, I perceived, with her head upon the bed.

I knelt on the floor and tried to detect footprints on the floorboards, but it was an impossibility, even for me. Dozens of feet had crossed this room since the crime had occurred.

"Who has been in here?" I demanded.

"Almost everyone, I'm afraid, sir," the footman said. "We did try to keep them out, but the master… that is to say, we were overruled."

"We?"

The boy took a long breath and let it out slowly. He said nothing and it was obvious he meant to keep whatever confidence he held. I exchanged a glance with Watson and I could see he agreed with my assessment: best not force the man too soon.

"It is of no account," I said, with studied indifference.

The examination of the room took only minutes to reveal it as a wasted exercise. The inquisitive and the incompetent had done an effective job of destroying all traces of value.

Watson rummaged through the dead woman's clothing. After a few minutes he said, "Holmes…"

I turned to see him holding an odd garment in his hands. I took it from him and examined it. I have never seen its like before.

It had the general appearance of an apron, complete with bib. However, the fabric was a thin sort of cotton which would have rendered the garment impractical for any sort of domestic purpose.

The dingy neck strap revealed the garment had been worn next to the skin. There was another strap that tied around the waist, again, in the fashion of an apron, and the whole thing seemed like an impractical version of every other such garment. However, a minute inspection revealed this was not the case. The skirt was twice as thick as the bib. Careful study revealed that the skirt was, in fact, a large pocket. There was a neat row of small buttons along the waist to keep the contents of the pocket intact.

"Ha!" I cried. "Well done, Watson, well done indeed!"

"Does this suggest anything to you?" my friend asked.

"It suggests four different possibilities, but it is premature to discuss them at present."

Rising to my feet, I said, "Where is Inspector Greer?"

The boy said, "He went into the village to see if anyone might have left on the train, sir. He said he'd be back by one o'clock. It's almost that now."

"Why should he be interested in train passengers?" Watson asked, anticipating me.

"Uh, Sir Christopher says no one in this house could have committed such a dreadful crime," the footman stammered.

"Bah!" I cried. "What idiocy! How could anyone else have gained access to this room? How would anyone outside know where the woman's room was? It is evident the room has been searched; even a cretin could see the deceased was murdered for something she possessed."

"What was that, sir?" the footman asked. "She was only a servant. The house has any number of treasures that must surely have been far more valuable than anything she possessed."

I studied the boy with some amusement. "Well, here is a brain, at least, Watson!" I cried. "What is your name, lad?"

"Stevens, sir," the youth replied.

"Well, Stevens, you can make yourself useful and tell us about this woman, the victim."

The youth beamed. "Yes, sir," he said.

Watson smiled, well aware of my technique. By inflating the footman's ego I was likely to learn far more than he intended to impart.

"Well, sir," Stevens began. "The woman, Liz Derby, has only been here a few weeks. She came with good references by all account and was approved by her Ladyship as a between maid."

Watson, taking notes in his attentive and efficient manner, said, "Where had she worked before?"

"Lady Redgrave's house in Eastbourne, sir. And before that she was with Sir Anthony Michaels in Cornwall. Miss Simms, that's the housekeeper, sir, can tell you more, I'm sure."

"How long had she been in these establishments, do you know?"

"Not long, I think," Stevens said. "But I believe her references were excellent."

"Were they indeed?" I said.

"What was she like?" Watson asked. "Miss Derby."

"She was all right, sir. Kept to herself. Her mother lived in Golders Green and Derby went to see her every week. Said the old woman was poorly and had no one else."

"Indeed?" I said. "Then pray tell, why would she come to an establishment so far away from the city?"

The youth could not answer and I moved on. "Tell me who was in this house last night."

A BIASED JUDGEMENT

As if he had been anticipating the question, the boy immediately replied, "The staff of course: Mr Reynolds the butler; Miss Simms, the housekeeper; Mrs Bracken, the cook; then there's a Lady's maid, a parlour maid and one footman, which is to say me, sir. Then there's Sir Christopher, Lady Summerville and the guests. That would be Mr and Mrs Beecham, Sir Edmund Villiers, Monsieur Perrot, and Lady Beatrice."

"And how many of these would have access to Miss Derby's room?"

"Everyone," the lad replied at once.

"Of course," Watson said with a groan.

"Well, sir," Stevens said. "Servants are not permitted to lock their doors."

Before I could reply, there was a tentative knock and a very thin, very precise man of about forty came into the room.

"Mr Holmes?" he inquired looking from me to the doctor and back again.

"Inspector Greer, I presume?" I replied. The man and I shook hands then I turned to the footman. "Thank you, Stevens, you have been of inestimable use."

The servant nodded and left the room with the greatest reluctance. I waited till I heard his footstep fade into the distance before turning to the policeman.

"This crime scene was not preserved, Inspector. Badly done."

"I know it, Mr Holmes," he replied. "Though in my defence I should point out most of the disarray occurred before I arrived on the scene. Once the alarm was raised, I think the entire house arrived here to gawp. Indeed, I believe more than an hour passed before I was even sent for."

"And the searching of the room: you were not responsible for that?"

"No indeed, sir."

"Who found the body?"

"The footman, Stevens. The lad who was just here."

"What time was that?"

A BIASED JUDGEMENT

"Just before six am. Miss Derby was expected downstairs by five-thirty in order to make tea for the servants, make the fires and so on. When she didn't arrive the housekeeper sent the footman to look for her."

"Whose room is adjacent to this?"

"The upstairs maid and the parlour maid share, Mr Holmes. But they deny hearing anything."

"Yet this disarray – it could hardly have been conducted in silence."

"If I may, Holmes," Watson interjected. "Many servants work sixteen hour days and much of it is heavy labour. In my experience very few of them suffer from insomnia."

I thought about that. "Yes, that's a fair point. Thank you, Watson: The font of knowledge for all things domestic, as always."

Watson wrinkled his nose, fully aware that the remark was as much insult as it was complement, but knowing me well enough to appreciate it was not meant unkindly.

"Inspector, I wonder if you have yet had the opportunity to inquire at the deceased's former employers for particulars of her character."

"Yes indeed," he replied, looking relieved that he had done something right, at least. "I sent inquiries right away, Mr Holmes. I should hear back this afternoon, I think."

"And do you have any theories as to the motive behind the crime?"

He swelled up with pride at being asked. Watson smirked behind the Inspector's back.

"Well, sir," Greer replied. "It does seem rather a crime of passion. Strangulation, I mean. It looked very much as if the woman and another, probably a man, were quarrelling and he lost control."

"But surely even the soundest of sleepers would have been roused by what would certainly have been a loud quarrel? In any event, this crime scene has been essentially silenced. We shall go and see the body – I assume it has been taken to the morgue?"

"It has, sir. I have a pony and trap outside; we can be at the morgue in no more than fifteen minutes."

A BIASED JUDGEMENT

"Let us away, then!"

Once in the trap I asked the man to explain his extraordinary behaviour in going to the train station. "It really was most inefficient, inspector," I said.

"It was, I know, Mr Holmes. But Sir Christopher insisted and he's a very hard man to deny. Besides, I had hoped to meet you there. I must have just missed you."

"So it would seem."

The morgue was in the bowels of the local hospital. We descended a stone staircase outside the building, our footsteps echoing in the stillness, and entered. There was an attendant on duty; a slovenly-looking man who stank. Within, the corpse of the victim lay upon a marble slab, a once-white sheet tossed indifferently over her.

I drew my magnifying glass and began my study.

The woman was about 27 years of age but looked much older. Every detail of her hard life was etched in the lines on her face and the course and reddened hands. As always, I worked methodically starting at the scalp and moving steadily down to her feet. I noted the curvature of her spine; the well-developed musculature of her arms; the rotting state of her teeth. She smelled of gin.

A discoloured brown stain around the back of her neck was unconnected with the cause of death. The ring of black bruises around the throat with two prominent beneath the jaws were, however. The hyoid bone was crushed and the course, fleshy tissue around the front of the neck showed eight well-defined bruises.

"Petechial haemorrhaging in the eyes... Manual strangulation, Watson," I observed. "You see: here are the prints of the killer's fingers beneath the jaw and the larger imprints of the thumbs on the back of the neck. He strangled her from behind."

"He?"

"The hyoid has been crushed, so the killer was likely a man; I doubt a woman would have had enough strength to cause such damage, though I would not completely rule out the possibility. The victim's fingernails are broken where the victim tried to fight him – or her – off. Inspector, was there any tissue beneath the woman's fingernails? I perceive she has been bathed and her nails cleaned."

"I don't, uh, recall," the man replied. He had, at least, the grace to look embarrassed. As well he might.

"Would anyone have noticed?" Watson asked, anticipating my annoyance. "Perhaps that footman?"

The Inspector bit his lower lip. I sincerely hoped he wasn't about to weep. "Uh, possibly," he said. "There was so much confusion, you see; servants weeping and Sir Christopher shouting… It's no excuse, I know. I'm really very sorry, Mr Holmes."

"Your sorrow will not solve this case," I said.

I turned my attention to the dead woman's clothing and here, at last, was a point of interest.

"Aha!" I said, picking up the woman's shoes, a stout pair of plain black brogues the soles of which were caked with dark red mud.

"What is it, Holmes?" Watson asked, peering over my shoulder to see what I was looking at.

I indicated the shoes, but the point eluded him. I motioned the beleaguered policeman to come forward. "You see here, Inspector," said I. "These shoes are curious, are they not?"

"A fine pair of shoes, hardly worn. What of them?"

"These shoes are manufactured by Church's. You will not find a better shoe in all of England. I doubt you will find this particular style for less than eighteen shillings; a small fortune for a between maid whose annual income is a mere six or seven pounds."

"Closer to five for her," the inspector said. "It's common knowledge Sir Christopher pays the very lowest end of the scale for servants. But how on earth could she afford such an extravagance?"

"How indeed?" I said.

I examined the small pile of clothes on the bench but there was nothing of consequence.

"This is what she was wearing when she was found?" I asked.

"Yes, Mr Holmes," the Inspector replied. "Her work clothes and her shoes."

"Getting ready to start her day," Watson mused. I shot him a glance.

"How long would you estimate the woman has been dead?" I asked him.

The doctor examined the woman's limbs and jaw. "About eight hours, by now," he said. "Give or take."

"Which puts time of death around three o'clock this morning. Rather early to begin work, don't you think? And these shoes have clear traces of mud on them. It is the same mud as I have observed around the grounds of the manor."

"Meaning what?" asked the inspector.

I glanced at Watson. "Meaning she was outside in the middle of the night," he said.

"Precisely," I said. "More than that, it suggests, does it not, that Derby had just returned to her room from her excursion outdoors when she was murdered?"

"But what are we to make of that, Mr Holmes?" The Inspector looked bewildered.

"We cannot say just yet. But these are, at least, points of interest and may prove to be key in solving this little puzzle."

There was nothing else to be gleaned, and so Watson and I elected to walk back to the house. By the time we began our approach along the distasteful drive, my glee at my discovery of the woman's shoes and her mysterious night-time excursion had already faded.

There was so much that room and that woman's body might have told me, and they had been rendered mute, either through stupidity or malice. Either way, it mattered not; the end result was the same. I had sunk back into a bottomless silence. Watson's voice cut into my reverie.

"Don't worry, Holmes," he said. "You'll solve it."

"How can you be so sure?" I asked.

"Because you always do."

6

I must confess my success in my chosen field owes much to friend Watson's unshakable faith. While it is not, in my opinion, always justified, it remains as resolute as the man himself. Often, when faced with an apparently impossible case, I have laboured on simply because I could not bear the thought of disappointing him. Not that I would ever confess such a trite and sentimental notion out loud, of course.

This case seemed particularly difficult for although I had a number of avenues to explore, I had none of the points of interest that generally sets my cases apart from the banal. None, that is, but the shoes. I amused myself by pondering what Watson would term this case in his annals: The Case of the Expensive Brogues, perhaps.

When we returned to the manor I asked to meet with all of the occupants, starting with the servants.

"It is decidedly chilly," I told Reynolds. "Can we have a fire?"

"I'm afraid not, sir," he said, smirking. "His Lordship does not allow fires in the house unless it is really cold."

"Really cold?" Watson spluttered. "I can see my breath, man."

"House rules, I'm afraid. I do apologise."

The odious creature looked positively smug at our discomfort. There was nothing for it but to sit at the library table with our coats on. Greer, with an odd mix of pleasure and nerves, sat with us. I glanced at Watson who said, "I have seen Holmes conduct these sort of interviews any number of times, Inspector. I find even the slightest word can be revealing."

"Oh yes," Greer said, breathlessly. "That is my experience too."

A BIASED JUDGEMENT

It is testimony to my forbearance, I think, that I did not roll my eyes.

Stifling his amusement admirably, Watson replied, "It's an education to me to just sit and watch."

To be fair, the man understood Watson's meaning at once. "Oh I shall say nothing, not a thing, Mr Holmes. You may count on me."

"I have no doubt of it, my dear Inspector," said I. Watson really does not give me enough credit sometimes. I am very gentle when it is warranted.

One by one the servants came to the library to answer my questions. Watson took notes and Greer sat in a state of commendable silence while I conducted my interviews.

The butler, Reynolds, came first. He is a cold and austere retainer with no information. A little man, both in stature and in personality. I suspect he could tell us quite a lot if he chose, but he is unquestionably his master's man, and his master does not approve of our presence.

Next came Miss Simms, the housekeeper. She is a middle-aged woman, about forty, with an iron spine and hair to match. Though unsettled by the violent death of one of her staff, I found her to be thoughtful and intelligent.

She sat before me with her gnarled hands in her lap. Observing her, it occurred to me that I must write a monograph on hands. So much can be learned from them: occupation, interests and even illness can be gleaned by the keen observer.

Miss Simms's hands belie her otherwise quite youthful appearance. Her fingers are hideously disfigured from arthritis. She wears no jewellery, but a depression at the base of her marriage finger indicates that at one time it bore a ring. That she is still a 'Miss' suggests that the ring was either her mother's wedding ring – unlikely as women tend to wear these items on the right hand, presumably so not to dissuade interested young men from making offers of matrimony, and they also would be unlikely to remove such an object – or, more likely, it was a promise of marriage that failed to materialise. A woman disappointed in love, then.

A BIASED JUDGEMENT

I believe her to be truthful if understandably guarded in how she discussed the household.

The dead woman, Simms said, had been employed by her eight weeks earlier. Liz Derby had been sent by one of those agencies that provide domestic help for the better English homes, and she had arrived with excellent references. Miss Simms had hired her on the spot and the woman commenced employment the following day.

"That was swift, was it not?" I asked. "Surely she had to work out her notice at her previous place of employment?"

Miss Simms flushed. "She explained that she had to leave her last employer rather suddenly because her mother had taken ill and needed care. However, her circumstances did not allow her to remain idle for long. Though her mother was not completely well, they could no longer afford to do without an income."

"And you needed someone urgently?"

"Quite so. The previous girl, Letty, had fallen... into a spot of bother."

"You mean she was pregnant?" Watson said.

Miss Simms nodded. "As soon as it became apparent she was summoned to Sir Christopher and he discharged her on the spot."

"And where is she now?" I asked.

"Dead, sir. She hanged herself. Awful, it was."

The good woman dabbed her eyes with a crisp white handkerchief and I saw Watson was much moved.

"It is deplorable that no help is available for young women in these straits, Holmes," he said. "It's just criminal! Did the child's father not have the means to aid her?"

"She never said who it was..." the crisp handkerchief was becoming mangled in the woman's fingers.

"But you know, do you not?" I suggested in my most lethargic manner.

Miss Simms stammered, "I cannot think what you mean, Mr Holmes."

A BIASED JUDGEMENT

"You need not speak his name, merely nod your head if I am correct: Sir Christopher?"

She bit her lip and nodded.

"O sir, you mustn't say anything. I have no proof and only a suspicion. It would mean the sack if he heard I was speaking ill of him. Indeed, it could mean gaol for slander."

"You may count upon our discretion," I said. "I take it there have been others?"

She nodded again. "But still, I have no proof, only a glance, a whispered word... it's the way he looks at these girls, sir. There's something... unsavoury about it."

"And one of the reasons you hired Miss Derby was because she was neither young nor pretty. She would prove no enticement to your employer."

"There, sir, I heard you were a clever man."

"And Miss Derby: what sort of woman was she?"

Again the hesitancy. "It is unchristian, Mr Holmes, to speak ill of the dead, and to be truthful I know of no harm in the girl, but I confess I did not care for her."

"Can you tell me why, Miss Simms? Come, you are used to dealing with staff. There must have been something that disquieted you?"

She measured her words carefully before she replied.

"I have worked for Lady Summerville for twelve years, Mr Holmes, and in all that time there was never any trouble. However, since that girl came here it seems there has been nothing but."

"Such as?"

"Such as the dismissal of Mavis, the young maid who was discharged for theft."

"You did not think she was the thief?"

"No, sir, I did not. She'd worked here for nearly five years and was as sober and continent as any young girl should be. She worked hard and I never had cause to censure her."

"And you believe she was incapable of this theft?"

A BIASED JUDGEMENT

"To be frank, Mr Holmes, the girl, hard worker though she was, just wasn't intelligent enough to steal. She was incapable of lying and I would swear she was as astonished as anyone else when that necklace showed up in her apron pocket."

"You believe Miss Derby placed it there?" Watson asked.

"I do."

"Why?" I demanded. "What would she hope to gain, except – ah!"

"Holmes?" Watson said. "Something has struck you?"

"A glimmer of an idea, Watson. Just a glimmer, and yet… yes, why not?"

I rubbed my hands together. Even with so little to go on, I might yet get to the bottom of this mystery.

"Tell me about the guests, Miss Simms," I said. "When did they each arrive?"

"M. Perrot came on Wednesday, that is the fifteenth, Mr Holmes. He and Sir Christopher had business to attend. Mr Wallace Summerville was here at that time too, but he left on Friday morning.

"On Thursday morning Mr and Mrs Beecham arrived and Mr Villiers that afternoon. Lady Beatrice arrived around noon yesterday."

"Thank you, Miss Simms. You have been very helpful."

After the housekeeper left, Watson and I continued to meet with the rest of the staff, but they either know nothing, or are prepared to keep their secrets. It was as discouraging a display of stupidity as I have ever seen. No, not merely stupidity. There is fear in this house and fear is a much more powerful motivator. The source of that fear is evident: Sir Christopher Summerville. In any event, I decided to turn my attention to the family and guests.

"Must we continue, Holmes?" Watson asked. "Couldn't we have something to eat first?"

I was loathe to stop but it seemed the household was about to sit down to their midday meal. There seemed no alternative but to join them.

A BIASED JUDGEMENT

Frankly, I almost expected Summerville to tell Watson and me to dine with the servants. Propriety ruled, however, and we were shown to the dining room with the other guests. As I sat, I pondered that it might be preferable, after all, to get to know the assembled players before interrogating them.

The meal was adequate if somewhat unimaginative. Certainly Watson seemed to enjoy it. He and I were greeted with undisguised curiosity as we sat at the table. Lady Summerville was bubbling with a barely suppressed interest and only the thinly veiled disdain of her husband kept her from asking all the questions that simmered on her lips.

The others at the table present an indifferent group. Monsieur Perrot is a fussy little man who reeks of garlic. In a pretence of poor English he asked about the progress of my investigations.

"Eet is quite a catastrophe," he said. "Tsk, tsk. I have never encountered so disquieting a thing before. We are all of us on tenterhooks, Mr Holmes."

For all his show of not knowing the language, I was amused to note that his choice of words was hardly that of an amateur. And only a proficient speaker would use an idiom such as "on tenterhooks".

"How do you get along, Mr Holmes?" Mr Edmund Villiers asked. "I too find it unsettling to think that someone could enter the house and slay any one of us in our beds."

"It is too soon to speculate," I replied. "And there are a few points of interest. It is a difficult case, very difficult. But I wonder, Mr Villiers, why you assume the killer entered from outside."

"Isn't it obvious?" Summerville demanded. To my silence he said, "The way that woman was slain was surely the work of a madman!" I remained silent and he forged ahead. "Well, you cannot think that any of my guests belongs in Coney Hatch! Or that I employ anyone who belongs in that infernal place?"

A BIASED JUDGEMENT

"Even if I admitted your initial premise that the murder was the work of a madman, or your second, that neither your guests nor your staff fall into that category, there are still three people in the house whom you do not excuse."

"Who—" Then, as the import of my suggestion struck him he demanded, "Mr Holmes! Are you suggesting I or my wife or my niece might have committed this monstrosity?"

"It is a ludicrous notion!" M. Perrot said. "My host is a gentleman. And women do not commit murders!"

"Indeed? I believe if you study the American chronicles you will find that just five years ago a young woman was considered the likely murderess of her father and stepmother."

"Ah, Lizzie Borden," Watson said, recognising my reference at once. "Yes, dreadful case."

"I believe you owe our host an apology, Mr Holmes," Villiers said with an uneasy glance at the apoplectic knight.

I waved an indifferent hand.

"You must forgive Holmes," Watson said. "He means no disrespect; this is merely part of his process."

"I call it an infernal insult!" Sir Christopher roared. He flung his napkin onto the table and stormed out.

Red faced, Lady Summerville said, "You must understand my husband is a very sensitive man, Mr Holmes."

Around the table the company stared disconsolately at their plates, almost as if they were too terrified to eat. Only one had continued to dine throughout the entire tirade and seemed unperturbed by Summerville's anger: Lady Beatrice. She had not spoken a word since I entered the room, nor had she even glanced in my direction. And yet my heart was as certain as it has ever been of anything that she knew far more about the death of Miss Derby than anyone.

After luncheon, I returned to the library with Watson to resume my examination. We were met at the door by Inspector Greer. He said, with obvious discomfort, "I'm afraid I have to leave you, Mr Holmes.

A BIASED JUDGEMENT

There's a disturbance at the local public house and I'm afraid it will take my entire station to handle it if it's the Lowry boys again. Those lads get very wild on a Saturday, but not usually until the evening. I'm so sorry to have to go."

"Oh what a shame," I said. From the disapproving look on Watson's face it was evident I had not quite managed to conceal my glee.

"I really wish I could stay here and watch you work. I've no doubt I would learn a lot."

Well, the man had sense enough to appreciate that fact at least. Still, I was quite certain I'd get nothing out of the sour inhabitants of Rillington Manor with him at my shoulder.

Watson said, with such warmth as to almost fool even me, "Perhaps we could meet up later and compare notes, Inspector? We really must not keep you from your other duties."

"Well, if you say so, Doctor. I shall hope to see you at the station, Mr Holmes. At your convenience, of course."

"Happy to, Inspector," I said. "Nothing would give me greater pleasure."

Thus relieved of the man's presence, Watson and I settled back in the library and worked our way tediously through the family and the guests.

I began with our host. He was, he declared, very busy and knew nothing of these matters. His wife was in charge of the household and, he made plain, he held her directly responsible for the catastrophe that had fallen upon his house.

He sat before me in the library, equal measures of belligerence and contempt. He is a man of poor temper and high ambition. There is no doubt he would be perfectly capable of committing murder, but I do not think he would do so in his own home. Notoriety.

In any event, he does not even know the dead woman's first name, let alone anything about her. Reluctantly, I have put him to the bottom of my list of suspects.

A BIASED JUDGEMENT

M. Perrot was next. He is a small foreigner with impeccable table manners and foul breath. He made a show of being unable to understand my questions. I therefore conducted the interview in French which was tiresome because Watson's command of the tongue has not the fluency of my own. After the loathsome little man had left I summarised for him:

"A corrupt and unsavoury sort, is our Monsieur Perrot, Watson," I said. "He claims to be a friend, a '*bon ami*' of our host, but could not tell me that gentleman's birth month."

"What do you suspect him of, Holmes?" Watson asked. "Is he our killer?"

"He is certainly capable of it, but of this particular murder, I cannot be sure. His purpose here is somewhat mysterious, but I suspect there is something sinister at the heart of it. There are too many inconsistencies in his tale. He claims to be from Paris but his accent is plainly from Quebec. Also, Perrot is not his real name."

"How do you know that?"

"He was wearing monogrammed cufflinks in the form of a W."

"Couldn't his first name start with a W?"

"Gentlemen tend to monogram their surnames; in any case, he claims his first name is Anton."

I stretched and lit a cigarette. "This is a nice household, is it not? Apart from the lad Stevens we have yet to meet anyone with either wit or conscience. Although…" I did not finish. I decided not to add that I was curious to speak with Lady Beatrice. I know Watson of old: he would instantly wander down the rose-scented pathways of romance. I need his attention.

Our next witness was Sir Edmund Villiers. A small, fastidious man with vague connections to the West End, he presented himself nervously and sat facing me, twitching like a chilly orphan.

"I am an old acquaintance of Sir Chrisopher's," he said. "We met one evening at the Savoy when he had the misfortune to have his pocket picked by one of the street urchins. I was privileged to assist him and he has repaid me with frequent visits here on occasion. I merely make up the numbers."

"So you were intended to match Lady Beatrice?" Watson asked.

"No, no. another young Lady, Miss Constance Longford was supposed to have made up the party, but she became ill at the last moment and had to cancel. I was supposed to match her."

"Then M. Perrot was intended for the Lady?" I asked.

This line of questioning suited him, and he relaxed noticeably.

"M. Perrot was not invited; he happened to call upon Sir Christopher and was asked to stay for the weekend. No, Sir Christopher's brother, Wallace, had that honour. Alas, he had some business in town that required his urgent attention, but I believe he is expected sometime today."

After the frightened gentleman left I turned to Watson.

"This is a curious state of affairs, is it not?"

"That the party was not that which was planned? Indeed. What do you make of it, Holmes?"

I shook my head. There were and are too many hypotheses; I need more data to sort through them. All I would say was, "Wallace Summerville has crossed my path a number of times, Watson. Though he has managed to avoid my net, I have no doubt the noose is awaiting him at some juncture."

"The brother of a knight? Good grief!" Watson exclaimed.

"The Summervilles are not high born, Watson. I might even go so far as to say they are not even gentlemen. I doubt they have a brass farthing to their name and young Wallace has expensive tastes. He is intemperate and becomes aggressive when in his cups. If memory serves he has also run up some quite substantial gambling debts. Very likely it was these that compelled him back to the city."

"They he cannot have been involved in this murder, surely, Holmes?"

"It is too soon to tell; I need data, Watson, data! Will you ask our next witness to come in?"

A BIASED JUDGEMENT

We were joined by not one, but two witnesses: Mr and Mrs Beecham. Their youth is amplified by their callowness. The young man is twenty-two and recently inherited a sizeable estate in Derbyshire.

"Alice and I hadn't been married very long," he said. "And we were finding it hard to make ends meet, weren't we, my dear?"

The girl, no more than eighteen, nodded. She clutched her husband's hand so tightly I wondered he did not wince. "Not that we minded, Mr Holmes," she said in a breathless, little girl voice I find immensely irritating. "But we're hoping to start a family…"

"And then came news that my uncle Charles had died and left me his fortune," the boy said.

"That would be the Honourable Charles Windham?" I said. "Yes, I remember reading about his death in the Gazette. You are to be congratulated on your inheritance. No doubt it will ease your path in life considerably. Tell me, how do you know Sir Christopher?"

"We met at my club, Mr Holmes," Beecham replied. "When he heard about my inheritance he offered to advise me about investments. I know nothing about business, I'm afraid. I am… that is to say, I was just a porter at St Guy's Hospital."

"He invited us here for the week," the girl said. Really, her speech seems all vowels and no consonants. "Sir Christopher, I mean."

Watson, seeing the signs of my irritation that, I flatter myself, no one else can detect, took over the questioning.

"So you hadn't known Sir Christopher or his family for long?"

"Lord love you, no sir," Beecham said. "Only just met him. He's such a… a forceful man, isn't he?"

Watson glanced at me and carried on. "Yes, I'm sure that's true. So had you ever met the dead woman before?"

"I don't think we even know who she was," the young man said. "We saw the body… Well, that is to say, I did, but I don't think we'd seen her before."

"It's just awful," the girl said and her huge eyes filled with tears.

"I really hope we do not have to stay here, Mr Holmes," said the boy. "This is so distressing to my wife."

"That will be up to the police, I'm afraid," Watson said. "But it will soon be resolved, I am sure. There's no better man for the job than Mr Holmes."

There seemed nothing more they could tell us so I dismissed them. As they rose to leave I added, "You would be well advised to stay clear of the Summervilles, Mr Beecham. Look for a reputable business manager to advise you and make sure you get excellent references from at least five sources before you entrust your financial matters to him."

The two stared at me and I saw the import of my words fill their eyes. "Thank you, Mr Holmes," the girl said. "I did say, didn't I, Edward, that there was something unsavoury about him?"

"You did. You certainly did."

The boy insisted on shaking my hand vigorously for several minutes. At last I was rid of them. Lord keep me from the passions of youth.

I expected Lady Summerville to be our next witness, but instead we were graced by the butler, Mr Reynolds.

"Sir Christopher's apologies, Mr Holmes. He does not think it appropriate that the ladies be… sullied with this matter."

I said, coldly, "I am afraid we must insist."

The man bristled and Watson said, "I am sure Sir Christopher is anxious to have this matter resolved as swiftly as possible. Who can say what snippets of information the ladies may have without even knowing. I am sure we need not detail them for long."

"Very well," Reynolds said in a sulky voice.

There was a delay of about ten minutes then Reynolds returned and announced her Ladyship. The retainer stood behind the sofa, intending to remain for our interview. I rose and showed him the door. He left spluttering indignities, to my great amusement.

Lady Summerville at the age of forty-seven is no less anxious and nervous than she was when she was Miss Winifred Jacoby and

A BIASED JUDGEMENT

affianced to my old friend Reginald Musgrave before his untimely death.

I was struck, as I had been over luncheon, by the way she tugged at the sleeves of her gown. As she sat opposite me the reason became obvious. However, I acted as if I had not noticed and asked some general questions about the household. She answered truthfully, breathlessly.

"How long have you and Sir Christopher been married, Lady Summerville?"

"Eight years," she said. This, then, was why Miss Simms said she'd been in the mistresses' employ for twelve years; she had been longer in this house than her master. But the Lady was still speaking and I paid close heed to her words.

"I had quite given up on the idea of marriage when I met Christopher at a dinner at Lady Bingham's home," she said. "He is a little younger than I, but we hardly notice the difference."

"And the estate was yours, I take it?"

"It was my dowry," she said. "But of course it is entirely my husband's now."

"And the staff? How many of them were here prior to your marriage?"

"They have all with me a long time except the poor dead girl and Mr Reynolds."

"Ah. And when was Mr Reynolds employed?"

"Oh he came with my husband. He has been in Sir Christopher's employ for many years."

"I see." The matter did not surprise me. I wondered what had happened to the previous butler. Still, it would not do to alienate our hostess with indelicate questions, especially when there are far more efficient ways of getting the answers. Instead I asked, "Do you ever involve yourself in the hiring of new staff?"

"No, I leave that to Miss Simms. She is perfectly capable, and my husband feels I have more important things to do with my time."

A BIASED JUDGEMENT

"Of course you do," Watson said in his genial way.

"And Lady Beatrice: is she your niece or your husband's?"

"Oh, mine. She is my brother Benjamin's girl. She's been quite alone since he died two years ago. I invite her here often; my husband is very generous in giving her free rein of the house, but she prefers the city, I think."

"Ah, she lives in London, then?"

"Yes, she has a house in Wimpole Street. My brother spent most of his time there, and Beatrice is surrounded by his books. I think that and the familiarity are a comfort to her."

"And how does she get on with your husband?" I asked the question as if it were no more than a formality.

"Perfectly well," she said, flushing.

"Come, Lady Summerville, we will get along much further if you are candid with me."

She laughed nervously. "Well, I don't suppose there's anything to be embarrassed about. Beatrice doesn't much care for my husband, if I am truthful. I cannot think why; he is always so genial to her."

"Perhaps she objects to his abuse of you, her aunt?"

Again she tugged on her sleeves and this time the flush on her cheeks coloured all the way down her neck.

"Mr Holmes!"

I leaned forward and peeled back the cuff of her sleeve. The purple bruise was still fresh and the imprint of a man's fingers clearly visible.

"Your husband's handiwork, I see."

"That is none of your business, Mr Holmes. My husband is merely playful. He forgets his strength, and I bruise easily…"

"So many excuses in one utterance, Lady Summerville. Why do you endure it?"

Tears, sudden and uncontrollable, filled her eyes and coursed down her plump cheeks.

"What choice have I, Mr Holmes? He is my husband, for good or ill, and I am bound to him. Besides, there are many much worse off."

A BIASED JUDGEMENT

I sat and stared at her for several moments in silence. Watson was brimming with fury but, good man that he is, contained his emotions in deference to my process. At last I said, "That will do for now, Lady Summerville, you may send Lady Beatrice in, if you would."

She sprang from the chair and I waited till she reached the door before asking, "Oh, about Lady Beatrice: I understand your husband is hoping to arrange a match between her and his brother?"

She shuddered, nodded, and escaped.

"Well, Watson," I said after the Lady left. "What a charming man this Sir Christopher is. I have seldom met a more convincing cad even in the vilest back alleyways of London."

"The man's a bounder, Holmes! It is a small step from wife-beater to killer, surely."

"He is a most unsavoury character, I agree, but you know my philosophy, Watson: we have few facts and I will not form a theory without more data. Still, it is an interesting household... ah, here is Lady Beatrice, I believe."

As we spoke, the young woman came into the room accompanied by Reynolds, the butler.

"Sir Christopher's orders, sir. I am to remain during the lady's interview."

The young woman who joined us in the library would be noteworthy in any circumstances; in a home such as this she is singular. Taller than most, she strode into the library exuding confidence and calm: two commodities that had been lacking in all our previous interviewees.

Meeting my eyes without demur she shook hands first with me, then with Watson, and then sat facing us, her hands on her lap.

Watson no doubt considers her a beauty. Even I must admit the intelligence in her eyes is intriguing, but at that moment I was more interested in what light, if any, she could shed upon the events of the previous night.

My hopes were dashed, alas. She told much the same tale as everyone else: they dined at eight, as usual, then she played the piano for the others in the music room before retiring around ten o'clock. She believed the gentlemen sat up for a while in conversation.

She did not know the maid, Liz Derby. She herself had not been to the manor for some months and had met the dead woman for the first time yesterday afternoon.

"Did anything about her strike you, Lady Beatrice?" I asked.

"I was much taken by her footwear," she replied. "Rather a handsome pair of brogues, I thought."

Her dark eyes met mine and I felt a thrill of recognition. Yes, here was someone who sees and hears and pays attention. I longed to get the odious butler out of the room, but I could not find a way of achieving the goal without creating difficulties for the girl. Given what we had learned of Summerville's behaviour towards women, I did not want to put her at risk.

At last, she rose and, as she took her leave, handed me a music manuscript.

"I have heard that you are a musician, Mr Holmes," she said. "I happened upon this some time ago; I think you will find it interesting. You may like to review it at your leisure."

I bowed and shook her hand and as she turned to leave she said, "Come, Reynolds, no doubt Mr Holmes has much to do. Perhaps you would pour me a sherry."

"Well, that was extraordinary," Watson said. "A beautiful young woman, if rather too self-sufficient for my taste. I wonder if that is why she is unmarried. Holmes?"

"Keep an eye on that door, Watson. I do not wish us to be interrupted or overheard."

He tiptoed to the door and peered through a crack. "No one there. What is it, Holmes? What did you learn from Lady Beatrice?"

I drew a large envelope out of the pages of the manuscript and strew the contents on the table. There was a letter and photographs, dozens of photographs of the dead woman.

And they were taken before the room had been trashed.

A BIASED JUDGEMENT

7

The photographs were remarkably clear and precise. The photographer had taken a close up of the woman's hands, and of the footprints on the carpet. Next to the latter was a foot-measure which enabled me to estimate the size of the shoe.

The pictures revealed a room that had been turned out by the killer, but was in nothing like the state of disarray that Watson and I had witnessed upon our arrival.

The dead woman's broken fingernails showed clearly a dark substance beneath them.

"What do you make of this, Watson?" I said.

"I cannot imagine Sir Christopher would allow a maidservant to be slovenly in appearance, Holmes," the Doctor replied. "And Miss Simms does not strike me as the sort of housekeeper who would permit dirty fingernails in one of her staff."

"I agree. So how do you explain it?"

He shook his head. "I'm afraid I am rather at a loss, Holmes."

"Come, Watson, the answer is clear enough, surely? The killer wore gloves, something black. The dead woman tore at them trying to save herself during strangulation. Have a look in that envelope; I cannot imagine our young friend had the foresight to save us a sample…"

"No, here, Holmes!" Watson cried, and handed me a piece of paper that had been folded around a black, suede-like substance.

"Excellent, excellent!" I cried. "Watson, this young woman has a brain. She has wit!"

"I wonder if it was she who took the photographs," Watson said.

A BIASED JUDGEMENT

I hardly heard him. I was busily examining the black substance under my magnifying glass. "Suede," I said. "Our killer wore black suede gloves. How very curious... Did you say something? Yes, perhaps the Lady herself is the photographer. Let us see what her letter has to say."

Although I have always maintained that gender can usually be determined by the quality of penmanship, I must confess I would have attributed the masculine gender to the author of this letter, if I did not already know otherwise. A fact I neglected to mention to Watson. The letter read,

Dear Mr Holmes,

I hope these photographs may be of some use to you. They are a poor substitute for an unsullied crime scene, I know, but they were all I could manage under the circumstances.

In addition to the pictures, I took some of the black substance that I found beneath the dead woman's fingernails. I only took as much as was necessary for your analysis, and left sufficient for the police, in the unlikely event that they would have wit enough to determine its importance.

It is doubtful that we will have a chance to talk during the day, but I shall come to the library at midnight tonight. There I will endeavour to answer your questions in full.

I need hardly say that if Sir Christopher were to learn of my involvement in this matter, the consequences could be extremely unpleasant for me and my aunt. I am sure I can rely upon your discretion and that of Dr Watson.

Your servant. B.J.

For the next several hours I lay on the library floor pouring over the photographs with my glass, scouring every detail. Though they were, as the photographer intimated, poor substitutes for an unsullied murder scene, they were, at least, vastly superior to the room we found on our arrival. Nor were they without points of interest.

A BIASED JUDGEMENT

As I had surmised, the dead woman was in a kneeling position by the bed with her head and shoulders lying upon the mattress. Her eyes were open and staring. She was wearing a coat and her expensive shoes. How curious. Why would she be dressed for outdoors in the middle of the night? There was a close image of the throat and I could clearly see the crushed hyoid bone. The dark bruises we observed in the morgue had not yet fully formed, but could still be distinguished. It seemed significant that the killer had not used a ligature, but had strangled Derby with his hands. These pictures must have been taken very soon after the murder.

"Holmes?" Watson said. "Well, what do you think?"

"I think we must consider using photography as a tool in the future," I said. "This is revealing. Yes, indeed. Very revealing."

"Then the girl has helped?"

I rose from the desk. "Yes," I replied. "I begin to see possibilities."

"But what is it you see?"

I handed him the stack of photographs and my glass. "See for yourself, my good fellow," I said. "What do you make of it?"

He was silent for several minutes, and then he said, "The room was searched. All those drawers are open, the cupboard, everything has been rifled."

"Yes. But what was our killer searching for? When we know that, we will know who he is."

"It is a man, then?"

"It certainly seems the most likely probability. It takes immense strength to crush the throat of a human being. Would a woman manage such a thing? Perhaps… But look at the marks upon the woman's neck. Such wide finger spread is beyond most of the women in this house except, perhaps, Lady Beatrice."

"Why her? I did not notice her hands to be larger than any of the other ladies."

A BIASED JUDGEMENT

"She is a pianist, Watson. That implies, does it not, a manual dexterity that would allow for such a broad hand spread? I find Lady Beatrice's hands immensely interesting."

He gave me one of his indulgent looks then said, "But surely if the girl was the killer she would not have offered to assist us."

"It is unlikely, certainly, but I will take nothing at face value. All the same, I am eager to hear what the young woman has to say when she is not being fettered by her uncle or his minions."

"Indeed. But the entire thing seems a bit rum. Why on earth was Derby wearing her coat and shoes?"

"A good question, Watson, but I have a better: Why was the killer wearing gloves?"

Watson thought for a moment before saying, "Perhaps he has read that no two sets of fingerprints are identical and was being cautious."

"Perhaps," I said. "In the future – the very near future if Scotland Yard will heed my advice – our police force will have a system in place to catalogue everyone's fingerprints. So far, only one country has established a fingerprinting bureau, and it is not England.

"I read an article on the subject by Dr Henry Faulds. You may have heard of him, Watson. He's a Scot."

"We don't all know each other, Holmes," he said. "Any more than all Englishmen do. But you have mentioned Dr Faulds before, I think. Wasn't he the fellow who wrote about the importance of fingerprinting in criminal detection?"

"He was, indeed. Well remembered, Watson."

"Hmph. Well as much as you have spoken about him, Holmes, I suppose I would have to remember something. But do you think the killer had that sort of foresight to wear gloves to avoid detection?"

"Perhaps. On the other hand, this is quite a cold house and last night was damp and chilly. It's more likely the killer was outside..."

"Holmes?"

"What if the killer was outside for some reason and he spotted the victim? He might have had a rendezvous with her... That footprint there

A BIASED JUDGEMENT

that the lady was kind enough to document – that does not belong to the victim. The shoe is larger and narrower. More to the point, the footprint seems to be damp, hence the discolouration."

"Well, if the killer was outside that would explain the gloves and the wet footprints, but I'm not sure how that helps," Watson said.

"No," I agreed. "There is not enough information to form a reliable theory. But I shall catalogue it. It will, no doubt, make sense when we have gathered some more facts."

19th September, 2am

This case has features of interest. Yes, indeed, I grow quite intrigued by it. But I digress: first I should record the results of my meeting with Lady Beatrice in the library.

She arrived punctually. Her footfall was so light as to be almost silent. Indeed, poor Watson quite started when she came into the room. We rose to our feet as she opened the door with great care. Then seeing ourselves, nodded and closed the door softly behind her.

She strode up to me and offered me her hand in a forthright way. "Mr Holmes," she said. "It is a great honour to meet you; I have followed your career with great interest. Doctor, how do you do? Please—" She indicated the chairs. She sat before me facing the lamp, and making no attempt to shield herself from scrutiny. I sat immediately opposite her in a leather armchair. Watson took the sofa.

"I must thank you, Lady Beatrice, for your most precise documentation of this unhappy event," I said.

She bowed slightly. I was pleased to see she neither denied the importance of her contribution nor blushed. Her response was perfectly matter of fact.

"A poor substitute for an undisturbed scene left for your scrutiny, I fear, but I hope you found it of use, Mr Holmes. I am sure you will have questions. Unfortunately, Sir Christopher's ah, protective nature…" she spoke the word with heavy sarcasm. "Makes it difficult to discuss the matter more openly. However, the library is little in use, even during daylight hours. At this time of night we may reasonably expect to have it to ourselves."

"Splendid!" I said, rubbing my hands together. At last I felt we were making progress. "Now, Lady Beatrice, would you mind elaborating upon your description of the finding of the body which you documented so admirably in your letter?"

"Certainly, though I recommend you speak with the young footman Stevens for it was he who found the body."

"A little before five o'clock, you said?"

"That's right. It was early for him to be awake. Usually he does not rise before six for he has no kitchen duties to attend. But he says something woke him. He sat up in bed for some minutes listening but he heard nothing further. He tried to go back to sleep but was unable to do so. Some instinct told him something was amiss, and so he crept along the hallway and found the body. I really recommend you speak with him again, Mr Holmes, but when he is alone. Find some reason to take a coach into town; Stevens will drive you. He will speak freely to you then."

"An excellent idea. Stevens acts as a coachman as well as a footman?"

Her reply was as contemptuous of her aunt's husband as before. "Sir Christopher likes the appearance of a wealthy household without necessarily wanting to pay for it. Most of the servants have extra duties from time to time."

"And this fellow Stevens," Watson said. "Do you trust him?"

"Yes, I do. I've known him since he was a very young boy and his mother came to work for my aunt. That was sixteen years ago."

"And your aunt's husband," I said. "Is it his abuse of your aunt you hold against him, or is there more?"

"You are that rarest of things, Mr Holmes," she said, smiling. "A man who is worthy of every superlative that has ever been spoken about him. You are right, of course. I trust your reputation for discretion is as reliable as that of your intellect."

A BIASED JUDGEMENT

"I can speak for Holmes's honour," Watson said, stoutly. "There is no man in England whose word is more reliable."

"Thank you," said the Lady. "Then I must have your word that you will treat what I am about to tell you with the greatest of confidence."

"You have my word," I said. I then and do find myself eager not to disappoint her. No doubt my experiences in Cornwall continue to leave traces of the maudlin upon me. I set aside the sentiment and paid close attention to the Lady's story.

"Well then," she said. "You will undoubtedly have surmised some of it yourself. My aunt is a good creature. She is, perhaps, rather nervous and foolish and her talent for avoiding unpleasant facts amounts almost to an art. But she has a good and kind heart and I am fond of her.

"Eight years ago when she was expected to remain a spinster – she was then thiry-six years of age – she announced to everyone's astonishment that she was going to marry. My father met with Sir Christopher and disliked him intensely. He pleaded with my aunt not to go through with the marriage, but given her age and her spinsterhood, she could not be dissuaded.

"Within a matter of weeks of the wedding I became aware that her husband was abusing my aunt quite outrageously. She denied it, of course, but she frequently cancelled lunches and outings that she ordinarily enjoyed. If I wanted to see her I had to come to her and what I found here troubled me. She had unexplained bruises – not just on occasion but every time I saw her.

"My father had, by this time, been diagnosed with the illness that eventually killed him and I did not wish to worry him with my concerns. I was exceedingly preoccupied with his care and I'm afraid I paid little attention to my aunt's concerns.

"Some time later my father was admitted to hospital. He did not want me to stay alone in London during that period, I therefore accepted my aunt's invitation to visit for a few weeks.

"As I have said, I had known Stevens since he was just a lad. I found him to be intelligent and honourable. One morning as I took a walk in the grounds he spoke to me of his concerns about my aunt's welfare. He observed first-hand the blows and the insults that she was subjected to on an almost daily basis.

"I pleaded with Lady Summerville to leave. Unlike most women in her situation, she had a home to come to and family who would support her. Our society is not kind to women, Mr Holmes. It is particularly harsh when they are victims of savage men. My aunt refused all offers of help. She had made her bed, she said, and she must lie in it. I believe, despite everything, she loves the brute.

"The best I could do was to ask Stevens to keep an eye on matters and to inform me if the violence to my aunt escalated. The young man has been good as his word and has often written to me when matters become acute. I have found that my presence here has, so far, tempered my uncle's behaviour. At least I can offer my aunt some respite from her husband."

She drew her hands to her mouth and was silent a moment. Despite the natural reserve of her caste, I could see she was greatly distressed by her aunt's situation.

I gave her a moment to calm herself before saying, "So you are quite sure, then, that young Stevens is above suspicion?"

"I have known him almost his whole life, Mr Holmes. But do not take my word for it. Speak to him yourself and you will see."

"Thank you, I shall. Now, tell me about that footprint that you photographed. In the picture it looked damp. Was that the case?"

"Yes, indeed. I put a ruler beside it so you could estimate the size. It was obviously not Derby's. Her foot was shorter and wider."

"As I observed…"

For another half hour we continued to discuss aspects of the housemaid's murder but she had little to add to the information she had already given us. Only one point emerged that surprised me.

"The black substance beneath Derby's fingernails was, I think, black suede," she said. "Ah, I see you agree with me."

A BIASED JUDGEMENT

"I do. I would like to examine it beneath a microscope to be certain, but my magnifying glass has convinced me."

"I also have examined the stuff under a glass," said she. "And I am in no doubt. I have asked Stevens to examine the men's drawers to see how many of them have gloves that fit that description."

"Capital!" I cried. "Well done, well done, indeed, Lady Beatrice! And what success has he had?"

"Moderate. Most of the male guests possess gloves of that sort, as do the butler, Reynolds, and Stevens himself. Also, Lady Summerville and I have black suede gloves. I have brought mine with me for your inspection."

I took the proffered items but even a casual glance showed there was no damage to the fabric.

"It is possible, of course, that I might have another pair. I can only give you my word that I do not."

She then splayed out her hands before me. "As a pianist, you will see my fingers have rather a wider span than most women. I also have better than average strength in my hands. Whether that would allow me sufficient ability to strangle another human being, I cannot say. But you cannot rule me out."

I rubbed my hands together. For the first time since arriving at this unhappy house I was enjoying myself. "And did you kill her, Lady Beatrice?" I asked.

"No, I did not," she said, rising to her feet. She smiled. "But I would be very disappointed if you merely took my word for it. Goodnight, gentlemen."

A BIASED JUDGEMENT

8

September 19th, 1897

    I find myself torn this morning between my need to learn more of Derby's background and my conviction that leaving Bitterne at this juncture would be most unwise. There is a killer in this house, of that I am certain, and he – or she – may strike again. I have particular concerns for Lady Beatrice. She plays the part of the indifferent socialite very well, but even a very small error on her part could be disastrous. Her every move is scrutinised by her uncle and I shudder to think of his retribution should she be discovered helping us. No, I must stay here in Southampton.

    Despite some misgivings about his safety, I have asked Watson to go to London and see what he can learn about Derby's background. He, good man, has agreed and I have given him a list of points to investigate. Frankly, Watson is likely to do a better job than I. His capacity for understanding the human heart is quite remarkable. In this instance, at least, that understanding is more likely to succeed here than all my cleverness. There, I have said it.

    It never fails to irk me how little credit the man does himself in his stories. If the public only knew what a mighty man John Watson is…"If it doesn't worry me, Holmes," he says, "why should it bother you? Besides, truth is a very precious commodity. Far too rich a thing for the general populace to digest."

    I am not appeased.

    In any case, I shall leave the London side of things in safe hands while I have a task of my own to accomplish: I must discover what the

A BIASED JUDGEMENT

killer sought in Liz Derby's room. The possibilities are endless, photographs or letters being the most likely, but I cannot make that assumption. Too many possibilities and too little evidence in any direction. Of one thing I can be sure: Derby's shoes will lead me to her killer.

This morning, as Lady Beatrice suggested, I requested the use of the trap to take Watson and myself into the town of Bitterne. I announced at breakfast that I felt the key to the housemaid's death lay in her past, and that I was sending my friend and colleague to learn what he may about her. This declaration caused considerable relief around the table as the family and guests made the obvious, but erroneous assumption, that none of them was under suspicion. I did not correct their error. Lady Beatrice reacted not at all. She is an accomplished actress.

Now expecting the matter to be resolved swiftly and with no blemish on his household, Sir Christopher has become what, for him, probably passes for genial. Of course we may have the trap, it would do young Stevens here good to get off his rump and do some work for a change.

The footman's face was implacable.

"You are very kind, Sir Christopher," I said smoothly. "We should be in the village by half past ten so Doctor Watson may catch his train. Stevens, can you convey us by… oh, let us say five minutes before the hour?"

"Certainly, sir," Stevens replied, and the illusion was complete.

Once we were on the trap and safely beyond the bounds of the manor, I reiterated my directions to the doctor.

"Take care to watch for reactions, Watson. These people will not willingly reveal their secrets. You must win their confidence and assure them that our only intention is to assist them."

"You can count on me, Holmes."

"I have not the slightest doubt of it, my dear fellow. I can think of no one better suited to the task. If you are delayed in the city, as I suspect you will be, I would be obliged if you could write to me of your progress."

"If I may, sir," Stevens interjected. "But letters to the manor may not be quite safe. Things have been... opened by the wrong person before now. You may do better having them sent to the local constabulary. Or you can send them to my old mum's cottage and collect them there if you like."

This raised a number of thoughts in my mind but I said only, "An excellent idea. Send them to the inspector, Watson. No, I have a better idea. Just telephone me at the manor. We should assume our conversation will be eavesdropped so tell me that Mrs Hudson sends her best wishes if you are able to confirm my suspicions, and that she is unwell if you have had no luck."

"I understand," he said.

Stevens dropped us at the railway station and was delighted at my suggestion that he go visit his ailing mother. As we waited for the train, I had the doctor outline his plan.

"I thought I'd start at Scotland Yard," said he. "If Lestrade is occupied with another case it might be wise to give him notice of what we need."

"Oh Lestrade can't possibly have anything more pressing than this case," I said. "You would do better to start at Baker Street."

"Lestrade has other priorities than yours, you know, Holmes," Watson said. "I shall go to Baker Street second and see if there have been any clients and if the Irregulars have any news for us. It's only been twelve hours since you called Mrs Hudson and gave her instructions for them. Not even they can have done all you asked in so short a time."

With an air of indifference I said, "Perhaps not; and yet they might. You know, Watson, if the Irregulars have been successful, your Scotland Yard trip may prove entirely unnecessary."

He gave me a look. "That's arrant nonsense and you know it, Holmes. And this isn't the first time you've been anxious for me to

A BIASED JUDGEMENT

spend my time with those urchins. They've dogged my path every time I've set foot outside 221B for weeks now. Then there's your recent insistence that I never travel without my service revolver. I can only conclude you believe me to be in some jeopardy. I have been patient quite long enough, surely? Come on, man. Out with it."

It was useless to quibble. Once Watson has his mind made up there's no stopping him. There is much of the bulldog in him. It is, at once, one of his greatest virtues and his most annoying failings. In any case, there was no hope for it but to tell him the whole story.

"It's a fool who underestimates you, my dear fellow," I said. "And in this instance, I have been the biggest fool in Christendom." Keeping nothing back, I proceeded to tell him the entire tale.

"But that's outrageous, Holmes," he cried when I was done. "I have seen the men across the street from our apartments, but I hadn't realised they were following you. Can they not be arrested?"

"They have broken no law as yet, Watson. So far they have done nothing more alarming than follow me. I was fortunate to be able to shake them when we took the train here, but it is extremely likely they continue to keep watch for my return to Baker Street."

"But what would they want with me?"

"Information, perhaps? Or they might follow you… Very likely I am being overly suspicious, but I should prefer to err on the side of caution."

"They must have a leader, these villains," Watson said. "Do you think this new Moriarty is behind it?"

Not for the first time, my friend's perspicacity surprised me. I said, as indifferently as I could, "Perhaps, but that makes such a man dangerous, not invincible. As you recall, I dispatched the original over the Reichenbach Falls."

"Yes, but at what cost?"

We fell silent for several minutes. Watson, though he perfectly understands why I kept silent for so long after my apparent death, still feels the sting of it. Not for the first time I berated myself that I did not confide in him sooner. It was done for compelling reasons as well he knows, but I bitterly regret the pain I caused him.

"Watson—" I began. He raised a hand to stop me, but I had deferred this for too long and I was determined to continue. "No one regrets more than I how shabbily I have treated you in the past. You have my word, I shall not lie to you again."

"Withholding the truth is not so different from lying, Holmes," he said and for once he made no attempt to disguise the depth of his hurt.

"You're right." I sighed, and stared up the track. The train wasn't due for several more minutes. I thought about changing the subject but this matter would lie between us. If it was anyone else it would not matter, but Watson…

"It seems I have committed the same error as before: My clumsy attempts to protect you ended up causing you pain."

He glanced over at me and said more gently, "Well, I've never doubted your intentions, my dear fellow. But yes, it was clumsy." He twisted the strap of his overnight bag around and around in his hand. He said, "Do you really think I might be in some danger?"

"I do not know. Probably not. But I should like you to be cautious all the same. And use the Irregulars. They will hinder those brutes from following you and insure your safety. Just please be exceedingly cautious. You know, you must know, I would never forgive myself if you were hurt because of me.

"In any case, proceed however you choose. I have complete faith in you, old man."

In the distance a whistle blew and the train thundered into the station. Watson and I said no more. I walked him to the train and as he turned to leave I said, "Watson," and held out my hand.

With some surprise he shook it. I said, "I am sorry. For this. For all of it."

"I know." He straightened his shoulders and turned to leave then paused, turned back and said, "It's about time you apologised. Still,

A BIASED JUDGEMENT

better late than never." He shot me a quick smile and winked then disappeared into the train's carriage.

Once Watson was safely on his way, I walked up the road to the police station.

Greer greeted me warmly. He was, I thought, anxious to redeem his reputation. He rose and offered me a seat and a cup of coffee. I accepted the former but refused the latter. I have drunk coffee in police stations before.

"The references came back, Mr Holmes," he said. "You may see for yourself."

He handed me a handful of letters written in varying hands on varying stationary. In content, however, they were virtually identical.

Liz Derby, they said, was sober and quiet. She did her work efficiently. It was with regret that they saw her leave.

"Does nothing strike you as significant about these, Inspector?" I asked.

"I'm not sure I take your meaning, Mr Holmes," he said.

"Come now, these references cover a year and there are eight of them. What member of the serving classes changes her employment so frequently?"

"But she must have been competent, Mr Holmes. Surely am employer would not have given her a reference otherwise."

"They would if they were afraid of her."

I turned the discussion to the members of Summerville's household. On this subject, the inspector proved informative enough.

"Lady Summerville I know well enough, sir. Though she is not so handsome as her niece, she is kind and very well liked in these parts. She used to attend local events pretty regular, and was quick with a smile and a word of encouragement to everyone. Not above putting her hand in her purse and giving a few pence to them that might need it either."

"You speak in the past tense, Inspector. Is that no longer the case?"

A BIASED JUDGEMENT

"I'm afraid not, Mr Holmes. A lot changed after her Ladyship got married. And not for the good, either."

"I understand the current butler came with the new master. What happened to the man who had the job before her Ladyship's marriage?"

"Ah, Mr Davenport that would be, sir. As fine a gentleman as you could ever meet. I believe there were strong feelings about his leaving. He'd been at the manor for any number of years, and very well liked he was too. He and the housekeeper, Miss Simms, had an understanding and we were all looking forward to the wedding. However, once Sir Christopher arrived Mr Davenport was sent packing, and that was that."

"Mr Davenport did not remain in the area?"

"No indeed, Mr Holmes. Not much work for butlers locally, I suppose, particularly not one who has been dismissed. I believe he went to London and opened a public house."

"Ah, I wonder if I might trouble you for the use of your telephone. I should like to leave a message for Doctor Watson that he should see if he can learn any more from Mr Davenport."

"How does that help us, Mr Holmes?" The man's entire face squashed itself into a frown of puzzlement.

"At the very least, he can give us some inside information on the workings of that house. Since he was close to Miss Simms, it is likely they have continued a correspondence. She will know far more than the footman Stevens, and may have confided in her former fiancé. The more we know of those inhabitants the better, do you not agree?"

"I would not presume to question you, Mr Holmes."

I left a message for Watson with Mrs Hudson and rose to leave. The policeman walked me to the door and said, "I can't tell you how glad I am you came to assist us. This seems a baffling matter to me, and that's the truth."

I smiled. "Well, well, if I am able to offer any insight, Inspector, you may be sure I shall do so. At least you are to be commended for recognising your need for assistance and contacting me."

A BIASED JUDGEMENT

"Well, to tell the truth, Mr Holmes, that was Lady Beatrice's idea. She said it was a puzzling case such as might tax even the great Sherlock Holmes and that's what made me think of it."

Half an hour later, well stocked on local gossip but few hard facts, I climbed onto the trap and sat beside Stevens. At my request, he drove us slowly to the manor. The air was chilly and I was glad Watson had tossed my scarf at me as we headed out.

I said, "Lady Beatrice suggested you had more to tell me about the morning you discovered Miss Derby's body."

"Yes, sir, she said I should speak plain to you. She's a fine lady, is Lady Beatrice. I was wanting only an opportunity to speak with you without having – well, certain people – listening in."

"People like Sir Christopher? You need not be alarmed, lad; my own observations of your employer have left me in little doubt as to his character."

"He's a hard man, and no mistake. I would have left this place years ago were it not for my mum's poor health and Lady Summerville needing someone to watch out for her."

"He is violent towards his wife," I said. The boy's lips tightened. If Sir Christopher, rather than Sir Christopher's maid, had been found dead I would have my chief suspect right before me.

"Brutal, sir," the lad replied. "If you could see the way he slaps and kicks and punches her. It would make you ashamed of all men, indeed it would."

"Why did he marry if he had so little affection for her? I have observed that even his manner of speech is often aggressive towards her."

"Well, sir, she had money and she was high born. This whole estate was hers; before they married Sir Christopher had nothing but a title. He and his brother are a pair, and that's a fact." He glanced at me. "You do know, Mr Holmes, that they intend Lady Beatrice to marry Mr Wallace Summerville? You may be sure, if she marries that... gentleman she will not survive a year."

A BIASED JUDGEMENT

"Surely she cannot be forced," I said. "In this modern age we do not compel young women to marry without their consent."

He reined in the horse and turned to look at me. "You think a woman has a choice? I'll tell you honestly, Mr Holmes, a lad like me, low born and with little education, has twice as many rights as a high-born lady. If her family insist she will have no option. And it will kill me to see it."

The thought of the spirited young woman who had so ably assisted my investigation being bound to so loathsome a creature as Wallace Summerville was a chilling one indeed.

I said, "Surely the lady has friends who would protect her?"

"Bless you, sir, she has many friends and they would help her if they could. But there are powerful people in this land who act according to expediency and not common sense. But there, I've said enough on the matter."

We had, indeed, got off topic and I changed the subject. "Tell me about finding Miss Derby's body," I said.

The lad's story mirrored the one told by Lady Beatrice. Something had woken him in the early hours and he had lain awake for some time listening. He tried to convince himself that he had imagined it but he could not go back to sleep. Some instinct told him to investigate.

He got up and went down the hallway of the servants' quarters to see if anything was amiss. He found the door to Derby's room ajar.

"I just knew, even before I looked inside, Mr Holmes, I just knew there was something really dreadful in there."

"Describe what you saw. Exactly, mind."

"Yes, Mr Holmes. Well, Lady Beatrice's pictures should tell you everything I saw."

"You did not go into the room?"

"No, sir. I saw at once the woman was dead. All purple, her face was. Made me quite ill to see it. There was no aid I could have given her. But I have read the accounts of your work, Mr Holmes, and I trust I am no stupider than any other man, so I did not go into the room and

A BIASED JUDGEMENT

I did not disturb anything. I stood in the hallway for some minutes, trying to decide what to do."

"What time was that?"

"A quarter to five, sir. I took note of the time."

The young man had all the details ready. Had it not been for his air of honesty coupled with Lady Beatrice's affidavit, I might have suspected him of being too well prepared. However, it was apparent he wanted only to be useful. He continued:

"I knew Lady Beatrice was the only member of the household who would not panic. I trusted that she would know what to do. I made my way to her chamber and knocked very softly on the door. I have observed her Ladyship in the past to be a very light sleeper, and so it was on this occasion. She came to the door looking tired but quite alert. I told her what I had found.

"Her Ladyship ordered me to fetch her photographic equipment and bring it to Derby's room. 'The household will trample this room like a prize bull, if I'm any judge,' said she. 'We must preserve the scene as well as we can.'"

"You assisted her Ladyship to take the photographs?"

"Yes, sir. I've helped her Ladyship a number of times in the past. She takes pictures of whatever catches her eye, if you know what I mean. I think I've become a pretty good assistant, though I say so myself."

"Yes, yes, but the murder scene… did either of you step in any of the footprints or disturb anything in any way?"

"No, sir," he said solidly. "And that's a fact. We were very careful, both of us."

"And after the pictures were taken, what happened then?"

"I brought the equipment down to the cellar. Her Ladyship has a darkroom set up down there… Ah, Sir Christopher doesn't know, and I'd be obliged, Mr Holmes, if you wouldn't tell him."

"Ha!" I said. "Your secret is safe with me."

A BIASED JUDGEMENT

I satisfied myself that Stevens had nothing further to add to the details of the murder. I turned my attention to the people within the house on the night of the murder. He confirmed most of my own suspicions.

"Mr Reynolds is a hard man and no mistake, sir. There's a rumour that he once did a man to death and Sir Christopher covered it up. All the servants are in terror of him. He tells everything to the master and takes great satisfaction in seeing the abuse and the threats that follow."

"I understand Mr Reynolds replaced a butler who had been in Lady Summerville's employ before her marriage."

"Yes, sir, Mr Davenport it was. He was as Christian a gentleman as you'd ever meet. Decent and kind he was and ever so fond of the mistress. It was a black day when that lady married, sir."

"What can you tell me about Davenport's departure? I gather he was dismissed and did not retire?"

"I never heard the whole story, sir," the lad said. He furrowed his brow trying to remember. "Miss Simms could tell you more; she and Mr Davenport were very close. But what I do know is that the gentleman was forced out and replaced by Mr Reynolds. It was all over in less than an hour and very upsetting to everyone."

I had the lad review the others in the house but he could do no more than confirm my own suspicions. Miss Simms was honest and kind; the cook worked hard and tried to keep out of everyone's notice; the other servants were too frightened of the master to put a foot out of line.

As to the guests: the lad's fondness for Lady Beatrice and his mistress aside, he had little information to relate. M. Perrot he disliked but that seemed more a matter of British pride than anything wanting in the Frenchman's person. His chief crime seemed to be that he reeked of cologne, as one might expect of a foreigner. And Steven's suspected Perrot often pretended worse English than he knew for some subtle reason of his own. He was, so far as the boy knew, a wine merchant. The Beechams he had never seen before, but Mr Villiers he knew quite well.

A BIASED JUDGEMENT

"He comes here now and then. The Master seems fond of him, though I'm not sure why. He's a very inoffensive sort, soft spoken and pleasant enough. He does rather fawn over Sir Christopher, though, and I suppose that might be enough to recommend him."

We had, by then, reached the gates of the manor and I had learned as much as I could hope. Stevens impressed me with his intelligence and resourcefulness. I said, "You have an interest in joining the police force, I understand?"

"Well, sir, I'd like to and no mistake. But my mum is ill, is dying in fact, and I'm all she's got. Then there's Lady Summerville... she's been very good to me and I owe her a lot. I'm still young; I have time."

"You do indeed. I have many reservations about the worth of the official forces, but they need all the intelligent young men they can muster. When the time comes and you are ready to make application, let me know and if it is in my power to assist you, I shall."

The lad blushed and would, I regret to say, have embraced me, so great was his pleasure, but I waved away his thanks and we continued on to the manor, he full of excitement, and I full of foreboding.

When we arrived back at the manor I said, "Tell me, Stevens, with everyone's letters being so carefully scrutinised, I assume the servants have found some means to avoid spying eyes?"

"Well, as much as possible, we have our letters delivered to other people in the neighbourhood, usually my mum's."

"And what of letters you wish to send?"

"We don't leave them out. We take them directly to the pillar box."

"Which is where, exactly?"

"There's one just a street over from the east wing. Uh, we servants take a short cut through the rose garden. There's a gap in the wall that we are able to get through. I'd be grateful if you wouldn't mention it to Sir Christopher or Mr Reynolds."

"You may count on me."

A BIASED JUDGEMENT

After giving me precise directions to the shortcut, Stevens returned to his duties. I stayed out in the grounds and followed the crazy-paving path through the rose garden. Fortunately, it rained on the evening of the murder but has been dry, if unseasonably chilly, since. The route through the roses was easy enough to follow. The trail wound through the white tea roses, and then cut off from the footpath where the blossoms turned pink and blowsy.

The tracks were perfectly clear. A broad, short foot had strode through these flowers after the rain. The soft ground readily preserved the print. Yes, that was Derby's foot. She walked steadily, there was no evidence of haste. It was dark; undoubtedly she was taking her time because she was not as familiar with this route as the other servants. Yes! Blue thread is caught on this rosebush. From her scarf, I believe.

I followed the footprints to the wall and found the gap behind the pale pink climbing roses through which the servants creep out. Beyond the wall was the public path and there were no usable prints. It did not matter. I had confirmed my supposition: the victim had come this way on the night she was murdered. There were no other footprints. The killer had not followed her here.

The clay beneath the roses was undisturbed in every direction. I traced Derby's steps from the gap in the wall back to the crazy paving. Here, the stone was uneven and did not hold a print. Did the killer confront her here?

No, I am missing something.

I searched back through the garden, combing through the roses looking for a man's footprints, but I did not see any. Am I wrong? Perhaps the killer kept the gloves on to avoid detection after all? No, his footprint was damp.

Heavy clouds obscured the light and it began to rain. In seconds the ground and all the traces were obliterated. I returned to the house in none too pleasant a mood.

I need to give this matter further contemplation.

This is a woeful house for contemplation.

9

Sept 20th 1897-- Bitterne

Well, well, yesterday transpired to become a study in contrasts: the utterly brutish on one hand, and the sublimely beautiful on the other. As to the case, I find myself with a surfeit of suspects. Indeed, I have only been able to eliminate two from my suspicions. No doubt Watson would remonstrate that women are unlikely stranglers but I have known a number of murderous females and will not eliminate anyone based on gender alone.

I have discounted Miss Simms because she suffers from a severe arthritic condition in her fingers. Even in the unlikely event that she found the strength to squeeze the life from the dead woman's throat, the bruises on the corpse would have reflected the malformation of her joints. There were no such signs, ergo, Miss Simms is not our killer.

Lady Summerville, too, I have removed from my list of suspects. She is overweight, soft in all her aspects, and I have no doubt the murdered woman would be well able to defend herself against so ineffective an opponent. Besides, given the huffing and panting I have seen her exhibit at even the gentlest of activity, I doubt she could manage the climb up the stairs to the servant's quarters.

Mrs Beecham might do the job credibly enough. Though slight of build her hands are strong. She lacks, however, the killer instinct… well, without suitable provocation. I believe she could be quite savage in defence of her loved ones. I keep her on the list with a question mark.

The others in the house I believe are all equally capable of committing cold blooded murder. I eliminate no one. True, the footman

A BIASED JUDGEMENT

Stevens and Lady Beatrice have impressed me with their intelligence and seeming honesty, but as someone once said, it is possible to smile and smile and prove a villain. I will not eliminate them just yet.

Then there is the matter of the footprints on the floor of the murdered woman's room. They reveal a shoe that is small in size, a man's size seven or a woman's size eight. The killer, then, was roughly five foot seven. Lady Beatrice is exactly so tall, but Mrs Beecham, Mr Villiers, Reynolds and young Stevens are of a similar stature. Sir Christopher, though he is some three inches taller, wears a surprisingly small shoe and cannot be eliminated.

I added another suspect to my list this afternoon. The frightful Wallace Summerville arrived on the four o'clock train. It was remarkable to see the atmosphere in the house congeal most unpleasantly upon his appearance.

He is a much smaller man than his brother. Where Sir Christopher gives the impression of being taller than his actual height and possesses an imposing mien, the brother is short, slight and bears an unhappy resemblance to a rodent. His hair is red and course and his moustache sits over his mouth like a dead mouse.

For all his lack of attractive physical features, they are nothing to his behaviour. He is course, abusive and savage, behaviours that are exacerbated by his intemperance. He had not been in the house five minutes before I heard him screaming at the unfortunate housekeeper.

"What do you mean, you have put me on the west of the building, Simms? As a member of the family I deserve better! I always occupy the eastern room."

The poor woman tried to explain that the other guests, myself included, had taken all the rooms on the eastern side of the house. I could not imagine that there was a significant difference between the wings, but Stevens tells me that Summerville's usual chamber, the one I am using, is immediately beside Lady Beatrice's. I conclude, therefore, it is more his being thwarted in his plans to spy on that young

A BIASED JUDGEMENT

woman than the inconvenience of being in the other side of the building that so vexed him.

Miss Simms made every effort to avoid saying she was acting under orders of Lady Summerville; she knew the consequence of such an admission for her mistress. I intruded upon the conversation and introduced myself.

"Ah, Mr Sherlock Holmes," the new arrival said with a sneer. "My brother told me you had arrived to pry into all our doings."

"Do you have 'doings' worthy of my efforts, Mr Summerville?" I asked, genially. "I assure you, I am already well acquainted with your reputation."

"Here," he cried. "Who has been speaking about me? If any of these young pups..."

"I believe your name arose in a conversation I had with Inspector Gregson of Scotland Yard," I said. "Like me, he has been interested in you for some time."

He fumbled for a reply, then a savage smile twisted his features as he said, "Well, now, Mr Holmes, you can't pin this woman's death on me. I wasn't even here yesterday. Anyone will tell you that."

"And where were you?"

"If you will excuse me, gentlemen," Miss Simms said, seizing her chance to escape. "I must see to Mr Summerville's room."

"You do that, you trollop!" he cried as she scurried away. Then his malign gaze was back upon me. "I was in London, if you must know. I have any number of people who can vouch for me, if I need."

I let the matter drop. Summerville has slithered away from justice at least twice before. If he is Liz Derby's killer, better to take my time and build an inescapable trap for him.

About half an hour later a telephone call came from Watson. He kept his conversation brief.

"Just to let you know I shall be staying in the city overnight, Holmes," he said, his voice crackling on the line. "I have learned a great deal that will interest you. Poor Mrs Hudson was under the weather when I arrived, but she seems to be improving…"

Though I had not expected him to complete so many interviews in one day, I confess I find myself disappointed at the delay in his return. I miss his company. As I have often noted, his presence and his knack for asking exactly the right questions often helps me to clarify my own thinking. Still, I needs must do without him for the evening at least.

The rain continues to pour down and it lashed the windows as we gathered in the dining room for supper. Though it is unseasonably cold, Lady Summerville had to plead with her husband for a fire to be lit. We therefore all kept our hands on the plates for warmth. Villiers, I noticed, was shivering uncontrollably.

"I really feel the cold most acutely," he said quietly, in obvious fear of offending our host. "I wish I'd brought a warmer jacket. My hands are quite blue."

They were indeed. The poor men seemed wretchedly uncomfortable, but so did we all. I think the Summerville's fortunes must be in a pitiful state indeed if he begrudges a few fists of coal to ensure his guests' comfort.

Wallace Summerville sat beside Lady Beatrice and made countless unproductive attempts to engage her in conversation. She remained silent and would not even meet his eye. He consoled himself with an astonishing amount of red wine.

Of one thing I am certain: the Lady fears him. And she does not strike me as the sort of woman to fear many people.

"How do you get on with your case, Mr Holmes?" Lady Summerville asked over the roast beef. "Have you – what's the phrase – eliminated us as suspects yet?"

"Some of you, yes indeed, Lady Summerville," I replied. "It is a process, of course, and a significant part of that is knowing as much as possible about the victim."

A BIASED JUDGEMENT

"So... you have nothing to report?" Sir Christopher said. He might have been accusing me of poisoning his prize stallion, so withering was his tone.

"On the contrary," I replied. "I think I get along very well."

"You do?" said Alice Beecham, breathlessly. "Oh, can you tell us?"

"It would be a mistake to say too much at this critical juncture," I replied. "But suffice it to say the killer left traces... they always do, you know. Even the cleverest."

"What sort of traces?" Villiers asked as breathlessly as any of the women.

"Oh, any number of things. The type of weapon is often revealing. In the housemaid's case the weapon was the killer's own hands."

"Which tells you what?" asked Wallace Summerville asked. He made no attempt to disguise his sneer.

"That the murder was a *crime passional*, a crime of passion, not premeditated." I paused, cut a piece of carrot and ate it before adding, "Of course there are other traces, too. Fingerprints, for instance."

They were all silent, spellbound, even Sir Christopher. He said, "Now, I've heard that. I remember reading somewhere that no two people have the same fingerprints."

"That is quite true. Thanks to the work of Sir Francis Galton we have learned a great deal about the usefulness of fingerprinting in revealing a suspect. A number of police bureaus around the world have started to catalogue and use them."

"Yes," Perrot said, slicing his venison with great precision. "They've begun to use them in Argentina." For the moment he seemed to have forgotten that his English was supposed to be poor. "I'm not sure with what success."

"The police in Buenos Aires have had a special fingerprinting bureau in place for some years now," I replied. "I believe they have found it quite successful. Do you know Argentina, M. Perrot? It is a place I have always wanted to visit."

A BIASED JUDGEMENT

"I have an interest in horses," the phony Frenchman said. "I spent a few weeks in Buenos Aires selecting some animals for my ranch a year or two ago. A fascinating place, not at all like Europe. I think you would enjoy it."

"I have no doubt," I replied.

"And this villain," Wallace Summerville asked, his voice already slurred. "Did he leave fingerprints?"

"Sadly no. He seems to have worn gloves."

"Then how do you proceed, Mr Holmes?" Villiers asked. "What is your next step?"

Again I took a moment to study their faces before replying. The Summerville men looked contemptuous; Lady Summerville titillated; Villiers, Perrot and the Beechams were curious. As before, Lady Beatrice seemed indifferent to the entire proceedings.

"As I said this morning, I think learning something of Derby's background may help."

"Ah, and that is why you sent Dr Watson to London," Beecham said. "He seems a very reliable chap, but I wonder you did not go yourself, Mr Holmes."

"I have every confidence in the good doctor," I replied. "And there is yet more for me to do here."

"Well, I hope it shan't take long," Sir Christopher said. "This isn't a guest house you know."

At that, Lady Beatrice raised her eyes from her plate and stared icily at our host. "I am sure, sir," she said. "You did not mean that to sound as ungracious as it did. I believe you owe Mr Holmes an apology."

There was a long pause and the gentleman's face grew progressively redder, more with choler than with embarrassment. His brother glared at the Lady but before he could say anything Sir Christopher said tightly, "No, of course I meant no offense, Mr Holmes."

"Here," his brother slurred, putting his hand on Lady Beatrice's arm. "You've no call to speak to my brother that way."

A BIASED JUDGEMENT

"I will address any member of my family any way I choose," she replied. "Now you will take your hand from my arm, sir, or I will most assuredly break your fingers." She picked up her fork and poised it over the lout's hand. He released his grasp at once.

"Please," Lady Summerville whimpered. "Please let us be calm. Please."

Lady Beatrice set down the fork and said, "I apologise, ma'am." Then, as if there had been no interruption, she calmly resumed her meal.

A silence then settled upon the company and I believe we were all relieved when we adjourned to the music room.

It would have been customary, of course, for the host to offer a cigarette and a cognac to the gentlemen after the meal but Sir Christopher did no such thing. In hindsight, I wonder if he was trying to limit his brother's drinking. He was much too late if that were the case; the lout was already well inebriated with the wine. At any rate, we were led into the music room and his wife begged Lady Beatrice to play the piano. There was a hushed exchange between the two women which ended with the younger sitting unhappily at the instrument.

My experience of 'talented' young women demonstrating their musical skills has seldom been pleasant. At best, they are dull. Frequently they are excruciating.

Lady Beatrice was extraordinary. She played Beethoven's piano sonata No. 14 with feeling and skill that I have seldom hear equalled even in the finest concert halls of the world. Certainly, her playing has never been surpassed. I listened in a state I can only describe as rapture.

She played without sheet music and yet she was note-perfect. I could see that she was quite transported to another realm, as all true artists are. As a violinist I can say with deep sadness it is a state I myself have never achieved.

I cannot say how the other guests responded to her playing; I was utterly transfixed and, I confess, in my rapture I forgot anyone else was present. The perfect beauty of the melody and the depth of feeling with which it was conveyed moved me as little else has ever done.

A BIASED JUDGEMENT

The last notes finally faded and the illusion of a world of civility and perfection shattered as Wallace Summerville shouted, "That's enough of the funeral rubbish. Play something lively."

Lady Beatrice said, "I must remind you, sir, there was a death in this house but yesterday. Lively tunes would not be appropriate. Indeed, I would not have even played the sonata save my aunt was so anxious to hear it."

"A servant," our host sneered. "What is that to us? Come on, you baggage, play something we can sing along to."

"I'm afraid I don't know anything that would suit," she replied, and rose from her seat. She went and stood by the window staring out into the darkness.

Villiers rose to his full five foot seven and said, "I know a few jolly tunes from the theatre. May I?" He sat and treated the company to a selection from Misters Gilbert and Sullivan. He played better than he sang, though he did well enough. Under other circumstances I might have enjoyed his performance. However, his forced jollity felt flat. After he finished his first song Lady Beatrice said, "Will you excuse me? I have a headache."

"Allow me to escort you to your room, Lady Beatrice," Wallace Summerville said rising unsteadily to his feet.

"That will not be necessary," she said. She left the room but he, undeterred, stumbled after her.

The party paid no heed but I observed Stevens silently slip out of the room. I admit I felt some relief in knowing Lady Beatrice had someone to protect her from whatever villainy Summerville had in mind.

"If you will excuse me," I said before Villiers could resume playing. "But I shall retire also. May I wish you all a pleasant evening?"

"Ah of course, of course!" my host said, clearly delighted to be rid of me. Frankly, I was equally pleased to rid of him too.

I left the room and ran silently up the staircase. A sound of a disturbance reached me from above. In a few seconds I achieved the landing and found Lady Beatrice struggling against the embrace of

A BIASED JUDGEMENT

Wallace Summerville. Stevens lay upon the floor with blood trickling from a cut forehead.

I grabbed Summerville and struck him across the chin. He crumpled like a discarded marionette.

"Blackguard!" I cried. "No one but a knave would behave so shamefully."

"You mind your own business, you Scotland Yard buffoon," he said, or tried to. His speech was rendered almost incoherent by rage and alcohol. He tried to get to his feet, but it took him several tries before he succeeded.

"Lady Beatrice," I said. "Are you all right? Come, that is a nasty bruise, we must see to it at once."

"There's ointment and such downstairs, sir," Stevens said climbing unsteadily to his feet. "I'll fetch it."

"Do," I replied. "Good lad. And have someone dress your own wound too." As the boy hurried away I gave Lady Beatrice my arm and assisted her to her room.

"You watch yourself, miss," Summerville cried. "I'll teach you to behave when you're my wife."

She made no reply but I felt her shudder convulsively against me as I led her into her chamber.

I poured her a glass of water and she took it from me with trembling hands.

"I wish Watson was here," I said. "He's far better than I at lending comfort to young ladies in distress."

She gave me a crooked smile and then winced. A deep bruise was forming around her right wrist. "You underestimate yourself, Mr Holmes," she said. "I am greatly in your debt."

"I sincerely hope, Lady Beatrice, Mr Summerville is not truthful when he says you and he are to be married."

"It is certainly not my wish, Mr Holmes," she replied. She would have said more but Daisy knocked on the door.

A BIASED JUDGEMENT

"Beg your pardon, my Lady," she said. "But Maurice – I mean Mr Stevens – said you needed this."

She came into the room and applied ointment to Lady Beatrice's wrist. The lady refused any attempts to bandage the wound.

"Thank you, Daisy," she said, smiling. "You're a very good nurse."

"Yes, my Lady," Daisy said, gathering up the supplies. "Are you sure you are all right? I could fetch you some medicine if you're in pain."

"Thank you, I shall do very well."

"I hope the injury will not impede your piano playing," I said. "I have rarely heard anything more exquisite. You are a remarkably accomplished musician."

Suddenly the lady smiled and her entire countenance changed. Where she had seemed somewhat listless and aloof, she now became animated. "It is just a bruise, and not my first," she said. "I am quite sure I shall have no difficulty playing the piano. I am very pleased that you enjoyed my performance, Mr Holmes. It is a rare thing for me to play for someone who has a knowledgeable ear."

I bade her goodnight and left her with Daisy to assist in her toilette. Then I joined Stevens in the hallway and asked him for a report of what had occurred.

"He's a brute, is Mr Wallace, sir, as I have told you. He is determined to marry Lady Beatrice and steal her fortune for himself. His attempts at love-making are crude, as you have witnessed this evening."

"Indeed so. Lady Beatrice is fortunate you were there to protect her."

"Her Ladyship has always been fair with me, sir, and to all us servants. It breaks my heart to think of her bound to such a lout as that young gentleman."

We stood at the end of the hallway and the sounds of the music below drifted up mingled with raucous laughter. Never has the sound of gaiety sounded more strained or inappropriate.

A BIASED JUDGEMENT

"Before you go, Stevens," I said. "One or two questions: the dead woman, Liz Derby's room looked from the photographs as if it had been searched."

"Yes, Mr Holmes. Her Ladyship thought so too."

"Have you had any thoughts about what the dead woman might have been hiding?"

"I have pondered that very questions, Mr Holmes. There is little enough privacy in a servant's quarters. Like many of us, Derby had a box for her treasures, but there was nothing in it of any note. Lady Beatrice went through it most carefully."

"Ah, one other thing: how often did Derby go to London?"

"She arranged with Miss Simms to take a full day off every Sunday. Her mother is ill, she said, and Derby needed to see to her."

"That seems very generous. Is not a half-day a week customary?"

"Indeed it is sir, but Miss Simms said she had no choice in the matter and, well, it's hard enough to get staff to stay here. Especially female staff. Miss Simms agreed and reduced Derby's wages accordingly."

"Excellent. Thank you, Stevens. That will be all. Make sure you take care of that cut on your forehead."

"Yes, Sir. Daisy will see me to rights. I was anxious to see Lady Beatrice was tended. Is there anything you need before I go, sir?"

"Thank you, Stevens," I said. "I believe I have all I need."

I returned to my room and saw at once that it had been searched. It had been skilfully done, with everything returned almost exactly as I had left it. But there were small signs only my eye would be able to detect: two newspapers I had left on the dresser had been opened and shaken out; the origami figure I left folded on my valise had been moved; and the shilling I had left in my coat pocket had been taken. I was, I confess, vastly amused. That anyone would have the foolishness to think he or she could deceive me. Me!

Happily, the steps I took to reveal any such intrusion worked exceedingly well. The organobromine compound with which I coated

A BIASED JUDGEMENT

my bag's lock will cause an unmistakable purple discolouration of the spy's fingers. The lock remained intact, and I am confident the false bottom of the valise is undetectable to all but the most acute observer. I know who the busybody is and I have no fears that he possesses the requisite intelligence for such a discovery. My journal and Lady Beatrice's letter and the photographs remain secure.

Since the rest of the party, other than Lady Beatrice, remained below playing cards, I took the opportunity to do some spying of my own.

The family and guest bedrooms rooms are laid out thusly:

Sir Christopher and his wife have adjoining bedrooms along the entire south wing. The bathroom on the southeast corner. The Summerville's suite and the bathroom overlook their beloved rose garden. The bedrooms share a small and architecturally ill-advised Venetian-style balcony.

Along the west is the Beechams' chamber, next to which is Wallace Summerville's. These overlook the stables.

M. Perrot and Dr Watson occupy the rooms on the north wing overlooking the lawn.

Finally, the east wing, overlooking the main drive, is occupied by Villiers, myself, and, finally, Lady Beatrice. As with the southern façade, the rooms on the east wing share an equally ill-considered balcony. I think I understand why Summerville junior wanted the room I occupy: The balcony with its array of ficus trees allows him to spy on the lady in her chamber with some measure of cover.

All of the rooms surround the main staircase and the landing.

I began my examination with my host.

Sir Christopher's room, though opulent and well ordered (by the servants rather than the man himself, I have no doubt), reveal an individual of no small vanity. His clothes are of the finest manufacture and his locked drawers contain a significant number of very expensive gemstones. I found no letters. Presumably he is too canny to hold on to anything that can compromise him. There are no secrets here; just

A BIASED JUDGEMENT

evidence of a man who is highly self-indulgent and, I suspect, living considerably beyond his means.

His gloves are, alas, intact and his shoes have narrow, pointed toes.

His wife's bedchamber is frilly and excessively decorated. She displays an unfortunate fondness for cats and these are embroidered onto every surface. Her correspondence is brief: 'Thank you for inviting me; I'm afraid I must decline' written over and over in a large rather childish hand. What strikes me is the frequency with which she refuses invitations. Is it her own choice or that of her husband's, I wonder. From what Stevens and the inspector say, she seems to have been a gregarious creature before her wedding. If not exactly forbidden from participating in these various social events, perhaps fear of her husband's behaviour dissuaded her from attending. I find myself torn between irritation and sympathy. Her clothes are of good quality but at least five years old, while her husband's costume reflects the very height of fashion. Her gloves are old and well-worn with little suede still attached to the surface.

I set aside my indignation on the lady's behalf and moved on to the Beecham's room. This proved to be as dull as the couple who inhabit it. They have no taste, no elegance. Their clothes, though clean and well maintained, are old and of poor quality. The man has only two suits in addition to the outfit he wears to dinner; his wife possesses a total of three dresses. These have all been let out at the waist in the past two or three weeks. I wondered if the husband has been told yet of the happy event Mrs Beecham is expecting.

They, too, have no correspondence, but that is unsurprising. They have no family except themselves. His shoes are round-toed and have a slight heel. The ones he wears each evening are of a similar style. It seems to put him out of contention as a suspect. His wife, however, has shoes that are of a comparable size and style to the killer's footprints. What lengths might a pregnant woman go to if sufficiently provoked? Yes, despite her milksop appearance, Mrs Beecham is a very credible suspect, I think.

A BIASED JUDGEMENT

The next room I searched was Wallace Summerville's. Unlike all the others, this was locked. Getting inside delayed me some fifteen seconds.

Junior has made an attempt at defeating any prying eyes: there is a padlock on his suitcase and all his dresser drawers are locked. It hardly seems worth the effort: the suitcase contains nothing more exciting than his (overdrawn) cheque book; and the drawers reveal nothing more alarming than the sort of smutty pictures that go for a song in Soho. I found no correspondence. His shoes – worn and down at heel – are round-toed.

Thus disappointed, I moved on to M Perrot's room on the south side of the building.

I moved hastily through this particular search. Perrot's fondness for perfume permeates his clothing and the room stinks. His gloves are a very expensive tan leather. His shoes are a square toed size 9, slightly larger than the footprints outside Liz Derby's room.

One point of interest: his valise contained a hidden compartment. It was very well designed and I might have missed it were it not for the peculiar signs of wear around the binding. The compartment contained two things of interest: a pistol and a selection of letters. These last are in French and Italian; nothing in English.

The Italian letters seem innocent enough on the surface. There are comments about the weather and various places in Rome. The first letter said, "Our customer would like to obtain a certain object. Since we release its acquisition may prove difficult, perhaps you might persuade the current owner to consider our terms?" The second letter contained the more sinister suggestion that a certain unnamed gentleman, identified only as "Caesar", has proved difficult and Perrot's services may be required at some point.

Two things about these letters excite my interest. The first is that innocent documents do not need to be hidden. Yet here, in this monolingual house, this correspondence is kept hidden. Secondly, the signatory on both the Italian letters is Romano, a Florentine gentleman

A BIASED JUDGEMENT

who was known to be a past associate of Hugo Oberstein. Thank goodness Herr Oberstein is still enjoying her Majesty's hospitality thanks, primarily, to his activities in the matter of the Bruce-Partington plans. For all the apparent innocence of these letters, I made a note of the contents and shall pass the information on to Mycroft as soon as I return to the city.

The third document was in schoolboy French and revealed at length the plans of the British government to address the situation in South Africa. Names, dates, locations: everything was revealed in horrifying detail. It was very evident that this letter was a continuation in a lengthy correspondence. The signature at the bottom of the letter made me seethe. I knew this bounder, this traitor. For a moment I was filled with incalculable rage. I am not, I think, a man much given to passion, but if that fellow were before me I would cheerfully have throttled him. It occurred to me that were circumstances just a little different, I too, might strangle someone in the heat of passion, just like Derby's killer.

There was not much time and I needed to act. For a moment I contemplated stealing this letter and sending it at once to Mycroft. However, I cannot risk letting the Perrot or his correspondents know that I have uncovered their secrets. Instead, I memorised the contents and then returned the letters to their hiding place.

Feeling in need of a bath to rinse away the filthy perfume, I hurried along to the next room, that of Mr Edmund Villiers. A raucous sound filtered up the stairs and I surmised the family were coming to the end of their entertainment and would soon retire for the night. I hurried on.

Villiers' room is orderly and immaculate. The only gloves I could find are an unfortunate canary yellow leather.

Like a schoolboy, all of Villiers' property is inscribed with his initials in a woman's hand; his mother's, I suspect. Even his lilac coloured silk scarves have discreet 'EStJV's embroidered in the corner.

His writing case is immaculate and expensive; his initials are embossed in the lower right corner of the calf leather cover. In the inside pocket there is a card that reads, "To Eddie, love of my life. From F."

A BIASED JUDGEMENT

The case is at least six months old and yet the card remains; 'F' is well-loved in turn then. I found a slight discolouration of the leather on the inside. Something, papers or a letter, had been here for a long time and only recently been removed. Though it is well stocked with expensive pale blue paper, stamps and notecards, there was no correspondence inside. That was a disappointment. There was also an unfinished and tear-stained letter addressed to 'Francis' which reads, "Why have you not replied to my telegram? You cannot be so cruel... Please, my dear, forgive me..." The letter was so badly stained with tears it was almost illegible. Still, I read enough to intrigue me.

I had just finished examining Villiers' shoes – size eight with pointed toes – when I heard the sound of footsteps coming up the staircase. I slipped back into my own room via the balcony and stood at my door, listening.

Sir Christopher and his wife were bidding each other good night. Banal wishes for a restful night were exchanged, my host seeming out of sorts and his wife declaring herself to have a headache. From this I concluded there would be no marital bliss awaiting Sir Christopher this night. Unless, of course, he forced himself upon the unfortunate woman, an act, I fear, not beyond him.

In any event he did not seem disposed to discuss the matter and I heard the door to his own room open and close a moment later.

As the guests returned to their rooms and the house fell quiet I pondered my discoveries. While there is nothing to definitely incriminate anyone, I could at least move some to the bottom of my list of suspects.

If my theory of motive is correct I can discount the servants. But what if I am wrong? It was a crime of passion, after all. That is all I can be sure of. But, then, the room was searched... Never mind. Start at the beginning. Consider the servants:

Miss Simms, I have already eliminated and I am satisfied with my reasons for doing so.

A BIASED JUDGEMENT

Daisy, though strong, has very small hands and I doubt her fingers could stretch around a neck as thick as Derby's.

The cook is nearly sixty years old; in good health, true, but hardly a match for a strong young woman half her age.

That leaves the men.

Now, Reynolds has the savagery and the strength to do the job. By all accounts, he has demonstrated his brutality in the past. But... he wears square toed shoes which are a size smaller than the killer's. He might be my man, but I really don't think it likely. Not for the first time I am struck by the vexing truth that killers are frequently good people driven to extremes by circumstances, while evil men manage to live blameless lives – at least as far as the courts are concerned. Ah, it is late. I should not wax philosophical at this sort of hour.

Stevens, then: he has the strength and, I think, under the right circumstances I believe he could be quite deadly. To strike down another human being, particularly a woman, seems out of character, but if provoked... He wears a narrow shoe of the right size, he has the strength. My heart tells me he is innocent, but I fear that is more my wish than facts. I cannot discount him. At least, not until I can be sure of the motive.

Lady Summerville I have already discounted since she lacks the strength to strangle a woman at least fifteen years her junior and in rude good health.

Mr Beecham has the strength, but it seems unlikely. What motive could he have? There is nothing to suggest he ever knew Derby before he came here. He is happily married, financially secure. His shoes are a broader fit than the prints suggest. I believe him to be an unlikely candidate.

Though it pains me to admit it, I do not think it likely that Wallace Summerville killed Liz Derby. There's no doubt about his savagery, nor the certainty that he has secrets to hide. But how could he have arrived in this sleepy town from London without being spotted, and then return

A BIASED JUDGEMENT

after the murder? Derby's murder was a crime of passion rather than one that was planned.

As to Lady Beatrice: the only one whose room I did not manage to search. Perhaps tomorrow when she is occupied elsewhere I may get my chance. I think it unlikely that she would leave anything incriminating in her room if for no other reason than she must know it is likely to be searched by Seaton or Summerville. Of course, my eyes are sharper than theirs. It's worth a look, anyway. She is another I cannot eliminate. Indeed, her demonstration at dinner tonight revealed a woman who would not shrink from any task, even murder, if provoked.

Of the other likely suspects, I have no reason to dismiss Sir Christopher, Mrs Beecham, or Mr Villiers. Each demonstrates the resolute nature, physical strength, and passion that combine to make a murderer. Were he here, I have no doubt Watson would add ruthlessness to that list of homicidal traits, but it has been my experience that passion will suffice where the cause is deemed great enough. As for Perrot – that gentleman has given me cause for considerable interest. He is too tall, wears the wrong sized shoes, and is left handed: I believe he is not my killer. But he is more certainly worthy of observation for other reasons.

September 20th, 1897

I have lain upon my bed for hours but sleep continues to elude me. I cannot keep my mind from retracing all the aspects of this peculiar case. The cold, too, has kept me wakeful. Around midnight, I got up and put my coat on top of the thin blankets, but even then I lay awake.

This case vexes me. Unlike most other murders I have studied where the motive becomes clear and, as a consequence, the killer becomes obvious; in this instance there is only one likely reason why the victim was murdered but, alas, that does not eliminate any of my suspects.

Then there is the question of the killer's wet footprints. It is most unfortunate that the weather intervened before I could conduct a proper search of the grounds. The rain continues to beat down and I must use my wits instead of my eyes.

I can see the events unfolding. Derby leaving the house in the middle of the night to go to the pillar box. It is too cold to merely put a coat on over her nightgown and so she dresses. It is late and all the house seems asleep. So, yes, she gets dressed and she takes the path through the roses. It is dark so she takes her time.

The killer sees her. How? Is he looking out his window? No, he's shoes are wet and he wears gloves...

Perrot knows something of fingerprints. He could have worn gloves to conceal his identity. His shoes could be wet for some other reason... No, it is not Perrot. You have already decided he does not fit into the evidence. Wanting him to be the killer will not make him so and it is sloppy thinking, unworthy of you.

Very well, the killer is outside. Perhaps he is distressed and takes a walk. He might have stayed close to the house where the ground is paved; that would not leave prints. Or he saw the dead woman from a window. The bathroom overlooks the rose garden... Yes. Assume that's the case. He sees her and determines to talk to her. He puts on his coat (he may have already been wearing it. It is a very cold house) and he decides to talk to her. He hurries outside but he cannot see her. Now it occurs to him he could search her room while she is gone...

As to the killer's search: There was frustration in the dumping of things onto the floor. The item he sought was not in that room. And he was unquestionably looking for something. Therefore my theory as to motive is correct.

Such were the thoughts that occupied my mind. It was, by my pocket watch, almost two o'clock when I heard a door softly open. Still dressed, I tiptoed to the door and opened it just enough to see Lady Beatrice slip out and head down the hallway. I gave her a minute then silently followed her.

A BIASED JUDGEMENT

My initial thought that she was headed to the library proved incorrect, and I was surprised to find her creep along the back hallways and take the staircase up the stairs to the servants' quarters. Her movements were silent, graceful as she crept up to the attic room in which Liz Derby had been murdered. I watched her take a deep breath and then open the door.

I tiptoed up behind her and stood watching as she as she searched in the drawers of the dead woman's dresser.

"This is an odd activity at so late an hour, Lady Beatrice," I said.

She started and just managed to suppress a yelp. "I couldn't sleep," she whispered, taking her hand from her mouth. "I was thinking about that woman, Derby, and wondering why the killer ransacked her room."

"Yes."

"She was a blackmailer, wasn't she? It all fits: The expensive shoes, her habit of being found in places she was not expected, the reason the room was searched... There can be no other explanation."

"You are correct, Lady Beatrice," I said. "And what conclusions do you draw from this realisation?"

"That the killer is almost certainly not a servant. Derby blackmailed for profit, I surmise. There would be little to be gained from one of the servant classes. Which means the killer is one of the family or guests."

"You do not think a servant might have killed her for another reason?"

I watched her work her way through this idea. "No," she said, after a moment. "If that were the case, her room would not have been searched. No, it had to be the person who she was blackmailing who killed her."

"Excellent," I said. I would have clapped my hands were quiet not so essential. "You do exceedingly well, Lady Beatrice. What else?"

She said, "Given the state of the room, it seems unlikely the killer found whatever documents his victim had stolen. So... what did Derby do with them?"

Her brow was deeply furrowed as she thought. I offered her a clue.

A BIASED JUDGEMENT

"Were you aware, Lady Beatrice, that there was fresh mud on Derby's shoes when her body was discovered?"

"Yes, I noticed that... Oh!"

Her brow cleared and her eyes sparked. "The killer could not have found the documents because she'd already posted them to her home address."

"Almost certainly. She must have been very reluctant to let the papers out of her sight, but she knew he suspected her. She was due to have her day off on Sunday and only had one day to fret about it. Probably it seemed the safer option. If she was challenged by her killer she could insist she was innocent. A search of her room would reveal nothing. I have learned first-hand that anyone's room in this house might be searched."

"Quite so," she said. "Reynolds has a light finger, and the younger Summerville is also apt to spy upon one. So... Derby underestimated his desperation. Possibly... now I think about it, almost certainly he killed her before he searched her room."

"Because..?"

"Because she could have calmly let him examine her belongings. She would have let him inspect everything. But he confronted her in a rage and... she turned her back on him, probably with an air of disdain. Yes. And that was the final straw. He grabbed her throat from behind and throttled her. That's why she was found kneeling facing the bed."

"Well done, well done, indeed, Lady Beatrice. Not even Dr Watson could surpass your ratiocination. Believe me when I say I could pay you no higher compliment."

"You searched this room already," she said. She sounded disappointed. "You realised all of this at once and it's taken me this long to work it out."

"But you did work it out, Lady Beatrice. No, I think you must congratulate yourself; you have really done very well.

"I believe Derby went out some time during the night to post the documents to her home. The killer saw her. He was either already outdoors or he came out to confront her, but he decided instead to search her room before she returned.

"Unfortunately, she came back much quicker than he expected and she caught him before he got very far."

She began to sit on the bed, realised what she was doing, shuddered, and stood up. "I just don't understand why she didn't calmly insist that he examine her room. He would have done so, found nothing, and that would have been that."

There was something in that. I was still missing something, but I would think over it later.

"By the by, did you see that strange apron-like garment hanging in the wardrobe?" I said.

Lady Beatrice shook her head and went to look. She held the item in her hands and studied it. "What a very odd thing," she said. "The fabric is too thin to be an effective apron. So why… Oh, the skirt is a large pocket! This is how she stole the items from her victims. She hid them in this pocket and she wore it under her dress." Suddenly she tossed the item aside. "What a filthy thing to do," she said and shivered.

"You are cold," I said. "Come, I think we have done enough for tonight."

In silence we returned to our wing. At her door I said, "How long will you stay here in Bitterne, Lady Beatrice? I confess the atmosphere here is unpleasant, even more so since Mr Summerville arrived. Your loyalty to your aunt is admirable but she has made her choice."

"She is my only family. We do not choose whom we love, Mr Holmes. Goodnight."

I thought at the time she meant her own affection for her aunt, but I have since considered the possibility she meant her aunt's affection for Sir Christopher.

10

I overslept but I was not the only one. I think most of us were too cold to sleep well. A disconsolate bunch we made over the breakfast table. Our hosts and Wallace Summerville elected to remain in bed and so Daisy and Miss Simms were kept running about to accommodate them. Villiers went for a walk; Perrot said he had letters to write. Edward Beecham prevailed upon Lady Beatrice to give his wife a piano lesson.

With the lady thus occupied, I took the opportunity to search her room.

My expectations were low and that was as well. There was nothing here of any interest. Her foot is narrow and the same size as the killer's. I have already seen her gloves. Her only other pair are made of a plain black leather.

Her stationary case is simple and unadorned. There were two letters; one from Mr Davenport thanking her for her assistance in setting up his inn and assuring her of an invitation to his wedding, "Should Miss Simms ever be prevailed upon to have me." The other was a plea for charity from a friend of her late father's who had fallen on hard times.

She had already drafted replies to both of these. To Davenport she sent her thanks and assurances that it was only a matter of time till Miss Simms succumbed to the gentleman's charms. To the second she sent her acknowledgement of the gentleman's friendship with her late father and a comment that she was sending a cheque for five pounds, which she hoped would help. The letter was unsealed and there was neither a bank note nor a cheque inside. I doubted she would have been careless

A BIASED JUDGEMENT

enough to leave either a cheque or cash lying about in this house. Presumably she would put the money in just before she posted it. But where did she keep her money? Her jewellery, too, seemed oddly absent. I observed the garnet earrings she wore to dinner were nowhere to be seen and she was wearing pearls this morning. There was no jewellery box to be seen; no cheque book nor wallet. I must conclude that she keeps these items on her person at all times when she stays here. What a way to live.

Watson has cabled that he plan to return to Bitterne on the afternoon train. Stevens took me to the station to meet him. It was still cold and wet and I wondered if I'd ever feel warm again.

Fortunately, Watson's train arrived promptly. I found myself very pleased to be reunited with my chronicler.

"My dear fellow," I exclaimed. "You look done in. I fear you have had a wearying time in the city."

"Indeed so," he replied. "But not without interest."

'Stevens," I said. "Why do you not drop us at the inn and then go see your mother? Watson and I will have an ale and get warm. You may collect us in an hour."

"I'm much obliged to you, Mr Holmes. Thank you, sir."

The inn was small, quiet and blessedly warm. The proprietor, a genial middle aged man whose ears revealed he was once a pugilist, served us at once. I commented on the shortage of drinking glasses.

"Those Lowry boys," he said. "Hardly a week goes by when they do not create some sort of disturbance. Half my takings go to repairs and restocking glasses and bottles."

"I would have thought an old fighter like you could handle them," I said.

"Why, bless you, sir, how did you know that? I did box, indeed I did, and very good I was too. But those years are long behind me, I'm afraid. Besides, there are six of them and only one of me. Takes every man in the police station to sort them out when they get started.

A BIASED JUDGEMENT

"Now, a meat pie, was it, sir? My Bertha will bring it to you. Just have a seat. Can I get you something to drink?"

We ordered hot rum and took our seats in the corner. The place was quiet enough given the time of day and the filthy weather so we could talk freely.

I waited till Watson finished eating before asking him to relate his tale. "I trust you had no difficulty in town?" I said.

"You mean your shadows? No, no difficulty at all, though they are still there, lurking opposite our flat. I suspect they might have tried to follow me but Billy had the boys distract them and I made off in a cab."

He sipped his ale and continued. "I did as you suggested and began at Baker Street. The Irregulars had already accomplished a great deal: they had tracked Derby's background and her current London address; they also found out about the former butler, Davenport. Young Billy then accompanied me when I went to visit the dead woman's last half dozen employers. I was fortunate they were all in the same two mile radius; much shoe leather it saved me.

"There is no doubt in my mind Liz Derby was a most unsavoury young woman. The despair and anguish she left in her wake is distressing in the extreme. Not one of the people I spoke showed even a modicum of distress at the news of her death. Indeed, several offered a prayer of thanks that they were rid of her.

"Each told the same story: They hired Miss Derby based on her excellent references. Initially she gave good and reliable service but as days passed and she learned the routine, she was often found in parts of the house where she had no business being. Before long, incriminating items disappeared: letters, photographs, and so forth. Then the demand for a 'gift', usually to the sum of several hundred pounds. These 'gifts' were given, in hardship, very often, and the woman's employment terminated. But demands for more money soon followed."

I interrupted Watson's tale to ask about Derby's pattern of employment.

A BIASED JUDGEMENT

"Always the same, Holmes," he said. "The longest she stayed at any place was three months. I assume because it took her longer to find anything of value in that house. It was the Mandeville's home in Golders Green. She always managed to get all of Sunday off each week. The story was always the same: her mother was ill and Derby needed to attend her."

"Ah, I think we can rule out religious devotion as a motivation for this extra time. She needed time to hide away her stolen treasures. Obviously she would not want them in her possession for more than a few days at a time," I said. "Even with the room to herself, there was too much risk of being caught."

"Oh, that reminds me: there is a pattern of the servant who shared her room being dismissed a short while after Derby's arrival. In most cases – though not all – Derby managed to keep the room to herself for at least a day or two. I suppose she needed to keep her stolen items in her room until she had time to take them to her home and did not want to risk discovery."

"An exceedingly unpleasant young woman, Watson," I said. "Indeed, this entire house is, almost without exception, quite vile."

He gave me a look and seemed about to comment. However, he said only, "So what's been happening while I was away?"

I related the details of my time at the manor and he listened attentively.

"I checked with Gregson as you asked," said he. "And he was unhappy to report Wallace Summerville was most definitely in London on the night of the murder. He was cautioned after he got into an altercation at the Suffolk club. He was extremely inebriated and smelled, according to the officer at the scene, 'like he'd just climbed out of a vat of ale' He is a most unsavoury character, Holmes. I fear for any woman who must endure his presence. If Lady Beatrice is indeed to marry him, her life won't be worth a moment's purchase."

I dismissed the matter with more indifference than I felt. "That is not our concern at present, Watson. We have a murderer to unmask; the romantic attachments of young women is beyond our remit. Once we find Liz Derby's secret collection of blackmail items we will have definite proof of the killer. There must be something there to reveal him – or her."

"Her? You cannot mean you still suspect any of the ladies? I am quite certain Lady Summerville doesn't have the physical strength. Given Mrs Beecham's current state, I would say she is equally unlikely; besides there can be no motive. And Lady Beatrice…"

"Yes? What of Lady Beatrice?"

"She's done nothing but assist us, Holmes. You said yourself you watched her reason out the blackmail. She wouldn't have done that if she were a victim, surely?"

"I have only her word that she went to Derby's room last night merely to test a theory. It's equally possible that she was making another attempt at searching for her own stolen documents."

"You don't really mean that?"

"I cannot afford to eliminate her from my suspect list just because she's beautiful and talented," I cried.

For a moment Watson said nothing, then he began, "I've been wondering, Holmes…" I waited. I know from old that when my friend has an unpopular opinion to express he cannot be hurried. I have also learned that these observations are often of immense value.

"Would it be so dreadful," he continued. "If the killer was not discovered in this case? I mean, the dead woman was monstrous; the number of lives she has destroyed or compromised… I confess, I have great sympathy for whoever was driven to such an extreme response."

I sipped my excellent hot rum before replying, "I understand your sensibilities, Watson. I even share them. But if the killer is not revealed, everyone in that house must be suspect for the rest of their lives. I confess I would not be too unhappy at such a fate befalling our unpleasant host or his revolting butler, but there are innocents there too. All we can do is our best and trust that justice may be done." I thought some more and added, "This case is not like the odious Milverton where the police had no clear suspect. Here everyone must be under suspicion."

"It's a hanging offence, Holmes."

"I know, Watson, I know. In any case, though I have two clear suspects I have no proof against either. All is mere theory until that proof is found. Ah, there's Stevens. I see his mother has died."

It required no great powers of deduction to see the change in the young footman's countenance. His face was blanched and tears were not far from the surface, though he did an admirable job of keeping them under control.

"Good God, man!" Watson exclaimed. "What is it? Stevens, sit down. I shall fetch you a brandy. How may I assist?"

"No, thank you, Doctor. You're very kind but I need nothing." He said. "I was in time to spend her last few minutes with her. Her neighbour, Mrs Pettigrew, was with her and had sent word to the manor to fetch me. Thanks to you, Mr Holmes, I was able to hold her hand at the last and close her eyes."

"You should not be here, lad," Watson said in his most gentle manner. "Go home and take care of things there. Holmes and I can take the trap back. If word has already been sent to the manor, they'll understand."

"Sir Christopher…"

"We shall see to your master," I said. "Watson is right, Stevens. Your first duty is to your mother and yourself. Is there anything we can do to assist you?"

The lad shook his head and ran the back of his hand across his face. "Thank you, Mr Holmes. I confess I am loath to leave her. This is the last duty I can ever do for her, my poor old mum."

"Take comfort in the knowledge that she is beyond all pain and suffering now, lad," Watson said, gently.

Watson and I returned to the manor and I informed Sir Christopher of Stevens' situation. "Confound the boy," he roared. Then, seeing Watson's expression added, "I suppose it cannot be helped. Well, we

A BIASED JUDGEMENT

shall be without conveyance until he returns. Can't have the housemaids drive us into town, now can I?"

Lady Summerville burst into tears when I told her of the death of old Mrs Stevens.

"Oh Alice," she cried. "She was with me for years, Mr Holmes, before she became unwell. Those were such happy days." She looked up at me with reddened eyes. "Deaths come in threes, they say…"

"I do not think you can count Mrs Stevens in this instance," Watson said, holding her hand and speaking with infinite gentleness. "The woman was old and she has not worked here for quite some time, I believe."

"But she's someone I know," she insisted. She began to sob.

In the end Watson had to give her a powder to calm her. Lady Beatrice, dry-eyed but, I think, upset, led her aunt upstairs to lie down.

This evening before dinner Watson and I took advantage of a break in the weather and went for a brief walk in the grounds of the manor. It was warmer outside than it was in the house. The gardens may not be large, but they are well maintained. Not for the first time, I marvelled that not only is Lady Summerville a keen gardener, but that her husband apparently shares her enjoyment. I would not have expected Sir Christopher to have the temperament for so wholesome, not to mention so invigorating a pursuit, but it is these little inconsistencies that enrich our lives.

At least here in the fresh air (spoiled, Watson said, by my "infernal cigarettes") we could discuss the case without fear of being overheard.

"You mean that butler went through your things? What a bounder!" Watson said.

I laughed. "You should have seen him at breakfast trying to hide his purple fingers."

"Serve him right."

"It is a nice household where private letters are read and one's belongings are searched and stolen." I bent down to inhale the scent of one of the last pink roses then, standing up and stretching my back I said, "What did Davenport tell you?"

Watson referred to his notebook. "He seems a very genteel, very respectable gentleman, Holmes. His inn in Pimlico does good business and the man himself is well respected and liked in the area.

"He tells me that initially all the servants were happy when Lady Winifred Jacoby, as she was, announced she was to be married. Sir Christopher seemed an honourable man. Then."

"Ah. And when did things change?"

"Within a day or two of the wedding. Sir Christopher summoned Davenport to the library and told him he had discovered some irregularities in the finances of the household. Though the charge was patently false he was dismissed at once.

"The staff were very distressed. They'd worked together for a long time. Davenport and Miss Simms were to be married. But it was done."

"And has he maintained contact with any of the staff here since he was sacked?"

"He still sees Miss Simms once a month when she has her weekend off. They meet in Southampton. He still wants to marry her but she's afraid to make so great a change. She's been in service all her life and I doubt she's ever even been inside an inn."

"So can he tell us anything about the inhabitants?"

"Nothing we do not already know or haven't surmised. One thing is certain: Rillington Manor was a happy house before the Summervilles arrived. Oh, he says Lady Beatrice was 'always a handful' but as straight and true as the queen's own guard."

We walked down to the gate and then slowly ambled back again towards the house. I said, "What did you learn of Derby's background in London?"

"The usual story: a founding, lived on the streets from a young age. Eventually was taken into service by a Jewish family in Golders Green by the name of…." He peered at his notes. "Yes, the Zeiss family. She was with them four years then almost overnight the entire family was wiped out with typhus."

"Four years?" I said. "Well, she had not learned her wicked ways yet, I suppose."

"By all accounts she was quite happy there. The Irregulars reported she was treated as one of the family. But it all changed after their deaths."

"She found another position?"

"Yes, quite quickly. A banker by the name of Longly took her on. She was there six months. Then followed her usual pattern."

"Ah…" I stopped walking and stared at nothing in particular for several minutes. Watson remained silent, letting me think.

"Where has she been living?" I said.

"A house in Brixton, Holmes. The Irregulars got it before Lestrade. I, ah, didn't mention it to him and don't you tell him either. He dropped everything to look into this case."

I waved a languid hand. "I have nothing but appreciation for the good inspector, Watson. Never fear."

The rain started again and we hurried back to the manor. Before we went inside I said, "I should like to take a look at the place Miss Derby called home. Have the police been there yet?"

"No, not yet. Strictly speaking, it's not Lestrade's case, after all. You shall have an untouched area to work in." With some reluctance he added, "I, uh, suppose you want to leave tonight?"

"I should like nothing more, but I do not think it is wise to leave this place unattended over night, not with a killer still at large."

"Well, I can keep watch."

I considered that idea. If I travel to the city this evening, Watson can surely keep watch here. I could accomplish my task overnight and return on the morning train.

On the other hand, Watson is obviously exhausted and though I do not doubt that he would spend the night in a chair, I am not convinced it is the best option. As tired as he is, he might well fall asleep. Besides,

A BIASED JUDGEMENT

a close scrutiny of Derby's house in the dark would not be efficient. This case has already been compromised by my inability to properly view the scene."

"You are done in, my dear Watson. You should sleep in a bed, even if it is such a bed as this wretched place affords."

"No, let us spend the night and travel to London in the morning."

"You mean me to come with you, then?"

"Of course, your assistance would be invaluable. We shall only be gone a few hours and will be back here before dark. No, I think we can risk it."

September 22nd, 1897

Yesterday morning Watson and I left the manor to return to London. So much has happened that this is my first chance to write up these notes.

I spoke with Inspector Greer before I left and told him of our plans. "If all goes well, I shall have answers for you tonight; by tomorrow morning at the latest."

On the train I fell into a brown study and Watson had to speak my name three times before I realised he was speaking to me.

"I beg your pardon, my dear fellow, I said. "You were saying?"

"I was asking if you had any fixed plan in mind. Did you want to go directly to Brixton or would you prefer to start at Scotland Yard?"

"Oh, Brixton, certainly. I sent word last night to Lestrade to ask him to meet us there." I fell silent once more. Watson wasn't having it however.

"Come, Holmes, these are dark thoughts which occupy your mind. What is it you fear?"

I released a long breath, lit a pipe and then said, "I begin to have second thoughts about leaving that house unprotected, Watson. There is violence and death there. It would take very little to unleash it."

A BIASED JUDGEMENT

"Come, Holmes, I am sure you worry unnecessarily. You said yourself, we'll be back by nightfall. What can possibly happen in just a few hours?"

"I do not know... I think I made an error in bringing you with me, Watson. If you had stayed there you might have kept an eye on things and I confess I would be easier in my mind..." I puffed disconsolately at my pipe before adding. "But the task ahead of us may require considerable deductive reasoning and I am forced to admit I find my abilities greatly enhanced by your presence, old man."

"Thank you, Holmes. I am always glad to be of help, as you know. But if this was a crime committed in passion and without premeditation, surely it is unlikely to happen again. What is it you fear?"

"Lady Beatrice," I said.

"Did you say Lady Beatrice? But for goodness sake, why?"

"Are you familiar with the properties of gunpowder, Watson? On their own, sulphur and charcoal and saltpetre are not dangerous, but when you combine them and then expose them to a flame they become deadly. That is what we have left behind us, Watson: a house full of gunpowder."

He stared at me in horror. Then, trying to lift my spirits said with an attempted laugh, "I cannot see that young Lady as sulphur, Holmes!"

"No, Watson, she's not. She's the flame."

For several seconds he said nothing, then, aghast, "You cannot mean she is the killer. Why, she's a girl. Taller than most, perhaps, and rather unfashionably athletic in her structure, but to imagine her in a life and death struggle..."

"What? Oh, Watson!" I slapped my hands together as all the pieces suddenly slid from their disparate places and slotted into a clear and startling picture. "Oh I am a fool,' I cried. 'Watson, I am a dolt."

'What, Holmes? What is it?'

'Oh if it is so... if it can only be so! On the face of it it seems improbable and yet... why not?' And I laughed long and loud.

11

Liz Derby's house is an unappealing building on the Brixton Road, a mere stone's throw from the place where, seventeen years ago, I conducted my investigation of the Drebber-Stangerson case, or, as Watson would have it, *A Study in Scarlet*.

Lestrade met us at the door and let us in.

"Thank you for your assistance, Inspector," I said. "Which flat is the victim's?"

"None, Mr Holmes," he replied. "She owned the building."

"Good gracious!" Watson said. "Working as a servant yet wealthy enough to buy a three-story house? Astonishing!"

"She did not accrue her assets from scrubbing floors, Watson," I observed. "Or rather, not directly."

"I'm afraid I cannot stay, Mr Holmes," Lestrade said. "I have other cases that require my attention and strictly speaking this one's not my concern, since the murder occurred in Bitterne and the local police are handling it. Still, if you would like to stop by the Yard around three o'clock there are a couple of other matters that I would like to discuss with you."

"An excellent notion, Inspector," I said. "We shall be glad to meet with you. Though perhaps you would rather join Watson and me for a late luncheon? Say, at the Rose and Crown?"

"That would be splendid, Mr Holmes. I shall see you then. Doctor." And with a touch to his hat he set off and left me and Watson to get down to business.

A BIASED JUDGEMENT

The house, despite its outer appearance, is clean, tidy and well-ordered within. The hallway was bright enough, despite the weather, thanks to the fanlight over the door. On the mat there was a large envelope addressed to 'Miss Eliza Derby.'

"This is what she posted just minutes before her death, Watson," I said, as I examined it.

I tore open the envelope and there, sure enough, was a love letter. The contents were so florid as to make even me blush. Watson took the pages from me with a shaking hand.

"Good God, Holmes," he cried. "I've never seen such filth…"

"The correspondents obviously do not share your opinion, my friend. Indeed, though I am hardly an expert, this seems like the product of a genuine, if, ah, passionate love affair. Certainly motive enough, is it not, for murder?"

"Unquestionably. But I am all astonishment. I really never suspected…"

"Which is why blackmail is so effective a weapon," I said. "Come, let us see if we can uncover this odious woman's secrets."

We followed the hallway into a large, comfortable living room. There were no books or newspapers, no musical instruments or any other form of amusement. The furniture was sturdy but otherwise uninteresting.

The only oddity was a collection of dolls, hideous things about eighteen inches high, with sinister porcelain faces and stuffed bodies. I pulled my jack-knife from my pocket and ripped open the back of one. It contained nothing but straw.

"You surely don't think Derby hid those stolen papers in a doll, Holmes?"

"Not papers, but perhaps a key."

"A key? Whatever for?" He was systematically going through every drawer and every cupboard. One of the things that impresses me about Watson is I seldom have to give him direction. Another virtue he refuses to acknowledge in his writing. He'd rather make me appear the all-

A BIASED JUDGEMENT

knowing hero. I've pointed out that as a result he sometimes makes himself seem a bit of a dolt but he laughs it off. "Poetic license, Holmes," he says. Such twaddle.

As we worked I said, "If the dead woman has amassed a collection of letters and photographs she's hardly going to leave them in plain sight. No, she'll have secreted them away. My first thought was she might have a security box in a bank..." I continued to examine the line of grotesque dolls as I spoke.

"Yes?" Watson urged. "I'd have thought she'd want to keep them close at hand. Holmes?"

"A key, Watson!" I exclaimed, retrieving the slender iron object from inside the head of a grotesque figurine that seemed to represent a harlot. A horrifying thing in a child's toy.

I flung down the doll and examined the object it hid.

There is no standard size for safety deposit boxes or their locks; each bank is unique. However, this was a large bridgeward key most commonly used for deadlocks. As I studied it I remembered Watson was waiting for my reply. I said, "What were you saying? Oh, the bank... Well, given her long absences she might have thought her treasures safer there. Still, you are right: blackmailers like to keep their stolen treasures as close to hand as possible. This key... Look at it, Watson."

"Heavy," he said. "And quite ornate. It would be hard to pick the lock that this key opens, I think."

"I think you're right, my dear fellow. And I think that was rather the point. Now, let us see if we can find that very lock."

I looked around the room, seeing the traces of Derby's living. She was not a careful housekeeper and the tracks of her footsteps could be clearly seen. There was nothing in this room to which she repeatedly returned, however. What did she do with herself here, I wondered. How can anyone live with things to read or music to hear? This woman seemed to have no interests at all other than her collection of revolting dolls.

A BIASED JUDGEMENT

"I'll start in the kitchen, Holmes," Watson said.

"Thank you, Watson; that would be excellent. This woman has undoubtedly accumulated a significant number of treasures so we are looking for a large trunk or a cupboard. Be systematic and precise. If you find any anomalies, do not touch them yourself but fetch me at once. Be careful to look behind things; if there is a door, it may well be concealed behind a picture or some such. I shall start upstairs and work my way down."

For the next three hours we examined every inch of the building. I climbed up into the attic, even though I knew it was highly unlikely: scaling an unsteady ladder with any regularity would not have been practical. On the other hand, I would not be easy in my mind if I did not let the evidence rule it out. Making assumptions with no hard facts is always an error.

I examined every inch of the three bedrooms. Two of the rooms were idle and there was no sign they had been used in recent memory. The third was obviously that of the dead woman. There were clothes in the wardrobe; a series of exceptionally ugly straw hats on the shelf; and a box of cheap and gaudy jewellery. I had, I confess, held high hopes for this room.

The dingy and under-used bathroom revealed nothing, nor did any of the cupboards or the hallway.

Watson joined me in the living room and shook his head.

"It is here somewhere, Watson. I'd stake my reputation on it," I said.

"I've combed every inch of the ground floor, Holmes. I've moved pictures, even dug through the food in the pantry. Nothing."

"Damnation!" I exclaimed. "I will not be bested by this small-minded, malicious guttersnipe."

"Holmes," Watson said in his most soothing manner. "You'll find it. Take a breath. Perhaps take a walk in the back yard. It is small to be sure, but it's stopped raining for the moment. Do go, it may help you clear your head."

A BIASED JUDGEMENT

"Yes. Yes, that is a sound idea. Perhaps you would be so good as to go through the bedrooms again. I may have missed something.'

"You, Holmes? Surely not!" he teased.

I smiled, recovering my humour. "You know far more than I about the habits of women, Watson. It is possible there was some anomaly that I could not detect. But I shall go outside for a few moments and gather my thoughts. What time is it?"

"Half past one."

"Well, if need be, we can come back after our meeting with Lestrade. All the same, I am loath to stay away from the manor for too long."

The rain had stopped for the moment, as Watson observed, and a fragile sun was trying to brighten the day. I wandered around the muddy and neglected yard for some minutes, thinking. At last I stopped and looked up at the building. I counted the windows: there were four which belonged to the two back bedrooms and the kitchen. The third bedroom, bathroom and living room were all at the front of the house.

I reviewed the position of each window and its corresponding room. The third floor was empty and unfurnished.

I kicked a stone. I had missed something. But what? I had searched the house from rafters to foundation... no, wait! I had not!

I ran back into the house and called, "Watson, Watson!"

The doctor came running down the stairs. "Have you found it, Holmes?"

"A basement, Watson? Did you find a basement?"

"No, come to think of it, I didn't. But there must be one, surely? At least a coal cellar."

"Exactly. It is a strange thing, Watson, but I find it is always easier to spot incongruity when an unexpected thing is present; far more difficult to notice when something that should be there is not."

I examined the fireplace: there was a plentiful supply of coal here in the scuttle but no sign of where it had come from. There were still ashes in the grate and though there was no telling how long they had been

A BIASED JUDGEMENT

there, it was a reasonable assumption that, given the recent bad weather, Derby had lit a fire the last time she was here, just over a week ago.

There was enough coal for one day's heating if she was careful with it, but no one buys coal in such a small amount. No, there must be a place where coal was kept.

I lay down on the floor and examined it with my magnifying glass.

"What are you looking for, Holmes?" Watson asked.

"Coal dust," I said. "Ah!"

The trail of small specks was not visible to the naked eye, but was clear enough under my glass. Thanking the stars that the dead woman was an unenthusiastic housekeeper I followed the trail into the kitchen. They led directly to the large china dresser. A glance at the floor showed faint scuff marks on the tiles. Ah, yes, that made sense. I felt along the shelves and dishes and there, behind a large blue pot, I found the handle embedded in the wood, almost invisible to the naked eye. I pulled it and the dresser swung easily out from the wall. Behind it was a flight of stairs leading downwards.

"Can you find a candle or a lamp, Watson?" I asked.

He took the oil lamp from the table and lit it, and then the two of us made our way down the stone steps to the basement.

"It is very curious, is it not, Holmes?" Watson asked as we climbed down the stairs. "I can understand her wanting to hide the papers, but why hide the entrance to the coal cellar?"

"An additional precaution. There's an old and filthy cart in the cupboard under the stairs. I saw it without giving it much thought. Now I realise she would have picked up the coal in it and brought it home in that thing. No one need ever know the basement was here; she wanted to make it as difficult as possible for anyone who came snooping. I've no doubt we shall find the door this key opens down here. Now, let us see what we may find."

The coal was piled in the corner to the right of the stairs. There was a plentiful supply, at least six months' worth. The rest of the cellar was filled with bric-a-brac: old prams, suitcases, and boxes all lay scattered about in a disorderly way.

"Does this not strike you as odd, Watson?" I said.

"That she should store things like boxes down here in a damp basement when there are two empty bedrooms? Yes, very odd."

"Not to mention the spacious attic. What does it suggest to you?"

He looked about him. "I would say Derby was making it difficult for anyone to find the secret door. I can't see it, can you?"

"Not yet. But I suspect this rubbish also served the purpose of revealing to Derby if anyone has been intruding here. There's no way of getting through these things without moving them, and it would take some effort to remember where each item had been. A decidedly paranoid person, was Miss Derby. Hardly surprising in a blackmailer. It must have rankled having to trust those stolen documents from Rillington Manor to the post."

Watson tiptoed through the accumulated junk with a concentrated expression on his face. "Odious creature," he said. "But you're right about paranoia being the normal state of being for a blackmailer. They have more insight into others' secrets, and a greater awareness of how easily those secrets can be uncovered than most."

"They have indeed. This is odd…"

"What, the mirror?"

"Mm. It's a perfectly adequate mirror. I'd expect to see it hanging in one of our larger mansions. It is enormous; far larger than the paltry square over the sink in the water closet. A cellar seems an odd place for such a thing, does it not?"

The mirror, it transpired, was not a freestanding object, but rather the door to a secret room. The lock was embedded into the side of the ornate frame and the key slid easily into it. With a cry of triumph I pulled it open and stepped inside.

The room was about six foot wide and eight foot long. It contained forty-two leather boxes. Most were clearly labelled with the names of some of the most illustrious people of the land. Some twenty or so others were unlabelled; I assumed these were empty, awaiting trophies she had yet to acquire. Never will acquire, now, thank God.

The boxes were neatly stacked upon a long table. In the corner there was what I first took to be a bench, but which further scrutiny revealed to be a trunk covered with a blanket.

I turned my attention first to the smaller boxes and went through the stacks. I chuckled as one name in particular caught my attention.

"Here, Watson! You see?"

"Good gracious, Holmes. How appalling!"

"Yes, well, we are all capable of foul things when we are driven by fear and despair. We shall take all these documents with us. No sense subjecting these unfortunates to further scrutiny and distress. First, let me open the lid of that trunk… I have some suspicions but perhaps I am wrong…"

I was not wrong. Inside was the mummified corpse of a man. Judging by his clothes and his hands, I determined he was a workman, though with a decidedly shady past. "Eddie 'Popper' Porter," I said. "Or so I surmise."

"How ghastly, Holmes," Watson said. "But you cannot possibly recognise him in this state."

"No, that birthmark on the back of his left hand that looks like a squib. It was the reason for his nickname, 'Popper'."

Watson looked about him and I waited as he put the pieces together. "He did this work for her and she killed him. I'm right, aren't I, Holmes?"

"It is as good a theory as any I can devise. Her need for secrecy was too great to risk anyone else knowing about this room. She probably persuaded him to do the work by suggesting he could hide his booty here. Porter was a notorious thief, you know. So she came here to review his work and then killed him. When he disappeared about five years ago I suspected he'd come to a bad end. I don't suppose you can determine a cause of death at this stage, Watson?"

A BIASED JUDGEMENT

The doctor examined the body with his usual thoroughness. "Yes," he said, after some moments. "There is a fracture along the back of the skull. Presumably she struck him with a heavy object."

"Yes, possibly one of his own tools. Would the fracture have been enough to kill him, do you think?"

"It would have knocked him senseless but it's impossible to tell if it was the direct cause of death without an autopsy. It's exceedingly likely the man was knocked out then she suffocated him."

"I suspect that's what happened. She locked him in the trunk and in that airtight container he never regained consciousness. In any event, it hardly matters. We shall inform Lestrade, but first let us remove these boxes."

"They're going to be difficult to transport, Holmes. There have to be about forty of them. They're not heavy but they are bulky."

"See if you can find a sheet or a tablecloth; we can wrap them up in that and leave them in Jermyn Street. We can go through them when we have more leisure. Give me a moment to check these unlabelled ones… Oh, they're not all empty. I wonder why there are no labels on them. Well, we'd better take the lot."

We did exactly that. There was barely enough time to deposit the boxes in my bolt hole before hurrying off to the Rose and Crown to meet Lestrade.

"You should have called me as soon as you found the body, Mr Holmes," the inspector said mildly as we related our discovery of Popper Porter's mummified corpse. "Though I suppose it hardly matters."

"Yes, I'm sorry about that, Lestrade. Though we left the body precisely as we found it. Here is the key to get you into the hidden room."

"Behind the mirror, you said, Mr Holmes? What I don't understand is why she would need a room like that in the first place."

A BIASED JUDGEMENT

Watson and I exchanged a glance. I said, "She was a blackmailer, Inspector. She hid the objects of her filthy trade in that room and she wanted to be sure no one else could access her secrets."

Lestrade knows me of old. He glanced from me to the doctor and back again. With a sigh of resignation he said, "I assume all evidence of this 'filthy trade', as you call it, is no longer there?"

"It does not good to sully people's names, inspector. Besides, your murderer is dead. What does it matter?"

"And I suppose there's no possibility that someone else murdered Porter?"

"None at all. You know my methods, Inspector."

"I should by now," he said. "Never mind. I'll take care of it. At least we won't have to worry about Popper making the Brixton Road a misery for everyone who lives there."

Satisfied that I had not corrupted evidence pertinent to his case, Lestrade turned his attention to another matter.

"Take a look at this picture, Mr Holmes, and see if you recognise him."

I took the photograph and studied it. "Ah, my old friend Gilberto Calvini." I handed the picture to Watson. "This is the villain who stabbed me in St James's Park. He is dead, then?"

"Dead as Mr Marley's doornail," said he, citing Dickens. "We found him on the Embankment with a broken neck. It was expertly done, very efficient."

"He's a savage looking brute, Holmes," Watson said. "You're lucky to be alive."

"Do you have any other information, Inspector?" I said. "When did this wretch return to our shores?"

"Three days ago, Mr Holmes. My man on the docks spotted him and followed the brute just as we planned. Calvini met up with a chap called Travis at the Old Bull the day he arrived."

"Algernon Travis, commonly called 'The Albino'? Yes, I know him. That is exceedingly interesting."

A BIASED JUDGEMENT

"Is it?" Lestrade said. "In any case, the two of them wandered about the docklands, getting drunk and carrying on, and from there made their way up the river to the Embankment. My constable thought they spotted him because they gave him the slip. The next morning Calvini's body was discovered in the Victoria Underground station."

"Hm... I do not suppose you were able to pick up the Albino's trail again, Inspector?"

"Ah, I thought you might ask me that. In point of fact, we did. We traced him back to the house of a gentleman by the name of Albrecht Porlock in Finsbury Park."

"Porlock," I exclaimed. "Ah, that is most interesting."

"Is it? I don't suppose you'd care to tell me why?" Lestrade always looks most ferret-like when he is curious. The resemblance at that moment was quite uncanny.

"It is a government matter, Lestrade," I said. "I'm afraid I can say no more than that. This Porlock gentleman, do you know anything about him?"

"Not much at all, I'm afraid, other than he owns a house in Finsbury Park and had a meeting with our friend here," he patted the picture of my dead assailant.

"I see. And I don't suppose you know where the Albino went after that meeting?"

"He took the boat to Ostend," Lestrade replied with some swagger.

"Ah, excellent. Well done, Inspector. And after that?"

"I'm afraid we have no means of tracking him beyond our shores, Mr Holmes," he looked crestfallen.

Watson said, "I think you've done splendidly, don't you, Holmes?"

He gave me a pointed look and I said, more enthusiastically than I felt, "Yes, indeed. Really excellent work, Lestrade."

A clear link between Porlock and Moriarty's old network. A small thing, to be sure, but many of my cases have rested upon small things. The depth to which parsley sank in the butter, I remember, helped me solve a particularly nasty murder. And there was the bloody fingerprint

A BIASED JUDGEMENT

that solved the apparent death of Mr Jonas Oldacre. My entire career has been built on small but significant details.

I was curious to hear that the Albino, a man as lacking in conscience as he is swift with a blade, should be in cahoots with the Professor's old university chum. From such unions fearful things are born.

"Yes, you have done very well, Lestrade," I said. "I am exceedingly obliged to you."

The inspector flushed with pleasure. It is ridiculously easy to elevate people.

I glanced at my watch and said, "Are you almost finished your luncheon, Watson? We really have no time to dawdle."

Watson gave me one of his faces and said, "Another ten minutes will hardly matter, Holmes."

Lestrade took advantage of the delay to say, "I, ah, don't suppose you'd care to tell me what you know about this Albino chap, Algernon Travis? Is he someone I should worry about?"

"He's most certainly worth keeping an eye on. It is a remarkable thing, but he has never been arrested and yet his name has been linked to some of the most dangerous men in England. That case of the screaming nun that I consulted on, you remember? Travis was behind it; well, he and some old friends of ours, yours and mine, Inspector."

"Do you mean the late Professor Moriarty's gang? We can never seem to stamp out that organisation entirely. We're making progress, though, with your help, Mr Holmes."

"That organisation is like the Lernaean hydra of legend, Inspector: for every head we chop off two more grow in its place. But have no fear, we'll get the better of the rascals if it takes every man in England and another decade to do it."

Watson finished his meal at last and we rose. "I will be happy to discuss this matter further with you upon my return, Lestrade, but I am anxious to get back to the manor before nightfall."

"Do you want to go to Baker Street, Holmes?" Watson asked when we were in the cab.

"Baker Street? Whatever for?"

"Greer might have left a message. The Irregulars may have news. I'd quite like to change my shoes."

"No, I'm afraid you'll have to put up with your footwear, Watson. We shall be back home soon enough, probably this evening. All that is left to us is to make an arrest. Besides, I have no wish to attract the attention of those shadows who keep watch on our apartments. If they had any intelligence they would have had someone keep an eye on Waterloo; they saw us leave from there. Even an imbecile would conclude we would most likely return the same way. We are fortunate that they are such dull witted fellows."

"Yes, I suppose you're right," Watson said, rubbing the side of his foot. "Still, I wish we did not have to make an arrest in this case, Holmes. It's such a sad situation. That Derby woman was as evil a creature as I have ever heard. Anyone might have been driven to extremes by her."

"I know, Watson. Believe me, I know."

On our way to railway station, I stopped to send a telegram to Mycroft. He will be most interested in the news about the Albino and Porlock. That duty done we were just in time to get the train back to Bitterne.

Watson waited until we cleared the station before saying, "What do you make of this meeting between Porlock and that albino person, Holmes? An odd thing, surely, for the man to arrive for only a few days."

"I suspect he was hired to murder Calvini. Porlock wanted no loose ends. The meeting between the Albino and Porlock was probably payment for services rendered." I leaned forward and said, softly, "Something is afoot, Watson. There are machinations behind this fellow's every movement. You may be sure I shall give the matter my full attention as soon as we return."

For the rest of our journey I remained in a brown study. Watson read the newspaper and then fell asleep. With each passing mile my

A BIASED JUDGEMENT

preoccupation with Porlock grew less and my anxiety about the Southampton case grew. I could not decide what exactly worried me, but I've learned to trust my instinct. By the time the train approached the Bitterne station darkness had fallen and I was in a fair lather. I leapt from the train before it had fully stopped. Watson stepped out behind me and said, "It feels like weeks since we've been here, Holmes."

"Come, Watson," I cried. "We must make haste."

"What is it that worries you, Holmes?" Watson asked. "We know the killer struck down Liz Derby out of fear and anger. Surely there is no cause for alarm now?"

"There is, Watson, of course there is. Don't you see? There is nothing more deadly than a trapped animal. The first murder is the hardest but it becomes easier after that. I am afraid there is more death to come."

"Death comes in threes," Watson muttered. At my quizzical look he said, "That's what Lady Summerville said, remember? That death always comes in threes."

"Superstitious twaddle," I said. And yet, and yet...

I ran down the platform in search of a hansom to convey us to the manor.

This small town had no such to offer, but fortunately the station manager's son was visiting and offered to convey us in his trap.

"As fast as you can go, lad," I cried. "Hurry! There may be lives at stake."

"Sit down, old man," Watson urged. "You'll do yourself nor anyone else any good if you work yourself into such a state. Come now, we're almost there."

We stopped at the gate and I gave the boy a handful of coins as payment. I did not even stop to count it but by his expression, I could see I had over-tipped him considerably.

"Come, Watson!" I cried. "There is not a moment to lose!"

A BIASED JUDGEMENT

The two of us ran up the drive. The curtains twitched at the windows of the third bedroom. That was our bird all right. "We may yet be in time," I said.

We reached the door and knocked loudly. After a brief but agonising moment, the housemaid Daisy opened it. "Oh, it's you, Mr Holmes, Doctor," she said. "Come in."

I rushed past her and saw Lady Beatrice on the staircase. She seemed to be frozen there, headed in no direction. Just standing.

Sir Christopher and his wretched brother came out into the hallway. "What is it, Mr Holmes? You have answers? Yes, I see on your face that you do. Come, who is it that has so disturbed our happy little home?"

"Happy, do you call it?" I demanded. Then, "Lady Beatrice—"

She remained in her frozen state and I ran up the stairs towards her. "Let it be, Mr Holmes," she said. "I implore you, let it be."

"You must know I cannot do that, Lady Beatrice," I said. I tried to continue up the stairs but she blocked my path.

"What is this?" Summerville demanded. "Out of the way, you wretched girl. Let the fellow do his work."

She remained unmoved, however. From the upper landing Stevens appeared and walked down the staircase. He stood beside her and the two made an effective blockade against us.

"What is this, you baggage?" Summerville continued. He raised his fist but Stevens struck first and Summerville fell backwards.

"You blackguard, you'll pay for that," the brother cried.

Before either Watson or I could remonstrate there came the report of a gunshot from above.

12

"Damn you, you baggage," Summerville screamed at Lady Beatrice. She stood and stared at him as if she had forgotten who he was. Though she was deathly pale she remained quite steady.

"Sir Christopher," I said tightly. "Do you go down and see to your guests. Have your butler call the police. You go down too, Mr Summerville. Stevens, stay here with the Lady."

"You'll need this, Mr Holmes," the lady said, handing me a key.

Then Watson and I ran up the stairs and along the hallway. The third door was locked but our key opened it easily.

Villiers was sat at the desk, his blood dripped onto the floor and a fine red mist speckled the room for several feet in every direction. Even the ceiling was spattered with it. The pistol lay upon the floor.

I shuddered. Watson felt for a pulse and looked at me shaking his head.

"Self-administered," he said. "This is what you feared, Holmes."

"No, Watson. I feared Lady Beatrice would confront him and he would turn on her."

"You were half-right, Mr Holmes," the Lady's voice came from behind me. "I found the gloves. He realised they were damaged and took pains to hide them. His monogram identified him."

"You should not be in here, Lady Beatrice," Watson said. "This is a terrible sight even for men to behold."

She shook her head and Stevens, standing behind her, tried to draw her away, but she would not leave.

"This is my doing," she said. "I ought to look upon it."

"Come, my Lady," the boy said. "It is not your fault."

"I think you should say no more before witnesses, Lady Beatrice," I said. I could hear the patter of footsteps hurrying up the stairs. "Stevens, take the lady to her room."

He nodded and took her arm. She made no further resistance and let him lead her away.

The next several hours were frightful and I cannot remember them without abhorrence, but in the interests of veracity I must go on.

Greer arrived and accepted my explanation of suicide without demur. "He was the killer, then," he said. "Guilt got the better of him no doubt. Robbed the hangman, but saved the Exchequer the cost of a trial. But why did he do it, Mr Holmes?"

Watson glanced at me and then occupied himself assisting the attendants prepare the body for transport to the morgue. I dissembled a little, saying only, "He was being blackmailed. We may never know why, but we do know Liz Derby was a most unsavoury character who had left a trail of devastation behind her everywhere she went."

"He left no note, I suppose?"

"Just this—" I handed the Inspector a sheet of paper that said only, "I killed her. I cannot live with myself. Forgive me. Edmund St James Villiers."

"Ah, well that's conclusive enough. Thank you for all your help, Mr Holmes. I will release a statement to the press this evening and you may be sure I will remember your contribution."

"Not necessary, Inspector," I said. "This matter essentially resolved itself. But I would ask that next time you find yourself faced with a murder you leave the scene intact and remember that you, and you alone, are responsible for the case."

"I'll do that, Mr Holmes. If I may say so, I have learned a great deal from watching you work. Thank you."

My vanity is no less than any other man's and I was pleased to hear this kind affirmation, unwarranted in this case though it was.

A BIASED JUDGEMENT

The household remained still until the body was removed. Then, like an exhaled breath, it all returned to shuddering life.

"What the deuce has that girl done?" Sir Christopher demanded. "Madam, that niece of yours is a menace."

"Trollop needs to be taught a lesson," the brother added.

"Mr Summerville," Watson cried. "That is hardly fit language to use in the presence of a lady."

Lady Summerville was sobbing quietly in the corner. The 'Frenchman' was muttering excitedly to himself; only the servants were silent.

"She may leave this house tonight," Sir Christopher continued. "I've suffered enough at her hands. She insults me daily in conversation, she shows me no respect. Had she not got in the way tonight we might not have the blight of a suicide in this house. And who will pay for the repairs to that room? Eh? Tell me that."

"Would the arrest for murder of one of your guests be preferable, Sir?" I said. "You are spared a court case; the indignity of testifying that a man you brought under your roof proved to be a killer."

"Nevertheless, I will not have it. She may leave my home this night and never return."

"Oh Christopher," his wife remonstrated. "There are no trains now till morning. Surely she can wait till then."

"This night," he screamed. "I am exhausted with all this nonsense."

I was tempted to reply that the Lady was hardly responsible, but Watson anticipated me and with his customary calm soothed the situation by saying, "Holmes and I mean to return to London; we can ensure your niece's safety, Lady Summerville."

He turned to me then and said, "Come Holmes, we should pack."

Before I left this repugnant house I had one more arrow left in my quiver and I prepared to shoot it.

"You have not asked the reason why your maid was strangled to death, Sir Christopher," I said. "She was a blackmailer. I hope she did not find any incriminating documents of yours or your brother's..." I was savagely pleased to see their faces blanch. Let them stew. They will fret about how much I know of their dealings. Ah, I shall be glad to read through Derby's papers. Who knows what secrets they hold.

Upstairs, Stevens was still at Lady Beatrice's door like a sentry.

"Stevens, Dr Watson and I are going back to the train station. Do you think you could convey us?"

"Gladly, sir," he said. "But you'll have a long wait for the train."

"It's all right, Stevens," Lady Beatrice said, coming out of her room. "I have no doubt the station master will let us sit in the lounge."

"Us?" Stevens said.

"I am leaving too. Come, Stevens, you cannot fail to have heard Sir Christopher even from this distance. Go, please, and prepare the trap. I shall be ready in fifteen minutes; I am sure it will not take Mr Holmes and Doctor Watson half as long."

And so, precisely fifteen minutes later, Lady Beatrice kissed and embraced her aunt and then climbed onto the trap. Watson and I climbed up beside her and we set off for the station. It was almost midnight and there was a chill in the air. I did not relish the thought of having to spend hours waiting on a cold, damp railway platform, but it couldn't be helped.

However, once we arrived, Stevens woke up the station master who, though curious and understandably irritable, opened up his lounge for us and lit the fire.

"First train won't be for another five and half hours," he said. "But you'll be out of the wind, in any case."

"Thank you, Mr Billings," said Stevens. I handed the man a shilling and his mood improved considerably.

"I can bring you some hot coffee, if you have a mind," he said. "Keep you warm till the fire picks up."

"That would be exceedingly kind," I said. "Thank you, Mr Billings."

At that, Stevens produced a basket that contained cold chicken, cheese and a variety of fruits and pastries.

"Miss Simms put this together for you."

A BIASED JUDGEMENT

"Excellent," Watson exclaimed. "I am ravenous. It's been a long time since that meat pie in the Rose and Crown, eh, Holmes?"

"Indeed it is. It was very thoughtful of Miss Simms, Stevens. Please convey our thanks."

With the case now over my appetite had returned and I did justice enough to the meal to satisfy even Watson's watchful eye.

"If there is nothing more I can do for you, my Lady, gentlemen, I must return to the manor."

"Surely you are not working, Stevens," Watson said. "Your mother's funeral cannot be over already."

"Not till next week, Doctor," he replied.

"Stevens returned to the manor when he realised you and Mr Holmes were not present to see to my safety, Doctor. It was very good of you, Stevens. Do not forget what I have told you."

"Indeed, my Lady, I shall not, and no mistake. It's been a real honour meeting you, Mr Holmes," said the boy and shook my hand.

"I have something for you, Stevens," said I, handing him an envelope.

He stared at it and then his eyes met mine.

"You may read it," I said.

He opened the envelope with such care I had to suppress a chuckle. He read the letter it contained and even in the lamplight the flush across his features was unmistakable.

"Stevens?" Lady Beatrice said.

"It says, 'Dear Inspector Lestrade, Allow me to recommend to your attention the bearer of this letter, Mr Maurice Stevens. His intelligence and powers of observation have impressed me greatly and he has been of considerable assistance in my investigation of one of my most recent cases.

"'Despite my reservations, he has his mind set upon a career in the professional police force. I have no doubt he would prove a considerable asset and I hope you will lend him whatever assistance you may in adding him to your ranks.

A BIASED JUDGEMENT

"'You may contact me at Baker Street if I can add to this affidavit. Sincerely yours, Sherlock Holmes.'"

The boy seemed on the verge of tears and I confess I had a moment's doubt of his possessing the necessary stability for such a career. However, he subdued his emotions and again thanked me before leaving for the manor.

Now at last I had the chance to speak with Lady Beatrice and ask all those questions which had so vexed my mind.

"So," I said. "We have much to discuss, Lady Beatrice. We can put these lonely hours to good use."

"Where would you like me to begin, Mr Holmes?" she asked. "With my discovery of Villiers' guilt or...?"

"Oh no, Lady Beatrice. I believe we should begin in February."

Her eyes did not leave mine, nor did she flinch. "Ah," she said. "What betrayed me?"

"February?" Watson interjected. "I don't understand. Derby wasn't at the manor back then, she was still working for the Lennox family in Waterloo."

"Bah, I do not mean this petty case; we shall get to that soon enough. No, I mean my assault in St James Square... and my rescuer, Jack. Lady Beatrice, it was you."

"Yes."

"Wait," Watson said. "Do you mean Lady Beatrice was responsible for your assault?"

"Of course not," I said. "She is Jack."

13

The lady smiled. "I'm afraid Mr Holmes is quite correct, doctor," she said. "I am Jack. But please explain to me, if you would, how you knew."

I rubbed my hands together as much in satisfaction as for the cold. "A host of things none of which on their own were significant but when put together formed an unmistakable picture. Your general height and demeanour were suggestive; your musicality too. I have often observed that those with a good musical ear are able to emulate various accents quite efficiently. I do it myself, as Watson will attest.

"When you were 'Jack' I noticed there was something not quite authentic about you. In my weakened state I could not pinpoint what it was that jarred, but once I saw you again I realised it was your hands that had given you away. Though your face and clothes were grubby, your fingernails were always manicured and clean. Your finger span – as you showed me yourself – was wide. Something else you shared with the boy, Jack. And when I met you again I recalled the boy bore a faintly chemical odour, the smell of the chemicals you use to develop your photographs.

"I had the individual pieces but none of it connected until Doctor Watson observed that you would hardly be able to defend yourself in a fight and he mentioned your aunt at the same time. That was when I realised you had been introduced as Lady Beatrice. But of course your aunt was your father's sister and so your last name must be Jacoby. And the idea of you being in a fight... "

A BIASED JUDGEMENT

"I see," she said. "I must be more careful, though I doubt there could be another man in England who could have identified me as readily as you. But I must implore you to keep my secret, Mr Holmes."

"Considering I owe you my life, Lady Beatrice, I am quite sure I can promise you that. But first let me understand the reason for your extraordinary actions."

"Extraordinary indeed," Watson said, pursing his lips and studying the woman before us in some perplexity. "Running around the streets of London dressed as a street urchin. I don't know what to make of it."

"I am happy to explain myself, gentlemen. But I cannot promise you will be satisfied with my explanation."

She sipped her coffee, took a moment to gather her thoughts, and then related her tale.

"As I told you, Mr Holmes, my father died two years ago. He and I were very close. You may have heard of Sir Benjamin Jacoby."

"Yes indeed. A man of many talents. He was a scientist of considerable merit. His study in toxins is the most authoritative in existence."

"I am pleased you think so," said she. "As befits a scientist of his calibre, my father was in all ways a modern thinker. He believed in education for everyone, and he did not exclude his daughter from that ideal. From my earliest age I was taught languages, the sciences, philosophy and any number of other things, in addition to the basic reading and writing that forms the foundation of all traditional education programmes.

"All was well while my father was alive. London was mine. Papa was very happy to accompany me to the opera or to art galleries. He encouraged me to play piano and took great delight in my small talent."

"Ah," I said. "He is to be congratulated. Your education has done you and him great justice. Certainly your piano playing is amongst the finest I have ever heard."

She bowed and continued. "Unfortunately, my father became unwell and after a long and unpleasant illness he died. My aunt was, by that

A BIASED JUDGEMENT

time, already married to Sir Christopher. She invited me to come and stay with her but as you have observed, I am ill-suited to life at Rillington Manor. I remained in London. However, my life as a single woman became circumscribed in a way I did not anticipate.

"Although intellectually I was aware of the constraints upon women in our society, I had never experienced them myself, not while my father lived. But as a single woman I found things I had taken for granted – going to the theatre, taking a walk whenever I chose, simple things – were no longer acceptable…"

"But why did you not marry, Lady Beatrice?" Watson asked. "You must surely have had offers."

She smiled. "Thank you, Doctor, I did. I have been honoured with three proposals of marriage, not including the repeated offers from Mr Wallace Summerville." A moue of distaste flickered across her face, invisible to all but the most attentive observer. "But while my father lived I had not any of the usual inducements to marry: I am wealthy, independent and not given to sentiment. I am convinced I should make a very poor wife."

"Yes, yes," I said impatiently. "But the rest of the tale, Lady Beatrice. You found your life restrictive…"

"And so one evening after the servants had retired I dressed in one of my father's suits and went out for a walk. I was astonished at how easy it was. I had no particular plan in mind, I just wanted to get out of the house and take a walk on my own. I walked up Oxford Street. No one stopped me, no one looked at me at all. It was… liberating."

"And instructive, I would imagine," I said.

"Yes. Yes, exactly. To see the world through different eyes, to be seen by it in a different light – it was magnificent. And I knew I must do it again.

"Over the next two years I refined my disguise. I conduct my changes in a series of stages. I start with a public toilet and enter as Lady Beatrice but I emerge as Madge, an old cleaning woman. It's surprisingly easy. Then I go to a boarding house where I keep a room and there I change into whatever male figure I wish to be."

"Surely the people in the boarding house have noticed?" Watson said.

"The lower classes know how to mind their own business, Doctor. I have prepared a story that these two people work shifts but I've never needed to use it. I have a locker at the railway station and I keep a supply of outfits there. I change in the public toilets from a street urchin into a gentleman. I put the clothes in a carpet bag and then reverse the process at the end of the day."

"Wait," Watson interjected. "You mean you use the gentleman's facilities?"

"Certainly I do. It was very difficult, the first time I did it. I felt self-conscious and uneasy. But it's really not that hard, not once you get used to it."

I laughed loudly – though whether it was more at the idea of the lady's nerve or Watson's discomfort I cannot say.

"Over time I began to modify my disguise. I got wigs, eyeglasses, costumes – whatever I thought would fit the character I was playing. There were two, primarily: Nigel Cuthbertson was the most usual. He's a young man about town with a fondness for music. When I am he I can attend whatever concerts I wish on my own. Then there's Jack, whom you met, Mr Holmes. My curiosity has, I confess, led me into some of the seamier parts of the city. As Jack I fit in and, well, I quite like him. He has a sense of humour that Cuthbertson does not..."

"Hang on!" Watson said. "You cannot mean to say you feel each of these... characters has a distinct personality."

"Why certainly they do, Doctor. As Jack or as Cuthbertson I am sometimes obliged to communicate with others. It is helpful if I know a little about the part I am playing beyond my wardrobe."

"Splendid, splendid!" I cried. "Ah, it was fortunate for me young Jack happened to be in the park that night. You took a grave risk, you know."

A BIASED JUDGEMENT

"I did not give the matter any thought. I recognised you, of course, Mr Holmes. I once watched you investigate the murder of my neighbours, Mr Addleton and his wife."

"Ah, the Addleton tragedy, Holmes," Watson said. "I do wish you'd let me write up the particulars of that case."

"The world is not ready for that story," I said.

"I could not leave you to that ruffian, even if you had not been Mr Sherlock Holmes I would have felt compelled to intervene."

"I do not think you appreciate the enormity of the risk, Lady Beatrice," said I. "If you knew more about the villain who attacked me… Still, I am greatly in your debt."

She flushed and bowed slightly. "My honour to have been of service, Mr Holmes. I do not count it a debt between us, but if you wish to repay me you can do so by keeping safe my secret."

"You have my word," said I.

"And mine," said Watson.

Thus satisfied, I added: "Now that we have addressed the matter of Jack, perhaps you would enlighten us upon the matter of Villiers' death."

She nodded. "I have no doubt you have surmised the matter yourself, Mr Holmes. The facts are plain enough.

"I continued my search for the gloves. I realised that the killer must have observed the scratches and tears in the fabric and have taken pains to hide or destroy the evidence.

"You will have observed the balcony that runs along the eastern terrace of the manor; I believe you used it when you were searching the rooms, Mr Holmes. No, no apology necessary. I'm sure you saw the ficus trees that decorate the balcony. This afternoon – I should say yesterday afternoon now – I searched the base of each and found the gloves buried in the soil of the one outside Villiers' room. He caught me and I confronted him with the evidence."

"You took a grave risk," I said. "You could not know how he would react."

A BIASED JUDGEMENT

"He caught me with the gloves in my hands; there was no point pretending I did not understand their significance. I know Villiers; I've met him several times and he's always been very kind to me. More than once his humour has deflected an unpleasant situation. Whatever secrets he kept, he always behaved as a gentleman in my presence.

"In any case, I presented my accusation as gently and as tactfully as I could. I was prepared to tell him I was working at your behest, Mr Holmes, if he became aggressive."

"How did he react?"

"He broke down in tears. Wept for forgiveness. He said he had not slept a wink since that dreadful night and I believed him. Oh, Mr Holmes, if you could have seen the way he suffered."

"He was a killer," Watson protested. "A cold blooded murderer."

"No Doctor," the Lady replied. "A killer he may have been, but not a murderer and certainly not cold-blooded. He did not go to Derby's room to kill; he went to search for a letter she had stolen from him. I suspect most people did not miss their stolen items until it was too late. But Villiers read that particular letter with great frequency and he spotted its loss at once."

"How did he know she was not in her room?" I asked.

"He saw her from the bathroom window. He was in there thinking about killing himself. Yes, doctor, even then he had begun to think of it.

"The night was cold and wet but the rain had stopped and for just a moment the moon shone on the rose garden. He saw her and recognised her at once. He already had suspicions about her. Some 'sixth sense', he says."

"Simpler than that," I said. "She had read his letter; she knew what he was. Ironic that Derby would show him such contempt and be oblivious to the evil in her own nature. But I interrupted you. He saw her and went down to confront her?"

"Yes. How did you know that?"

"His footprints in her room were damp; he had been outside."

A BIASED JUDGEMENT

Watson said, "So did he speak to her?"

Lady Beatrice sipped her coffee before replying, "He stood there, in the cold and the wet waiting for her to return. Then it occurred to him that he had a golden opportunity to search her room."

"But how could he know which was hers?" Watson asked.

"He couldn't. He opened two other doors before finding the right one. It was the middle of the night and everyone was asleep. None of the servants' doors have locks so he was able to proceed with some degree of confidence."

"Surely he knew she must return at any moment?" I said. "What on earth did he think she was doing at that hour?"

"I asked him that but he had no answer. I don't think he even thought about it. He saw the opportunity and took it."

"Ah." I too sipped my coffee and said, "But she returned almost immediately?"

"Within minutes, he said. They did not speak, just stared at each other. Then she laughed."

"What?" Watson said. "She laughed?"

"Yes, with considerable contempt. 'You won't find it,' she said. Then she called him some vile word and turned her back. 'I'm going to bed,' she told him. 'Go on, hop it.'"

"It was the word she called him that did it," I surmised. "To be treated with such contempt by the likes of Liz Derby. Yes, I can fully understand why he was driven to violence."

"That and the fact that she turned her back on him," Lady Beatrice said. "It unleashed something... He says... said he didn't even remember strangling her. One moment she turned away and the next she was lying face down, lifeless, on the bed like a wretched Desdemona."

"And then he searched the room," I said. "But to no avail. She'd already put the letter into the post. It is a shame he didn't think things through more clearly."

A BIASED JUDGEMENT

"He was distraught," Lady Beatrice said. "People in great distress seldom think clearly."

"That is true," I said. "What a study in contrasts: Derby a woman consumed by hate and Villiers a man consumed by love."

"I'm sorry, Holmes? Love did you say?" Watson seemed utterly perplexed.

"Certainly it was love. The half-written letter that I found when I searched Villiers' room revealed the truth to me. I knew the man's nature from the salutation."

"The salutation?" Lady Beatrice seemed as puzzled as Watson.

"It was a love letter to Francis."

"That's a girl's name too, Holmes," Watson said.

"Yes, but it is customary for men to spell Francis with an 'i'; women with an 'e'. The half-written letter I found in his room, a love letter that was covered with tears, was addressed to a man.

"People in our society are not kind in how they treat those who share what Mr Wilde calls 'the love that dare not speak its name,'" Watson said. "But Villiers told you all this, Lady Beatrice? It seems a most inappropriate thing to discuss with a young woman."

"Certainly he told me," Lady Beatrice said. "I wonder at your surprise, Doctor. I find people often confide in me, I seem to inspire trust. But I have known Villiers for two years and I have never been under any illusion about what he was."

"It is not fit for a young woman's ears," Watson said.

She smiled. "Hardly as young as all that. We do not choose whom we love, Doctor, and Villiers did love that young man. Given the restrictions I have faced as a result of societies, ah, mores, I can hardly judge another for functioning outside those same traditions."

"It is hardly the same," Watson persisted. I could see the debate would rage on for some time, so I raised my hand.

"Be that as it may," I said. "He confessed his guilt to you. What then?"

A BIASED JUDGEMENT

"I tried to persuade him to confess his crime but he could not. His mother is a widow and he is her sole support. The shame – more of his intimate relations with a young man than that of the killing – would ruin her. No, he said, the only option open to him was the gentleman's way."

"Gentleman!" Watson snorted.

Lady Beatrice gave Watson a disapproving look and continued. "Yes, he was a gentleman in my eyes. Would you prefer a brute like Christopher Summerville, Doctor? A titled man who beats his wife and abuses his servants? Is he more a gentleman than Villiers? I rather think not.

"In any case, I agreed with Villiers' plan and told him I would give him until your return, Mr Holmes, to do the deed. As it happened, while I was still speaking to him we heard your voice and realised there was no moment to delay. I went to stall you while Villiers… Well, you know the rest."

"And the weapon?" I asked. The lady stared at me and did not answer. Ah… so the weapon was hers and she had given it to him to perform the hideous act. It made her culpable in the eyes of the law, but in truth I could not condemn her. I have, in the past – even very recently with the Abbey Grange case – followed the dictates of my own conscience before that of the courts. Justice need not always be wigged and gowned.

"He must have brought the pistol with him," Watson said. "A man like that…"

I did not point out that if he had a weapon in his possession he would have used it to threaten Liz Derby. No, I knew I was right and I saw confirmation of it in Lady Beatrice's eyes.

"I know he wrote a letter admitting his guilt, but he did not explain why. Was there another letter?" I said. 'Perhaps one he did not want the official police to see?"

She drew it from her purse and handed it to me. It was unsealed and was addressed to his mother.

153

A BIASED JUDGEMENT

"He told me to read it," she said. "And extracted from me a promise to look after her. I do not suppose he will mind you reading it."

The letter was plain enough:

My dearest mamma, it said. *I hardly know how to beg your forgiveness. I fear I have been a grave disappointment. I cannot live with my shame or with the pain my actions must cause you. Know me to be your eternally loving and devoted son. Edmund.*

"No direct admission of guilt in this, or explanation for his actions," Watson said. "The grief of having her son commit suicide will be a hard burden for the woman to bear."

"Kinder though," said the lady, "than the ignominy of a court case; of seeing a son labelled homosexual and seeing him hang. This is truly the lesser of two grotesque evils.

"Mr Holmes, I pray you find the rest of that foul woman's store of blackmail items and inform their owners their secrets are safe. From just a few days of seeing the results of her villainy, I cannot bear the thought of anyone having to suffer such torment as Villiers did."

"It is already in hand, Lady Beatrice," said I.

A BIASED JUDGEMENT

14

September 30th, 1897

Oh what drama we had this morning. Drama, or comedy.

I was at the breakfast table drinking my coffee when Mrs Hudson brought in a plate of kippers and said, "I do not understand what Mr Weiss can be thinking. Expecting workmen to paint in this weather."

"What workmen are they, Mrs Hudson?" Watson asked.

"The men painting the front of Mr Weiss's shop," said she. "You must have seen them. All day every day and hardly a lick of work done. You just can't get good workers any more. Though I suppose the weather being so bad of late must be delaying them."

"Painting, you say?" Watson said. "Seems odd in this weather." He looked at me but I refused to meet his eye.

"Kippers, Mrs Hudson?" I said. "Ugh, I could not eat a thing. Just coffee."

"Well, the doctor likes a nice kipper, Mr Holmes," she said, setting down the dish in a most decided manner.

"Thank you, Mrs Hudson, they smell delicious," my friend said. Then he rose and went to the window. "Ah, just as I thought," he said. "Holmes—"

"Thank you, Mrs Hudson," I said. "Perhaps you will bring us another pot of coffee? We seem to have finished this one."

"I have other things to do with my day than fetch you an endless supply of coffee, Mr Holmes," she protested. Then, with a sigh. "I suppose I shall have no peace until I do. I'll send the girl up presently."

"They're not painting," Watson said as soon as the door closed.

A BIASED JUDGEMENT

"Hmm?"

"Come on, Holmes. That pair across the street. They might claim to be painting Mr Weiss's window, but it's pretty obvious what they're really doing."

"And what is that?"

"Watching our flat. That is to say, watching you."

"That's hardly news, Watson."

"Well?"

"Well what?" I said. He really was in the most decided mood.

"Well, aren't you going to do anything about it?"

"Such as?"

"Such as confront them. Thrash them. Have them arrested."

"You really should calm yourself, my dear Watson. It's not worth risking an apoplexy. There is no point in confronting or thrashing them. I don't suppose you've noticed, but it's not one individual nor even a team of the same people: There are many of them and we seldom see the same man twice. Even if I managed to frighten off one or two, there would be more to replace him. Do you not see?"

"Have them arrested then."

"On what charge?"

"Oh really... You cannot mean to do nothing."

I rose. "No, there is something I mean to do."

"At last!" He rubbed his palms together in anticipation. "What?"

"I'm going to visit Mycroft."

Half an hour later we made our way through the sneezing and dripping city to Whitehall. Watson insisted on accompanying me because "Someone has to look after you."

Well, I suppose two men, both armed, are a more difficult target than one alone. Even if that one is, as Watson says with dry wit, "the Mighty Sherlock Holmes."

Frankly, I have not felt very mighty this past week. I caught a chill in Bitterne, no doubt because of the wretchedly cold conditions of the

A BIASED JUDGEMENT

manor, and I awoke on my first morning back in London with a fever and a sore throat. For a medical man, Watson was exceedingly unsympathetic.

"You will insist on wearing yourself ragged when you're working on these cases, Holmes," he said. "It's not surprising you've caught a chill. You're lucky it's not much worse."

"Not much worse?" I croaked. "You have no idea what I suffer."

"It's a sore throat and a cold," he said, dismissing my ailments. "Stay in bed and I'll have Mrs Hudson bring you up some tea."

Off he went in rude good health, and left me to ponder the decline of the so-called 'caring' professions.

After three days bed rest – I will not elaborate on my sufferings; suffice to say there were intense and plentiful – I felt well enough to start looking through the Liz Derby papers. Still coughing, still miserable (Watson has hidden my pipe and refuses to tell me where) I had no option but to distract myself by going through each wretched box.

In addition to the letters and photographs, Derby kept a ledger sheet for each purloined document in which she documented the amounts she received for it. At first the amounts were small enough, a shilling or two a week, but by the time of her death she was demanding several pounds at a time.

If Watson had his way I should toss all these filthy papers on the fire unread. I confess, part of me agrees with him; it is a vile task delving through this lot and I wish I were done with it. Such an age it takes to rummage through other people's dirty underwear. The photographs are the hardest. At least with letters I can make some determination of the correspondents' identities: there is an address, a salutation, a signature; at least one, if not all three. But the photographs reveal very little beyond an excess of corpulent flesh. Three hours it took me yesterday to realise that the big-breasted woman in a picture was not the person being blackmailed, but rather the Member of Parliament whose reflection could just be made out in a glass-covered painting behind her.

A BIASED JUDGEMENT

Derby's system, though accurate enough when it comes to figures and cash receipts, is wanting when it comes to identifying her victims. She used nicknames which she, no doubt, thought amusing: "Mr Jockey" turned out to be Sir Sidney Rider; "Lady Pink Blancmange" is Lady Prudence Barnsley (though I must say, the nickname seems appropriate if her photograph does her justice); and "The Fish" is Cuthbert Salmon.

I would be inclined to just toss the lot on the fire and have done with it, but I determined to make sure the victims are guilty of nothing worse than slight indiscretions. So far, I've managed to process a mere dozen of these relics. As expected, almost all of these documents relate to illicit love affairs, some of a startlingly prurient nature. What a sad indictment of the state of matrimony in this country.

After I finish examining each letter or picture I burn it, then Watson writes to the former victim saying that their former employee, Liz Derby, has died and all papers in her possession have been destroyed. Watson's literary talent enables him to phrase these letters in such a way as to convey sympathy and yet leave the reader in no doubt that their worries of blackmail are over.

Thus far, only one of the letters has revealed a scandal worthy of the courts. HL, the prominent barrister, poisoned his late wife. Given that his current bride is exhibiting the same symptoms, I wasted no time in forwarding the incriminating letter (ironically from the killer to the present Mrs L) to Scotland Yard.

Anyway, this morning, feeling much better and utterly bored with both the task and my bedroom walls, I decided it was time to call upon my brother.

Whether because of Watson's presence or for some other reason, our journey was uneventful. The watchers followed us, but at a distance. Their aim seemed only to monitor my movements, which is irksome, but I am conscious that matters could be far worse.

A BIASED JUDGEMENT

"I don't see why we couldn't have taken a cab, Holmes," Watson grumbled.

"And I don't see why you couldn't return my pipe. Come, Watson, it's only rain. I'd have thought you'd enjoy the fresh air and exercise; you're forever extolling their virtues. Besides, I have good reason for walking."

"Which is?"

"It amuses me to see my two shadows look so disconsolate."

Our journey took us through the West End and it was pleasant to be back in the hustle and bustle again. Watson held his temper far better than I expected and it wasn't until Haymarket that he turned suddenly to challenge our shadows. Brandishing his umbrella he shouted, "Hey, you there!" and gave chase. Oh, I did laugh! Watson, his head wet, the umbrella bobbing above the heads of the startled shoppers and tourists as he ran through them.

The two villains did not wait but vanished into the crowd. I leaned against a lamppost and chortled until I could scarcely breathe.

A few minutes later my companion returned and gave me a withering look which, I am ashamed to admit, only made me laugh the louder.

"Cowards," Watson cried into the throng.

"It does no good to get upset, Watson," I said once I'd caught my breath. "It is certainly unsettling but thus far, as I have already reminded you, this pair have broken no laws."

"Well there should be a law."

"Have you forgotten that I, myself, have been known to follow people on occasion?"

I spoke more nonchalantly than I feel. I very much doubt I've seen the last of the attempts against my life. All my instincts tell me the danger, far from being past, is greater than ever.

I am filled with foreboding, but this villainy must be met with wit and guile; not a spontaneous outburst of annoyance. It does no good to

A BIASED JUDGEMENT

sever the limbs when the beast has so many others. It is the head we must destroy."

We reached Mycroft's offices without further incident. Though I'd never have admitted it to Watson, it was a relief to get indoors away from the rain and my odious shadows.

"Bad day, Mr Holmes," Gillespie said. "Would you like me to take your coats? I've a nice fire going in here so they should be dry by the time you leave."

"Thank you, Mr Gillespie. This is my friend and colleague, Doctor Watson. Watson, if my brother Mycroft is the cog that keeps the British government working, Gillespie is the oil that enables him to function."

"Ah, it's very kind of you to say so, Mr Holmes." Gillespie shook my friend's hand and added, "I enjoy your stories very much, Doctor. What adventures you have."

Watson, I fear, would have stood chatting about his tales for some time. I interrupted with, "Is my brother free?"

"He is, Mr Holmes. You may go right up. I shall bring you some coffee directly."

Watson and I made our way up the stairs to the top floor. For a busy government building it was extraordinarily silent and our footsteps echoed in the wood and marble halls. It was Watson's first visit and he was agog with curiosity.

"What goes on here, Holmes?" he whispered.

"Decisions that decide the governing of the empire," I replied. "You may speak normally, you know."

Mycroft called out an *entrée* at our knock. He was seated by a merry fire in an enormous armchair with his foot up on a stool. I heard Watson's intake of breath as he beheld the magnificent view of Westminster Bridge through the rainy window.

We had barely sat when Gillespie arrived with a tray of coffee and cake.

A BIASED JUDGEMENT

"A whole week without a pipe, Sherlock," Mycroft said, as soon as the old man left. "That will make a sinner of any saint. The doctor's doing, I suppose?"

"Nothing is worse for a cough than tobacco," Watson said.

"No doubt," Mycroft said. He nodded his head and I rose, went to the door and checked. We had the floor to ourselves.

Thus satisfied, Mycroft began at once to review Perrot's letters that I found in Bitterne.

"There is not enough in those Italian letters to work with, Sherlock. Still, it is interesting to know who this so-called 'Perrot' fellow calls his friends. Romano is as unsavoury a piece of work as I've encountered. Worth keeping an eye on the situation. I have alerted the Italian government.

"As to this other." He picked up the letter I had copied. "You duplicated the contents precisely?"

"To the comma, I assure you."

"Good, good. I did not doubt it, but as you know, it's important in my business to be precise."

"Mine, too."

He smiled. "Quite. Well, then... I entirely agree with your analysis, Sherlock. Just as no good deed goes unpunished, it seems that no bad one cannot benefit someone. That Derby woman did the nation most excellent service by inadvertently drawing your attention to these documents."

"Her greatest service was her death," I replied, without humour. "It far outweighed anything she accomplished in her life."

"I cannot believe a British gentleman would write such a letter," Watson said. "To betray his country like that..."

"I'm afraid not all British gentlemen have your integrity, doctor," Mycroft said. "This particular gentleman shall face the noose."

"You have arrested him then?" Watson asked.

"Oh no, he's still here. He's hard at work just one floor down."

A BIASED JUDGEMENT

"You cannot be serious," Watson exclaimed. "Surely, Mr Holmes…"

Mycroft raised his hand. "He does not know we have unmasked him, doctor. He has no reason to suspect his secret has been revealed. This man is only one small cog in a much larger machine. We shall see where his treason may lead him. I assure you, justice has him in her sights and he will not escape. Unfortunately, the worse of the damage is already done. He has dealt us so grave a blow that we shall suffer the deadly consequences for many years to come."

"The South African situation?" I said.

"Indeed."

"Can nothing be done?" Watson asked.

"No. No, it's too late, I'm afraid." Mycroft spoke calmly but I could see his anger in the tightness of his jaw.

"Then… war?"

"I'm afraid so, Doctor. It's inevitable. That our friend," he picked up the offending letter and smacked it with the back of his hand, the first outward sign of his rage. "That our friend should have betrayed his own government in this manner is… Well, the matter would very likely have come to war without his help. Still…"

"So many lives will be lost," Watson said. He rubbed absently at his left leg and I could see he was thinking of his own unhappy military experience.

"Yes. Unfortunate," Mycroft said. "Most."

We sat in silence, feeling the full weight of this pronouncement. Then Mycroft poured the coffee and said, "At best we might hope to delay it. I shall speak to the queen and see if the Kaiser may be invited for a visit. Her majesty has powers of persuasion that even Wilhelm's mother cannot match. We might mitigate the problem if we are very lucky and very careful."

Mycroft folded up the letter and slid it into his breast pocket. "It was exceedingly fortunate you unmasked this creature, Sherlock. There's a knighthood in it for you, you know."

A BIASED JUDGEMENT

I dismissed the honour with a wave of my hand. "I am not interested in such matters, as you know, Mycroft. But you will put your best men on this job? We cannot afford to let this creature slip away from us."

"You need have no fear on that account. I've spoken to Bradstreet; you know there's no sounder man in Christendom, save ourselves, of course." He laughed, but the sound was somehow hollow and lacking in mirth. The unmasking of a man who had been a colleague, even, I dare say, a confident, is a heavy blow.

"There is enough here to justify an arrest, but I think we'll keep the gentleman under surveillance a little longer," he said.

"It explains his deception about Porlock's return to the capitol, I think. Watson and I owe that gentleman for those bad moments with the dogs."

"Quite right," Watson said, shuddering.

"A small matter, brother, given the enormity of his other crimes. Fortunately you and the good doctor suffered no more than momentary alarm. Tell me, what did you make of this Perrot fellow?"

Watson spluttered and I gave him a sympathetic look. All very well for Mycroft to be so dismissive; he had not been there.

I replied, "Loathsome. A liar and a traitor and utterly without morals. I cannot say I was at all surprised to see he was the recipient of correspondence such as this. He was armed, too, as I wrote you. Although the weapon had not been recently fired, it had most definitely been used since its last cleaning."

"How can you tell that, Holmes?" Watson asked.

"Because two bullets were missing from the chamber."

"You think he's Canadian?" Mycroft said.

"There is no mistaking the accent. No one but a clod could mistake him for a Frenchman."

"Summerville did," Watson said.

"Which rather makes my point, I think."

Mycroft laughed again and sipped his coffee. He said, "It is unfortunate we do not know his true identity. I have sent inquiries to

A BIASED JUDGEMENT

the Royal Canadian police service. I hope they shall be able to put a name to this villain. But we shall have him. It may take a little time, but we shall have him, Sherlock."

"I hope you are right, Mycroft. And I hope we capture him before he does any worse harm."

"As do I. Now, this fellow Porlock, I've had Bradstreet run down some particulars which I think you shall find interesting."

"Well?"

"Like Moriarty, his training is in mathematics. He was a student of Weierstrass."

"The German mathematician? The so-called 'father of modern analysis'?"

"Never heard of him," Watson said.

"No? Well, it's possible many people outside his field have not. He is exceedingly well known in the world of mathematics. His papers on elliptic functions are quite remarkable…"

"Quite right, Sherlock," Mycroft said. "But perhaps it escaped your notice that Weierstrass died in February."

"Did he, indeed? No, I was otherwise occupied in February; I did not hear. But surely the death of a tutor would not impact Porlock?"

"By all accounts Porlock viewed Weierstrass as more than a mentor; he was almost a father-figure. I have it on excellent authority that Porlock was deeply upset by the loss.

"However, Porlock's wife is English and her mother has been unwell. It seems that for many months Mrs Porlock has been urging her husband to return to London. He would not go while Weierstrass was dying, but once the man passed on, Porlock was eventually persuaded. They returned at the end of May."

"Ah, a man subjected to the whims of domesticity once again."

"Oh tosh, Holmes," Watson said. "You make it sound like a disease. Anyway, what is the old lady's condition? Will Porlock take his family back to Germany when she dies?"

A BIASED JUDGEMENT

"All excellent questions, Doctor. I gather the woman has been unwell for several months and is not expected to live out the year. She occupies a room at the top of the house in Finsbury Park.

"Our friend Porlock is having some improvements done to his home near Munich so it seems very likely he means to return as soon as it is possible to do so."

"He's been having me followed," I said. "At least, I assume it is he."

"He fears you, Sherlock. He knows you defeated Moriarty, a man he thought invincible, and that makes you dangerous. I suspect he is merely keeping an eye on you in order to try to anticipate your movements. For the present, I do not believe you are in any danger."

"How can you be so sure?" Watson asked, anticipating me.

"Because for the moment, the man must stay in London. He dare not risk anyone inquiring into his activities. If you die, there is a very real possibility he may have to flee, and whatever else you may say about him, there's no denying he is devoted to his family."

"Hmph," I snorted. "You seem to have forgotten, Mycroft, the man has already made an attempt against me."

He laughed and stretched his back. "I assure you, I forget nothing. No, my dear brother, I remember the incident quite clearly, but my interpretation of the events is a little different from your own."

I felt, rather than heard, Watson growl.

"Well then?" I said.

"Calvini was hired to watch you, nothing more. However, he had a particular regard for Moriarty, and Colonel Moran too. No, I think his own passions got the better of him and he decided if he killed you he'd be considered a hero in his gang of cutthroats."

"But he failed and inadvertently called attention to Porlock's activities," I said, following his thought. "Porlock hired the Albino to kill Calvini, not because he wanted to tie up loose ends, but because he was livid that Calvini had upset his plans. Yes, that theory holds true."

A BIASED JUDGEMENT

Watson and I took a cab back to Baker Street followed, as before, by two thoroughly soaked shadows. As we trundled through London, my friend said, "What's going to happen to Perrot, Holmes? I know that Frobisher..." he spoke softly so the cabbie would not hear, "is guilty of treason, but surely Perrot is culpable too?"

"Of course he is, Watson. He's Canadian, remember, not French. He will be charged with treason in due course, but he's more valuable at present as a free agent. You may be sure Mycroft will keep close watch on him. Perrot's friendship with Summerville puts that gentleman's into question as well."

"Summerville commit treason? But he's a knight of the realm."

"Pah, some of the worst men I've ever known were knights of the realm. Our friend Summerville beats his wife. Such a man might do anything."

A BIASED JUDGEMENT

15

October 15th, 1897

    For the past two weeks I have divided my time between processing Derby's trophies and keeping watch on Porlock's house in Finsbury Park. It's an easy matter to leave my flat by the back window – well, less easy than it was seven years ago, but I manage well enough – and so thwart my pair of watchers across the street. They have finished 'painting' and now pretend to fix locks they themselves have broken. I have warned Mrs Hudson that she is by no means to trust them if they come to ply their trade here. Fortunately, she is canny enough to accept my word in matters such as this without demur.

    Once free of Baker Street I head to my bolt hole in Jermyn Street where I change into my costume-du-jour. This week alone, I have been a beggar, a street-sweeper, and a rag-and-bone man. When I have not been able to keep watch myself, I've had the Irregulars take turns. And the result of all this effort: Nothing. Well, perhaps 'nothing' is a slight exaggeration. A few small crumbs have been my reward.

    The governess leaves the house every day at two o'clock unless the weather is particularly unpleasant. She brings the two little girls out to the park for precisely forty minutes.

    The lady of the house, Mrs Porlock, seldom goes out except with her husband. I assume she is kept much occupied looking after her ailing mother.

    Porlock leaves the house on Sunday mornings to escort his wife and daughters to church. I won't even comment on the Almighty's likely response to that evil man's prayers. Twice he visited our new National

A BIASED JUDGEMENT

Gallery of British Art and spent several hours examining the Pre-Raphaelites. Monday last, he escorted his wife to the opera and this week to the theatre; and on Tuesday, Thursday and Friday of both weeks he attended his private club in Piccadilly. This last is exclusive to German men and I was given short shrift when I attempted to gain entry. I managed to slip in via the kitchen dressed as a valet.

On the face of it, the place is typical of any such facility. There is a smoking room, a room where cards are played and another for billiards. Alcohol is available without charge. (I suspect the dues must be prohibitive).

The members are magnates of industry, stockbrokers, and the wealthiest members of German society. I understand even the Ambassador is a member, though he was not present during my, ah, visit.

Porlock confined himself to the smoking room. He immediately dominated the best seat in the lounge and over the course of the next thirty minutes he received a succession of gentlemen who came and whispered in his ear. Circumstances did not permit me to overhear these conversations, but from the fear with which he is approached – even by the powerful – I perceive Porlock is a fearsome creature indeed.

This afternoon, knowing the master of the house would be occupied elsewhere, I contrived to gain access to his home. I waited until he had left and then, with a schoolboy's slingshot, broke a window on the first floor.

Two hours later, a glazier called upon the house and was admitted by the maid. A brief and tense conversation ensued between her and the mistress of the house. Then, sighing at life's cruelties, Mrs Porlock accompanied me to the front bedroom and showed me the damage. The dogs, mercifully, were out in the back yard but their baying was an unpleasant reminder of my last visit.

"I cannot think how this happened," the woman said. "I have not seen children playing ball – and this room is too high up and too far from the road in any case."

A BIASED JUDGEMENT

"Birds," I said in a rich West Country accent. "They do fly right into the windows sometimes. No one knows why. It's an easy fix, missus, and I shall have it set to rights in no time."

"Excellent," she said. Then sat in the chair and watched me.

"I don't like to keep you from your work, missus," I said. "You've better things to do, I'll warrant, than to sit and watch old Festy play with putty."

"I'm sorry, but my husband is very strict on who he allows into the house. It's nothing personal, you understand, but leaving you alone is out of the question."

That was unfortunate but served to confirm my suspicions of the man in question. I made a production of moving the new glass pane into position. "Can you ask your manservant to help me hold this, missus?" I said. "It's a bit awkward for one man."

"I'm afraid we don't have a manservant," she said. "Mr Porlock does not allow men to work in his home. He would not be pleased to know that I let you in."

"Well now, that's unfortunate. Still, we'll do our best, eh?"

"Can you work quietly, please? My mother is very ill upstairs."

The job did not take long and I chattered as I worked. The lady was not very forthcoming and refused to laugh at any of my little jokes.

One of the little girls came in and watched me work for a while.

"Margaret," said the mother. "You should be at your lessons."

"It is lunch time, mama," said the child. "Madame de Pury went out to post a letter. She said we will continue at one o'clock."

"You can leave the little one here with me, ma'am," I said. "If you have things to do. I don't mind."

"I do have things to do," Frau Porlock replied. "But I will stay until you are done." Then, in German, said to her daughter, "Margaret, go and practice the piano until Madame returns."

The child skipped away from the room and a few moments later I heard the sound of scales being played fairly competently.

A BIASED JUDGEMENT

"A blessing, is children," I said. "She's a handsome girl, and no mistake. Do you have many little ones, missus?"

"I have two daughters. Are you almost done? My husband will be home soon and I do not want him disturbed."

"Just a few minutes more."

Nothing else could I get out of the woman. Still, by the time I left the house I knew some things I had not known before: that only women are permitted to work in the Porlock household; that anyone who enters that house is watched closely; and that the governess has more freedom than any of the other servants.

Searching this house will be difficult, but I will find a way. I must, if Porlock is to be brought down.

October 17th, 1897

I have spent the weekend continuing my work on the Derby papers. As luck would have it, in quick succession I discovered cold evidence of embezzlement by one of the City's most respected bankers and two letters inculpating the writers in murder. The next four or five were tawdry love affairs. Very banal.

After several hours I was irritated, bored and fatigued. Watson suggested dinner at Simpsons and an excellent suggestion it was. Isaiah Collins led us to our favourite table and served us himself.

I was vastly amused to see the waiter's amazement when I asked him why he was so sure his next child was going to be a boy.

"Why bless you, Mr Holmes," he said. "You never fail to astonish me. However did you know that? My wife is indeed expecting another. I suppose I can't help hoping for a boy this time, though all my girls are wonderful. But however did you know?"

"You have been muttering boys' names under your breath since we arrived, Collins. After your last child was born you told me how much you had hoped for a son. It was not a difficult deduction."

"Well, Marta had a difficult time of it with this pregnancy, Mr Holmes. It seemed like every day there was a new complication. Then just last week she suddenly seemed to improve and we're finally able to get excited about it."

"How much longer has she got?" Watson asked.

"Just a couple of weeks, Doctor," Collins said. He poured out the port with some satisfaction. "I know it's just superstition, but since everything went so well when she was carrying the girls, I can't help hoping all the problems this time mean it's a boy."

"No doubt your morning run is helping you deal with the anxiety," I said. "No, no, it's not witchcraft – you told me two years ago how running in Hyde Park every day helps you cope with the demands of your position."

We had the lobster as Collins recommended and I returned home in good spirits. Except that we were followed the whole way there and back.

October 21st, 1897

I finished reviewing the last of the Derby documents last night. Thank God I am done with it at last.

Just before midnight I took the last letter from the last box and read it through and then read it again.

"Here, Watson," I said. "See what you make of this."

He took the document and read it aloud:

"Dear Mr Winters,

You will forgive, I am sure, my addressing the debt which you now owe.

By my calculations, with interest the current amount stands at five thousand and twelve pounds, seventeen shillings and four pence. I believe your creditors are becoming anxious for the remittance which you are yet to make. Furthermore, my sources tell me you do not have sufficient funds to pay even one-tenth of the amount due.

I should not wish to see such an old friend come to ruin, and you would, you know. Utter ruin. Therefore I remind you of the generous

A BIASED JUDGEMENT

offer I made to you last April. It is such a little thing I ask; so very little a thing.

Do think it over, Mr Winters. If you do the job carefully no one would ever imagine anything was amiss. Not given the lady's extreme old age. In a way, you would be doing her a kindness. Has she not longed for release for almost forty years?

Surely a man like you cannot have such tender scruples as to blind your sense of pragmatism. Think of your family, do.

Give careful thought to my offer, but do not think too long. Should your plans to satisfy your debts fail, you and your family must face utter ruin.

I remain yours, most cordially...

"This signature is most peculiar. It looks like two letter S's one on top of the other."

I held the letter up to the light and examined it. "Hmm... Written in blue-black ink on heavy paper of Bavarian origin. The writer is a middle-aged man, right-handed, with some Austrian heritage and who has been educated in one of England's smaller universities, possible in Oxford."

"Who do you think this W.E. Winters is?"

"No idea at all, I'm afraid. It was in one of Derby's unlabelled boxes so there is no clue there. I suspect she found it in one of her homes and held onto it. There is no ledger sheet for this as there were for all the others. Very likely she did not know who the recipient was either, which suggests an alias."

"I'm sorry," Watson said. "But why do you think that?"

"People don't generally give their personal correspondence to others, Watson," I said. "The person from whom this letter was stolen was almost certainly the recipient."

I steepled my fingers and closed my eyes, thinking. I mused, "Derby may not have been sure that Winters and the person she stole the letter from were one and the same. Or she may have been quite certain it was the same person, but wasn't sure she could blackmail him because it's not actually his real name on the letter. She would have expected it to make him uneasy though, and that might have been enough to amuse her."

"That symbol, Holmes..."

"Yes?"

He stared at it and said, slowly, "Something about it looks familiar."

I sprang back into alertness. "It does? Where have you seen it?"

"Well, if it had a line down the middle it could be a staff of Asclepius," he said. "Sorry, that doesn't help much."

"The staff of Asclepius? Preferred by many over the caduceus of Hermes as a symbol of medicine." I looked at the signature again and saw exactly what the doctor meant.

"I think you're exactly right. Watson! Do you know what that means?"

"Means?"

"You recall our old friend Porlock's full name is Albrecht Stefan Porlock. ASP."

Watson blinked, a little startled at his own brilliance, perhaps. He said, "Do you really believe this letter was written by Porlock, Holmes?"

"I do. It all fits: the Austrian background, the Bavarian paper. Yes, ASP... if we are right, it changes the complexion of this letter entirely. We must see Mycroft tomorrow."

October 22nd, 1897

I awoke with a stiff back, probably because I spent most of the night sitting in my chair, thinking. Watson persuaded me with very little effort to have a sauna before we called upon Mycroft. In addition to my knotted joints, I felt I needed some sort of cleansing after my recent activities, keeping watch over Porlock and, more particularly, wallowing in Derby's filth.

Watson accompanied me and we had a splendid time relaxing and talking about music.

A BIASED JUDGEMENT

"You know," I told him. "I have been privileged to hear some of our finest musicians play extraordinary compositions, Watson, and yet it is Lady Beatrice's performance of Beethoven's piano sonata No. 14 that I return to most often in my memory. Ah, it is a pity you never got to hear her play. It was an unforgettable experience, I assure you."

I was sitting on the bench with my eyes closed and I was able to recall every note of her performance. It was a moment before Watson replied and when he did it was with a rather too casual, "You could call upon her, you know, Holmes. I'm sure she'd be delighted to play again for you."

"Dear friend Watson," I said. "You never tire of trying to marry me off, do you?"

"It's not good for you to be alone, Holmes. Oh I know you have me and Mrs Hudson and as much of a social circle as you feel comfortable with but it's not the same. Surely from time to time you miss having a wife and children like any other man?"

"Yes, I do miss it in occasional moments. Then the moment passes and I congratulate myself that I am free of those burdens. I am not any other man, and I must forge my own path."

"Even if you're lonely? Never mind, forget I spoke."

Afterwards, when we were dressed and out in the fresh air heading for Whitehall, I found myself haunted by his words. I am not and never have been a sentimental man. There are very few women whose company I can tolerate for any period of time, and while Lady Beatrice is one of them I have no romantic inclinations towards her. No. I am ~~almost~~ certain I do not.

I should like to hear her play the piano again, though.

A few minutes later I set the foolish notion aside for we had arrived at our destination: Mycroft's office in Whitehall.

"Well, well, Mr Holmes and Doctor Watson," said Gillespie. "What a treat to see you gentlemen again. You're looking a lot less peaked than last time you were here, Mr Holmes. Just been to the sauna?" He chuckled and I confess I was, for the moment, bewildered.

A BIASED JUDGEMENT

"Ah, the doctor and I look rather flushed," I said.

"And the unmistakable scent of the oil used in massage," he said, smiling.

"Well done, Gillespie," I said, laughing. "Is he free?"

"Yes, sir. You'll find your brother alone at present, although he does have an engagement in," he checked his pocket watch, "forty minutes."

"We shall not delay him."

"Who is that man?" Watson whispered as we climbed the stairs. "That Gillespie chap?"

"He's a funny fellow, isn't he? You know, I've always said, Israel Gillespie is the cleverest man in England after my brother and myself. Oh, don't look at me like that. It would be false modesty for me to claim otherwise. As to that old man, he served in two overseas campaigns, was attached to the Queen's private guards for a while, and has survived two shootings. He's almost eighty now – you'd never think it to look at him, would you? As he refused to retire, he took the position of clerk for Mycroft's department. He's one of the most dependable men I've ever known, save for your good self, Watson. Ah, here we are…"

Mycroft glanced at his watch and said, "You're very welcome, Sherlock, Doctor, but I really do not have a great deal of time. I have a meeting with the Prime Minister shortly."

"This won't take long, Mycroft, and I think you will find this interesting."

He took the document and said, "Is this the last of those dreadful documents, Sherlock? I hope you found the sauna soothing to your spirits. Now, what is it you have brought me? Something curious, I think."

He examined the letter, then read it through twice.

"An excellent find, brother. What a treasure… And what a curious signature. Have you drawn a conclusion as to its meaning?"

"I have not, but Watson observed it resembles the medical insignia."

A BIASED JUDGEMENT

"The staff of Asclepius, yes, I see what you mean." His eyes, very blue in the morning light, met mine. "So we're saying the twisting line represents a snake. You are thinking an asp?"

"Precisely."

"Hmm... It's a little juvenile, but from everything I've heard about Albrecht Porlock that's exactly the sort of thing that would amuse him."

"The elderly woman, and the almost forty years..." I began.

"Yes. Yes, Sherlock, I think you and I are thinking along the same lines."

"What?" Watson said. "What lines?"

"Think about it, Watson," I said. "What lady is elderly and has longed for death for almost forty years? Since 1861, in fact."

"You mean the queen? Good God!"

"It seems likely," Mycroft agreed. "It's not much to go on, you know." He picked up the letter again and stared at it. "There may be another explanation, of course, but I believe your analysis is correct. In any event, we cannot afford to dismiss the possibility."

"From everything I've learned of the man, I am not surprised if he, too, indulges in the infamous activity of blackmail, and I will not even comment on the irony of a blackmail letter being stolen by a blackmailer, but something malevolent is being planned here. I am certain of it."

"I wonder if some of the other people who committed assassinations had been blackmailed by Porlock," Watson mused. At my and my brother's startled expressions, he added "Well, people will go to extraordinary lengths to protect their loved ones."

"That's a leap," I said. "And yet such leaps are often the result of brilliance. You really are on quite splendid form of late, Watson."

Mycroft said. "ASP is an appropriate monogram for one of the most lethal reptiles ever to slither through the London streets: Albrecht Stefan Porlock. A man who will work for the highest bidder, who starts wars to line his pocket, and whose anonymity is at distinct odds to his infamy. Yes, I can see him blackmailing poor wretches to do his dirty work. It's cheaper than paying them, and is a better guarantee of their silence if they're caught. Well done, doctor. I think you may have hit upon the truth."

"But, Sherlock, who is this Winters person? Do you have any idea?"

"None at all, I'm afraid," I said. "I do not believe Derby knew either. There was no ledger notation attached. Unfortunately, I have no way of knowing when or where she acquired the letter."

"Yes, it's unfortunate it is undated, that might have narrowed the possibilities down a little. The letter raises too many questions: Who is Winters and when is this assassination to take place?"

"And by what means," I added. "Well, since I have not yet managed to gain entry into Porlock's house, I shall try working from the other end. I shall look for Winters."

Mycroft rose and put on his coat. "How shall you proceed, Sherlock?"

"I shall begin with the one thing we know about him for certain: he gambles."

We walked together to the door of his office but before he opened it, Mycroft turned to me and said in a low, urgent voice, "I do not have to stress the importance of this, Sherlock? It is imperative we learn everything we can about this plot and prevent it from being carried out. The queen's own life may be at stake."

"I know, Mycroft," I said. "Believe me, I know."

"Shouldn't she be warned?" Watson asked. From the look in his eyes I could see that he'd single-handedly defend the lady against all comers if needed.

"Not yet," Mycroft said. "There is the smallest margin of doubt here; a miniscule possibility that our conclusions are incorrect. We need to be sure... I shall alert all the necessary people, of course, but best not alarm the queen unnecessarily."

16

October 29th 1897

    I have spent the past week working my way through the more extravagant gambling places in the city. I lost a small amount but won two thousand pounds. Watson is somewhat peeved that I would not let him come with me. No doubt his knowledge about various gambling practices would prove useful, but I dare not subject him to that vice again. Not after last time.

    My indolent queries after a fellow going by the name of Winters were met with anger by two gentlemen with whom I played a few hands of poker. "We'd like to find him, and all," said a certain Admiral, his face flushed as red as his tunic. "Scoundrel owes me a small fortune."

    "You too?" I said sympathetically. "What is the world coming to when a gentleman will not pay his debts?"

    "No gentleman at all," said another. "A puffed-up pipsqueak. He pretends to airs but his suit is two years old."

    "I am very anxious to have him settle his accounts," said I. "Can either of you gentlemen suggest where I may find him? You can be assured, I shall be happy to deliver him to you too."

    "Not been seen for six weeks or more," said the fellow, a banker by the name of Carstairs. "And I have it on good authority he's being sought by every club in the city. My guess is he's hopped it."

    "Hopped it?"

    "Canada," said the Admiral. "If you can believe a word out of his lying mouth. Said he had business deals in Montreal and Toronto."

A BIASED JUDGEMENT

Armed with this information I approached the shipping lines, but no 'Winters' is on any of the passenger lists for Canada. Given his circumstances, if he has, indeed, left the country, I assume he's traveling under a false name. Unless Winters is also a false name, which I rather suspect to be the case.

In other news, I have received a number of gifts – bottles of wine, a rather nice set of diamond cufflinks, and some other trinkets – with cards that say only, "Thank you". None of them is signed but it is obvious they come from Liz Derby's former victims.

November 8th, 1897

Poor Watson received a telegram yesterday evening saying his brother is extremely ill. After a wretched night and a hurried breakfast, I saw him off at King's Cross on the train for Edinburgh.

I confess I felt very sorry to see him go. I would have gone with him, of course. I know he would have been glad of my company, but this business of a possible attempt against the queen requires all my attention. Still, I dithered, a state I dislike in the extreme.

"Perhaps I should come with you, Watson," I said. "Just long enough to see you safely home and I can return in the morning."

"That's nonsense, old man," he said. "You really need to keep an eye on things here. Don't fret; I shall probably sleep on the train. Promise me you will look after yourself, Holmes. I really wish you'd ask Mycroft to get some guards for your protection."

"You need not be concerned, my dear Watson," I said. "I shall manage very well, I am sure. My trusty Tranter revolver shall have to substitute for your presence.

"I hope you have a safe journey and find your brother much improved upon your arrival. Goodbye, my dear chap, goodbye."

With some misgivings I stood on the platform and watched the train pull out of the station. To be entirely frank, part of me was relieved to have a sound excuse for remaining in the city. Truth be told, I'd rather face a pair of brutes in a dark alley than spend an hour with Watson's

A BIASED JUDGEMENT

pious family. The poor chap always returns from Scotland in a sour temper which, I am surprised to report, does not improve when I attribute his ill humour to a surfeit of haggis. "Not funny, Holmes," he says. Then I suggest he was struck by a wayward caber or fell into a loch... Eventually he brightens. He's generally of a cheerful disposition (which, Lord knows, I test to the maximum on occasion), and our little ritual helps set him to rights. I like to think so, anyway. I really could knock the blocks of all his clan. It's outrageous the way they treat him. As if living in London was some form of treason. Ridiculous! That said, if he loses his brother he shall be inconsolable and I am ill equipped for lending comfort.

This evening after yet another fruitless day searching for the elusive Mr Winters, I decided to attend a concert at the Royal Italian Opera in Covent Garden. The music was disappointing, but the real pleasure was when a young gentleman at the bar asked me for a light for his cigarette.

I was vastly entertained to realise the 'young man' was, in fact, Lady Beatrice. Indeed, my mirth quite overshadowed the concert (a banal offering of the most insipid Caroline concertos.)

The Lady has invited me to dinner tomorrow and I have accepted. The opportunity to break the boredom is most welcome. Besides, I am curious to hear the news about the peculiar inhabitants of Rillington Manor.

November 9th, 1897

Precisely at eight o'clock this evening, I arrived at Lady Beatrice's home in the City and was surprised to see the door opened by young Stevens. Since the death of his mother he has nothing now to keep him in Southampton. A couple of months ago he applied to the Metropolitan Police and is waiting to learn his fate.

"I am sure you will do very well, Stevens," I said. "I only fear the duties of a police constable may be too far beneath your abilities."

"I don't mind, Mr Holmes," he said. "As long as I work hard I can make my way up the ranks."

A BIASED JUDGEMENT

"And how do you come to be here, in Lady Beatrice's home?"

"Her Ladyship was kind enough to give me a job while I'm waiting to hear back. The work here is light enough; I drive the carriage and help out a bit, but to be honest, Lady Beatrice doesn't really need me. She just gave me the job out of kindness. She'd do well enough without me."

He'd have said more, I warrant, but the Lady herself joined us in the hallway.

"You are very punctual, Mr Holmes," she said. "I see you and Stevens have been renewing your acquaintance."

"We have indeed," said I. "It is rare for me to see again people I have met on a case. I was greatly surprised to see Stevens ensconced so happily in London."

"He is here temporarily," said the Lady. "An engagement that suits both of us. But we should not linger in the hallway. Come," and she led me into the dining room.

The Lady sets an excellent table and, more to the point, is a highly engaging conversationalist; something I would not have guessed from her dull appearance at Rillington Manor.

For some time we discussed music. Her knowledge on the subject is as broad as it is deep. "I hope," I said. "That you will honour me with a performance on the pianoforte this evening."

"I would be delighted," she said.

"Ah, it is a pleasure to discuss music with someone whose knowledge is equal to my own," I said.

She said, "Doctor Watson does not share your taste?"

"I'm afraid not. The good doctor prefers less lofty entertainment. Ah, it is a great pity he did not get to hear you play in Rillington Manor. You might have converted him to the joy of Beethoven, at least."

"That was a dreadful evening," the Lady replied. "Isn't it strange how some houses seem to attract bad luck or unhappiness? Or is that too romantic a notion for your rational mind, Mr Holmes?"

She smiled as she spoke and I realised I was being very gently teased. I laughed loudly.

"Ha!" I said. "Well, some houses do seem particularly unhappy. Baskerville Hall, for instance, over the centuries seems to have brought nothing but misery to its inhabitants. As for Rillington Manor, a great deal of the misery there must rest at the feet of Liz Derby of unhappy memory."

"Well, it was an unhappy house even before Derby arrived, but she certainly added to its wretchedness. Tell me, what did you do with the documents you found at her house?"

I responded by telling her, in very broad terms, what I had found in Derby's secret room and my current investigation.

"And this person, Winters, you say you're looking for, Mr Holmes, I assume it's a matter of some urgency that you find him, given the extent of your efforts."

"It is indeed, Lady Beatrice. I regret I cannot be more explicit about the reasons, but I can assure you it is a matter of the greatest urgency."

"How old is the letter? Is there some way you can narrow it down and so determine in which house she was working when she stole it?"

"I have been through every moment of Derby's career going back five years. The 'Winters' letter is quite recent, I believe, judging by the condition of the paper, but I cannot narrow it beyond roughly two or three years. Since it is best to err on the side of caution, I have extended that period to five years. The likelihood is that it is much, much more recent than that. I do not suppose you ever heard of such a person visiting Rillington Manor?"

"No one by that name, I'm afraid," she said. "But if you cannot narrow down the period by the paper, is there a test you can make on the ink?"

"Ha!" I cried. "You have the mind of a scientist, Lady Beatrice. It is a great pity you were not born a man.

"The letter is written in ink made of iron gall in Schlutigg and Neumann's formula."

A BIASED JUDGEMENT

"I'm afraid I'm not familiar with it. Ink is made of iron salt and a binder of some sort, isn't it?"

"Yes. Generally inks have three basic ingredients in common: Iron salt, as you say, usually ferrous sulphate; plant tannins which are extracted from the likes of oak tree galls; and a binder like gum Arabic which keeps the particles in suspension and enables the ink to flow. Iron gall ink does not fade, not even over extremely long periods of time. This permanence makes testing for its age almost impossible."

"I see the difficulty," she said.

"If we were dealing with decades perhaps I could devise some sort of test..."

"I can make discreet inquiries, if you like," she said. "If the matter is so grave as you seem to think I should like to help."

"Thank you, Lady Beatrice. You must be very discreet indeed. I am fearful that this fellow, if he is still in London, may flee if he learns that I am looking for him. It is a matter of the gravest importance that I speak to him."

"I shall be very circumspect, I promise."

Her cheeks flushed with pleasure or excitement. I suppose she does not have many opportunities to make a meaningful contribution beyond donating to the church fund.

Over dessert she asked about the assault that had been the means of introducing us. "Who was that man? Did you ever find him?" she asked.

"His name was Alberto Calvini," I said. "I believe he was hired by the same villain who wrote the letter to this Winters fellow. Calvini was found dead on the Embankment some months ago."

"He was hired to attack you?" She put down her spoon and I could see her reason through a number of possibilities and dangers. After some moments she said, "Then I infer this villainous overseer is still at large since you are hoping Winters will lead you to him. Have there been other attempts made against you?"

I made a show of nonchalance and said, "No, none."

"Come, Mr Holmes, I think there is more to the story than that."

A BIASED JUDGEMENT

It is really most unsettling to find a woman with such insight. I need to be on my guard with her as much as I am with Watson, although I suspect I shall have no better luck concealing my fears from the lady than I do the doctor.

"I am being watched and followed. Thus far the brutes have not raised a hand against me since that night in February, but it is unsettling and inconvenient. I have had to devise other means of egress from my home in order to conduct my researches. Do not be alarmed, Lady Beatrice. I assure you I am quite capable of looking after myself."

"But you cannot mean these villains continue to prey upon you, Mr Holmes," the Lady said. "Surely they can be arrested?"

"You and Doctor Watson take the same view of things," I said. "He would have me arrest all of them who show up in Baker Street to spy on me. But, you see, these men are nothing, are mere foot soldiers in a huge army. Besides which merely following me is not illegal."

"No, I see your point." She sipped her wine thoughtfully. "What do you know of the leader?"

"Not nearly as much as I should like. The man who now leads that villainous gang has ties with some of the most unscrupulous characters in Europe and even in the North American territories. He would like nothing better than to see our nation destroyed…" I paused. It was rare for me to discuss such matters outside my most trusted circle; unheard of for me to discuss anything approaching politics with a woman. However, something about this particular woman seems to invite confidence, in both senses of that word.

"What makes a man forget his principles?" she mused, her meal forgotten in her utter focus on the subject. "He cannot always have been evil, surely? What is his background?"

I said, "He is, outwardly, a perfectly ordinary Englishman though with a pronounced Germanic flavour. He is highly intelligent and well educated. He is fluent in several languages, has a fine appreciation for music, and wide knowledge of a number of subject, particularly politics."

A BIASED JUDGEMENT

"You could be describing yourself, Mr Holmes," Lady Beatrice said, smiling.

"In outward things, yes. But dig deeper and you find many differences. This individual began his life of crime when he was hardly more than a boy. Despite his education, he was expelled from at least half a dozen schools, here in England and abroad. Only family name and money enabled him to go to Oxford where, I confess, he excelled in his studies of politics and languages. Despite these and other accomplishments, even then he was befriending men as unsavoury as himself.

"His name has been linked to a number of political scandals, including a number of assassinations, and yet he is a family man, a devoted father and, so far as I can tell, a faithful husband."

Lady Beatrice shook her head. "What a creature. It worries me to think of you at risk, Mr Holmes," she said. "I wonder..." She took a moment to select her words and then said, "As you know, Stevens is with me for a few months. Even after he is accepted by the police force, as I have no doubt he shall be, he will have to wait for the next admission period before he can join. I really do not have enough to keep him occupied, but perhaps he might be of assistance to you? You could use the carriage to convey you to your destinations. Do please say you will, Mr Holmes. I confess it would greatly relieve my anxiety to know you were not walking alone through darkened streets. I know Stevens would be delighted to be of service; he holds you in the very highest regard."

I hesitated only a moment. "I am happy to use the carriage and Stevens on occasion," I said. "So long as my doing so does not inconvenience you, Lady Beatrice."

For the next ten minutes we haggled over the arrangement and finally decided I would call when I needed Stevens and he would come to Baker Street to convey me whenever I wished. In thanks for the Lady's generosity, I offered to escort her to the symphony next week, an outing that pleases both of us.

A BIASED JUDGEMENT

Over cheese and biscuits I said, "What news of your aunt and the rest of the company in Rillington Manor? Have you heard from that household or have you lost all contact with its inhabitants?"

"I'm afraid I know very little, Mr Holmes. Stevens tells me my aunt was well when he left, but I have had no news from her directly. The rest of the household seems... unsettled from what Stevens says. Or rather, from what he contrives not to say. Neither he nor Derby were ever replaced and that has put some strain on the remaining servants. Daisy will be leaving soon, too. She and Stevens mean to marry just as soon as he begins his new position. As for Miss Simms, I believe she and Mr Davenport expect to marry next year."

"And Wallace Summerville? Have you heard any more from him?"

She shuddered. "I have heard from him, but I would prefer not to discuss that matter, if you don't mind, Mr Holmes."

"As you wish," I replied. "Tell me, do you play any other instruments..?"

After dinner we adjourned to the drawing room where my hostess required little persuasion to take her seat at the piano. She happily played every piece I requested: Bach and Beethoven, Mozart and Brahms. She played with such skill as I have rarely heard even in the finest concert halls of Europe. I told her so and she said, "Alas, I have never had the opportunity to attend any concerts save the ones here in England. I should love to go to Italy and hear my favourite pieces played there."

At the end of our very pleasant evening, Stevens was delighted to convey me back to Baker Street and he chattered away quite merrily as we went. He was full of excitement about his new career prospects.

"Between ourselves, Mr Holmes," he said. "Inspector Lestrade said with your recommendation and his own I should have no difficulty being accepted. Lady Beatrice too has been kind enough to give me a reference – a good thing since I doubt I would get one from Sir Christopher. All I can do now is wait."

"And have you heard anything from your old friends in Southampton?"

"Miss Simms writes me, sir, and so does Daisy. They say it has got very bad and they all envy me my happy new position. I think Miss Simms will not stay there much longer. She has accepted Mr Davenport's proposal and they are to be married next June."

"And you and Daisy are making plans too, I hear," said I.

"Yes, sir. I have hopes to marry as soon as the job is secure and we can find a place. Lady Beatrice is extremely kind. She has given me a roof while I wait to hear back from the force. But she really has few needs and there's little enough for me to do. I was glad when she suggested I convey you in the carriage tonight. I am happy to assist you in any way you need me, Mr Holmes. A man likes to feel he is earning his keep.

November 15th, 1897

Watson called this morning to say his brother was starting to show signs of improvement. "I feel I should stay a while, though, Holmes," he added. "He needs a lot of care yet and I know I should worry if I were to leave him."

"Of course you must stay, my dear fellow. Your brother must be your first concern."

"I knew you'd understand. How are things there? Are you making progress?"

"Slow, Watson. I make very slow progress. I have concluded that Winters is most definitely a false name. I have a description of him which is too vague to be of much help, but it suggests an idea. Just an idea. The bird is lying low, but if I am right he cannot stay away from London for much longer. Indeed, I suspect he will be back within the next month.

"As to Porlock, I have a rather audacious idea for getting into his house... It will need some preparation and careful planning. I shall write you the details. Stay warm and make sure you wrap up in your woollen scarf. We cannot have you getting ill too."

It is unfortunate that my friend must be away at this period. I miss him, I confess. Still, Stevens has proven himself quite invaluable. He calls every morning and takes me wherever I need to go. Despite his youth and lack of education, I find him very eager to learn. He has accompanied me to Scotland Yard twice this week alone and seems to be making friends among the younger constables. He has that ready knack for socialising that remains a mystery to me. It is a relief to travel without fear. I feel far more secure in the carriage and Stevens himself seems a very capable fellow.

He tells me he is to go to Bitterne next week to see his fiancée, Daisy. He added, "I hope you will not think me impertinent, Mr Holmes, but I wonder if I might ask a favour?"

This is exactly the sort of thing to raise alarms with me but I said, as casually as I could, "What sort of favour?"

"It's about Lady Beatrice, Mr Holmes. She'd no doubt be very cross with me for telling you, but the lady needs protecting, and that's a fact."

"Protecting?" I exclaimed. "From what?"

"That Wallace Summerville. He's been calling upon her Ladyship fairly regular, like, and he always leaves her in distress. Of course, she'd never confide in me, Mr Holmes, but she might tell you."

"I shall look into it, Stevens. Thank you for letting me know."

November 21st, 1897

My two shadows have vanished. I would like to think they have given up the task of spying upon me since I've been travelling by carriage, but I am not so naïve. I am, I confess, somewhat unsettled by their absence.

Unfortunately, Stevens is away in Southampton visiting his fiancée and with Watson still in Scotland I am feeling an unfamiliar and most unwelcome sensation of vulnerability. Still, I will not let this unease keep me from my work or my tasks.

A BIASED JUDGEMENT

Since I was in the City conducting some business at my bank I decided to call upon Lady Beatrice, ostensibly to thank her for the use of her carriage and her young footman's time, but also to keep my promise to see she is safe.

I was alarmed to find her much altered since last I had seen her, though it has been a mere couple of weeks. She greeted me affably and invited me to stay for lunch, an invitation I accepted with pleasure. Still, her distress, though well contained as one would expect from a member of her caste, caused me much concern.

"Are you well, Lady Beatrice?" I asked.

"Thank you, Mr Holmes," she replied. "I am healthy enough."

"Come, you must not dissemble with me. Surely you can trust me with the truth?"

She bit her lip and waited till the maid had finished serving the coffee. Then she said, "It is foolish of me to try to conceal anything from you, of all men. The truth is I am... frightened. There. It galls me to have to admit it. A healthy, educated and financially secure young woman living in the heart of the greatest metropolis in the world and I am as frightened as a child."

"Wallace Summerville?" I said.

She nodded. "He came by late last night and was in rather a pitiful state of inebriation. He comes here from time to time, but when he last visited Stevens showed him the door rather forcefully. I was foolish enough to think I was finally rid of him. His timing is curious what with Stevens being away for a few days. I am not sure if Summerville's appearance is merely coincidence, or if he has been watching the house. In any event, last night he arrived in high dudgeon and declared all sorts of nonsense—"

"Nonsense?"

"Of a romantic nature. Or what he thinks passes for romance. I have no patience with such conversation even when it is heartfelt, Mr Holmes. How much more repulsive is it when it is cloying and self-serving."

A BIASED JUDGEMENT

"And what happened?"

"I told him to leave. I could have cried out but I hate seeming weak. Though I suppose I am…"

I could see that tears were not far from the surface but the Lady controlled herself magnificently and they did not spill.

"He became abusive and pushed me down. I told him I would scream and have him arrested. At that he seemed to recover himself somewhat. He rose to leave but said it was merely a matter of time until I succumbed to his 'charms' as he put it."

She shuddered.

I gently peeled back her sleeve to examine the fresh bruise on her wrist. "He did this?"

She nodded. "Mind, I left a mark or two of my own. I struck him with my fist. I fear I shall pay dearly for my resistance when I marry him."

"Marry..! You cannot mean it, Lady Beatrice. What could possibly compel you to marry such a creature?"

"I have family obligations…" She bit on her lip so hard I thought she would draw blood.

I rose and paced the floor. "I am reluctant to leave you so defenceless against this creature," I said. "Surely you have friends or family who will protect you."

"My aunt is all the family I have."

"You cannot mean your aunt would compel you to marry the brute?"

"No, not she. My godmother."

"Who is?"

"The queen."

"Oh."

For some moments we sat in silence, then I asked, "You'll forgive me, Lady Beatrice, but I see no evidence that Summerville has any particular fondness for you. Why, then, should he be so anxious to marry?"

A BIASED JUDGEMENT

"His fondness is for my fortune, Mr Holmes. His brother has already gone through my aunt's dowry and is about to lose the house to creditors. Wallace Summerville is in equally dire circumstances, from what I understand. If he cannot pay his debtors and swiftly... I would just give him the money if I thought I could be rid of him."

"You must not do that," I said. "Such a creature will spend every penny in a matter of days and then come back for more."

"I know... I know..."

We ate a rather morose luncheon, both of us too preoccupied with our thoughts to engage much in conversation.

For the rest of the afternoon I paced the streets of London. As evening fell I found myself walking through St James's Park on my way towards the Diogenes Club. I shivered when I passed that spot where the Albino had attacked me; it was here all my adventures with Lady Beatrice began so many months earlier. Fortunately, there were no assailants lying in wait this evening.

Mycroft and I dined together and I laid the Lady's difficulty before him. Though not interested in domestic matters, as he would term them, my brother has an exceptional ability to see to the heart of the problem. To my surprise he was already familiar with Lady Beatrice's predicament.

"I know her quite well, Sherlock," he said. "Indeed, I have the pleasure of meeting Lady Beatrice on a few occasions. Once at a dinner for the French ambassador, and twice at the Palace when she and I were invited to dine with the family. She is Her Majesty's godchild, you know. In fact, she was named for the queen's youngest daughter, Princess Beatrice."

"Yes, yes. But surely the queen will not countenance so unpleasant a union between her goddaughter and that oaf, Summerville. He is grotesque, Mycroft. As dangerous a ruffian as ever stalked the streets of Whitechapel."

"And Lady Beatrice is twenty-seven," he replied. "Moreover she is an independent thinker."

A BIASED JUDGEMENT

"What has that to do with anything?"

"The queen is old, Sherlock. Though the news has not been made public, she is ill; I doubt she will see many more years – even without Porlock's assistance."

"Yes, but—"

"The Queen does not like loose ends. She believes all young women should be married, particularly those who have attracted her notice. While Sir Benjamin Jacoby lived, Lady Beatrice was secure. Her father would not see her shackled to an imbecile or a fortune hunter. But the queen knows only that the girl has not married and here is – in the queen's eyes anyway – a perfectly sound proposal."

"You cannot let this happen, Mycroft. The girl will be dead in six months if she has to marry that villain."

"It is out of my hands, Sherlock."

"But surely… The queen will listen to you, Mycroft. Or if you are so unwilling to speak to her perhaps you can arrange for me to do so?"

"Absolutely not. I forbid it. I mean it, Sherlock. The queen's health is too delicate for such an audience. She cannot be distressed by this melodrama."

"Melodrama! Mycroft, a young woman's life is at stake."

But he would hear none of it.

November 23rd, 1897

Very unexpectedly this afternoon, Watson returned home.

"My dear fellow, I am delighted to see you," I exclaimed. "Why did you not let me know you were coming?"

"It was rather spur of the moment," he said, dropping his bag on the floor and sagging into the armchair.

"What happened? Your brother was much improved when last we spoke but you were planning on staying a little longer."

"True, true," he said. "Once he turned the corner he mended with great speed and I… could not think of my friend Sherlock Holmes in London, all alone, and at the mercy of violent men."

"A lovely sentiment to be sure," I said. "And I'm sure your quarrel with your sister-in-law had nothing to do with your sudden departure from Scotland."

He shot me a look. "Why do you think I quarrelled with Bertha?"

"Because you always do. To tell the truth, I wonder that anyone can tolerate that woman's company... But there, it's none of my affair. Suffice it to say I am very pleased to see you. Does Mrs Hudson know you're back? She'll set a big table for you to celebrate."

"I saw her when I came in. I'm surprised you did not hear me."

"I was asleep," I admitted. "I was keeping watch until very late last night."

"Over Porlock's house?"

"No, over a house in Wimpole Street."

I told him about Lady Beatrice's encounters with Wallace Summerville and concluded, "I was afraid he might return and so last night I kept an eye on the place. By four o'clock I decided it was safe to come home but, I confess, I was in a state of such vexation it took me until after dawn to get to sleep."

"My dear fellow, you must go back to bed. No? Well... When does Stevens return from Southampton?"

"This afternoon. But I hear from Lestrade that he has been accepted into the metropolitan force. In just a few weeks he must leave his current position and Lady Beatrice will be utterly at the mercy of those insufferable Summervilles."

"It's insupportable, Holmes. A woman's life is so little valued in our society. But there must surely be a solution. Could she leave the country?"

"Abandon her home? And for how long?"

"Well... the queen cannot live for ever. She is a good age and you tell me her health is not the best. A king may be more sympathetic. Lady Beatrice could return when there is a new monarch on the throne."

A BIASED JUDGEMENT

"I cannot see her agreeing to abandoning her home and being driven out by this creature. She has people who depend upon her... I can suggest it to her of course, but I do not see that as a reasonable option."

"Can the police not help?"

"I spoke with Lestrade and Gregson last night. That is how I learned of Stevens' happy news before the young man himself. At my request, they will place a man outside her house in Wimpole Street."

"Well, that's something."

"Perhaps. I have no great faith in underpaid public servants, Watson. You and I know only too well how unreliable many of them are. Of all the people working Lady Beatrice's home, other than the soon to depart Stevens, only one is male: Mr Fallon, her late father's valet. He is a man of some age and I doubt he'd be much match against the wiry and savage Summerville."

"You say she has bruises, though; could she not bring charges against him? He can hardly harangue her when he is in custody, and it might make him a less attractive candidate to the Queen."

I thought about that. "I will suggest it to her. I rather doubt that she will though; there is that family pride to consider. I suspect she would deem it a matter of distress for the queen. Besides, there is the likelihood of repercussions against her aunt."

"You'll think of something, old man," Watson said. "Why don't you go back to bed for a while and sleep on it?"

November 24th, 1898

As Watson suggested, I slept on this unpleasant situation Lady Beatrice faces, but badly. I awoke in time for dinner in a querulous mood. There are too many random pieces of information all fighting for attention in my brain. I confess, I am irked at having to devote even moments to the safety of a privileged young woman. Then I remind myself that Lady Beatrice, as Jack, saved my life and I am chagrined.

I picked up my violin, disconsolately I confess, and started to play a sad piece by Schubert when from below I heard the doorbell ring. I

A BIASED JUDGEMENT

continued to play but my attention was riveted by the light footsteps coming up the stair. As I completed the last movement I turned at last to see Lady Beatrice standing in my doorway.

"You play very well," she said.

"I misfingered the last movement," I said.

"Yes. I distracted you."

Watson sat in his usual chair by the fire looking from one of us to the other. Then, belatedly, realised his manners and rose to his feet.

"I beg your pardon, Lady Beatrice," he said. "Do please sit down by the fire. It's rather a filthy evening. Shall I have Mrs Hudson bring up some coffee?"

"Do, please, Watson," I said. While he went to do just that I sat in my seat facing the Lady. "Now then," I said. "You need my help?"

She was very pale and the flush that rose to her cheeks suggested illness rather than comeliness. Despite that she met my eyes calmly and said, "You are, of course, correct, Mr Holmes."

"I am at your completely disposal. If it is in my power to serve you I shall."

"Stevens received a letter this morning telling him his application to join the metropolitan police force has been approved. He is to report in January."

"You will feel his absence keenly," I began. Then, seeing her expression, I added, "But it is not that which troubles you. He has offered to forgo his position and remain in your employ."

"He has. He is tremendously loyal and honourable, but of course I cannot permit such a sacrifice. He has much to offer our police force and, besides, he has hopes to marry some time next year. I cannot possibly allow him to give up his long-held ambition."

"No. No I quite see that."

"The thing is, Mr Holmes, after Stevens leaves I need to be able to defend myself. That is the reason why I came…"

A BIASED JUDGEMENT

"Yes?" I waited. I was almost afraid of what she might ask me but her request, when it came, was not what I feared and yet it alarmed me almost as much.

"I wondered, Mr Holmes, can you tell me where I might be able to get a gun?"

17

I vow, for a moment I could not catch my breath. When I could speak I said, "Since I first met you, Lady Beatrice, you have shown a remarkable talent for surprising me. I was not expecting that."

"I need to be able to protect myself. It is only a matter of time until Summerville's behaviour becomes... dangerous."

"You cannot believe a firearm is the answer? Is it not more likely that he would overpower you and take the weapon from you? You yourself might be the victim."

"What else am I to do?" she cried. She rose and paced the floor.

"You could leave the country," I began.

"Out of the question. I have responsibilities here, Mr Holmes. I have two houses, my father's business interests, and a number of people who are dependent upon me. Also, I want to be on hand in case my aunt should ever need me."

I frowned. It seemed all my best ideas were being thwarted. At the time I was annoyed but now, in the calmer moments of today, I respect and admire her loyalty. But at the time I said rather irritably, "You could bring charges against Summerville for his assault."

She smiled. "Let me tell you a story, Mr Holmes. When I was a young girl I wanted to be a professional musician. Thanks to my father I had an excellent education and studied the piano under some of the finest teachers in the world. They all agreed I had talent enough to tour as a concert pianist. It was also what I wanted."

"And why didn't you?"

A BIASED JUDGEMENT

"My family objected. That is to say, the queen objected. She felt travelling the world and 'attracting notoriety' would disgrace my family. As you see, I am not a concert pianist."

"A loss to the world," I said, and meant it. "So you believe bringing charges against Summerville must also be seen as bringing notoriety? Surely the queen would not want to see her goddaughter so abused."

"I am sure she would not, but she will not hear of Summerville's abuse from me nor from any of my friends. She is old and becoming frail. Although we do not always agree I am very fond of her. Besides, even were she not my godmother, she is still the queen."

"But surely shooting a man would be even more notorious than bringing charges," I persisted.

"I wouldn't use the weapon, Mr Holmes. Just the threat of it would protect me, I am sure."

I was less certain. I suspected the Lady spoke more in hope than in fact. From what I know of Wallace Summerville I believed there was very little evil he will not do. Any man who would strike a woman might be capable of anything. On the other hand, leaving Lady Beatrice without some means of protection was unconscionable.

"You had a weapon before, I think," I said, remembering the sad end of Edmund Villiers.

She met my eyes and said, calmly, "I was in the habit of bringing my father's revolver with me to Rillington Manor, but… I seem to have mislaid it."

For a moment neither of us spoke. Then the Lady continued, "I do not expect an immediate answer, Mr Holmes. I realise my request places you in a difficult situation. And if you feel you must decline I will of course understand."

Before I could respond Mrs Hudson accompanied by a hesitant Watson came into the room with a tray.

"There now," said our housekeeper. "A pot of fresh coffee to keep out the cold. Can I bring you some supper, Lady Beatrice?"

A BIASED JUDGEMENT

"Thank you, I'm afraid not. I really must get home pretty soon, but I am very grateful for the coffee, it is just the thing." She smiled at Mrs Hudson and that old woman flushed with pleasure. Not for the first time, I marvelled at the natural talent some people possess for making others feel at ease. It is a talent I have never possessed. Watson says I just need to set my mind to it. I flatter myself my mind has better things to employ it.

For a long time after Lady Beatrice left I sat with my violin resting on my knees but with my bow silent. After waiting more than an hour for me to speak, Watson at last said, "Are you able to help our young friend, Holmes?"

"She wants a weapon, Watson. She wants me to tell her where to get a gun."

"To protect herself; I see." Absently, he rubbed his leg. The dampness of the season has been causing him some pain, I perceive, but he never complains. He muffled a wince as he eased back in his chair and said, "Firearms are a tricky business, even for an experienced man. Is it a good idea to put one into the hands of a young woman, no matter how competent she appears?"

"I confess I share your apprehension," I replied. "I am afraid that a slight young woman could so easily be disarmed and have the weapon used against her."

"Yet her options, as you said yourself, are rather limited. What other choice does she have?"

What choice, indeed? That is the question that vexes me. It dances around my brain and keeps me from sleep. It is almost three am and I am no closer to either rest or a solution. I can forgo the former readily enough, but the second... what am I to do about the second?

November 24th, 1897

All night I wrestled with the question. Were Lady Beatrice merely some acquaintance made in the course of an investigation I would be

A BIASED JUDGEMENT

sympathetic, but feel under no obligation. But the fact remains, I almost certainly owe her my life. Surely that gives me some responsibility for her protection?

I spent the day in Finsbury. Tommy has been keeping close watch on Porlock's house but has nothing to report. The governess comes out each afternoon with the little girls, regardless of the weather. They spend precisely half an hour walking around the park and then, punctual to the minute, return to the house. Albrecht Porlock's routine has not changed. Mrs Porlock is seldom seen outdoors save on one occasion when she and her husband left in a carriage, presumably to a concert since Tommy reports they were dressed formally.

I sent the boy away to get some food and rest and kept watch until the next Irregular, young Kevin, arrived. I sat on a park bench and had a clear view through the ground floor front window, despite the lace curtains. Husband and wife were at the piano. She was playing and he was turning the pages of her music. In that instant I had a sudden flash of inspiration. An idea so startling, so outrageous it quite took my breath away.

Kevin arrived and I gave him his instructions and then walked back to Baker Street, thinking hard as I walked.

Watson was out somewhere so I had supper alone. I hardly tasted the food. My idea consumed me.

No, I have thought it through from every angle. It cannot be helped. A great sacrifice to be sure, but there is no other way.

I know what I must do.

November 25th, 1898

This morning I called upon Lady Beatrice. She greeted me with her customary grace, and no casual observer would ever suspect her anxiety.

"You should have had Stevens come and fetch you, Mr Holmes," she said.

A BIASED JUDGEMENT

"My shadows have vanished for the moment," I said. "And I took a cab without any difficulty."

I sat facing her in her library and said, "I have been thinking over your request, Lady Beatrice."

"You have qualms about giving a firearm to a woman. I understand."

"It is not because you are a woman. You are as capable as any man; more than most, I dare say. But I am reluctant to give you a weapon that can be so easily turned against you."

She said, too brightly, "It was a foolish thought. Thank you for considering it, Mr Holmes."

"I have an axiom: once you have eliminated the impossible, whatever remains must be the truth."

"I believe I have heard the phrase," she said.

"It may also be applied to life's problems: once you have eliminated all impossible or impracticable solutions, whatever remains is the one you must take."

"So, then, you suggest I marry Summerville," she said.

"By no means! No, no, such a course would at best be a slow suicide. No indeed, you cannot marry that worm. But I do think you should marry. It is the only way to ensure your safety."

She laughed though there was no mirth in the sound. "Mr Holmes, I am twenty-seven years of age and although I am wealthy I no longer have long lines of suitors waiting to propose. Where is such a husband to be found?"

I took a breath and said, "I will marry you. If you will have me."

She stared at me in utter astonishment for several silent moments and then she threw her head back and laughed. She laughed so long and so hard that I was afraid she would become hysterical. However, she recovered herself then managed to say, "I had not labelled you a prankster, Mr Holmes, but I thank you for that laugh. It was sorely needed... Wait, you cannot mean you are serious? Forgive me, but... Why?"

201

A BIASED JUDGEMENT

"I am not proposing a traditional marriage, Lady Beatrice," I said. "Our living arrangements need not change save as much as is needed to present a show of convention to watchful eyes. I would continue to live at Baker Street and you here in Wimpole Street. We need see no more of each other than we do at present. You may rest assured I would never make any demands of you... and of course your property would remain yours to manage as you have always done."

She leaned forward, her eyes bright. "What an extraordinary suggestion! Oh, it is a generous offer, Mr Holmes, and as brilliant a solution as I can imagine, but really, I cannot allow you to make such a sacrifice."

"There is no sacrifice," I said. "There is nothing sentimental in my nature. I have no need of romantic attachments. This marriage would simply be a matter of convenience."

"But the benefit is entirely on my side, Mr Holmes. Certainly you would be entitled to my fortune, which is considerable, but you have already said I would continue to control that."

"I am a wealthy man and my needs are simple. I have no need for anything more. But I have not forgotten the great debt that I owe you – no, do not demur."

"I was not about to. I was going to point out that sacrificing your freedom seems... excessive. As for the happy accident that enabled me to aid you, I do not require recompense."

I confess this was not the response I had expected. I had thought – inasmuch as I'd thought of it at all – that the Lady would be delighted at the offer, would accept with alacrity. Her refusal to do so was surprisingly unsettling.

"Then," I said, rather coldly. "What is your solution, Lady Beatrice?"

"You know I do not have one. But how can I buy my own security at the expense of your liberty?"

"My liberty? Come, you make too much of a trifle. Do you think you would want me to play the traditional role of the husband?"

A BIASED JUDGEMENT

"Of course not."

"Then you think we should live under the same roof?"

"Not at all."

"Ah, then perhaps you are hoping to find for yourself a husband more suited to your taste."

"By no means. Mr Holmes, my only scruple is to refuse to allow you to pay a cost greater than the odds."

"The odds, in this case, is my life."

"That is by no means certain..." She broke off and I saw her struggle. She rose from her chair and paced the floor. I sat, waiting.

After several minutes she sat before me again.

"You would really do such an extraordinary thing?" she said. "You know I would never ask more of you? If we are to engage in this extraordinary... engagement we should sit and design a contract so we are both clear on the point."

I laughed. "If a contract is what you wish, Lady Beatrice, a contract is what you shall have."

We debated the matter then for another half an hour. It was, I thought, an academic exercise for the lady; she was still reluctant to accept my offer. I was confident, however, that once she had taken the time to ponder the matter she would see there really was no other choice.

For the next half hour we amused ourselves by listing the parameters of our contract, focusing on the absurdities. We have agreed upon the following:

Our living arrangements shall not alter save on the occasion when some measure of outward appearance is necessary. In the unlikely event that either of us must stay at the other's home, we shall, of course, have our own bedchamber.

We each keep our own bank accounts and management of our own funds.

I am to escort the Lady to the theatre at least once a month. (We did harangue over whether the opera or symphony should be specified, but

A BIASED JUDGEMENT

these things are dependent upon the vagaries of the Opera House and the musical calendar so we have agreed to be no more specific than that.)

My fiancée (how strange!) agrees to play the pianoforte for me at least once a month. We discussed a reciprocal arrangement whereby I play the violin for her, but ultimately decided this should be on an ad hoc basis. I find I cannot play to any sort of schedule.

The Lady's unusual nocturnal activities are to remain at her own discretion. In any event, she has had to curtail them, of late, as it is likely that Summerville is keeping her watched.

Our engagement, should the Queen approve, is to be of at least a year's duration. Longer, if possible. If Her Majesty should not survive to see our wedding day, we shall quietly terminate our arrangement.

I am to call the palace tomorrow to see if I may have an appointment with the Queen. First, though, I must relate my news to Mycroft. I am not greatly looking forward to either encounter.

November 26th, 1897

This morning I went to meet my brother for breakfast. It was only right that he should be the first to hear news of this sort, and from my own lips.

We dined at the club and I told him of my marriage proposal to Lady Beatrice. He stared at me for several minutes in silence. It is the first time I have ever seen Mycroft stunned. At length he said, "You have no great attachment to this woman do you, Sherlock?"

"I have the greatest admiration for her mind," I said. "But there is no romantic attachment, if that is what you mean."

"Good, that is good."

"Why so?"

"Because it will not cause you too much pain to learn the Lady is to be married. I had it myself last night from Harris. Summerville has been to Windsor and has received the Queen's permission to marry her goddaughter."

18

To Mycroft's considerable astonishment and embarrassment I jerked to my feet, upending the tea cup as I did so and sending a small spray of milk across the table.

"Sherlock? Good God, whatever is the matter?"

"This cannot be permitted, Mycroft. He will kill her... but first he will make her suffer in unimaginable ways. It is not to be borne, you must excuse me."

In less than half an hour I was knocking on the door of Lady Beatrice's home in Wimpole Street. The Lady was in the library and she greeted me stoically.

"Well," she said. "So you have heard."

"From my brother. It is true? I see from your countenance it is. Please sit down, you look very ill."

She obeyed me and I called for the maid to bring some coffee.

We sat then in silence. I do not deal well in these situations. I have not Watson's unerring ability to find the right phrase, to offer comfort. So I said nothing and we sat there until the coffee was brought and poured and the maid left and we were alone again.

We sipped our coffee and then I said, "It is not too late. I will go to the Queen and make my own application for your hand. Or if you prefer we could elope?"

"I cannot elope; it would embarrass the Queen. You really are determined to go through with this plan? To marry me, I mean. Now that you've had time to sleep on it, perhaps you have changed your mind?"

A BIASED JUDGEMENT

"My mind remains unchanged. And the matter has become one of some urgency now, I think."

It was a measure of her distress that her hair was untidy. An auburn strand had fallen loose from its pins and curled onto her shoulder. She tends to such precision in her dress and toilette as a rule, that one curl spoke volumes. Absently she twirled it around and around her fingers.

She said, "You must be sure, absolutely sure, Mr Holmes. If we approach the queen and ask her permission, there will be no going back. At least, not without scandal and a great deal of unpleasantness."

"My mind is quite made up," I said.

"I still have qualms about allowing you to make such a sacrifice, despite our most amusing contract. But…" She bit her lip and looked at me. "If you are certain, then, yes."

"I shall make application to Her Majesty at her earliest convenience."

"I think I should come with you," she said. "If I add my voice to yours she is more likely to be swayed. The queen has a strange affection for the Summervilles. Their grandfather was a close friend of Prince Albert's and Her Majesty is very loyal to the people her husband loved. However, she holds you in esteem too, I know. I believe I can convince her that I will be happy with you."

She managed a fleeting smile and I was pleased to see some colour return to her cheeks.

"The queen likes me well enough," I agreed. "Though she is vexed at my repeated refusal of a knighthood. Still, I do not think she will hold that against me.

"If I may use your telephone I shall make the call now. It is fortunate Her Majesty has not yet left for the Isle of Wight."

It was all arranged with remarkable ease and a few hours later Lady Beatrice and I sat in a large, elegant but impersonal room waiting to be admitted to the Queen's presence. Her Majesty's private secretary, Sir Arthur Bigge, said softly, "I do hope you will not cause the queen any anxiety, Mr Holmes. Her health is not good, and this time of year

A BIASED JUDGEMENT

weighs heavily upon her with reminders of the loss of her beloved husband."

I assured him that we had only good news and a few moments later we were summoned into Her Majesty's chamber. She sat, as she always did, in a small chair. She was dressed in the same black gown she had worn every time I have seen her. The left cuff had been replaced and the collar had been repaired. It seemed odd that the most powerful woman in the world should continue to wear the same gown. Then I realised I was focusing on trivia because I was, astonishingly, nervous.

"You said this was a matter of some urgency, Mr Holmes?" Her Majesty said following our greeting. "Well, what is it?"

"I understand your majesty has granted Wallace Summerville permission to marry Lady Beatrice," I said.

"What of it? This is a family matter, Mr Holmes. We are mindful of how much this Empire owes you but it does not allow you free reign over one's private matters."

I glanced at Lady Beatrice. Though pale she was perfectly calm. She nodded almost imperceptibly.

"I ask your indulgence, ma'am," I said. "But if Your Majesty is not irrevocably decided upon Mr Summerville I believe I can suggest a more appropriate candidate."

The queen glanced from me to her goddaughter and back. "More suitable than the grandson of one of dear Albert's most beloved friends? I have already agreed to the union, Mr Holmes," she said.

Beatrice, deathly pale, said, "Please, Your Majesty…"

The queen studied the young woman at my side with shrewd eyes. "So, you've been taking matters into your own hands, have you, my girl? I told Benjamin he should not give you so much liberty. Nothing good can come of it. Come, come, do not distress yourself…"

The queen sighed and stretched her back. She was in pain, I thought, and I felt a surge of sympathy for her. She can be difficult at times. She can be dogmatic, and is often humourless and demanding, but I suppose that's understandable. After all, she has reigned over this land for the past sixty years. Besides, I have found her to be capable of great kindness and generosity. She can be exceedingly gracious to the people she likes, and she likes me. Well, usually.

I said, "I mean no disrespect to the Summervilles, Ma'am, and no one understands better than I how remarkable a woman Lady Beatrice is. It is a mark of Wallace Summerville's good taste that he should have formed an attachment to her. She is a credit to her father and to everyone who has nurtured her."

There is no doubt that the queen knew I was buttering her up, but she seemed pleased nonetheless.

Less fretfully she said, "Well, well, my only concern is to leave this world in full knowledge that I have secured for all my family and loved ones a position of trust and stability. Who is this more appropriate candidate you suggest?"

"I suggest... myself."

Sir Arthur Bigge, standing at the Queen's side, forgot himself enough to exclaim, "Good God!" In other circumstances I might have laughed.

"I was not aware that you and my goddaughter were much acquainted, Mr Holmes," the Queen said, ignoring Sir Arthur. "Do you mean to tell me an attachment has formed between you?"

"Mr Holmes is the best man I know, your majesty," Lady Beatrice said.

The queen looked shrewdly at the two of us. After several moments she said to my intended fiancée, "Well, I have often said you should marry a man at least as clever as you are."

Smiling at me, relaxing now, Beatrice replied, "Indeed, ma'am. Though I seem to have overshot the mark."

"Quite. So you want to marry my goddaughter, Mr Holmes... Sir Arthur, tell cook we have two guests staying for dinner. No, no, we cannot arrange all these matters so swiftly, Mr Holmes. You and Beatrice will dine with me this evening and we will discuss the matter thoroughly as we ought."

A BIASED JUDGEMENT

Bigge left the room and, now alone, the queen said, "Well, this is sudden. It pleases me. I promised your dear papa I would take care of you, Beatrice. I think settling into the life of a married woman will satisfy you once you adjust to it. Your future husband is one of the finest men in this or any other kingdom. It will do him good to marry.

"And you, Mr Holmes: you know, I suppose, that we hold our young goddaughter in the very highest esteem. God gave her more wits than a woman needs – you need not frown, Miss – and her father indulged her with considerably more education than any woman deserves. It has made her rather more choosy in her spouse than I would have wished but, then, if she has selected one of our finest subjects I am well pleased. Better a late marriage to the right man than an early one to the wrong, eh?"

"Indeed, ma'am," I said.

The Queen took it upon herself to inform Summerville of the change in plans for her goddaughter; that is to say, she had Bigge telephone the wretch with the news. A lesser man would have shown his abhorrence of the task on his features, but the queen's private secretary is above such things. Still, I could tell from his pallor and the dew on his upper lip when he completed the task, the news had not been well-received.

Over an indifferent meal the Queen said, "I am seventy-eight years old, Mr Holmes. I want to see my goddaughter secured before I leave this world and join my beloved Albert. It will not be long now, I think. I wrote out the plans for my funeral a few months ago. There is nothing now but to wait for God's will, and that could be any time.

"So, I would prefer not to delay. We shall have you wed here at Windsor. Yes, I believe that is just the thing. Mr Bigge will make the arrangements. I think next Tuesday will suffice."

"Next Tuesday!" Beatrice glanced at me in alarm. "A quiet wedding at Windsor would be perfect, Ma'am, though there is no need for such haste, surely? Would not a year's engagement be more seemly?"

"Short engagements are best. They do not allow young people time to overthink things, nor to see each other's faults.

A BIASED JUDGEMENT

"I want the matter settled before I leave for Osborne House," the queen said. "That does not give us much time. Next Tuesday suits my schedule. You won't want a big fuss, will you, Beatrice?"

"Uh, no, ma'am," my fiancée replied.

"Next week will be excellent," I agreed, since there seemed no alternative. "However, your majesty, there is one point of which I must make you aware."

The two women looked at me expectantly, my future bride with sudden panic. I hoped my demeanour calmed her nerves.

"I have for some months been followed by members of an extremely dangerous organisation. I have thus far managed to avoid serious injury at their hands, but I am concerned that were these men to become aware of my attachment to Lady Beatrice they might harm her to avenge themselves upon me."

"That is most alarming, Mr Holmes," Her Majesty said. "Do you have enough assistance? Can I lend you any support?"

"Your majesty is most kind," I said. "But I believe I can manage as I have done. My only concern is for my fiancée."

"What is it you suggest, Mr Holmes?"

"I wonder if your majesty would mind if we kept the marriage as quiet as possible; that is to say, it should not be go beyond the immediate family circle?"

"Your scruple does you much credit, Mr Holmes. I wonder if approving your marriage is wise after all…"

"I assure Your Majesty I will allow no harm to befall Lady Beatrice. My only wish is to protect her."

"Quite right too," the queen said.

"I should prefer a life of peril with Mr Holmes than a safe one with anyone else, Ma'am," my fiancée said.

"The heart will not be denied. You are very much in love, I see."

Neither the Lady nor I could bring ourselves to look at each other.

A BIASED JUDGEMENT

19

Later this evening when we returned from our visit to the Queen, Beatrice and I stopped at Simpsons to supplement the paltry meal we had partaken in the royal presence. Since we are now formally engaged and shall be married in a few days I thought we could stretch propriety enough to dine in public together.

With the shadow of the hateful Summervilles eradicated, my fiancée was more relaxed and at ease than she had been since I had first met her. I did not have the heart to point out Summerville is unlikely to allow the small matter of our engagement to derail his plans. Indeed, I suspect the risk to both of us has greatly increased. At least I can take comfort in the knowledge that she will soon be completely beyond that creature's grasp.

Determined not to trouble the lady with my gloomy thoughts, I committed myself to keeping the mood light and cheerful.

After an hour of merry conversation and good food Beatrice's demeanour suddenly became sombre.

"You are very good to do this for me, Mr Holmes," she said. "I am sorry her majesty insists on such a speedy marriage."

"I rather suspected that might be the case," I said. "But it is no matter. It's not as if I had other plans for my bachelorhood."

"What you said being followed: have there been other attempts you have not told me about?"

"No. In fact, my watchers departed quite suddenly a few days ago. That has made me more on my alert than ever. At least when they were openly watching me I was able to watch them in turn, whereas now…

A BIASED JUDGEMENT

But you must not concern yourself. I assure you, I am quite capable of protecting myself."

She seemed not appeased and I added, "I admit it is annoying to have to take extra precautions, but I am an observant man and other than the occasion when we met, have managed to avoid any injury. In any case, I am confident I shall live long enough to stand beside you at the altar, if that is any comfort."

"Holmes!" she cried, forgetting the honorific for the first time. "That is unworthy of you. I do not deserve it."

"Forgive me," I said, truly chagrined. "No matter how many times you have proven otherwise, I still sometimes think of you only as a woman."

"I hardly know how to take that," she said. She picked at her venison and we fell silent. For the first time I doubted the wisdom of my reckless action.

After several moments I said, carefully, "It occurs to me that you, too, should take precautions. We cannot tell how Summerville will respond to his plans being thwarted."

She said, "I am already taking as much precaution as possible. I have not gone out on my own since that day when we met in the Opera House."

"That is as well. Is there someone you might stay with until the wedding? I am sure the Queen would be happy to have you stay at Windsor if there is nowhere else."

"I shall not be driven out of my home," she replied.

We had become awkward with each other and I felt a sudden and almost irresistible urge to flee. As I struggled to find something mild to say, Beatrice said, "Would you mind if we left? I'm suddenly feeling very weary. I'm afraid I've not been sleeping very well."

"Of course," I said.

A few minutes later as we stepped outside the restaurant, I spotted young Billy running up the Strand towards me.

A BIASED JUDGEMENT

I handed Beatrice into her carriage and said, "Would you forgive me if I let you return home unescorted? I'm sure Stevens will see to your safety."

She observed Billy and merely nodded. I said, "Look after the lady, if you would, Stevens," I said. "Keep her safe."

He assured me he would do so and they sped away.

As soon as the carriage left, I turned to the boy. "Something has happened," I said. "What is it? Porlock?"

He nodded his head, still gasping, and said, "That's it, Mr 'olmes. Three visitors 'e's 'ad this evening. A toff arrived first, about seven o'clock it was, and 'e were there a good while, nigh on an hour. Then before 'e left two other chaps came. I knew them, Mr 'olmes, and you do too: 'acker and Smiley. The toff left and the other pair a short while later."

"This 'toff', was he a small man with a thin, rodent-like face and an unfortunate reddish moustache?"

"That's the chap. Do you know 'im, Mr 'olmes? Young Kevin said 'e 'eard Mr Porlock call 'im 'Winters'."

"Yes, he's the man I've been looking for. Ah, if only I had not been so waylaid today... Seven o'clock, you said? Why did it take you so long to find me?"

"Been all over the city looking for you, Mr 'olmes. Then young 'arry said 'e'd seen you on the Strand, so I came 'ere. Guessed you might be at Simpsons. And I were right." He grinned, and I couldn't help but laugh.

"You did exceedingly well, but I see you've brought company."

"Company?"

"Don't look around, keep your eyes on me. Across the street outside the Vaudeville Theatre: Harold Smiley."

"I'm sorry, Mr 'olmes," Billy said. "I only just got 'ere though, so 'ow could 'e 'ave followed me?"

213

A BIASED JUDGEMENT

That was a reasonable observation. "You're right," I said. "He may have been following me. He could not have picked up my scent until I got back into the city though; I'd have spotted him in Windsor."

I thought for a moment and gave Billy careful instructions. He's a bright lad and I seldom have to explain or repeat myself to him. He listened intently, grinned and said, "Ah, I gotcha, Mr 'olmes."

"Now, here's sixpence. Act like you've been paid for your work and off you go, as casual as you please."

My whole day wasted on domestic trifles and I missed my opportunity to grab the very man I'd been looking for. And a chance to see Winters and Porlock together. It was infuriating. Well, it could not be helped now. I turned my attention to the brute across the street, though I pretended not to notice him. He held back in the throng of people leaving the Vaudeville theatre, waiting.

How curious that after lying low for six months, Smiley should choose this moment to appear.

Mr Isaiah Collins, Simpsons' head waiter, came out and said, "Is everything all right, Mr Holmes?"

I said, "Be so good as to keep your patrons indoors for a few minutes, Mr Collins. Or if they must leave, have them do so by the rear entrance. I hope we will be able to avoid trouble, but it's best to be safe."

"Thank you, Mr Holmes. I shall see to it at once."

Across the street I saw two policemen advance on Smiley. Good work, Billy!

Just at the last moment, Smiley realised his danger and ran across the street, risking terrible injury under the passing horses and carriages.

He ran diagonally, towards the Savoy, no doubt hoping he could either cut through the lobby or go down Carting Lane and escape along the Embankment. It might succeed too, given the Friday night crowds that still spilled out from the theatres and the restaurants onto the Strand.

A BIASED JUDGEMENT

I fled after him, and saw that Collins had joined the chase. The two of us, as well as the policemen and Billy, tore up the busy thoroughfare as our prey made his terrified way towards the Embankment. Sergeant Mulligan anticipated the wretch and ran ahead to block the steps leading down to Carting Lane. In almost the same instant, Collins, leaping like the gymnast he had once been, soared through the last several feet and landed on top of Smiley, bringing the wretch to the ground.

Smiley struggled but soon realised he was considerably outmanned.

"Thank you, Mr Collins," I said. "You've lost none of your speed nor your athleticism, I see."

"Glad to help a good customer, Mr Holmes," he replied with a laugh.

"A fine beauty, these, Mr Holmes," said Mulligan, in his thick Cork accent. "Wouldn't it be a grand thing now if all the rest of these brutes fell into our hands so easily?"

"It would indeed, Sergeant Mulligan," I said.

"'Ere," said the permanently-grinning Smiley. "Wot you fink you're doing? I ain't 'armin' no one, am I?"

"Harold Smiley," I said. "You did the Notting Hill job. You remember, Sergeant? The artist and his wife who were stabbed to death back in May."

"Oy, you can't 'ang that on me!" Smiley said, his face still set in a grotesque grin.

"I found your tooth marks in the apple you left behind, Smiley," I said. "Your bloody footprints were on the floor. Inspector Hill has been combing the city looking for you and your friend Herbert Hacker. How kind of you to make it so easy for us."

The words had hardly left my lips when I thought, Yes, it is too easy.

Billy cried, "Look out!" and pushed me to the ground as a carriage hurtled by. A hand appeared through the window and a pistol-shot rang out.

A BIASED JUDGEMENT

Blood gushed like a fountain, drenching me and the policemen. At our feet, Isaiah Collins lay still. A woman screamed and there were cries of, "Help, police!"

I bent down to see if there was anything I could do for the unfortunate waiter, but he was beyond all aid. I closed his eyes. It was the only service I could do for him.

Sergeant Mulligan blew his whistle and his colleague ran up the Strand after the carriage. There was too much traffic, too many people and the policeman re-joined us within minutes, shaking his head.

"Well, Harold," I said to the gibbering villain. "What nice people you associate with. This is what happens when you play with the big boys."

"That bullet was meant for you, Mr 'olmes," Smiley said. "Shame 'e missed."

"A shame for you," I replied, glancing back at Collins's body. "That man was a husband, a father of four children. He was a friend..."

I could hardly speak for anger. My words came spitting out of my mouth as I said, "You were nothing more than a decoy, meant to keep watch so the gunman would know where to find me. And yet, as you see, I'm still here."

"Steady there now, Mr Holmes," the Sergeant said. "This is a nasty business, and no mistake. Now you," he added to Smiley. "You'll go a long way to helping yourself if you tell us who hired you and what the plan was."

"I don't know nuffin'," Smiley said.

"It doesn't matter, anyway," I said. "I know who hired this creature. Did Porlock pay you, Harold, or hold the Notting Hill murder over you? Then again, perhaps he paid you to do the Notting Hill slaughter too?"

"Here, that weren't me what done the Notting Hill job, Mr Holmes," he said, stuttering in terror. "As God is my witness. I was there, right enough, and I kept watch for 'erb while 'e did 'is business. But the killing of the man and 'is old lady, that weren't me. 'e said if I stood

A BIASED JUDGEMENT

'ere just to lure you over, 'e'd 'elp us leave the country for a bit. Been awful 'ard layin' low and 'erb gets mean if 'e can't use 'is blade."

"Who is it who hired you?"

He hesitated for only a moment before spitting out, "A gentleman in Finsbury, by the name of Porlock."

"Ah, Albrecht Porlock…"

"But where is your friend Hacker, Smiley? It's rare to see you separated from one another."

"'e's got another job, does 'erb."

"Another job?" Some presentiment sent icicles down my spine. I forced myself to stay calm. "Well? Who else does Porlock want murdered?"

"Not Mr Porlock, Mr 'olmes. It was another gentleman. Though perhaps gentleman's too strong a word… It was summat I overheard… You'll speak for me at trial, Mr 'olmes, sir? Tell 'em I never lay an 'and on them two in Notting 'ill. As God's my witness, I never."

"Yes, yes, if your information is helpful. Now speak!"

"There's a fellow calls 'isself Winters though if that's 'is real name, I'm a Dutchman. 'e was there with Mr Porlock when 'erb and me arrived. We 'ad to wait in the 'all until they was done. They was talkin' all soft, like, but I got good ears. What makes me so good with safes, innit?"

"And what were their words? Exactly, mind."

"You'll put in a good word for me at the assizes, Mr 'olmes? Say I was 'elpful. They'll 'ang me for sure if you don't speak for me."

"Yes, yes," I said. "But Porlock and Winters: what did they say?"

"Winters, I've seen 'im before. Evil bugger 'e is, beggin' your pardon. Anyway, 'e said 'e'd do Mr Porlock's job if only Mr P would do 'im a favour first. 'e said if a lady could be got rid of all her money would go to 'er aunt's 'usband, and this 'usband was Winters' own brother.

"Then 'e said it would have all gone according to plan if you, Mr 'olmes, 'and't meddled. 'e said 'e really didn't want to kill the lady, but

A BIASED JUDGEMENT

'e 'ad no choice now. And Mr Porlock, 'e said 'e was right fed up with your meddling, and it was time to fix you for once and for all.

"So this Winters fellow leaves and me and 'erb was brought in and given our orders. I was to keep you stood 'ere so 'e could shoot you and 'erb was to go to Wimpole Street to 'teach 'er a proper lesson,' that's what 'e said.

"I don't 'old wiv 'urting a Lady. I got my standards. Might not be the same as yours, Mr 'olmes, but I got 'em right enough."

I thought my heart would stop in horror. Stammering in my haste. I said to Billy, "With all haste, find me a cab." As he ran to do my bidding, I turned back to the odious creature. "You, Smiley," I said. "Have you told me everything? Anything you tell me could save you from the noose."

He gibbered, tears and snot coursed down his sallow face even as he still grinned. "As God's my witness, Mr 'olmes, I'd tell you if I knew."

"All right," I said. It was too much to hope for more. "Sergeant—"

"Wait!" Smiley cried. "I did 'ear summat, I just remembered. Don't know what it means, but Mr Porlock was saying about it would 'ave to be done before she went to the island and it would be a proper Christmas treat for 'is friends in dutch-land."

"Dutchland? Do you mean Deutchland?"

"That might 'ave been it," he said. "That's all I know. It is truly, Mr 'olmes."

"Very well. You may have saved your skin, Smiley. I shall remember your help in this matter when you come to trial. I have no time to spare now, but be assured I shall speak to you later."

"God bless you, Mr 'olmes, for a gentleman," he cried. Several constables arrived and took him away.

I leaped into the waiting cab and directed Billy to come with me. I gave the driver Beatrice's address. "With the greatest of haste," I said. "A woman's life may be at stake."

The carriage clattered through the streets, sending theatre-goers leaping from its path.

A BIASED JUDGEMENT

My thoughts went through a series of acrobatic leaps and landings. I was right but for once there was no satisfaction in the realisation... I had correctly surmised Winters' true identity. A man in debt, desperate to find money. He had tried to marry a fortune, but I had prevented him. Now he saw his only alternative was her death so her aunt's husband would get everything. No doubt he thought it a poor second, but at least it meant he would be able to pay his debts...

And the lady, oh dear God, the lady, the lady, the lady...

The carriage lurched dangerously as we took a corner. It had started to rain and the road was deadly. Some part of me was aware that Billy was holding on to the door for dear life. The thought was an intrusion... I must concentrate.

But the next thought made me ill: the artist's wife in Notting Hill, the butchery to which she had been subjected... Dear God if Hacker harmed Beatrice...

I felt the bile rise in my mouth and forced it down.

Think of something concrete: Winters is Wallace Summerville. You know now; all the suspicions have been confirmed. You have a witness in the form of Harold Smiley.

Smiley eating an apple as Hacker slashed and stabbed...

Oh God, Beatrice...

We sped along the terrible roads and at last turned onto New Cavendish Street. There were two policemen outside her home on Wimpole Street. Oh yes, I'd asked Lestrade to post someone for the lady's protection... I'd quite forgotten. Bless the man for keeping his word.

After my anxiety in getting to her, I was disconcerted to find an utterly relaxed, even giddy atmosphere prevailing at my fiancée's home.

Stevens waved to me with a bandaged hand as I leaped from the carriage. I ordered the cab driver to wait, and left Billy sitting there too.

"What is it?" I asked. "Is Beatrice safe?"

"Perfectly safe," Stevens said. "Thanks to these good gentlemen."

A BIASED JUDGEMENT

"Just doing our duty, sir," said one pimple-faced officer. (Are policemen now being recruited from the nursery?)

"What happened?" I demanded.

Stevens said, "We got home and everything seemed quiet. The lady said she'd stay up for a bit and bade me goodnight. I was going to just go to bed but your caution was ringing in my ears, Mr Holmes, and I thought I'd check the house first.

"I found a broken pane in the basement and, using your method, sir, I followed the footprints. That's when I found this evil brute hiding in the pantry. Leaped on me with a knife and I shouted for help.

"Lady Beatrice let in these fine gentlemen and we eventually got the villain subdued, though it took all three of us."

"The lad took a slashing to his hand, but no real damage done," said the police officer.

"And the lady is safe?" I said.

"Quite safe," replied the other officer. "This young man deserves a medal, Mr Holmes. You should have seen him wrestling with that brute. Young Mr Stevens will be a fine addition to the Force. A big arrest to his credit and him not even an officer yet."

Stevens beamed. Well, I suppose he should.

"And Hacker? Where is he now?"

Stevens said, "Officer Bradstreet here called for a car and the villain's on his way to the Assizes, not ten minutes ago."

An attempt against Beatrice, Hacker detected, disarmed and arrested, and all of it done without me. Well.

"I'm sure the lady would like to see you, Mr Holmes," said Stevens. "Though she's not in the best temper."

"A spirited lady," Bradstreet said.

"It's a filthy night," I said. "The boy Billy is in the cab, Stevens. Will you see he gets something hot to drink? And ask the cabby to wait."

"I'm happy to take you wherever you want to go, Mr Holmes," Stevens said.

A BIASED JUDGEMENT

"Thank you, Stevens. If you feel well enough, I shall certainly need you. But I shall need the cab as well."

I got to the door and turned. "Bradstreet? Are you related to Inspector Bradstreet?"

"His son, sir," said the man, proudly.

His son? Surely Bradstreet – my Bradstreet – is hardly old enough to have a grown son. I really have become the Elder Statesman.

What a loathsome thought.

Beatrice was in the library drinking a brandy. She poured me a glass and as she handed it to me, said, "Well, you have heard all our news? Vile creatures hiding in my pantry and policemen at my door... I assume that's not your own blood behind your left ear?"

"It is not," I said and wiped at it with a handkerchief. "It is what remains of an unfortunate gentleman by the name of Isaiah Collins."

"I am sorry for the gentleman. Is he all right?"

"He is dead."

She stared at me in silence. "So a good man is dead while I am perfectly safe. Do you know three men came to my defence? Stevens had his hand sliced by the wretch. I, of course, could not be trusted with the information that I was at risk nor the measures taken to protect me."

"It is fortunate that you were so well protected," I replied. "I shudder to think what the consequences might have been otherwise."

"A visit from a drunken, abusive Wallace Summerville I was prepared for," she said. "But a knife-wielding killer? I do not understand why someone would hate me so much..." She downed the contents of the glass in one gulp and wiped her mouth with the back of her hand like a schoolchild.

"It was not hate," I said. "But greed. Desperation, even."

"You know who was behind this? Greed... you can only mean the Summervilles. Has it come to this? They hired someone to kill me?"

"You should sit down."

"I don't want to sit down. I'm too angry."

A BIASED JUDGEMENT

I smiled. She said, "Well? I amuse you?"

I laughed out loud. "I was thinking any other woman in the nation would be reduced to tears and terror. My Beatrice becomes pugnacious. It is delightfully refreshing."

A brief smile flickered at the corners of her lips but she fought it back. "Don't make me laugh," she said. "I want to stay angry."

She really is too delightful for words.

After a few more moments pacing she stopped and sat down, facing me. "Greed?" she prompted.

"You remember I told you I was looking for a fellow called Winters who had amassed considerable gambling debts? Well, I have suspected for some time that Winters is Wallace Summerville.

"Today he was seen at the home of Albrecht Porlock, the man who is, I believe, the head of that deadly organisation. Summerville agreed to do something for Porlock if he, in turn, would arrange your death."

"Good God!"

"It is distressing, I know. But perhaps it helps to realise he is not acting out of malice but out of desperation. I cannot say why there is a distinction, but I believe there is one."

"Yes. Yes, I think so too." She smiled at me and suddenly I felt warm. "I know this will come as a great surprise to you, Holmes," she said. "But you're a great comfort."

We sat quietly, each occupied with our own thoughts. The November rain beat against the window panes.

After some moments I said, "I must ask you to pack a bag. May I use your telephone?"

"You may of course use the telephone and anything else you wish, but not until you've explained why I am to pack."

"I cannot risk another attempt against you. I am going to arrange for you to stay at Windsor until the wedding."

"No, Holmes, absolutely not. It is out of the question."

"Hush and listen. There are several good reasons why I need you to do this. Be still, and hear me out.

A BIASED JUDGEMENT

"This man Porlock means to make an attempt against the queen and he plans to act before Her Majesty goes to Osborne House for the holidays on the seventeenth of next month. If you are in the Castle for a few days you can keep watch; be my eyes and ears. It allows me some time to put another plan into motion.

"Secondly, I need you to be safe. I find myself worrying about your well-being and that is distracting. No, I understand that concern is not of your making, but you must know it is beyond my control.

"I need you to do this, Beatrice. And there's more."

She took a deep breath and slowly released it. It sounded like steam hissing from a kettle. I was subjecting her to a lot of information very quickly but she seemed to be following me. I continued. "I need you to help me with something, but it could be dangerous. Very, very dangerous."

Her eyes sparkled and she said, "You can count on me."

It wasn't until much later I realised we'd been holding each other's hands throughout this entire conversation.

20

November 27th, 1897

A little after midnight, my future wife and I were in her carriage being whisked through the streets of London back to Windsor Castle.

Billy, happy because of the hot soup Beatrice's cook had given him and the two shillings I had added to his sixpence, took the cab to Mycroft's Pall Mall apartments with a letter updating him on the evening's events, and then back to Finsbury Park with new instructions for the Irregulars.

The streets were quiet now, and only the destitute and the drunks still wandered about.

"What does the queen make of all this?" Beatrice asked.

"I did not speak to her directly. Sir Arthur Bigge did not want her to be disturbed. I have no doubt she will have many questions."

"Does she know about the plot against her? What may I say?"

"She does not yet know anything of the danger and Sir Arthur Bigge has asked that we say nothing for the moment. If all goes well, we can tell her after the holidays."

"Surely she ought to be put on her guard?"

"I agree, but it is not up to me."

She frowned and, after a moment's deep thought, said, "I suppose it is for the best. And no point in worrying her about Summerville either, but you do realise if the queen knew of his involvement in this assassination plan she would have him arrested and you might not have to marry me."

A BIASED JUDGEMENT

"I don't think there's any way of getting out of the marriage now. We are committed. Come, Beatrice, it may not be so odious as all that.

"As to your erstwhile suitor: We do not as yet have any real evidence against Summerville. He was seen entering Porlock's house, but that alone means nothing. He could argue it was merely a social call. It will take Smiley's statement of what was said between the two men if we are to make a charge stick. When it comes down to it, Wallace Summerville is from a well-respected family and his brother is a knight. Were he just a common man we might be able to have him arrested regardless, but he still has powerful friends. We must proceed carefully. It is, in part, why I need you to do that job we discussed."

By the time I had seen Beatrice safely ensconced at Windsor and got back to the city it was 5am.

Stevens was happy to drive me and despite the hour did not seem fatigued. Not even the weather, which was filthy, seemed to dampen his mood. He would have chatted quite merrily if I had given him even the slightest encouragement. Fortunately, he forced himself into silence. I sat with my chin on my chest and my hat pulled down around my ears. The clatter of the carriage as we wound through the empty streets helped me to think.

Mycroft was none too pleased at being awakened at such an "unholy" hour. I built a fire in his living room as he dressed.

"I don't suppose there's any breakfast?" he said morosely as he joined me.

"I fear not. Please, Mycroft, sit down and let me tell you what's been happening."

"I got your note. That urchin brought it here a few hours ago. So Winters is our old friend Wallace Summerville? Well, well."

"I sent word to Lestrade to keep watch on his lodgings. The police are not to enter until I am present. I cannot risk them destroying evidence through their clumsiness."

A BIASED JUDGEMENT

"I must call Bigge and arrange a meeting to discuss the Queen's security." He frowned and I could see he was already reviewing those details in his mind.

"Bigge prefers we say nothing to Her Majesty for the moment," I said. "With the anniversary of Prince Albert's death in a couple of weeks and the state of her health, he does not want Her Majesty to be burdened unnecessarily."

"Hmm... I will speak to him in any case. Windsor is as secure as any other royal dwelling, which means it is difficult to penetrate but not impossible."

"I agree, but your word will undoubtedly carry more weight than mine."

I went on to tell Mycroft about the Queen's approval of my engagement to her god-daughter, the attempt against Beatrice, and that I had placed her in Windsor.

"She has been given instructions to say only that I want to ensure her safety; she is to say nothing at all of Hacker or Summerville. While she is there, she can also keep an eye on the queen's well-being."

He stared at me in astonishment and for several seconds said nothing. Then he spluttered, "She's just a woman, Sherlock. No, no, I understand she is exceptional, but you cannot think she can circumvent an assassination."

"She needs only observe," I said. "And I can attest that her talents in that area are quite exceptional. Besides, she knows Summerville and she will be on her alert as soon as she sees him."

Mycroft went to his cupboard and pulled out a tin of biscuits. He offered me one and I shook my head.

He sat again, sinking heavily into his big armchair and pulling a heavy tartan rug close around him. The fire was taking a long time to catch; I poked it again.

Nibbling on the iced biscuit Mycroft said, "We cannot be certain Porlock will trust to Summerville alone. I would be very surprised if he doesn't have a back-up plan already organised."

A BIASED JUDGEMENT

"I have thought of that. It makes getting into Porlock's house even more urgent."

"There isn't much time, Sherlock. What do you have planned?"

"I shall see Hacker and Smiley and get a formal statement from both of them. That should be enough to get a warrant for Summerville's arrest. With any luck, he'll tell us what he knows about Porlock. But if that plan fails, I have an alternative which is already in motion."

"And your marriage? Do you mean to go through with it?"

I hesitated. "I don't see any way out of it, Mycroft. I've rather committed myself."

"You have indeed," he replied. His shrewd eyes studied me. "Perhaps you feel more regard for this young woman than you are willing to admit?"

"Nonsense," I replied.

I continued to poke at the fire and the embers started to catch at last. I said, "How do things stand with your own vile creature?"

"You mean Frobisher? Oh he is ever so polite and helpful. He is, on the face of it, the most dedicated man in the British government."

"He does not know he's been unmasked?"

"He has not the slightest suspicion. I suppose I should see how your own plans progress before I have him arrested?"

"Yes. If all goes according to plan, we should be able to move within a few days. We shall know soon."

I rose and pulled my coat tightly around me. I was still damp and cold and, though I hate to admit it, tired.

"What time is it?" I said.

"Almost six. You look done in, Sherlock. Perhaps you should go back to Baker Street and sleep a couple of hours."

I yawned and stretched. "Yesterday was very long and today promises to be no better. Perhaps a couple of hours sleep wouldn't go amiss. I'm sure even the redoubtable Stevens is flagging by now.

"Very well, Mycroft. I hope to have good news for you very soon."

A BIASED JUDGEMENT

"Goodbye, Sherlock. And be careful: Porlock may try again to snuff out your life. It would be a pity if he were to succeed. Have young Stevens ferry you about - at least his mistress won't need him for a few days. I must say, I don't envy her having to stay at Windsor. That castle is hardly the homeliest of places and the food is never sufficient."

Stevens looked like he was half asleep, sitting in the driver's seat with his head nodding on his breast. He perked up as soon as he saw me however and said, "Where to now, Mr Holmes?"

"Back to Baker Street if you would be so kind, Stevens. I need to talk to Doctor Watson and I've no doubt a couple of hours sleep will do you some good. You will not object to the sofa, I trust?"

"Bless you, Mr Holmes. I could sleep on the floor if need be. I'm that tired, though I hate to admit it."

The streets were starting to come to life though dawn had not yet broken. As we turned onto Baker Street I said, "We should be very careful going into the building. There may be dangerous men watching."

"No worries, Mr Holmes. I'll see you safely indoors before I take care of the horses."

The street was quiet enough and I got inside without any difficulty. Stevens followed a short while later. He stretched out on the sofa and was asleep in seconds.

I woke Watson to update him on all my adventures. He stared at me in complete silence for a full minute after I finished. Then he spluttered, "Engaged? Married on Tuesday? And someone shooting at you and trying to kill Lady Beatrice..? Good God, man! Did it not occur to you to telephone me?"

"Whatever for?"

"I could have helped. At the very least I could have kept watch to ensure your safety."

"But I am safe, as you see. Stevens did a splendid job, Watson. Oh, he's sleeping on the couch so try not to wake him. You might want to

A BIASED JUDGEMENT

have a look at his hand when he does waken. He got stabbed protecting Beatrice from the detestable Hacker."

"Yes, yes, of course."

"There's something else... Isaiah Collins is dead."

"Collins? Our friend from Simpsons? Oh, Holmes, that is dreadful. Such a gentleman and always so happy to see us. What happened?"

"The gunman who aimed for me... Billy pulled me down in time and Collins was shot. The bullet tore through his chest and I suspect punctured his heart. He died instantly."

"His wife just had a son," Watson said. "That boy they'd been hoping for. We must find this gunman, Holmes."

"We shall. Never fear, Watson. We shall."

"I'll call upon his wife this morning and offer condolences from both of us. I'll offer her whatever assistance she needs, poor woman. What are you going to do now?"

"Right now? Think. So much has happened so quickly, I need to sort through it all. I'll write my journal; that usually helps me focus. I'll let Stevens sleep a few hours, then head off to interview Hacker and Smiley. It's strange, Watson, given their propensity for antisocial behaviour, but that pair share a terror of prison. Perhaps a couple of hours behind bars will loosen their tongues still more. I will get their statements, and, with any luck, conclude the day by arresting Wallace Summerville.

"If all goes well, Summerville's arrest will encourage him to tell all he knows about Porlock. I hope, Watson, I fervently hope that by the time the sun sets this evening, Albrecht Porlock will be in chains.

"I would be exceedingly obliged if you will accompany me today. I feel in particular need of my friend Watson's strength. Collins's death weighs heavily upon me, as does the planned attack against Beatrice."

"You know I'm your man, whatever you need, Holmes. But it wouldn't hurt if you took a few hours rest yourself. You look all in."

A BIASED JUDGEMENT

"Well, I shall lie down for a while, but I doubt I shall sleep. I will have these creatures before the day is done, Watson. I will not rest until I have them in chains."

Watson said, "Well, at least try to sleep even if it's just for a few hours. I shall take my breakfast downstairs with Mrs Hudson."

I rose and went to the door. Just as I was about to leave he said, "There's an old Scottish saying, Holmes, that I think is worth remembering: There's many a slip twixt the cup and the lip."

Watson's words turned out to be prophetic.

I woke the weary Stevens at two o'clock, had some coffee, and the three of us headed to Scotland Yard.

Lestrade would not meet my eye and I knew at once something had gone amiss.

"I need to see Hacker and Smiley, Inspector," I said. "As soon as possible. Can you arrange it?"

"Uh, no, Mr Holmes... I'm afraid there's been a problem."

"Problem?"

"The truth is... they're dead."

I felt as if the floor had given way beneath my feet and I was falling, falling into some sort of bottomless pit.

"How?" Watson said.

"Murdered."

"What, both of them?" I said.

Lestrade studied the papers on his desk. To them he said, very quietly, "Yes, I'm afraid so."

"That's not good enough!" I cried, slamming my fist on the desk and causing his teacup to rattle. "Those two men were in custody. They were my only link to one of the most dangerous men not only in the country, but in the world. Lestrade, Lestrade, if you only knew the true horror of this news..."

He looked up at me then, his face gaunt with misery. "It's a terrible thing to have a man die in custody, Mr Holmes. I know it happens more

A BIASED JUDGEMENT

often than we like to admit, but usually those deaths are due to disease or some natural cause. To have two men murdered within minutes of each other is shocking. I don't blame you for being upset. Tavistock Hill is pretty hot about it too, and I can't say I blame him either."

"What exactly happened?" Watson asked. He gave me a troubled look. He, at least, appreciates the appalling weight of this news.

"Hacker had his throat cut and Smiley was stabbed in the heart. No one seems to know how it happened and we have no way of knowing who was responsible."

I balled up my fists and rubbed my eyes hard. This was no time to surrender to fatigue. I needed to think. I needed time. Everything lost. My two witnesses dead. The only hope I had of saving the queen. No... I still had another possibility.

"Lestrade," I said. "I need you to do me a favour."

"Anything at all, Mr Holmes. You know that."

"Bring in Wallace Summerville for questioning. Have two of your biggest and ugliest policemen arrest him. I'm not sure where you'll find him; perhaps at his home sleeping off a hangover, but he could be at Bitterne staying with his brother. Can you see to it?"

"I certainly can. I shall see to it at once, Mr Holmes," Lestrade said, rising. Then, more hesitantly, "He is the brother of a knight..."

"We only want him for questioning."

"Regarding what crime?"

"Regarding a number of complaints regarding his gambling debts. That should hold him until I can gather some more information."

With London's police force alerted to look out for Summerville, Lestrade, Watson and I headed to Pimlico. Thanks to police bureaucracy – it is the one thing at which they excel – and two previous cautions for drunkenness and assault, we had Summerville's address.

I knew we would not find him there. A man who is hiding from his creditors is hardly likely to return home, but I could not pass up the opportunity to search the place.

A BIASED JUDGEMENT

Wallace Summerville had apartments on the top floor of a very elegant building in Pimlico. The view of the river was breathtaking as was the spaciousness of his rooms. Sadly, his housekeeping was an offence to the fine architecture. Dirty clothes, still stinking of alcohol and something worse, lay strewn around the floor; unwashed dishes grew mould in the kitchen; and a film of grey dust covered every surface.

Watson kept Lestrade busy, suggesting he interview the other tenants. Lestrade, who is not nearly as dull-witted as he sometimes affects, was happy to comply, knowing full well the real intent was to give me some latitude to act rather beyond the law.

Thus left alone, I carefully and methodically went through every centimetre of the wretched place. The flat was barren of books, letters, everything that might reveal something of the man. It was evident Summerville had not been here for several weeks.

The landlord, summoned by Lestrade, confirmed my conclusions. "He owes me twelve weeks' rent, sir," said the man. "Indeed, I've already arranged to have his things taken to the dump. Property like that won't stand idle for long."

"Tell me," I said. "Why did you wait so long? You would have been within your rights to evict him months ago."

"Strictly speaking that's true, sir. But he's a warm character, is Mr Summerville. Not someone you'd like to cross. Besides, his brother Sir Christopher could make things unpleasant... But I really cannot wait any longer. I'd be obliged if you'd let him know when you find him."

We left, defeated. Outside, Watson said, "Well, you were right, Holmes. It doesn't look like he'll be returning to Pimlico any time soon."

Lestrade said, "Well, I'll post a man here for a few days, just to be sure. And his picture has been circulated all over the city. If he's still in the country, we'll find him."

"Post a man if you wish, Inspector, but I believe there is somewhere else you should look first."

A BIASED JUDGEMENT

"Yes? And where's that, Mr Holmes?"

"Southampton, Inspector," I replied. "I suspect he's staying with his brother. Send word to Baker Street as soon as he is found. I want to be present for his questioning. In the meantime, I have other avenues to explore. Stevens, will you be so kind as to drop me at Jermyn Street?"

A BIASED JUDGEMENT

21

I sent Watson, ever my touchstone for all things domestic, off with Stevens on their task.

"You need to be very discreet," I said. "Be sure to do nothing to arouse suspicions."

"No, I understand, Holmes," Watson replied. "Although I still don't see how you mean to pull this off. Still, you'll let me know eventually, I suppose."

"Of course. Don't I always? Stevens, do not drop your guard. I doubt you or the good doctor are at risk, but we cannot take it for granted. Be on the alert, for both your sakes."

"You can count on me, Mr Holmes," he replied.

The two set off in the carriage and I walked down Jermyn Street to my old secret flat.

I've only been here twice since 'Jack' nursed me back to health after my attack by Gilberto Calvini; Once to drop off Derby's papers and again to collect them. No doubt Watson would expect me to have some sentimental reaction, but I felt nothing. Well, perhaps a fleeting moment of gratitude towards the woman who saved my life.

Half an hour after I entered the place, an old man with rheumatism and a crooked back emerged. He walked the one and three-quarter miles to Baker Street by way of Piccadilly and New Bond Street. The man sat for a moment in Portman Square and there encountered a young man called Billy.

"Lawks, is that you, Mr 'olmes?" the lad said. "That's a fine cough you've got there." He grinned broadly.

A BIASED JUDGEMENT

"You gave the Irregulars their orders as I instructed?" I asked him.

"Yes, sir. They should be doing it right now, I'd guess."

"I do not want her badly hurt, just enough to lay her up for a while."

"You can count on Tommy and Kevin, Mr 'olmes."

"Good. I shall head up to Finsbury Park and see how they've got on. How are things on Baker Street? Any activity?"

"Nuffink so far. Just the usual for a Saturday."

"Very well. Well, I have another job for you. That man 'Winters' – I need him found and watched. Spread the word."

"Usual rates, Mr 'olmes?"

"Of course. I shall come back to Baker Street in a few hours. Report to Doctor Watson if you have any news; he'll likely return before I do. If neither of us is around you may leave word with Mrs Hudson."

"As you say, Mr 'olmes. Ta-ra for now."

It was already dark by the time I shuffled up the Seven Sisters Road. Tommy and Kevin were in the park ostensibly playing ball, but keeping watch on the house.

I coughed and sank onto a bench. It took a few minutes for the boys to realise it was me. When they did they sauntered over and sat down near me, as if they were tired from their play.

"Well, boys," I said. "Report."

"It went just as you said, Mr 'olmes," Tommy said. "Well, almost.

"We kicked about this old ball for a bit 'cos we knew she'd be out pretty soon. Every afternoon, regular as clockwork she takes those little 'uns out for a walk. Mr P., 'e went out in an 'ansom this mornin' and ain't been 'ome since. The missus is inside though and what a noise she did make when she saw they carried that lady back inside."

"You didn't hurt her too badly, I hope?"

"Well, it was a bit rougher than we'd planned," Kevin said. "I kicked the ball good and 'ard like and it 'it 'er right upside the 'ead. I didn't mean to do aught but knock 'er out but she fell onto the street."

"Good God!"

"Right in front of a carriage," Tommy said. "They reckon she's got a broken leg, but she was out cold. She's out of the game for now, that's for sure."

Not for the first time I was struck by the heartlessness of youth. Then again, I could not be too dismayed. The woman had to be got out of the way, and the boys had been ruthlessly efficient.

I paid them and told them to continue their watch.

"Any young woman who comes to apply for the job," I said. "Make sure you do a good job of frightening her off. Mind, most governesses are not easily alarmed so you'll need to be pretty… unpleasant."

Tommy laughed. "That's as easy as breathin' for us, Mr 'olmes," he said.

Some time later I lumbered down Baker Street and knocked on the door of my apartment.

Mrs Hudson did no more than roll her eyes at me as she let me in. "Is Doctor Watson back yet?" I asked.

"Just a few minutes ago, Mr Holmes. I was about to bring up supper."

"What, is it that late? Oh all right, he'll complain if his meal is delayed. Just coffee for me, if you please."

"Oh, it's you, Holmes," Watson said as I let myself into our flat. "I thought it was Stevens. He's just taking care of the horses."

"Is he staying here?"

"Yes, unless you have other plans for him."

"No, no. It's probably as well to keep him and the carriage available. Have there been any messages?"

"A few." He picked up his notepad and read. "Lestrade called just a few moments ago. He says Greer down in Southampton reports seeing Wallace Summerville just yesterday. Lestrade and he are going to go pick him up and question him."

"Damnation!" I cried. "They will not know what to ask him. They ought to have waited for me."

A BIASED JUDGEMENT

"Don't get yourself into a lather," Watson chided. "Lestrade knows full well you want to be present. He's bringing Summerville back to Scotland Yard. He'll have Tavistock Hill with him so there will be plenty to intimidate that gentleman."

"Gentleman," I snorted. "Well, if they can delay him long enough he'll miss the last train home. Excellent. That gives me a little time. Anything else?"

"Your brother called. He's been in touch with Bigge and they have agreed to say nothing to the queen for the moment about her danger. I, uh, don't think Mycroft is very happy about it. And I don't think Lady Beatrice is very happy either."

"No?"

"No. According to your brother, the queen has been making all sorts of arrangements for her – that is for your and the lady's – wedding."

"Beatrice won't like that. She's not a woman to make a fuss. Nothing else? Splendid. Now, tell me, how did you get on?"

"Very well, Holmes. I said my name was Ward and I needed a new governess to take care of my three children. I said that my neighbours, the Porlocks, had recommended the agency. The first two places seemed bewildered, but I got lucky on the third one, an agency called Winthrop's. Miss Winthrop herself immediately knew the name and said she had placed Madame du Pury with the Porlocks and the family were well pleased with her. A difficult family to please, she said. They wanted someone who spoke French as well as English and played the piano. Rather curiously, she added, they insisted the right candidate should have no German."

"Excellent!" I cried, clapping my hands together. "Ah, you have excelled, my dear Watson. Well done, well done, indeed."

There was a knock at the door and Mrs Hudson came in with her maid carrying the supper. Stevens followed immediately behind.

"Come in, Stevens, I said. You can have my seat. Where's the Bradshaw? Ah, here it is…"

A BIASED JUDGEMENT

"At least have some coffee, Holmes," Watson said. "I know it's pointless to try to persuade you to eat, but you must certainly drink."

"Oh, very well. What's the matter with you, Stevens? We do not stand on ceremony here. Sit, sit."

"Please do join us, Stevens," Watson said. "No point in food going to waste. You're off out, Holmes?"

"Yes. I want to catch the next train to Southampton."

"Southampton, Mr Holmes?" Stevens said. "Do you want me to come with you?"

"No, no. I shall do very well on my own, I think. You and the good doctor please stay here and deal with any questions or other issues that may arise. Watson, young Billy may report in with news. If there's anything urgent leave a message for me at the inn in Southampton. I shall use the name Mead. And if Lestrade calls tell him I hope to return to London on the last train. Tell him to delay his, uh, guest until I arrive."

Happily, I missed Lestrade and Hill at Waterloo. Undoubtedly, they took the earlier train, a fact that suited me very well. I thoroughly dislike chatter. Small talk on a train is a waste of an environment which I have always found so conducive to thought. So, here I sit in the stuffy compartment, packed with Saturday evening travellers, mulling over the events of the day and days, writing my journal. My handwriting reflects the syncopated rhythm of the train's motion.

I am not optimistic of finding anything of interest in Rillington Manor, but with so much at stake I can hardly ignore the possibility, no matter how slight it might be. If I am happily wrong I shall be able to dispatch Summerville and Porlock alike into the arms of justice. If not...

My plan for breaching Porlock's bastion worries me. Not because I doubt its potential for success, but because the risk is so very great. Were the risk mine alone I should cheerfully accept it, but this risk is not mine. What sort of a husband shall I be if my first act is to put my

A BIASED JUDGEMENT

wife in the gravest possible danger? What sort of man does such a thing? And yet, and yet… For all my cleverness, I cannot devise a better alternative.

Evening had fallen by the time I arrived at the inn in Bitterne. Dressed as I was, still, as an old man with rheumatism, no one recognised me. The landlord said there had been no messages for a Mr Mead.

For some time I sat in the lounge drinking a pint of bitters. There was a good crowd present, and all was merriment and laughter. The air was thick with tobacco smoke and the backdraught from the fire. In the centre of the small room six young men sat around a crooked table. They were very tall, almost as tall as I, and burly with it. Their bulk was given voice by their boisterous conversation.

"Strapping young lads," I said to the innkeeper as he poured my pint. He glanced up and made a wry face. "That's the Lowry boys, Mr Mead," he said. "Good boys as a rule but they get very wild when they've had a drop. They're always worse on a Saturday night since they've just got their wages… You might want to make yourself scarce if things start to get ugly. Wouldn't do for an old gentleman like yourself to get hurt."

"I thank 'ee for the caution," I replied. "But why don't the local police handle those matters? It's not right for a respectable businessman like yourself to have to put up with such nonsense."

"You're right there, sir, but I can't blame Mr Greer. He's a decent gentleman and he takes care of matters sure enough, but he can't arrest them until they've done something. Besides, he's a bit busy tonight."

"Busy?" I sipped my drink and looked innocently over the rim of my spectacles.

"Some gents from London arrived about an hour ago. They've headed up to the manor with the inspector. Still, he'll be along soon enough, I'm sure; I just hope those London gentlemen don't delay him

A BIASED JUDGEMENT

too long. Just watch yourself there, sir, and give the Lowrys a wide berth."

Over the next hour the tension in the inn gradually increased as the Lowry men sank deeper and deeper into their cups. Fortunately, just as they began to throw things at one another, Greer arrived, looking harassed and tired. Immediately, the mood in the inn cracked and the tension dissipated. It was impressive to see a man carry such respect.

As the crowd in the inn shuffled and formed into new groups I slipped out and walked up the hill towards the manor.

22

Twenty minutes later I walked up the familiar driveway. It was remarkable to see the difference a few months had made to the estate. The blowsy pink roses were gone now and not merely due to the weather and the season: every one of the bushes had been hacked down. Indeed, most of the garden had been trampled and, though the damage had undoubtedly occurred weeks ago, the signs of destruction remained fresh. There was malice in this devastation, I thought.

I made my way around the back to the servants' entrance. Daisy was just coming out and she said, "Oh I beg your pardon. Were you looking for a bite of food? There's not much in the house, but no doubt cook could give you some soup."

"Thank 'ee," I said, selecting Dorset for my accent purely on a whim. I like to vary it. "Quiet night," I said. "I 'oped to 'ave a word with your master about some work."

"I'm sorry, sir," she said. "But the master and his brother are on their way to London. I doubt they'll be back before morning. Now, you sit there by the fire and I'll see if Mrs Bracken has some food she can spare you."

I went into the kitchen where, just a few months ago, I spent a pleasant evening hunting for a key with the woman I shall soon marry, and found myself alone. An easy matter to slip up those stairs and begin my search.

I quickly stole up the back staircase and made my way along the family hallway towards the room which had been Wallace

A BIASED JUDGEMENT

Summerville's customary bedchamber; the one I had the use of when last I stayed here.

The house was still, almost as if it were holding its breath. Although I am not a superstitious man, I confess I felt something unwholesome in the stillness. I strained my ears for a sound. After a moment's intense concentration, I could make out a muffled whimper in Lady Summerville's room. If the mistress of the house was unwell, that might explain the preternatural quiet. All the same, the message of that destroyed garden suggested something far more sinister than a minor ailment.

I could not investigate that matter now, however. I must focus all my attention on uncovering Summerville's secrets.

His room was neat and tidy, though not by his hand. I have seen how he lives when left to his own devices. Conclusion: the housemaid has restored him to order.

I began with his suitcase, but it contained nothing more than a newspaper from three days earlier and, curiously, a cameo brooch with what appeared to be my fiancée's profile carved in onyx. I examined the brooch closely but it was clearly of more sentimental value than monetary. For the first time it occurred to me that Wallace Summerville may have some genuine regard for Beatrice. I found myself strangely unsettled by this realisation, but was determined not to let it distract me from the task at hand.

For a moment I considered taking the cameo; I suspected it had been acquired by unscrupulous means, but on reflection decided to let it be. After all, I could not be certain the trinket was not Summerville's own. I had already turned the door handle when I thought further about the newspaper. It seemed odd that Summerville should have one three-days old in his possession. He is, as I have observed, slovenly in his habits and very likely he had merely forgotten it. Still, on the chance that it might be of worth, I rolled it up and stuck it in my coat pocket.

A BIASED JUDGEMENT

The house remained still and I stealthily made my way into Sir Christopher's room. It was clean and orderly, though a sour smell suggested illness... or alcoholism.

Something in this room seemed changed since my last visit. I stared at the wall and after a few moments, realised the picture that hung there was new. I went to take a closer look – the painting itself was an amateurish attempt at a vase of lilies – and found it concealed a wall safe. Obviously Sir Christopher had learned his lesson from the late, unlamented Liz Derby.

Opening the lock took a few minutes, but eventually I heard that satisfying click and the door swung open.

The safe contained legal documents: the deeds to the manor and his will, nothing of consequence. The letters were more interesting: most of them were from creditors, but three were from his brother. These I slipped into my pocket then I closed the safe and slipped from the room.

I was just about to head down the back staircase when my attention was caught by a low whimpering sound.

I hesitated, but only for a moment. Then I went back and knocked on Lady Summerville's door.

A weak voice bade me enter.

My fiancée's aunt was in bed and she started when she saw me.

"Hush, Lady Summerville," I soothed. "It is I, Sherlock Holmes."

She began to cry; indeed she had been crying. Not for the first time I wished Doctor Watson were with me. He has such a happy knack for dealing with distressed ladies.

I dithered for a moment. I dislike dithering. It shows a want of intelligence. In my defence, it probably was of very short duration. I said, "What has happened, Lady Summerville? You are unwell, I see. Your niece is very concerned for you."

She blinked and, through muffled sobs said, "Beatrice? Is she all right? Oh, Mr Holmes, I have been so fearful for her."

"Because of your brother-in-law, you mean?" I said. "He will not trouble her again."

A BIASED JUDGEMENT

"Christopher was so angry today. Word came from London that Wallace, that Wallace..." but what words followed, if there were any, were drowned beneath a vat of tears.

Her condition was pitiable and, indeed, I did pity her. But it was pity conjoined with irritation. What on earth could possess the woman?

"What happened to your garden?" I asked. "Your husband destroyed it because he was angry with your niece for refusing his brother's proposal of marriage?"

She nodded. Still weeping.

"You cannot stay here, Lady Summerville. Your husband is a brute of a man."

"I am his wife," she spat back with more determination than I would have expected. "I made my bed..."

"But you do not have to stay," I pointed out. "I can take you with me to join your niece. I give you my word that none of the Summervilles will ever harm you again."

Suddenly her tears stopped and she stared with me with such hope that I almost forgot my irritation. She reached out and grasped my hand. "You are a good man, Mr Holmes. Not just a gentleman... heroic," she concluded. "Like a Lancelot."

There was no answer to this extraordinary statement and I attempted none. But she said, "I cannot leave; not because I am afraid – though I am afraid. You see, I'm going to have a baby. I know I must seem much too old for such a thing; my doctor is amazed. But I must stay for the sake of my child. Christopher will be a new man when he holds his son in his arms. Oh yes, it is a boy. I'm quite certain of it.

"The garden... it was upsetting indeed, the act of the moment. He is a passionate man, my husband, and he deeply regretted his actions as soon as his temper waned. If you could only have seen his tears of remorse... He loved that garden too, after all. Many a happy hour we spent together with our roses.

"I know what a low opinion you have of him. You're not alone, you know; I see how people look at him, hear what they say. But you don't

A BIASED JUDGEMENT

know him the way I do. I love him, Mr Holmes, and he loves me. It's just that he's been so worried…"

"About money?" I said.

"Money, yes, but mostly about Wallace. He loves his brother, Mr Holmes; he worries about him. Some years ago young Wallace fell in love. She was wholly inappropriate, a woman with the most dreadful reputation, but Wallace truly loved her. He lived with her and despite everything he was happy. Christopher should simply have let them be but there was family honour at stake, do you see?"

"He separated them?"

"Yes." She had stopped crying for the moment but her sadness had immeasurable depths. "That was a turning point for Wallace. He began to drink and gamble. Then, six months later the girl died in childbirth… we do not know who the father was, but Wallace was adamant it was he. Since then his life has been one of increasing debt and disaster. He's forever begging my husband for money, and Christopher… He blames himself. Can you see, Mr Holmes? If he'd just left well enough alone perhaps it would have worked out, but now Wallace hates Christopher and cannot forgive him."

"And now they are in such debt they see your niece as their only hope," I said.

Lady Summerville wiped her face with an inadequate lace handkerchief and said with surprising dignity, "Please tell Beatrice that I am very well and I hope we may see each other again after my child is born."

There was no help for it. I left the room and went back down to the kitchen. Daisy was alone, sitting at the table polishing the silver.

"Oh," she said. "I wondered where you'd got to. What were you doing, anyway? I'll catch hell if you've nicked something."

"I assure you, Daisy, the house is exactly as I found it," I said in my normal voice. "But I thought you were going to London to marry young Mr Stevens."

A BIASED JUDGEMENT

"Oh, la, it's Mr Holmes!" she cried. Then, at my gesture, lowered her voice to a whisper. "I'm due to go to London in February, once Maurice finishes his training and gets settled. But what are you doing here, Mr Holmes? Did Lady Beatrice send you?"

"It's a secret, Daisy. Tell me, what has been happening here? Where is everyone?"

"Well, Mr Greer came with two other gentlemen a few hours ago and hauled off Mr Wallace Summerville for questioning, they said. Sir Christopher said it was outrageous and he wouldn't stand for it. So off they went to London together. I can't imagine we'll see them before morning."

"And the staff? Where are they all?"

"Well, Maurice left to go with Lady Beatrice – but you know that, already. And no one was hired to replace him or that awful Derby person. Miss Simms is getting married to Mr Davenport so she's leaving at the first of the year. All the grounds staff were let go weeks ago – you saw the rose garden? Terrible business that was, with the master shouting and saying he would take an axe to the whole country if he could.

"Who else did I forget? Oh yes, cook. Mrs Bracken is ready to retire. There's only Mr Reynolds left really."

"And where is Reynolds this evening?"

"He's gone to bed. Had a spot too much to drink and turned in right after the gentlemen left."

I couldn't imagine how a house of this size could manage without staff. Certainly Lady Summerville wasn't capable of running it. In response to my question, Daisy's voice dropped and she said, "Now, this is a big secret, Mr Holmes. Even the staff aren't supposed to know: they're leaving the country. Sir Christopher and the mistress and Mr Wallace – they're off to Canada in just a few days. They wanted to slip away without telling anyone. Probably mean not to pay us, neither. I'd be gone already if I had a place in London but I can't expect Lady Beatrice to put me up and all, can I?"

A BIASED JUDGEMENT

"How did you find out about Canada if it's a secret?"

"Mr Reynolds got drunk one night and told us everything. About how he was going to live it up in Canada and how England was done for…"

"Do you know when they're planning on leaving, Daisy? Or what ship they're sailing on?"

"I'm sorry, sir, I don't. By the first of the year, I'd guess, but it's only a guess. I think the mistress will want to spend Christmas in her home."

Her eyes teared up and drops hovered on the lashes before spilling down her pale cheeks. "She's lived here her whole life, Mr Holmes. It's not right that she's being forced away from her home."

As soon as my train pulled in at Waterloo, I hastened to Mycroft's offices at Whitehall. It was now dark and the building seemed empty, other than old Gillespie. He said, "Ah, good evening, Mr Holmes. He's still upstairs, working late as usual. Can I bring you a cup of tea?"

"That would be most welcome, thank you, Gillespie. Your son is still unwell, I see."

"There, now, only you and your brother would notice such a thing. Mr Mycroft Holmes said he spotted the stub of my ticket to Woolwich in my pocket. You do have sharp eyes, the two of you."

"As do you, Mr Gillespie. You're the only man I know who can instantly see through my disguise, no matter how cleverly applied."

He chuckled and I hurried up the narrow wooden staircase to Mycroft's office on the top floor.

"Come in, Sherlock," he said before I even reached his door.

Mycroft looked up from his desk and made a moue of distaste as I entered.

"I realise you're playing the part of one of London's unfortunates, my dear brother," he said. "But surely you could have taken a moment to bathe?"

"No time," I said.

A BIASED JUDGEMENT

I sank into his armchair by the fire and took off my scarf. It had begun to rain and was very cold. I longed for the hot cup of tea promised by Gillespie.

Mycroft continued to work at his papers for a few minutes, then he came and joined my at the fire.

"You look done in, my dear brother," he said. "You'll wear yourself out with all this running around, you mark my words."

"Needs must, Mycroft," I said, rousing from my doze. "May I use your telephone?"

He nodded and I dialled Scotland Yard's number. After some moments an irritated Lestrade said, "Yes, yes? Who is it?"

"It is Sherlock Holmes," I replied. "I understand you were successful in Southampton?"

"Yes, we have the bird here, but I do not know how long we can keep him. We really do not have too much to go on with. Young Hill's managed to put the wind up him proper though, sort of hinting that we know all sorts about the man's dealings. And his brother, Sir Christopher... well, that's a man to make you long to see the end of the nobility and no mistake."

"I shall be along in an hour, Lestrade. You can keep them there for that long, can you not?"

"Yes, I think we can just about manage that. I'd be obliged if you'd make haste, though, Mr Holmes. We're really about out of ideas."

"Well, ask young Wallace to tell you about the Piccadilly Club. Imply your investigation is related to his gambling debts. Tell him a number of people have filed complaints against him; you do not need to give him names. That should keep him occupied until I arrive."

I sat back by the fire with Mycroft and felt my eyes close. I could not remember a time when I was so tired. There was a tap on the door and Gillespie brought in a tray.

"This'll keep the cold out, gentlemen," he said. "Is there anything else I can get for you?"

"Thank you, Gillespie," Mycroft said. "This will suffice, I think."

A BIASED JUDGEMENT

The old man left and Mycroft poured the tea. I held the hot cup between my freezing hands and sipped. Once I was sufficiently warmed and my thirst quenched I reviewed the events of the day. Mycroft listened in silence. He kept his eyes closed and tented his fingers; it struck me, not for the first time, that we employ the same methods of concentration.

When I finished he said, "What was in the letters?"

I handed them to him. "Just requests for money, as you see. The last one is the most interesting: Wallace talks about his house in Canada. I suspect the three Summervilles will be going together, and soon, if the housemaid is correct."

"It might not be a bad thing to let them go," Mycroft said. "This land will be better for their absence."

"It will be hard for Beatrice though to be without her aunt."

Mycroft gave me a look but only said, "What of the newspaper, the one you found in Summerville junior's bag: was there anything of interest in it?"

"I didn't think so, at first. Then I found this—" I pointed at an article that had been circled in pencil. It was a story about the Queen's scheduled return to Osbourne House for Christmas. I see that the date has been underlined...

"It may be nothing," I said. "But it tallies with the information Smiley gave me. I understand Bigge still refuses to alert the queen to her danger?"

"I'm afraid so. No, you need not explain to me again why it is a bad idea. You know I agree with you. Even I can be overruled on rare occasions, Sherlock, and this happens to be one of those times. Bigge has the Prime Minister in his corner. There is nothing I can do. At least they've increased the security at the Castle quite considerably." He sighed, then said, "Summerville is being questioned? I wish it was anyone other than Lestrade. That man does not fill me with much confidence."

A BIASED JUDGEMENT

"He has his strengths: a rare tenacity being foremost. It doesn't make up for his lack of imagination, but I suppose he can't help that. Anyway, young Tavistock Hill is with him. He's a newly promoted inspector, Mycroft, and is one of the best I've seen. You might want to keep your eye on him. All the same, I do not expect much from their interrogation. We would have more leverage if we could charge Summerville with treason."

"Out of the question, I'm afraid, Sherlock. I've spoken with the DPP and he points out, quite rightly, that there just isn't enough hard evidence. I'd go so far as to say there is no hard evidence whatever."

"What's the point in creating a department of Public Prosecution if the Director is going to impede our efforts? Have you told him the particulars?"

"In great detail, I assure you. If Summerville was a grocer or even a bank clerk we might not have a problem, but he has powerful friends. The Department is too new for them to take these sort of risks, Sherlock. I'm sorry. Get some evidence and he will be glad to act."

"What about Frobisher? There's plenty of evidence against him."

"Yes, but only against him. His link to Porlock is tenuous. No, I don't doubt its existence, Sherlock, but unless he talks we have nothing. We can put the noose around Frobisher's neck and let the bigger fish escape, or we can be patient."

"He might talk, though. If he's frightened enough."

"Is that a risk you are willing to take, brother? Possibly losing all chance of capturing Porlock, of ending his organisation…"

He waited while I thought about it. He's very patient, Mycroft. Far more so than I. Finally, though, I was forced to concede his point. "We shall wait for now. Perhaps I shall get what I need from Summerville."

With that, Mycroft yawned and stretched then he rose from his seat. "Time for me to head home, my dear brother. Are you going back to Baker Street now?"

"No, I need to go to Scotland Yard and see if I can squeeze any information out of Summerville."

A BIASED JUDGEMENT

He teased the crease between his brows with his thumbnail, a sure sign that he was troubled. "We are no further along than we were before, Sherlock," he said. "If Summerville refuses to talk…"

"I have one other option. It is dangerous and I really do not wish to put it into action, but if Summerville fails us we may have no other choice."

"Indeed. I do not have to tell you what is at stake, do I? The queen's very life; the collapse of the Empire. I assure you, brother, it is worth any sacrifice we have to make."

23

Even late at night, Scotland Yard stays open. Although it was almost midnight, the building hummed with conversations over long tables, muffled oaths and slamming doors, and, from somewhere far below, a repeated wail of despair.

Several of the policemen greeted me as I made my way to the Inspector's Division on the third floor. Lestrade was at his desk and looked as weary as I felt.

"Well, Lestrade," I said. "What progress have you made?"

He peered up at me with drooping eyes. "None at all, Mr Holmes. It's been a devil of a job to keep him here. We really don't have anything to hold him on. It's a pity you could not get here sooner."

"I have not been idle, I assure you," I replied. Really, the man should be grateful I had gone out of my way to change my clothes at Jermyn Street. Still, I suppose he wasn't to know that. Instead I said, "I am here now, in any case. Where is Summerville?"

"In the interview room. Hill's really been laying it on him, but the man hasn't budged yet."

"Can you call Hill? I'd like to hear his report before I begin my own questioning."

A few minutes later, a bright and energetic Tavistock Hill bounded into the office.

"Mr Holmes, sir," he said warmly. I shook his proffered hand and tried not to growl at his enthusiasm.

A BIASED JUDGEMENT

"Good to see you again, Hill," I said. "A shame about Hacker and Smiley evading the courts, but at least the streets are safer without them. Now, tell me how you got on with the delightful Mr Summerville."

"Not well, I'm afraid, Mr Holmes. The difficulty is it's a man called Winters who ran up these gambling debts and the late Mr Smiley was the only one who could identify him and Summerville as one and the same. I've made a production of having witnesses brought in, but he still insists he's not the man we're looking for."

"This matter doesn't really seem to be worth all the effort, Mr Holmes," Lestrade said. "I don't suppose you'd care to tell me what your real interest in Summerville is?" His sharp little eyes glinted and I smiled.

"You're right of course, Lestrade. The gambling debts are merely a ruse to detain him. You'll forgive me, I'm sure, but I cannot divulge the true nature of his crimes. All I can tell you is they are deeper and muddier than you can imagine. May I see him?"

"Of course, Mr Holmes. This way."

I was annoyed to see Summerville had not been separated from his brother. From the look that exchanged between the two policemen, I perceived this was something they had discussed and, I surmised, Hill had been overruled. Well, it couldn't be helped.

I said, "I'd be obliged if you would take Sir Christopher to another room, Lestrade. See if you can get him to give you a formal statement about his brother's activities for the past... oh, let's say three months. That should keep him busy for a while."

Lestrade went off to do as I asked. One thing about the man, he's no respecter of persons. Lord or street sweeper will receive precisely the same response from him.

Hill unlocked the door and said, "Do you want me to come in, Mr Holmes?"

"No, thank you, Inspector. I'm afraid I must do this task alone."

A BIASED JUDGEMENT

Summerville looked up in alarm as I entered the room. The bravado and arrogance he displayed at Bitterne was all but gone. The man who faced me was terrified.

Good. I could use that.

I sat down facing him and said, "This is a bad business, Mr Summerville. Your best bet, if I may use that word, is to make a clean breast of it."

"I told those gentlemen," he said, still striving to sound assured. "That I am not this Winters person they are looking for."

"Oh come, Mr Summerville, you and I both know that is not true. But it is not your gambling debts that interest me. It is your relationship with Albrecht Porlock."

The colour slid from his cheeks leaving him ashen. For a moment I feared he would fall into a faint. I waited and watched him squirm.

"I've met Herr Porlock," he said at last. "In fact, I owe him money. Ours is purely a business relationship."

I remained silent for several minutes but he did not fall into the trap of filling in the silence with more information. I said, "Your engaging Porlock to kill Lady Beatrice: was that merely a business arrangement?"

"No!" His pallor had gained a greenish tinge. He now seemed more likely to vomit than to faint. It could go either way.

"I have witnesses, Mr Summerville. You were heard." I gave him a moment to digest that before adding, "Your entire conversation was heard."

I could see him calculate the odds. He had two choices: he could admit his involvement in a plot to murder the queen, or he could say nothing. I was counting on his fear, or on some deeply buried sense of patriotism and decency.

"Bring forward your witnesses," he said, folding his arms and glaring. "I have done nothing wrong. Either charge me or release me."

A BIASED JUDGEMENT

"Whatever this business is, Mr Holmes," Hill said, later. "It seems to be worrying you considerably. Is there anything we can do?"

"Thank you, Hill. I confess I am very disappointed. I had hoped Summerville might have cracked after your lengthy questioning and my own but he's a tougher bird than I thought."

"Well, there's no help for it. Release him. But if you could arrange to keep him under close watch for the next... well, we'd best say for the next three weeks, I would be grateful. You need not be subtle about following him, either. There's a chance, a very slender chance, that fear may yet lead him to panic."

"You alarm me, Mr Holmes," said Lestrade, joining us. "But as my young friend says, we will do our part."

"I know I can count on you, both of you," I said. "I don't suppose you got anything more out of Sir Christopher?"

"Nothing, Mr Holmes. Man claims his brother has been unwell and staying with him for the past several weeks. He made a point of reminding me that he's one of the gentry. He thinks I really had some neck by even speaking to him."

"I don't doubt it. As to his giving an alibi for his brother, well, he'd swear on holy writ that the sun rises in the west too, if it suited him. It's no more than I expected.

"One last thing and then I must get back to Baker Street: Can you keep tonight's interrogation quiet from your colleagues? You know I would not ask if the matter were not a very grave one indeed. The fewer people who know of this the better."

"If you think it's important," said Lestrade. "Then certainly."

Hill added, "What should we tell the officers who follow Summerville?"

"Tell them he's suspected in the assault of the queen's goddaughter."

"But if that's the case, Mr Holmes," spluttered Lestrade. "Surely we have grounds to arrest him?"

A BIASED JUDGEMENT

"The lady refuses to press charges. I do not wish to embarrass her or the illustrious person who is her godmother. Discretion, gentlemen."

"You can count on us and no mistake," Lestrade said. Perhaps I was fatigued, for I believed him.

November 28th, 1897

I slept very late and Watson was already eating the midday meal with Stevens by the time I arose.

"Ah, Holmes," he greeted me. "Which would you prefer, breakfast or luncheon?"

"Neither," I replied. "Just coffee and tobacco."

"You had a late night of it, I'd guess, Mr Holmes," Stevens said.

"Late indeed. I'm afraid you weren't too comfortable on that sofa, Stevens. I perceive you have a crick in your neck."

"Just a bit of a pinch, Mr Holmes. You got something for me to do today?"

"No, I need to go to Windsor. I have another job for you, however. How would you like to visit Daisy?"

He brightened at her name. "I'd love to, Mr Holmes. What do you need me to do?"

"Just get the lay of the land. Talk to Daisy and see if she managed to hear anything between the Summervilles after they got home about their plans or anything else. It's possible there was some discussion about the day's events and their course of action, or Lady Summerville may have said something. Any information you can glean would be helpful. I shall not need you until Tuesday morning.

"If there are any significant developments, telephone. If I am not here you may leave a message with either the good doctor or Mrs Hudson."

"I shall leave directly," the young man said.

"After luncheon will be fine," Watson said, frowning at me. Then, "Do you have anything for me to do, Holmes?"

A BIASED JUDGEMENT

"Yes, indeed. I would be obliged if you would write a reference for a governess..."

An hour later, Watson had written a glowing reference for a Miss Elizabeth (Betty) Jones, a governess of discretion and many talents.

Stevens left in high excitement, whether for eagerness to see his fiancée or the thrill of the hunt, I could not say. After he left I told Watson about my visit to Rillington Manor and my conversation with Lady Summerville.

"Things are in a bad way there, Watson..." I told him about the eerie silence of the place, the destruction of the garden, the appalling state of Summerville's bank balance. "Can she really be pregnant?" I asked.

"It's possible. She's in her mid-forties or thereabouts? It could be anything: false pregnancy, the onset of menopause, a tumour... But certainly she may actually be pregnant. Perhaps if she is her husband might modify his behaviour."

"You have more faith in humanity than I do, Watson. It's unfortunate that they plan to leave the country. If Summerville does not mend his ways his wife will be essentially alone in another country, possibly with a child to care for."

"It is most unfortunate that the lady means to go with her husband," Watson agreed. "And will undoubtedly be upsetting to your fiancée. She is very fond of her aunt."

"She is indeed." I lit my cigarette. "I find it incredible that any woman could remain devoted to a man of such little worth. I will never understand..."

"Women? Or love?" Watson asked.

"Both."

He smiled at me almost as if he had a secret. "You're probably right about women, Holmes. But, then, why should you have insight that has eluded all men since the beginning of time? As to love, I suspect you know far more than you are willing to admit."

A BIASED JUDGEMENT

With this bewildering comment teasing my thoughts I left to get the train to Windsor.

Beatrice was decidedly unhappy. The queen had been very vexing. She insisted Beatrice should have a new gown made for the wedding, and demanded considerably more pomp than my future bride wished. "Do you know I was not even permitted to unpack my own bags?" My fiancée seethed. "Such nonsense!"

The rain beat down on the squat castle and kept us indoors. We were not allowed to be alone together, Lord only knows why, and so had to sit with one of the queen's ladies as chaperone. She pretended to be busy with her embroidery but her mere presence constricted our conversation. As a result, everything we said had to be in code.

"I was worried," Beatrice said. "With not hearing from you. I trust all is well?"

"Things are progressing rapidly," I replied. "By the way, that gentleman you encountered in Wimpole Street has met with an unfortunate accident."

"Indeed? Serious?"

"Extremely."

"Well, that is... surprising. How are your, ah, preparations going?"

"Very well," I replied. "That matter we discussed... You are still willing?"

"Of course."

She glanced at the woman who sat near the window, apparently engrossed in her needlework, and said softly, "The queen has invited some guests to dine with her on Thursday the ninth. It is an informal gathering of close friends and relatives. My aunt's husband and his brother are expected to attend."

Her eyes met mine and held. I said, "Well, at least now I have a time-frame. Thank you, Beatrice."

A BIASED JUDGEMENT

"The queen has been very generous with her time," she said. "Indeed, I am hardly out of her company." The enthusiasm of her words belied the irritation in her eyes.

I laughed and said, "Make the most of it. After all, this," I waved a hand to indicate her opulent quarters, "must end on Tuesday."

"Thank heaven," she whispered.

"Tell me, have you seen anything of Sir Arthur Bigge?"

"Yes, quite a lot. He is devoted to Her Majesty." Softly: "I have tried to persuade him to let me tell the queen about the plot against her but he will not change his mind."

"He is an excellent if stubborn man," I replied. "I should like to see him before I leave."

"Let us see if we can find him."

We rose and left the room with the queen's lady following at a discreet, yet still irksome, distance. Ironic, really, since Beatrice and I are the last two people on earth to need the presence of a chaperone. Still, we must maintain the fiction, I suppose.

Bigge greeted me warmly. "It's very pleasant to see you, Mr Holmes. Come sit by the fire. It's a wretched day, I'm afraid."

"It is indeed."

To our chaperone Bigge said, "It's all right, Lady Alice. I'll take over from here."

Once the three of us were left alone I prepared to chastise Bigge for his refusal to speak to the queen about Porlock and Summerville. He raised a hand before I could say a word, however, and said, "I know what you're going to say, Mr Holmes. I've already heard it at length from your brother and from Lady Beatrice. Believe me, I am not unmindful of your concerns, but I have a larger issue: My first concern must be for the queen.

"Will telling her of this plot aid her in any way? No. You say you want her to increase her vigilance: do you really think that is possible? She is already closely watched by people who will protect her no matter what the cost to themselves.

A BIASED JUDGEMENT

"No, Mr Holmes, alerting her will only cause her distress and anxiety. She is much advanced in years and her health is not good. This time of year weighs heavily upon her because of the loss of her beloved consort, Prince Albert.

"You must trust me to do my job, Mr Holmes. As I am trusting you to do yours."

The day was well advanced by the time I returned to the city. I went to Finsbury Park and found Tommy. "Not much going on today, Mr 'olmes," he said. "The lady of the 'ouse sounded cross. She kept shouting at the children. I could 'ear 'er from across the street. No sign of anyone applying for the job yet, but I suppose it's too soon."

"That, and the fact that it's a Sunday. They'll start arriving tomorrow, I've no doubt. And you know what to do? I cannot risk the wrong person being employed."

"Yes, we've talked about it. Billy worked up a story about the last governess being carried out on a stretcher and sort of suggesting who knows what 'appens in that 'ouse... Well, it's got the advantage of being true. Mostly."

I laughed. "No sign of the family?"

"Naw, just church this morning. They always go to church, the lot of 'em. Suppose they've got a lot to pray for."

November 29th, 1897

Despite my plaintive objections, I was forced to endure all sorts of rituals in preparation for tomorrow. There was a suit to adjust, a sauna to take, gifts for the bride and the bridal party as well as the queen. I do not know why men endure such trials. Watson would not be gainsaid, however, and he had no sympathy whatever for my sufferings.

"It's your own fault, Holmes," he said. "Leaving everything to the last minute. Ah, Mrs Hudson, have you fixed those cuffs? Excellent! Now, here are the gifts for the bridal party... what do you mean, you don't want to see them? Oh very well... Here's the gift for the queen.

A BIASED JUDGEMENT

Well, she likes jewellery so she will be pleased with it. Of course you must give something to your bride. It would look pretty odd if you did not…"

And on and on until I was quite demented.

Around ten o'clock this evening Stevens arrived. He whistled when he saw me. "Don't you look dapper, Mr Holmes? Quite the gent and no mistake."

At last I was able to sink into my armchair with a pipe and listen to his report.

"Not much in the way of facts, I'm afraid, Mr Holmes. Daisy says there's been a lot of slamming doors and tears. Sir Christopher keeps saying they're ruined and Mr Summerville has threatened suicide."

"That might be the best solution for everyone," I said.

"Holmes!" Watson remonstrated.

I said, "Come, think of the alternative, Watson. What else can he do? Has Daisy heard any more of their plans to leave the country?"

"She says there are crates and trunks being packed, mostly with valuables. Lady Summerville's not even able to take most of her clothes with her."

This was as much as I was allowed to ask then I was bundled off to bed like a child.

24

November 30th, 1897

The vows have been said, the ring placed on the finger and the toasts all drunk.

I am married.

How odd a thing that is to acknowledge. It is something I never thought to hear myself say.

I had expected Beatrice – my wife – to arrive at the chapel in high solemnity in light of the occasion. Nothing could be further from the truth. She was in a giddy, even foolhardy mood and she teased the Prince of Wales (who, I may say, enjoyed it rather more than he ought) and even kissed the queen's cheek. Her majesty was less taken with this liberty than the prince but I do not think she was really upset. She said with good humour, "Since this is such a special day, child, I will allow you this liberty. Once."

Watson stood witness for me; Mycroft wasn't sure he'd get away from affairs of state in order to attend, though he managed it in the final moments just as my bride was walking up the aisle. But I was happy to have Watson stand at my side as he has at every perilous moment of my life. Surely there could be no occasion more perilous than this.

My bride looked very well. Not beautiful, necessarily, though she is handsome enough I suppose. She has exquisite eyes and lustrous hair, and her features are perfectly regular. But I mean she looked confident and completely at ease.

I found her sense of the ridiculous quite contagious, and we exchanged vows in a riot of laughter. Then when the business was done

A BIASED JUDGEMENT

and I was invited to 'kiss the bride' she merely held out her hand and shook mine like a comrade in arms.

All in all it was a delicious occasion; far more than I would ever have expected.

Vows said, celebratory meal enjoyed – well, eaten - we left the palace and returned to Beatrice's home on Wimpole Street.

It was necessary to greet the servants and I did so briefly but, I think, in good humour. I gave each of them a guinea to remember the occasion and they all drank a toast to their mistress and nominal new master. Then, at my request, the lady played some Mozart for me upon the piano.

Really, it was a splendid day.

Tomorrow the real work begins.

December 1st, 1897

As the hansom drew close to the park, I said, "You have the letter from the agency and the references I gave you? Excellent. Everything has been arranged so even if the Porlocks decide to contact the families you have listed here, the story will hold firm."

"And that agency? You can trust them to maintain the fiction, too?" she asked.

"You need not concern yourself on that account. Mrs Pennyfeather owes me a favour and she was very happy to send you for this job. You are over-qualified, of course, but Porlock will like to think he is getting a bargain. You remember what to say if he asks about your circumstances?"

"I should imply my former employer has been taking liberties and I am anxious to leave his employ in a hurry."

"Yes, he's a puritan of the first order, is our friend Porlock. Murder and treason are his pastimes, but impropriety is abhorrent to him. Such is the fickleness of the human nature.

"Watson has been well prepared to answer if there is a phone call, as I rather suspect there might. The doctor is rather good at this sort of

A BIASED JUDGEMENT

thing. I think they appeal to him. I hope he will not stay out too late this evening. But there, he knows what's at stake and I trust him as much as myself."

We went over her story one more time and at last, satisfied that she was completely prepared, I alighted from the carriage and let her continue on alone to the house. Young Kevin at my nod let her proceed unmolested.

By the time I walked to the park and found my seat, Beatrice had already been admitted to the house. I could see nothing through the lace curtains but I did not have very long to wait. Less than an hour later, she left and made her way down the hill to find a hansom to take her to the train station. I kept close watch but she was not followed and we met again in Leicester Square as arranged. She was excited to tell me everything that had happened.

"It is a very curious house," she said. "And I mean that in every sense of the word. The questions they asked! Every detail of my life from my childhood – do not worry, I was very well prepared and told my story exactly as you directed me. I let my behaviour suggest an improper advance from my former employer."

"And have you secured the situation?"

"Yes, I think so. They wish to check my references. From the detailed questions Mrs Porlock asked I suspect the check will be thorough. It will stand up, won't it? I should hate all this hard work to have been in vain."

"Have no fear. It will all be well. You are ready to go into the lodgings we arranged? There cannot now be any direct contact between us. I suspect your job there will run for several days. It will take some time before you learn the position of the safe. Given that Summerville is not expected to see the queen until the 9th, that gives us a little more than a week.

"I do not wish to attract attention, but I shall keep close watch on the house as much as I can. I will have the Irregulars help, too. There

A BIASED JUDGEMENT

will always be someone nearby if you need to get a message to me. And you can write to me as your aunt Lavinia too."

As Beatrice turned to leave me at the train station I felt a qualm. "You can still back out if you wish," I said. "I will think no less of you. It is a dangerous job – really, too dangerous—"

"Please do not finish that sentence, Holmes," she said. "Or we shall quarrel. I am well prepared and I am not, I think, foolhardy. I shall take no unnecessary risks and shall update you as often as possible. Now, stop worrying."

December 2nd, 1897

I received a phone call. "Please tell Aunt Lavinia I am employed by the Porlock family and will let her know when I am situated."

My plans were all laid out then and there was little more for me to do but wait. This I did. I am a patient man when needs must (granted, Watson is unlikely to agree with this self-appraisal). And so I went to Finsbury Park and prepared myself for a long wait.

December 4th, 1897

Only two days and yet this wait feels interminable. The weather turned inclement on Thursday night and it has rained steadily since. It is difficult to lounge in a park during a rainstorm and unproductive too. My wife and the children who are her charges did not leave the house and there were no letters or any other form of communication from within.

The Irregulars are disconsolate and I paid them double their usual rate. Though I am loath to admit it, I feel uneasy. I remind myself that there was no cause for concern. Beatrice knows her part and she will not be foolhardy. All the same, the endless silence from within that wretched house wears unpleasantly upon my nerves.

"Why don't you go home, Mr 'olmes," Billy said. "Me and the lads will take turns watchin'. Anyway, won't nothing much 'appen now. It's too late for folks to go out and who'd leave the 'ouse in this weather 'less they 'ad to?"

I could not argue the point and so returned to Baker Street. It was seven o'clock but the black storm clouds turned the city into midnight. I stood at the window looking out at the downpour flooding Baker Street and tried unsuccessfully to shake off the sense of disquiet that engulfed me.

"What is it you fear, Holmes?" Watson asked. "The girl is safely tucked up in a bourgeois house and is probably suffering no worse than boredom. Besides, Billy and the lads will keep watch and send word if there are any problems."

All of this was sound enough and yet, and yet...

By half-past-ten I could stand it no more. "I'm going out, Watson," I said.

"At this hour? In this weather? What do you expect to find?"

"I do not know. I just know I cannot stay here. I must go back. I cannot explain it, Watson, but all my instincts tell me she is in difficulty."

He let out a long sigh and rose from his comfortable armchair.

"All right," he said, putting on his coat.

"You do not need to come with me, Watson. It is, as you say, a filthy night."

"You may need me. But perhaps you would prefer to go alone?"

"By no means!" I cried. "I should be very glad of your company, Watson. Come, I think we must hurry."

It was not so easy a matter as all that. The weather had driven all men of sense indoors and there wasn't a cab to be seen the entire length of Baker Street. The strong winds made a mockery of our umbrellas. Watson said, "We're not thinking straight, Holmes. Why don't we go back indoors and call Stevens? It might be a good idea to have the carriage handy anyway."

A BIASED JUDGEMENT

Though I fretted at the delay I had to recognise the wisdom of his words. If we needed to make a swift departure from Finsbury Park, we would be glad of a carriage.

Twenty agonising minutes later Stevens arrived and we climbed aboard. I sank into a morose silence as the unfortunate horse clomped its way through the filthy London streets.

"You're really worried," Watson said. "What is it you fear?"

"I do not know. Something weighs on my heart, Watson. It is not rational but I cannot shake it."

"Perhaps it is merely the circumstance – knowing your wife is in the house of this Porlock fellow, and the restrictions imposed by the weather. But you and I know there is no more resourceful woman in all of England than Mrs Holmes."

Despite my mood I smiled. "Good old Watson!" I said. "You can always be relied upon to find sunshine – even on a day such as this."

It took a long time to reach the Seven Sisters Road and the weather showed no signs of improving. It was approaching midnight, and the night was as black as any coal mine. I told Stevens to wait for us a few hundred yards away from the house and Watson and I walked up the road along the side of the park.

To my alarm Billy was nowhere to be seen.

"What can have happened, Watson?" I said. The house was as we had left it, with a light burning in every window. The three-story detached house looked, at first glance, unchanged. But closer inspection showed the drainpipe was damaged and the water from the gutter ran like a waterfall down the side of the house. On the steps were bits of broken shingles and part of the metal that should have anchored the drainpipe to the house lay upon the verge.

"There is something very wrong here, Watson. Look at this – this required violence." I scoured the small, uninspired lawn and the path. There was nothing to be seen. Whatever signs there had been were silenced by the rain.

"Come, Watson," I said. "Let us see what we can find out here."

A BIASED JUDGEMENT

I knocked on the door which, after an interminable wait, was eventually opened by a frightened looking young maid, the same who had admitted the glazier just a few short weeks earlier.

"Good evening," I said in my most charming manner. "Is your master at home?"

"No sir," she said. "There's no one here but me and the sick old lady upstairs."

"Good gracious, I was expecting to speak to Mr Porlock. I'm quite sure he was expecting me. Where can he have gone in this weather?"

"I don't know, sir." And at this she burst into tears.

"Perhaps we should come in and wait," Watson said.

"Lord bless you, sir, the master would have my life if I let any gentleman in."

"Then where is Mrs Porlock?"

"I do not know, sir," she wailed. "She packed up the children not twenty minutes ago and left by cab."

"They left in a hurry, then?"

"Yes, sir."

"And I suppose the governess went with them?"

"I don't know, sir. Miss Jones, the governess, is not anywhere to be found."

"Perhaps you should tell us from the beginning, child," Watson said in the gentlest possible manner. "Come now, you are quite distressed. We are old friends of your master and he would not want us to stand on the door step like tradesmen. Come, we will go in – hush, you can say we gave you no choice – and you shall tell us all from the beginning."

Watson led the girl inside. I whistled for Stevens and he brought the carriage up to the house.

"Stevens, there's no time to lose. I need you to go to my brother immediately. If he's not at his apartment in Pall Mall try his office or the Diogenes Club – you know all the addresses? Good. Tell him Porlock has fled. He'll know what to do. Once you have delivered the

A BIASED JUDGEMENT

message, to Mycroft Holmes and no one else, mind, come back here with all speed."

Off he sped and I went into the house.

They were in the opulent drawing room. Watson had found a decanter of brandy and poured a glass for the girl.

"Now," I said, joining them. "Tell us what happened this evening – start at the beginning and omit nothing."

"Well sir, my mistress and master had made plans to go to the theatre and dinner. It was their wedding anniversary. Mr Porlock, he tried to talk the mistress into changing their plans on account of it being such a dreadful night, but she'd have none of it. She'd already given cook the night off since they had planned to be out and there was no one to prepare a meal. So just after seven, the two of them headed out.

"Miss Jones put the little girls to bed and told me to take it easy. She said she would look after anything that needed to be sorted. It was awfully good of her and I confess I was glad to let her. I went down to the kitchen and warmed up some leftover stew and then I fell asleep by the fire.

"Next thing I knew the master and mistress were home. It looked like they'd quarrelled and they had left their meal early without bothering to go on to the theatre. I was helping Mrs Porlock get out of her wet things and the master wanted to know where everyone was. Well, I didn't know, sir, and I said as much. He went running upstairs – I thought he was looking to the children, but then I heard him in his study and what a roar he let out. As far as I could gather, sir, someone had been in his study and stolen his private papers from the safe."

The girl took another eager gulp of brandy and continued.

"Next I heard a crash and a scream – I think the burglar was trying to climb down the drainpipe and it gave way. Then I heard…"

"Yes? What?"

It was all I could do not to shake the wretched girl.

"A loud crack, sir. Like a pistol being fired."

"And then? For the love of God, what happened then?"

A BIASED JUDGEMENT

"The master told Mrs Porlock to get the children and leave at once. Then he went and got the dogs and ran out into the night. That was hours ago, sir. The mistress had me run out and find a carriage, and then I helped her pack up the children's things. By ten o'clock, she was gone and I've seen and heard nothing since."

"And Miss Jones? Have you seen her or spoken to her since?"

"No sir, not a word. I'm that frightened, sir. I'm not used to being in the house on my own, truly I'm not. What if the old lady dies?"

Watson looked after the maid and the old woman while I searched the house. There was nothing extraordinary to be found until I reached the study.

A small Friedrich painting sat on the floor and the wall safe it had evidently been hiding was open and empty. It was a simple enough lock; any decent burglar could have broken into it. I could have managed the job myself in just a few minutes. I stopped and closed my eyes. My emotions were making me leap ahead of the facts and make suppositions. I needed to clear my mind and just focus on the evidence before me. Resolutely shutting out all my fears of my wife's safety, I began again.

An examination of the house revealed no evidence of a break in. All the doors and windows were carefully shuttered. The only exception was the window in the office. The window that overlooked the park. The window that was next to the now broken drainpipe.

I lay down and examined the carpet. The signs were there: a woman's footsteps from the door to the safe. Then... what next? Flight to the window. The window pulled open and then escape down the drainpipe. A woman in skirts climbing down the drainpipe? And in a downpour too. She would not have been prepared for a sudden departure; the Porlocks had been expected to stay at the theatre for the evening. Undoubtedly she thought she had ample time. But the master of the house had returned suddenly. Given the noise of the storm and Beatrice's close attention to the tumblers in the safe, she would not have

A BIASED JUDGEMENT

heard them till it was too late. Likely she was so close to victory that she continued with the task even after she knew the risk.

Of course, I could not know that, but it fit with my knowledge of the woman.

And what of the safe? Had she succeeded in opening it? Yes, she must. The papers were gone and the safe stood open. If she had failed and simply fled Porlock might well have let her go, had her arrested. Or had he taken the documents and his family and left the country? No. he fired a shot after her.

I felt a wave of nausea flow through me. Oh God, if he hit her... no, don't think of that. Think about the events as they unfolded. What next? Think, man!

He fired a shot. It was dark, wet, chances are the shot went wild. She would have relied upon that to help her. What next?

If she had the documents she would have fled, knowing her life was not worth a moment's purchase. She might have waved down a cab – no. Considering the difficulty Watson and I had in finding a hansom it was unlikely in the extreme that Beatrice would have been so lucky to find one at the exact right moment. No, she would have made for the park. There was plenty of cover there and she might hide easily enough. And Billy... Yes, Billy, good lad, would have seen the whole thing. He would have helped the lady to safety.

But that was... almost three hours ago. Where were they now? Had Porlock chased after them? Yes, I had the maid's word that that was exactly what he had done. And with the dogs too. No, don't think of that. Had he found them? Billy is resourceful and with no one else to think of I have no doubt that he could look after himself. But Beatrice... a gentlewoman hardly used to running around the city... no, she was used to dressing as a boy and doing who knew what... She was resourceful and far better equipped to handle the situation than any other of her sex or station.

So... another look outside. There was little enough to see: the rain had taken care of all the traces. The drainpipe listed at an alarming angle and I reasoned that a person climbing down would have fallen into the holly bushes. Her gown would be torn and she would have tears in her skin from those thorns. Out here in the cold in this endless downpour with a dangerous man, an armed dangerous man with those savage dogs, looking for her. And she without coat or money or any form of defence other than her wits and a boy.

I released a breath I did not even realise I'd been holding. No, those were good odds. I'd stack Beatrice's wits and Billy's resourcefulness against a great many threats.

By the time I finished, Watson had sent the maid to bed. "We'll find her, old man," he said. "Not to worry."

I shook my head, unable to find words. He squeezed my shoulder and though I cannot begin to say why, I found comfort in the gesture.

Watson said, "Did you want to call Lestrade? Put them on the alert for Porlock?"

"I sent Stevens to Mycroft. I need to start looking. She went into the park; I'm sure of it."

"All right, so we shall start there."

"No, Watson, I shall start on the park, I need you to wait here for Stevens."

"That's an awfully big park for one man alone, Holmes. I can help."

"You are. You are helping, my dear friend. Stay here for Stevens. I doubt it shall be very long. He understands our need for haste. Then I need you to take the carriage and make a complete circuit of the park. I very much doubt she will be on any of the roads, but I cannot completely discount the possibility.

"Once you've done that, go back to Baker Street and see if she has made her way there."

"You do not think she would she head for Wimpole Street?" Watson asked.

"She is being hunted by a dangerous and armed man. She has papers that I am most anxious to have. No, she will go to Baker Street. I'd stake my reputation on it."

"So what should I do if she's not there?"

"See if you can find any of the Irregulars – they should be sleeping down by McClancy's – and send them here in the carriage. They can help me search the park. As to yourself," I looked into his kind and worried face. "Get to bed. You look done in."

He frowned at me. "And leave you to search alone? You know that's not going to happen, don't you? I'll get my service revolver and come straight back."

Good, solid, reliable Watson! "Your service revolver?" I asked.

"You said there's an armed and desperate man at loose. Not to mention those blasted hounds. Best we should be prepared."

"Well, Porlock is probably on his way to one of the ports. Still, best be prepared. Meet me at the park's main gate at—" I checked my watch. "Three am."

He took off for Baker Street and I sprinted into the park and began my search.

25

I called out Beatrice's name, Billy's name as I made a circuit around the howling park. The wind and the rain seemed to be conspiring against me and I doubted anyone would have heard me even if they'd been only a few feet away. Still, I worked my way systematically along the periphery and slowly began to work in towards the middle.

The rain continued to pour down and even with my sou'wester I was drenched. The thoughts of what Beatrice must be like in no more than a gown I did not care to think.

They would not have stayed here, in the park, at least not for long. They would have made their way back up the road and towards Baker Street. Given it had been several hours, it was almost three o'clock, they would surely be long gone by now.

I headed back up to the gate and arrived just in time to see Watson alight from the carriage with three of the Irregulars.

"Well, boys," I said. "I am sorry to wake you so early, but I assure you I will see you all well paid for your trouble."

"Usual rate, Mr 'olmes?" Tommy asked.

"Double the usual rate," I said. "Given the hour and the weather. And a guinea bonus to the boy who finds the lady."

They exchanged excited looks and were eager to start looking.

"Now, Tommy, I'm putting you in charge until Billy can be found. Start here in the park, but they may have left and started back towards Baker Street. Given they were being hunted by a dangerous man, I think they may have sought shelter somewhere along the way. Somewhere to wait out the storm."

A BIASED JUDGEMENT

"I know a couple of places they might have gone, Mr 'olmes," Tommy said. "I'll send Albert. He's quick and he's well known in all those haunts."

"Excellent. I shall try the side streets starting on Adolphus Road. We shall meet at... six a.m. where Camden Road meets York Road. You all have your whistles? Excellent. The usual drill if you find anything."

For the next hour and a half Stevens drove Watson and me through the wretched streets of Islington with no success. Just after five the rain finally stopped falling but left a sodden, dispirited world behind. We searched side streets, back alleys and every inch of the neighbourhood. But the Seven Sisters Road is almost five miles from Baker Street as the crow flies. The truth was, she could be anywhere.

At six we all rendezvoused as arranged but there was no news, nothing to work with. Albert returned and had nothing to report.

I would have continued regardless but I could see Watson was on his last legs. Stevens aided where he could, but he, too, was exhausted.

"Very well," I said. "Let us return to Baker Street, Watson. We shall get some sleep and start again later. Tommy, you and the boys keep looking. Get the rest of the Irregulars to help."

"Still double rate, Mr 'olmes?"

"Yes, yes. Send the lads to all the hiding places, even places you would not expect a lady to go. Off with you!"

I felt a cad for keeping Watson out the whole wretched night. Stevens went to stable the horse, and then returned to take his usual spot on the sofa.

"I hope I did all right, Mr Holmes," he said when he returned. "But I saw a cabby I know from the stables and I asked him to pass the word on to the others in his trade to keep an eye out for her ladyship. Mrs Holmes, I should say."

"Excellent," I said. "That was a first-rate notion, Stevens, well done."

He beamed.

A BIASED JUDGEMENT

"Let us all try to get some sleep," I said. "We shall start again at... let us say two o'clock."

"That doesn't allow much time for sleep, Holmes," Watson said trying not to sound too miserable.

Reluctantly I said, "Yes, all right. Make it four."

Watson went to bed. I bathed and sat sleepless in my bedroom. The newspapers were worthless. Not that I'd been expecting anything, but part of me had hoped.

December 5th, 1897

I wrote my journal and then dozed for a short while. At last, troubled by grotesque nightmares, I rose, dressed and went out.

Lestrade knows me well enough not to ask any unfortunate questions. "We'll find the lady, never fear," he said. "It's an awfully large area, but every man is on the alert. We'll take proper care of the lady when we find her." He put his hand consolingly on my shoulder. "We will find her, Mr Holmes. It's only a matter of time."

Another man who thinks I need comforting.

I took a cab back to Islington and found a couple of Irregulars searching the more unseemly parts of the area. They had nothing to report but as I was about to return to the search, young Albert came and found me.

"Mr 'olmes, sir," he said, panting. "I was about to send to Baker Street to find you."

"What is it?" I asked. "Have you news?"

"We left Kevin in the park, Mr 'olmes. Searched every square inch of it, 'e did. Found this in the bandstand." He handed me a torn piece of black cloth obviously ripped from the gown such as a governess would wear. It was sodden but still sticky with blood.

And right through the middle was a bullet hole.

"'ere, you best sit down, Mr 'olmes. You look proper green."

I was really getting irked by so much solicitation.

"Where is Kevin now?" I demanded.

A BIASED JUDGEMENT

"Still in the park, sir. He's very thorough, Mr 'olmes. If there's aught to be found, Kevin's the one to find it."

I left the boy abruptly and ran back up the road to the park, pushing my way past startled gentlemen taking their morning walks, and governesses tending to their charges. Governesses... no, I had to focus.

I found Kevin just a few hundred feet from the bandstand.

"Where did you find this, lad?" I said. "Show me."

I examined the corner of the bandstand the boy indicated. There really wasn't much to be seen, except under the wooden seat that curved around the perimeter of the structure there was evidence of blood. I knelt down and examined the ground beneath the seat where the rain had not washed away the signs. There was blood here. Yes. A fair amount I thought. I followed the very faint traces of footsteps. Two sets: a woman and a boy. Yes, just as I had thought. The woman's footsteps were weak and uneven: the boy was supporting her, then. So she was hurt sufficiently to need to lean on him. Dear God...

No! Stop! That will avail nothing. Think, man!

Right... At least she was walking. Unsteadily, it is true. She had been shot; she had lost quite a bit of blood, but she was still able to walk. Good. Hold on to that.

But where was she? With the storm and the darkness, they could have hidden in the park for some time undetected. Of course, for every moment they stayed there she lost yet more blood. What did Billy do? He might have left her and run to get help... but where? None of the usual safe houses reported seeing him. Besides, he wouldn't have left her there alone and bleeding. No, he'd have stayed with her. Good lad, Billy. Solid. Dependable.

Right then, he would have stayed with her. They found shelter of sorts in the bandstand but it was too open and exposed. They knew it was not safe. Probably they could hear the dogs barking. The rain may have obscured enough of her scent.

They stayed long enough for Billy to check the wound and give whatever first aid he could... in the night, in a storm, with no instruments. No, they tore the garment. It was Beatrice who did that. She would have exposed the wound so Billy could treat it, and she had left the fabric for me, to let me know she was still alive.

Probably they had used some of the torn fabric to make a tourniquet and sling? It wouldn't do much beyond slow the bleeding and perhaps ease the pain a little.

O God, was she in much pain?

Stop that. Think!

I worked in a circumference around the bandstand but there was nothing to see. The rain had obliterated all traces.

Kevin was watching me with a distressed look on his face. "I'm really sorry, Mr 'olmes."

I forced a smile. "You've done excellent work, Kevin. This is the first evidence we have that she and Billy were here. Here's some money. Go get something to eat. Take the other boys with you. We'll start again in an hour."

"Cor, thanks, Mr 'olmes!"

The boy scuttled away, and I sat in the bandstand thinking. What did Billy do? What would I have done? Cut through the park and tried to get as far away from Seven Sisters as possible. All right, yes. But they were gone – I checked my watch – fifteen hours.

I walked back along the side streets and the back roads around Islington. I do not even know what I was looking for. Not even I could see traces the deluge had washed away. No, there must be reason. If only I could think.

The only possible solution was they had either taken shelter somewhere, an empty house perhaps, or had managed to get a ride on a cart. Yes, that was likely. There weren't too many cabs about last night, but there would still have been the odd cart making deliveries or conducting the business of trade. So supposing they did that... the driver might not even know he'd picked up a couple of passengers. And Beatrice and Billy wouldn't have cared where they were heading as long as it took them away from the danger area. Yes. That was very

A BIASED JUDGEMENT

likely. Good. Now the only problem was to figure out where they had ended up. And that was when my pretty theory hit a brick wall. There was no way of knowing. There were far too many variables for me to anticipate. The only comforting thing about the theory was it explained, at least in part, why we had not yet found any traces of them. There was, of course, a far more sinister explanation, but I refused to acknowledge it. After all, if Porlock had found them all was lost and there was nothing I could do save avenge their deaths.

No, I had to believe they were safe and proceed under that assumption. Yet I wondered why, once they were safe and secure from the area of danger, they did not attempt to contact me. Surely they could have alerted a policeman and asked for help. But they had not done so. Why?

I realised it was almost four o'clock so I hurried back to Baker Street.

Watson still looked fatigued but he was dressed and ready to continue our search.

"There you are, Holmes," he greeted me. "We've just had some interesting news."

"News? Well?" I demanded, more sharply than I ought.

Stevens said, "I went around to get the horse ready, Mr Holmes and one of the cabbies told me that he was on the Seven Sisters last night around ten or so. He saw a young woman and a boy hurrying up the road. He thought it odd because the young lady had no coat and they were right in the middle of the roadway."

"In the middle..? Did he not stop to offer them a fare?"

"He already had a fare, sir, or I've no doubt he'd have done so. After he dropped off his passenger he turned back but the two were gone."

"I see. Thank you."

"I'll bring the carriage around if you're ready to leave, sir."

"Thank you, Stevens. Please do."

After he left I stood at the window looking out at the muddy street.

A BIASED JUDGEMENT

"At least we know she got away from the park, Holmes," Watson said.

I nodded. "Yes, that's something. You look done in, Watson. I really think it would be best if you stayed here. I have the Irregulars on the job. To be frank, I do not think there is much we can do."

"Can I be of assistance?"

"Of course! You know how much I rely upon you. But I would be a poor friend indeed if I let you wreck your health—"

"And I would be a poor friend if I let you go through this alone. Anyway, we have a stop to make."

"A stop?"

"I'll tell you in the carriage."

Stevens was waiting for us. Baker Street was its busy, bustling self again and horses, carriages and people hurried by. One of the new motorised cabs hissed and spat up the street, frightening the horses and causing amazed stares from onlookers. Soon all our traffic will be replaced with motorised vehicles. Well, at least we won't have to step over manure...

"Manure," I cried.

"I beg your pardon?" Watson looked not only surprised but a little repulsed by my outburst.

"It's why they were walking down the middle of the street. They were walking through the manure in order to throw the dogs off their scent. This woman, Watson, this woman!"

For some reason that realisation lifted my spirits as little had. A woman of such intelligence must be a match for a wretch like Albrecht Porlock. So I told myself.

As we left Baker Street Watson told me news of a potentially more enlightening sort. Lestrade had paid a visit.

"Lestrade? Did he have news? What did he say?"

"He had a report from Billingsgate Markets of a couple of stowaways on a delivery lorry. The officer who investigated didn't think much of it. There was no sign of the people concerned and he

A BIASED JUDGEMENT

wouldn't have mentioned at all, except Lestrade had sent very particular word out to all the stations in the city."

"Oh well done, well done indeed, Lestrade. We are on our way to Scotland Yard now?"

"Yes, I thought you'd like to ask him about it yourself. The officer involved will be at the station too."

"You have done far better than I, Watson, without even leaving our apartment. My entire morning was a waste. No, there was one thing..."

I showed him the bloody sleeve and he examined it closely.

"Well," he observed. "The good news is this looks like part of a sleeve. A wound to the shoulder is unlikely to be life-threatening. She will be in a lot of pain and there will be some blood loss, but she will be all right. We'll find her, Holmes."

And again my shoulder was squeezed sympathetically. Was it merely the fact that Beatrice was my wife that inspired such consideration, or did I appear distressed? I did not ask. I was not sure I wanted to hear the answer.

Lestrade was puffed with pride when we arrived at Scotland Yard. I refused his offer of tea and sat down to listen to the report of the young policeman from the docks.

"Tell me every detail, Constable," I said. "Omit nothing."

"Well, sir, I was on duty last night at the market – Billingsgate Market, that is, sir – and a long, weary night it was. The wind and rain were dreadful and there wasn't so much as a cat out. The weather is raw there on the docks and the stink of fish... "

"Get to the point!" I snapped.

Nervously the young man continued. "Anyway, it was around two o'clock and I was doing my rounds outside the arches. A delivery lorry arrived and I exchanged some words with the driver. He was glad to get in out of the rain, he said. Then he added that he thought he'd picked up a couple of unwanted passengers along the way and said I should keep an eye out. 'Thieves will be glad of an opportunity to slip in here and help themselves,' he said."

A BIASED JUDGEMENT

"He did not look for them himself along the way?"

"No sir, he did not. I did ask him but he said with it being such a raw night he just wanted to finish his round and head home. Can't say as I blame him, sir."

"And you looked for the stowaways?"

"Yes I did, sir. I was very careful and checked every inch of the place. There was no doubt there had been someone on that lorry – you could see where the tarpaulin had been flattened in some places."

Lestrade said, "The market is a very large area and if someone didn't want to be found it would be easy enough to hide."

"It would indeed," I said. "You didn't check the vaults, I suppose?"

"I just shone my torch, but I didn't go down."

"And you did not see anyone during the rest of your watch?"

"No sir."

"Very well. Thank you."

Lestrade led the man outside and spoke to him for a moment, then he returned and said, "He really should have been more thorough, Mr Holmes. We missed an opportunity there."

"Yes, perhaps," I said. "But it is a very large space and hard for one man to find someone if they do not wish to be found. Well, Watson, I think a visit to the market is in order. Are you game?"

"Of course!"

"Do you want me to come with you, Mr Holmes?" Lestrade asked. He seemed torn between enthusiasm to be included and the bane of his duty.

"We would welcome your company, Lestrade, but I should not keep you from your other cases. Thank you again. Good-bye."

At that, Watson and I hurried back to the carriage and set off for the docks. The weather was starting to turn again and the dark clouds rolled over the city turning everything to gloom. At least it was still dry, though it was cold and there was a strong wind.

The stench of the market hit us almost a mile before we reached the place.

A BIASED JUDGEMENT

The building is vast and at that time of day was crowded with fishmongers and customers. I spoke to each of the traders but none of them had seen a woman and a boy.

I led Watson down to the vault. The homeless and disadvantaged often took shelter here, hiding from the elements and the unkindness of the outside world. Today was no exception. A scurry of footsteps greeted us as the occupants hid.

"My name is Sherlock Holmes," I called. "I am looking for someone. I will pay a shilling for good information."

At that, three men and a woman slithered forth from their hiding place. "Show us the money," said the first man.

I jangled the change in my pockets. "Not till you tell me what I want to know."

"What is it, then?" said the woman. "We'll tell you whatever you like."

"There was a woman and a boy came here during the night. She was wearing a black gown and she was injured. The boy is about thirteen years of age, wearing a black pair of trousers and a blue jacket."

"They were here," one of the men said. "Came just after the third bell rang. They hid in the back there. We heard the bobby look about up above and he shone his torch down here but didn't come down."

"And the woman and the boy, are they still here?"

"Naw," the youngest man said. "They slept a bit then left just as the market was starting to open up to the public."

"Did they speak to any of you? Tell you anything."

"She did," an old woman said stepping out of the shadows. "She said I was to give a message to Mr Holmes should he come looking and he'd reward me. That's what she did say."

I appraised the woman and shone my torch onto her face. She seemed genuine enough. While I appraised her, she appraised me in return.

"What did she say? You shall have your reward. All of you. Now, tell me."

A BIASED JUDGEMENT

"She asked if I'd like to make some money. I said I would of course. Then she said I was to keep watch for a Mr Sherlock Holmes. I would know him as a tall, thin gentleman, dressed like a toff. She said likely he'd have another man with him, a stocky chap. That would be you, then," she said to Watson.

He bowed formally. "Your servant, ma'am."

"Well, now, ain't you got nice manners?"

"And the message?"

She thought a moment. "How much is it worth then?"

"Half a crown now. If I find the lady and if she is unhurt another half-crown then."

"Here, here, what about us?" demanded the others.

"A shilling for each of you, as I promised. But now, my good woman, tell me what she said."

"She said to tell you she was all right. That she had the stuff you wanted and was keeping it safe. She said there wasn't no one she could trust and she was going to make her way back to Baker Street but not till after dark... It wasn't true though," the old woman added after a brief pause. "About being all right. She was hurt. She had scratches all over and her gown was torn. She had her arm wrapped up but she was still bleeding and she walked with a limp. The lad – Billy, he said his name was – was right worried about her. He wanted to stay till you got here, but that bobby put the wind up her right proper and she'd have none of it. She said for you to go home and she'd be there soon as she could."

"Thank you, my good woman." I handed her a crown and gave a shilling to each of the others. They cheered and bowed and offered us any other help we might desire.

Watson said, "Come Holmes, we must let the Inspector know we have news. Good day to you."

We hurried back up the steps to the main floor. After the stench of misery in the vaults below it was a relief to breathe even the fishy stink of the market.

A BIASED JUDGEMENT

"Very dangerous waving money about in a place like that, Holmes."

"Calm yourself, Watson. I knew what I was doing. Well, I will say I am very relieved to know they found shelter. I am worried about her being injured though. Is it dangerous for her to have lost a lot of blood, Watson? Tell me truthfully."

"It's not good, Holmes. If she loses too much blood, she could pass out..."

"She could die."

"Yes. But she was still well enough to walk around this morning and she had tied off the wound. She's a bright girl, Holmes. She said she'll meet us at Baker Street; I have no doubt she will. Indeed, she may be waiting for us already."

She was not waiting for us. We were greeted at the door by a very unhappy Mrs Hudson. She shook her head at the sight of me and Watson – you'd think she'd be used to us by now – and handed me a note. Mycroft had called and left word that he had men placed at every port from Scotland to Cornwall. No sign of our prey yet, but it was only a matter of time.

As soon as Watson and Stevens had eaten supper, I asked our reliable coachman to return to Scotland Yard and tell Lestrade to call off the search.

"Are you sure, Holmes?" Watson said. "It might be helpful to have someone keep an eye out. After all, she is hurt and it won't be easy for her to get back here."

"I know, Watson. Don't you think I know?"

"Then why?"

"Use your head, man! She cowered in that vault when a policeman came by. Why didn't she ask him for help?"

"I don't know. I hadn't thought of that. Why didn't she, Holmes?"

"Because those papers she took from Porlock's safe undoubtedly list some members of her majesty's police force as members of that vile organisation. Beatrice cannot be sure who to trust and so she will trust none of them."

A BIASED JUDGEMENT

"Good gracious, Holmes, surely men who have sworn to protect the people of this island couldn't be in league with such evil. And yet I cannot deny the likelihood of what you say. But it means something else too – it means that Lady Beatrice is able to concentrate on reading and is able to reason. That's encouraging."

"Do you want me to bring any message to your brother, Mr Holmes?" Stevens asked.

"Yes, thank you, Stevens. I would be obliged if you would update my brother on everything we have learned so far. Then return here, if you would."

He hurried off. I stood at the window and looked down into the dark street. New rain battered down and the road was awash. In the distance, in the direction of the river, there was a lightning flash and a roll of thunder. Even supposing my wife had been well enough to read and reason at Billingsgate, that was seven hours ago. How much blood had she lost in the interim? Why did she not come? The storm covered the city in darkness. Surely she could have found a cab to take her here. Did she doubt me? No, of course she didn't. She had known I would trace her to the vaults and had taken care to leave me word. No, she had done admirably to this point. I needed to have faith that she would continue to justify my belief in her.

December 6th, 1897

The wind has died and the house no longer rattles. Outside, the street is silent, save the drips and splashes of the steady rain. Night is upon us.

And still she has not come.

Watson ought to be in bed but he will not leave me.

"Why don't you at least lie down, Holmes?" he says. "I can sit up and wait if you like. You're fairly done in."

"I couldn't sleep, Watson. But don't let me keep you up; you haven't had as much rest as you ought. I have already compromised the health of one of my friends; I will be damned if I harm the other."

A BIASED JUDGEMENT

"Come, you make too much of it," Watson said. "Your wife is an intelligent and resourceful woman. If anyone can survive these difficult nights it is she. She'll come. Before the night is out, I'm sure she'll come. She gave her word, Holmes."

I have never known such agonising indecision.

Beatrice promised to come to Baker Street so I ought to be here to greet her, but why does she take so long? Is she hurt? In danger? Should I go and search the streets once more? No, the Irregulars are scouring the city. They can cover more ground than one man alone. And what if she comes just minutes after I leave?

So I sit and I wait. Watson fell asleep in the armchair half an hour ago and his snores are now forming a beat to Stevens' own nocturnal noises.

I am still here, still sitting by the window looking out into the street, jumping at the sound of every carriage that passes. There are few enough at this hour. All I hear is the rain, not so intense now, but constant, and the chimes of the interminably passing hours.

Around three o'clock I could stand it no more. I put on my coat and was headed down the stairs when a knock came to the front door. I fled to answer it. There stood Tommy, wet through and weary.

"I found them, sir," he said. "You'd better come."

Half way down Baker Street, I thought I should have brought Watson, but I couldn't bring myself to disturb another night's sleep for the poor man. No. She was found. All would be well.

She was in Park Square West. I would not have recognised her. Billy sat on the grass holding her in his arms. He was shivering uncontrollably.

"Well done, boys, well done indeed!" I cried.

I knelt down and called her name. Her eyes opened and after a moment focused. She managed a smile and said, hoarsely, "Dear Sherlock... I knew you'd find me."

I picked her up and carried her. The two Irregulars trailed behind.

A BIASED JUDGEMENT

"Tommy," I said. "See if you can find a cab. It's not a long way, but Billy can't walk much further, I think."

"Yes, sir," said the boy and he scurried off. We continued to walk back towards Baker Street, I carrying my exhausted and drenched wife in my arms. I swaddled my coat around her and held her close to me. I could feel ice where her cheek touched mine, and my heart failed.

Tommy flagged down a cab and we all bundled in. Beatrice's head rested on my shoulder and I found myself utterly mute in the face of her heroism.

Back at Baker Street, Watson and Mrs Hudson, roused by the sound of our arrival, sprang into action at once. The boys were dried by aggressive parlour maids; soup was heated; clean, dry clothes found; and then the boys were bundled up to sleep in Mrs Hudson's parlour.

I carried Beatrice into my bedroom and lay her upon my bed. Watson and Mrs Hudson tutted in there for some time while I, a mere husband, was forced to wait outside for news.

After several minutes, Mrs Hudson came out holding the relics of my wife's tattered garments in her hands. "Only fit for burning," she muttered and I am not sure if she meant the gown or me.

Still I was not allowed into the room. I paced the living room. Stevens said, "Let me pour you a brandy, Mr Holmes. Come now, you'll do her no good like this."

"No," I said. "Thank you, but no... I need to call Mycroft."

The hall was cold and I realised belatedly that I was still in my soaked coat. After an age, Mycroft's landlady answered and a few minutes later my brother came to the phone.

"We found her," I said. "That is, the boys did... She's badly hurt, Mycroft..."

"And the papers? Does she have the papers..? Sherlock?"

"I didn't think to look," I admitted. "She didn't have anything in her hands." I closed my eyes, remembering. "No, nothing..."

"Damnation," he said. "That is... unfortunate. All right, thank you for letting me know, Sherlock, though it could probably have waited for

A BIASED JUDGEMENT

a more civilized hour. Never mind, I'll stop by in the morning. Perhaps she managed to read some of the documents and maybe remember something of significance. Well, I'm going back to bed for a bit. Tell her... well, thank her for trying."

As I set down the receiver I found myself shaking with fury at my brother's indifference to Beatrice's sufferings.

Back upstairs, Stevens put a brandy in my hand and, to appease him, I drank it. I felt it warm me and I said, "Thank you, Stevens. That has helped."

"Let's get you out of that wet coat, too, Mr Holmes." He began to unbutton the soggy garment even as he spoke. He said brightly, "I've known Lady Beatrice all my life, sir, and I can tell you for a fact, there's no one stronger. She fell off her horse when she was twelve and broke her arm. She never made a word of complaint, not for all the nasty treatments they put her through. She'll recover from this too, and faster than you can imagine. Now, let's change those wet shoes for some slippers. There, that's better, isn't it? Let me see if I can build this fire up a bit."

He continued to prattle as he worked and I found myself soothed by the steady drone of his cheerful voice. A moment later my bedroom door opened and Mrs Hudson summoned me to my wife's side.

I winced to see Beatrice lie so pale and so still upon the bed.

My friend closed up his bag. "Watson?" I whispered.

"Don't keep her talking for long, she's been through a horrendous ordeal."

"She will be all right?"

He frowned and said, "Your wife has lost a great deal of blood. I've stitched up the shoulder wound and dressed it. She also has a fractured bone in her ankle; I've bound that up too. She's in pain, and has been exposed to the elements. She needs a lot of rest, good food and a great deal of care. But yes, in time she should make a complete recovery. Be very gentle with her, Holmes. Her only fear is disappointing you." It

A BIASED JUDGEMENT

seemed like he would have said more but he did not. Instead he went to join Stevens in the living room and left me alone with my wife.

I sat at her bedside and said her name. At last her eyes opened.

"Well, husband," she said. "I've made a bit of a mess of things. I'm sorry. I'm so sorry…" She bit her lip, but tears still spilled down her pale cheeks.

"Hush, now," I said. "It's not as bad as all that. I was a cad for asking you to take such a risk."

"No," she said. "You trusted me. You trusted me with something important… you cannot know what a compliment that is."

"You did very well. It was a fearful thing to do, to enter the house of one of the most dangerous men in Europe. As to the papers, if you could not save them…"

"But I did," she said. "They're over there, on the dresser."

"What? You saved them? But how..? You had nothing in your hands when I found you."

"I took a leaf from Liz Derby's book and had a shift made for the very purpose of carrying the papers. I must say it worked well."

"Very well. But you have been extraordinarily successful. Why do you say you failed?"

"Because if I hadn't been so clumsy, so precipitous, you would have been able to arrest him. Instead, I suspect he managed to flee. Now he can continue his evil work."

"Not so, not without these papers. And we shall track him, never fear. You really have done extraordinarily well. Sleep now, and dream only good things."

"Good night, my dear," she said. Then, "Holmes…"

"Yes?"

"Don't let the queen know what I've been up to."

I chuckled. "You have my word. Now, sleep. Good night, my good wife." And I sat in the chair at her bedside and watched while she slept.

26

Beatrice slept. Once she cried out but I spoke to her and she fell asleep more restfully. Watson came in, urged me to rest, but I shooed him away.

While she slept I went through Porlock's documents. There were letters, passports, lists, timetables, blueprints, and his diary.

There were names here, important names that would shake the very foundation of the empire when their owners were arrested. Police officials, too. Lestrade would have his work cut out for him, but the arrests would earn him great credit. No wonder Beatrice had hidden from the policeman in Billingsgate.

Three more assassinations are planned over the next six months. If successful, entire nations could topple. Indeed, the face of Europe could become unrecognisable.

Mycroft whistled as he read page after page. "No wonder he was so careful about keeping strangers out of his home. Your young wife has done this nation an extraordinary service, Sherlock. Some of these men hold positions of great power. This chap is a close friend of the Prime Minister's." His lips tightened and I could almost pity those men who would feel the full brunt of his anger.

"Take a look at Porlock's diary entry for November 26th."

He did so and smiled. "You have to admire a man who keeps his diary in Latin... Ah, so Summerville agreed to poison the queen's food. Ah, *mortifer albino mos operor officium:* The deadly albino will do the job. Not very elegant Latin... So that's his backup plan. He doesn't seem very confident of Summerville, does he?"

A BIASED JUDGEMENT

"With good reason. Daisy telephoned Beatrice's Wimpole Street house on the day before yesterday to say the Summervilles have all disappeared. Beatrice's butler called Mrs Hudson but she forgot to mention it until this morning."

"That was Thursday morning? So their flight had nothing to do with Porlock's discovery?"

"Their flight was discovered on Thursday morning, but I suspect they left some time Wednesday night. No, there seems to be no connection to Porlock. Not directly, anyway. I think Wallace Summerville is fleeing him and the terrible agreement he made. The lot of them fled with no word for the staff, and no wages either."

"Well, let them go. I hope for his sake he escapes Porlock's clutches. That man has a well-developed sense of vengeance, I think… Something about this amuses you. What is it, Sherlock?"

"Just that they left without the butler, Reynolds. I'm sure that will put his nose out of joint. As for this organisation, I fear we have missed our opportunity in arresting them. No doubt Porlock will have sent word to his underlings and sent them scattering far and wide."

"I do not think so. I believe his only thought was for himself. Frobisher was in the office first thing this morning as usual and I see from these records that he is a key figure in this organisation. If he is unaware of his danger you may be sure the others are too. Well, these letters and the other documents will see them all hang. And I have no doubt that once they are arrested, most of them will be happy to talk about their leader's activities. No, we shall have Mr Porlock in our grasp very soon. I shall deal with it, Sherlock. Have no fear. Every port is on heightened security."

I rubbed my eyes with my knuckles. When did I last sleep a full night in a proper bed? I can't remember. "Yes," I said. Then, "You know, Mycroft, I keep thinking about Mortimer Granger."

"Who?"

A BIASED JUDGEMENT

"The artist who was murdered with his wife in Notting Hill. He also had a side line in forgery. These passports Beatrice found in Porlock's safe are undoubtedly his work."

Mycroft studied the documents. "Forgeries, indeed. All for different countries, and all with different names. But I'm not sure I take your point."

"Porlock kept all his passports in that safe, Mycroft. Getting out of the country without one will prove difficult. However…"

"…However, he doesn't need a passport to go to Ireland. And from there, he can have one of his allies send him a replacement."

"Which means…"

"…Which means we can focus our attention on ports used by Irish ferries. Excellent! I shall send out word at once." He glanced at his pocket watch. "This shall keep me busy for quite some time, Sherlock. I'd better be off."

"Do you need my assistance?"

"You have done enough, my dear brother, you look quite exhausted. Get some rest and take care of that wife of yours. She should be given the Royal Victorian Medal for her work. Your place is at her side."

"We do not have that sort of marriage…" I began, then let it drop. Instead I said, "Beatrice does not want her involvement in this matter made known. The queen would undoubtedly disapprove her activities."

He rose and smoothed his jacket over his enormous belly. "No? No, I suppose not. Very well, Sherlock, I shall keep the secret." He smiled. "It's what I do best, after all. Keep secrets."

"What shall you do next? Arrest Frobisher?"

"Sending word to the docks is my first task, then, yes, Frobisher. The risk to the queen remains until the Albino is found. Possibly Frobisher may be willing to give us some idea where we may find him. I want to review these documents thoroughly before I start the arrests, and I want to make sure they are all coordinated so no one escapes. It probably won't be until this evening that we are ready to act. I shall aim

A BIASED JUDGEMENT

for six pm. You're welcome to attend my questioning of the wretch, Sherlock."

"Thank you, I should like to be there. And I think Watson has the right to attend also."

"Well... yes, if you like. He's a solid sort of chap. It would be no harm for Frobisher to see what a true, honest man looks like. I'll send word if there are any changes, Sherlock, but if you don't hear from me I shall see you at Whitehall at six. Thanks again to you and your wife."

"And when you find Porlock..."

"I shall call you at once."

"How are our guests, Mrs Hudson?" I asked.

She wrinkled her nose. "Nothing a bath wouldn't cure, Mr Holmes," she said. "But they're good lads for all that."

They all jumped to attention as soon as I came into the little parlour. Even Billy, though he was a mere shade of the boy he usually was.

"Well, boys," I said. "I hope you're all being well looked after?"

"Very well, Mr 'olmes," Tommy said.

"Smashing grub Mrs 'udson makes, Mr 'olmes," said Kevin.

"Well you have all done exceptionally well. Here are your wages." I handed them a fistful of riches, with the lion's share going to Billy.

"Cor," Tommy said. "Thanks awfully, Mr 'olmes."

"I shall ask Mrs Hudson to give you dinner before you leave, and then I have another job for you, if you are interested."

Billy said, "Thanks, Mr 'olmes, but do you mind if Tommy and the others do it? Only I've not been 'ome in days and me old mum'll be that worried."

"You've done all I could ask, Billy. Of course you must go home, but get something to eat first. As for the rest of you boys..."

"Count us in, Mr 'olmes."

"I need a man found. The Albino. You know who I mean? On no account approach him, just let me know if you find him. I shall be here

A BIASED JUDGEMENT

until about half-five, then I shall be at Whitehall. Send word for me there if you spot the creature."

I doubt they shall succeed, but it's worth trying.

Beatrice woke a short while after Mycroft left and with help from Mrs Hudson was able to eat some food. Then she fell back asleep.

"Are you sure this is normal, Watson?" I asked later. "I know she did not sleep when she was fleeing Porlock, but she seems so weak."

"She's lost a considerable amount of blood, Holmes," Watson said. "That has debilitated her. Besides which the amount of pain medication I gave her has made her very drowsy. Sleep is what she needs. It wouldn't do you any harm either."

"I'm perfectly sound," I said.

"No you're not. Your nerves are all afire and you're worn out from the past few days. Why do you not take my bed for a few hours? I might stretch out on the sofa for a spell myself."

"That makes no sense," I protested. "Why should you be uncomfortable? Besides, what is Stevens to do?"

"I sent Stevens to meet Daisy and Miss Simms at the station and take them to Wimpole Street. They shall stay there for the moment. Your wife can make other arrangements if she wishes when she recovers, but this is the best solution for the moment. As for the sofa, well, you are much taller than I am. You really need to sleep in a bed."

"Yes, it is good to send Stevens back to Beatrice's house. As soon as she is well enough, she will undoubtedly want to return home… As for my sleep: I'll not leave Beatrice's side in any case," I said. "It is the least I can do. I can doze here in the armchair while she sleeps. I would not want her to waken and need something… go get some rest, Watson. I promise to call if I need you."

"This isn't your fault, Holmes. It's unfortunate, but there is no lasting harm done. You must not blame yourself. I am quite sure she will not."

A BIASED JUDGEMENT

"Regardless, I am responsible. She would not have been in that position were it not for me. In any case, she is lucky that shot did not find a more vulnerable target than her shoulder." I stopped, afraid to say more. There were and are deep feelings there I neither recognise nor trust.

Watson frowned, then said, "Very well, I shall go lie down for a spell. I do not like it, but I can see there is no arguing with you. Do please call me if the lady needs any medical attention. I shall see you later, Holmes."

"Sleep well, Watson."

It was just a little after noon. Our erratic activity over the past few days had worn us out. I sat back in the armchair and in the space of a few minutes fell asleep.

Still yawning, Watson and I arrived at Mycroft's office at five minutes to six. The door to the building was locked but Gillespie admitted us and then locked it again.

"Mr Holmes's orders, sir," he said.

He nodded at two burly security men. They took their position in front of the locked door. They and Gillespie himself were all armed.

I glanced at Watson and had a glimpse of the soldier he had once been: John Bull personified. Of all the strange, horrifying and deadly crimes we have handled, nothing stung his heart as deeply as treason.

Gillespie led us, not to Mycroft's office, but to a large meeting room at the back of the building. Its tall, barred windows were shuttered. The gas was lit and threw sickly green light onto all our pale faces. Four burly men stood at attention and two others sat at a long table. The seated men were my brother and the Prime Minister.

"Have a seat, gentlemen," Mycroft said. "I believe you know everyone, Sherlock?"

"I do. We are ready to proceed?"

"We are. Lestrade, Gregson, Bradstreet and all the other best of Scotland Yard are acting…" The clock chimed six and he said, "Now.

A BIASED JUDGEMENT

"Mr Gillespie, if you will be so good as to ask Mr Frobisher to join me here for a conference. Tell him I apologise for the lateness of the hour but a matter of extreme importance needs to be addressed. Do not let him see that you are armed. But if he resists..."

"He won't resist, Mr Holmes. Thinks me a doddering old fool. Young pup."

Gillespie left and we sat in silence. Waiting.

A few moments later we heard footsteps coming down the hallway and the low, easy tones of Gillespie's voice. Frobisher laughed. The door opened.

"Come in, Frobisher," Mycroft said.

The man turned a ghastly colour, like candle wax. He turned and would have fled, but Gillespie had his pistol drawn and pointed at his temple.

"Sit," Mycroft said. "Gillespie, will you see no one enters this room?"

Gillespie nodded and left, shutting the door softly behind him.

Frobisher swallowed and forced himself to walk the three paces to the table. Once he was seated the four large men stood behind him.

"Best to make a clean breast of it," Mycroft said.

"I don't know—"

"No, no. Lying will accomplish nothing. We already know, you see." Mycroft indicated the documents that spread out before him like a ruinous poker hand. "Letters in your own handwriting; diary entries by your friend Porlock: it's all here. You have nothing to say? No explanation? Vindication?"

"Lies... I never..."

"Enough!" Mycroft's hand slammed down on the table and thundered through the room. The Prime Minister jumped and dropped his fountain pen. It bounced on the table and made a low grumbling noise as it rolled across the walnut.

"Do not play me for a fool," Mycroft said, his voice adding a new layer of chill to the cold room. "There is no question you will be found guilty of treason and will face the hangman before the year ends. However, I may be able to help you if you tell me what you know about the plot against the queen."

"Your time is over, Mr Mycroft Holmes," Frobisher hissed, abandoning all pretence. "You and your filthy empire will come tottering down. It's you that doesn't have much time left. Even now my friends are putting plans in motion to destroy more monarchs than your stupid old woman."

"How dare you!" Watson cried. I put a restraining hand on his shoulder without which, I fear, he would have lunged across the table and throttled the wretch.

I said, more calmly than I felt, "If you mean Bradley, Purfroy, Chambers and the others, they are being taken into custody even at this moment. Your new world order will have to wait a while."

"Take him down, gentlemen," Mycroft said.

Two of the men pulled him to his feet and all but dragged him to the door. As one of them opened it Frobisher turned suddenly and cried, "Death to you all!" He drew a dagger from inside his jacket and would have hurtled it towards the Prime Minister, I think, but Gillespie, sharper than four men who were less than half his age, knocked it from Frobisher's hand and held him at the point of a pistol. At that, the traitor began to scream threats and evil predictions. The door closed behind him and his voice grew steadily fainter until at last we could not hear it any more.

"Villain," Watson said, pocketing the revolver I had not even seen him draw. He was, quite literally, shaking in fury.

"I think we could all use a drink," the Prime Minister said. "Mr Holmes?"

"I agree," Mycroft said. He rose and went to a cabinet in the corner and poured a glass for each of us.

"A pity he would not be more forthcoming," Mycroft said as he sipped his brandy. "Not that I expected it."

A BIASED JUDGEMENT

The Prime Minister downed his drink and said, "I must get back. You'll keep me informed of the evening's events?"

"Of course."

Over the next four hours reports came in from all over the kingdom as policemen, magistrates, and public officials were arrested. Two-hundred-and-forty-two arrests were made on charges ranging from corruption to high treason.

On the continent, too, a further twenty-six anarchists and would-be assassins were arrested in Spain, Italy and Germany.

By the end of it, of the leaders only Porlock remained at large.

Poor Watson could hardly sit upright in the cab by the time we reached Baker Street. It was almost midnight and neither of us had slept sufficiently in several days.

"If you want my bed—" he began.

"I thought we'd settled that argument. Go get some sleep, Watson. I shall stay with my wife."

She did not stir when I went into the bedroom. Her colour was slightly improved, I thought. I sat in the armchair and pulled a rug around me. I had hardly done so when I fell into a deep sleep.

I was awakened to the sound of a muttered "Damn!"

Beatrice was trying to climb out of bed. I hurried to her side.

"What in the world are you doing?" I said.

"I need to go to the bathroom," she said.

"You must not put any weight on that ankle," I said. Then I picked her up and carried her to the lavatory.

When I put her back in the bed she said, "What time is it?"

I glanced at the clock on the mantle. "A few minutes before two. Did you want anything else?"

"Some water, please."

I poured her a glass and handed it to her.

"Why are you sleeping in the chair? Oh, I have your bed. I'm sorry."

A BIASED JUDGEMENT

"Hush," I said. "You have had a dreadful ordeal. You need your rest."

"I've been a wretched nuisance," she said sharply. "Really, Holmes, how do you put up with me?"

"How do I—?" Then I realised she was teasing me, and I laughed. But the laughter was bitter. "You might have been killed, Beatrice. Can you ever forgive me?"

"My dear Holmes," she said. "You entrusted me with a matter of national importance. You gave me an opportunity to serve my country and you let neither my sex nor my station compromise that. You cannot know what an enormous honour you have done me. Please do not blame yourself. The fault is mine for being clumsy. I could have left that study when I saw the Porlocks return and tried again later. But I had heard them speak of leaving the country for Germany and I was anxious not to miss the opportunity. Then the drainpipe collapsed as I was climbing down it... if it had not been for young Billy I am not sure what I would have done. He all but carried me through the park and helped me hide. I found it difficult to put weight on my ankle."

"I do not wonder. Watson says you broke a bone."

"Ah, that would explain it then," she said, "Please do not be so hard on yourself. Really all that matters is that we have the papers. I hope that means you will be able to put an end to that dreadful organisation for once and for all."

"We have already begun to do so." I told her about the evening's activities and the search for Porlocks.

"I was startled," she said, "to see so many men of influence on that list. And several members of our police forces. It made me reluctant to trust any of them."

"You were wise to be cautious. But come, you must sleep. Watson has given strict orders."

"I cannot sleep while you sit in a chair. Come, there is room enough for two. Oh, don't look so scandalised. We are husband and wife, if a rather unorthodox couple. I dare say we may share a bed without shocking anyone."

She was determined and I did as she bade. And for the rest of the night, we slept in each other's arms. As if our marriage was no different from any other couple's.

27

December 7th, 1897

No word of Porlock. No word of the Albino.

Have I come so far only to fail now?

He cannot have left the country yet. Every port and every vessel is being closely watched. I believe he will be found in either Liverpool or Anglesey. The former is closer and a busier place and the port services ferries to Ireland. On the other hand, Anglesey is much further from the capitol which may make it feel safer. Though it is not as lively as Liverpool, it may be easier for a careful man to keep watch for anyone who may be looking for him. I long to join the hunt but Mycroft wants me to stay in London.

"Other men may not have your wit, Sherlock," he says. "But they are strong and well-prepared to handle any sort of resistance from our Bavarian prey. I should prefer you focus your attentions on the Albino. As long as he remains at large the queen's life is in danger."

"You have seen that all the arrests are being kept quiet? If the Albino gets word that the network has collapsed he may panic. There is no telling what he might do."

"Not a word has been said. From his standpoint everything appears as it ought. The only possible difficulty will be if the assassin is expecting final instructions from Porlock."

"No, Porlock is far too clever to risk implicating himself in that way. I think we may safely assume the Albino has been left to his own devices and will not expect to speak with any of that odious organisation until after the queen is dead." I stood at the window of his office looking down at the Thames. It is such a grey dull day, which perfectly suits my mood. "I do not share your faith in the police authorities, Mycroft. It takes only one man to make a mistake and Porlock will escape."

"Even you, my dear brother, cannot be in two places at once," Mycroft said. "You concede finding the Albino is the more urgent problem?"

There are very few people who can best me in an argument, but there's no denying my brother is one of them.

Back at Baker Street my wife continues to sleep for long periods. She refuses the laudanum Watson offers her for the pain and insists she will mend quicker without it. She wants to return to Wimpole Street, and Watson believes she will be more comfortable in her own bed. Well, tomorrow is soon enough.

I am tired but I cannot slow my mind down enough for rest. I long for the quiet of the syringe but I have given my word. Besides, this case is some way from being over.

At two o'clock Watson urged me to go out. "See if the Irregulars have any news, Holmes," he said. "Perhaps go to Windsor to check on their security measures. If nothing else, it will ease your mind."

"And get me out of the way," I said. Even as I spoke I knew I sounded like a petulant child.

Watson didn't take the bait. He said, "I shall stay here and look after your wife. I shall send word to the Castle if there is any news on Porlock or if the Irregulars find the Albino."

I had to admit he had a point. I put on my coat and headed out into an icy fog for the train station.

Bigge was worried. Despite all his protestations, I could see anxiety was carving new lines on his face.

"I confess I had hoped this entire matter would have been resolved by now, Mr Holmes," he said. "The dinner is just tomorrow evening. You and your good wife are attending, I hope."

A BIASED JUDGEMENT

"I shall certainly attend," I said. "But with the queen's permission, I shall bring Dr Watson with me. I'm afraid my wife is unwell and confined to bed."

"Oh, I am sorry to hear it. Her majesty will be disappointed. Still, one must be careful with influenza at this time of year... unless she is confined for a happier reason?"

"No, there is no happy event on the horizon. It's... something quite different."

He gave me a quizzical look and said, "Well, I'm sure there will be no difficulty in bringing Dr Watson. Please send Mrs Holmes my warmest wishes of the season. Let me know if there is anything she needs."

I turned the conversation to the arrangements for tomorrow's event. Since it is for friends and family only, there would not generally be exceptional measures taken. However, in light of the threat to the queen, Windsor's staff have been at pains to review every detail.

"Only invited guests will be attending," Bigge said, handing me the guest list. "It is a small party, as you see."

"And who is handling the catering?"

"The queen's own staff, as usual. All the food will be inspected before it is served."

"What of gifts for the queen?"

"They will be examined by me personally."

I sighed. "I cannot find a flaw in your arrangements, Sir Arthur. I shall arrive early tomorrow morning and conduct my own examination."

"That would be an extraordinary task," Bigge said. "The grounds run to some thirteen acres and the castle itself is 484 thousand square feet."

"And the meal is to be served in the Gothic private dining room?"

"That's correct."

"Well, I shall confine my examination to the Prince of Wales tower."

A BIASED JUDGEMENT

For the next four hours I scoured the building, identifying possible weaknesses. I met with staff and checked every entrance. Although the Castle's Constable and his staff assure me it is impregnable, I have identified three possible means of access. Extra guards shall be placed at each location and yet, and yet...

December 8th, 1897

We have him! A telephone call came from Mycroft just after ten o'clock last night. His agents in Holyhead spotted Porlock and his family in a local hotel. They were presumably waiting until he decided it was safe to travel. He was arrested without difficulty and sent to London on the boat train, flanked by two policemen and a formidable number of army officers. Porlock's wife insisted on returning to the capital with him. They took the night express and so arrived in Euston by half-eight this morning.

Lestrade and Bradstreet were already on the platform, talking with Mycroft. My brother was determined to see that Porlock would not escape. The three greeted Watson and me with considerable warmth, and shook our hands.

"It is a fine piece of work you have done for this nation, Mr Holmes," Bradstreet said. "The gaol cells are stuffed to overflowing."

"They won't be stuffed for long," Lestrade said with a sinister smile. "The hangman will thin their numbers right enough. But my friend Inspector Bradstreet is right enough: this case will make your name, Mr Holmes. Not that you need any more acclaim than your cases have already earned you."

"I cannot take credit for other people's work, Lestrade—" I began then, remembering the need to preserve my wife's secret said, "You and your colleagues and many other people have worked as diligently as I. But as for acclaim, the world must never know any of this. What an embarrassment it would be for the queen and her government."

"It would shake the Empire to its core," Lestrade agreed.

A BIASED JUDGEMENT

"The Empire will never hear of it," I replied. "It is impolitic to make the matter public."

"Indeed," Mycroft said. "And I must ask you, Inspector, to keep what you know to yourself. This is a delicate time for us, politically. It would not do if any foreign agents were alerted to our actions. It is a matter of national security."

Lestrade, puffed with patriotism, replied, "Not a word shall pass my lips, on my honour, Mr Holmes."

Watson blew into his gloves and hopped from foot to foot. It was exceedingly cold on the platform though at least it was not raining at the moment.

"How long till the train gets in?" he asked.

"About ten minutes," I said. "If they are on time."

"They're on time right enough," Bradstreet said. "I checked just before you gentlemen arrived."

And so we stood and we waited while all around us the station bustled with trains arriving and departing; friends and families greeting one another; all of humanity gathering, ebbing and flowing.

"Here she comes," Watson said as the train came into view.

The passengers alighted from the train and merged into the mass of London's populace. Only when the crowd had cleared did the military force arrive. They cordoned off the area and, a few moments later, Albrecht Porlock, manacled and scowling, was bundled off the train onto the platform.

"You!" he hissed. "You have more lives than a cat, pestilence-Holmes."

"Which is more than I can say for you," I replied. "The noose shall finish you once and for all."

"Wait!" he cried as the officers put the manacles on him. "Let me say goodbye to my wife and my children."

"Time enough for that later," Mycroft said. "You can say your farewells from your cell after the judge has pronounced your verdict."

A BIASED JUDGEMENT

He glared at my brother and me. Then, smirking, he said, "A shame my revenge on you was not as thorough as I should like, Mr Holmes. But I have hurt you and I am content with that."

He was carted away, snarling, and flung into the back of the black Maria. On the pavement, his wife and children stood sobbing. Not for the first time, I wondered at man's stupidity.

As soon as the vehicle left, Mycroft, Watson and I began the long and weary journey to Windsor.

We met with Bigge and the Windsor Constable, Lord Lorne, and reviewed again the security details. Their attention to detail was commendable.

Watson and I were led around the Queen's private apartments by Lorne. We examined the queen's private chapel where she attends services every Sunday. It is a monstrously gloomy place, dark, with ugly Gothic designs. Decidedly not to my taste. I can't imagine Her Majesty likes it any better than I; Lorne tells me Sunday service last no more than thirty minutes. Ha! More to the point, however, the chapel is two stories high, with alcoves, a choir loft, and any number of places where a clever man might hide. There is no service today, however, and Lorne was happy to have the chapel locked and sealed.

We spent most of our time reviewing the Gothic-style octagonal dining room. This is a much more pleasant place, painted in a rosy cream and with pilasters decorated with carved gilded oak leaves. The gold plate from George IV is on display and, Lorne tells me, it glitters most delightfully on a sunny day. It being December, however, there was no sun. The gloom seemed to glower inside the castle as much as on the land around it.

There is a heavy chandelier which, I confirmed, is very well secured. Nor is there any way a foe could access the room from the windows.

I am more concerned about the so-called Grand Corridor. It runs some 550 feet and is well-nigh packed with cabinets, corners and heavy drapes, all of which could hide a man.

"This room must be swept by your officers immediately before the queen walks through," I said. "They should check behind the curtains, examine the larger cabinets, and look behind every corner."

"I confess, this is an area that has concerned me, too, Mr Holmes. My wife, Princess Louise, tells me that she and her brothers and sisters often played hide and seek here." He frowned at the expanse of the hallway and added, "It might help, Mr Holmes, if you could tell me something about this man you call the Albino. If we knew who we were looking for…"

"I thought Scotland Yard sent you a photograph of the villain?"

"They did indeed," he said. "But there is more to a man than his face."

"True," I said. "Well, then. He is called The Albino but it is a misnomer. Recent studies suggest true albinism is a result of an absence of pigment in the hair, skin and eyes due to a lack of tyrosinase. However, Archibald Travis is merely extremely pale. His hair was originally brown but turned completely white when he was twelve years old. He has been killing for as long as his hair has been white. He is now twenty-eight, but can look much younger and at least once escaped from a mob by dressing as a schoolboy.

"Despite this apparent youth, he kills with ruthless efficiency. Poison, firearms, the garrotte: he will select his weapon based on the circumstance. His preference, however, is the blade. One of his intended victims, the only survivor, reported that after stabbing him, Travis licked his blood from the blade and said he liked being close enough to inhale his victim's last breath."

Lorne stared at me in horror. "Good God!" he cried. "And this is the villain who means to make an attempt against the queen?"

Watson said, "But Holmes won't let it happen, Lord Lorne."

A BIASED JUDGEMENT

Later, as we walked down the Grand Corridor, the queen said, "I was sorry to hear of your wife's illness, Mr Holmes. Please convey my best wishes for her recovery and for a most pleasant holiday season."

"Thank you, Ma'am," I said. "I shall certainly do so."

"Dr Watson, I have been enjoying your tales of Mr Holmes's adventures for many years now," she said. She was leaning on his arm as we walked to the dining room. I swear I have never seen my friend more proud than he was at that moment.

"You are very kind, Your Majesty," he replied.

The Queen nodded towards the guards who flanked the hallway at regular intervals. "I seems unusually secure this evening, Mr Holmes," she said. "And having you and Dr Watson escort me in also quite out of the ordinary."

"We are merely being overly cautious, Ma'am."

She gave me a look such as a governess might bestow upon a naughty child, but said no more. We entered the Gothic dining room and took our seats.

For an hour we dined in regimented fashion. Every course was served at precisely the right moment. Oh how wearying it was. Watson, I could see, was bitterly disappointed in the food. I myself did not eat more than a mouthful, but I knew from past experience that the taste, temperature and quantities of the meal would be unsatisfying in every respect.

We had just finished the fish course when a cry came up that there was a fire in St George's chapel.

"I ordered the chapel locked," Lorne cried. He sprang to his feet and belatedly apologised to the queen.

"Go at once," the queen said. "The chapel must be preserved at all costs."

Half the room emptied. Mycroft stayed where he was, as did Watson and I.

"You know something about this business, Mr Holmes," the queen said. "Perhaps it is time you shared your information with me."

A BIASED JUDGEMENT

My brother said, "Please do not be alarmed, Ma'am, but we have information that there might be an attempt made against your life this evening."

The ladies, lords and princes who remained at the table all began to talk at once. The queen chinked her water glass with her fork, and silence fell.

"This fire is an attempt to divert attention from the dining room," I said. "The idea is that the would-be assassin will be able to slip in and out without being noticed."

There were more squeal and shouts from the assembled guests.

"Perhaps we should dismiss our guests?" the queen said.

"No, ma'am," I replied. "If you will forgive me, that is precisely what the killer is hoping for. Better to continue with the meal, surrounded by people you know and trust. The army and Lord Lorne's men can handle the fire. Dr Watson and I will speak to your safety. As will my brother," I added, as an afterthought. Mycroft gave me a somewhat peevish look, but there was no malice in it.

And so we sat and forced ourselves to dine upon an indifferent meal in the company of cranky and frightened guests.

Watson asked the queen about the sapphire brooch she wore. "It was a gift from your late husband, was it not?" he said.

"Yes, a wedding gift," the queen replied, touching the large oval stone. "My dear Albert gave it to me the day before our wedding. I wore it on my wedding gown."

She and my friend went on to discuss the day of her wedding and I was pleased to see the queen distracted from the anxiety of the moment. There is no doubt she remained distressed but I flatter myself she had faith in my ability to protect her.

By the time the dessert was brought in the atmosphere in the room had calmed slightly. The queen was still talking about the late Prince Consort and Watson continued to distract her with his questions observations.

A BIASED JUDGEMENT

"You would have liked him very much, Doctor," the queen said. "He was the wisest, kindest, and most devoted of husbands. You know, you rather remind me of him."

The footmen stepped forward to serve the dessert to each guest. They were as precise as an army. The young man who leaned forward to serve the queen was, I noticed, two inches shorter than he had been. And just behind his left ear I observed a brown splodge.

I leaped to my feet and grabbed his wrists.

"Watson," I cried. "Search him for a blade."

It was in his sleeve. A stiletto so thin as to be hardly more than a barber's razor, but twice as sharp. If he had plunged that into the queen's side she might not even have noticed it at once, and he could be out of the room and gone long before the fatal hurt was realised.

The dining room was a riot of screams and confusion.

"Sit down and be silent!" Mycroft roared. They instantly obeyed him.

Lord Lorne came flying into the room and stood in bewilderment.

"Is this the man?" he said. "But you said his hair was white, Mr Holmes..."

"And so it is. Hair dye, you see? That spot on your ear was enough to give you away, Travis."

"Sherlock Holmes," the Albino hissed. "How did you know I'd be here?"

"You can thank your friend Albrecht Porlock," I said. "He and the rest of his rabble are under arrest. You shall all keep the hangman very busy for the next month or so, I think."

"This job was a bad lot from the start," he said. "I told Porlock, but he said if Germany is to ascend England must fall. But things went badly almost at once. This job was never even meant for me. Some blasted Englishman was meant to poison a dish of cherries... I was only supposed to act if his nerve failed. Englishmen do not do assassination well, Mr Holmes. I mean no offense."

Watson snorted.

A BIASED JUDGEMENT

28

December 12th 1897

I have been fairly exhausted after the events of the past few months and Watson confined me to my bed. Secure in the knowledge that the Queen and the Empire are safe, for now, anyway, I slept, and then I slept some more. Now and then I woke and took some food and drink or tobacco. Each time I woke my eye fell on the gem upon my dresser: a diamond ring, a gift from a grateful monarch.

"We are fortunate to have so remarkable a man as you in our service, Mr Holmes," the queen said when she gave it to me.

"I did not work alone, ma'am," I said. "There are others who deserve your commendation far more than I."

"What, has married life made you humble, Holmes?" said the Prince of Wales. "All down to the power of love, eh, eh?"

Watson was given a fine set of sapphire cufflinks. "A reminder of our conversation about dear Albert," the queen said. For one ghastly moment I thought my friend was about to weep. He held himself together in proper military style, however, and merely bowed and said thank you.

He has worn them every day since. They flashed in the light this morning when he shook me awake.

"Watson? What is it? Am I needed?"

"Your wife just arrived, Holmes," he said. "It's bad news, I'm afraid."

A BIASED JUDGEMENT

I flung on my dressing gown and hurried into the living room. Beatrice stood at the window leaning on a cane. She did not look at me but simply handed me a letter.

Dear Madam, it read,

I regret to inform you of the deaths of your aunt, Lady Summerville, her husband and his brother. Their bodies were discovered this morning by the agent who was sent to follow up on the non-payment of the rent on their cottage where they were staying. All three had died of a gunshot wound to the head. The lady was, alas, about five months pregnant. The victims had been dead at least two weeks.

Please let me know what disposition you wish us to make for the remains. Sincerely, Marcel du Place, Royal Canadian Police.

"Porlock," I said. "He told me he was glad he had hurt me... I can only imagine this is what he meant. Perrot is behind this, I'll warrant. I shall cable the Canadian authorities..."

Watson shook his head at me and I realised I should not burden my wife with such things.

"What sort of a monster murders a pregnant woman?" Watson said.

Beatrice shook her head. She was still pale and, I thought, suffering from her recent wounds. I urged her to sit down and she sank into the armchair in a state of utter dejection. There were no tears, however. She has remarkable strength. Her only concession to grief was to hold my hand tightly.

December 25th, 1897

Watson and I spent Christmas with Beatrice at Wimpole Street. She invited Mycroft too and, to my very great surprise, he accepted and arrived a few minutes before dinner was served.

Stevens and Daisy served at the table, for what must be almost the last time. At the beginning of the year he starts his new career with the Metropolitan Police. Daisy will be moving into the Green Thistle Inn to work for Miss Simms and Mr Davenport after they are married, at least until she is married herself.

A BIASED JUDGEMENT

That is two weddings I shall be obliged to attend in the next few months.

Beatrice has been at pains to see that the Rillington Manor staff are paid up to date and have been given references, all except Reynolds who seems to have vanished.

After an excellent meal – Mycroft said, with some justification, that we dined far better than royalty – Beatrice played Mozart on the pianoforte.

I was pleased to see my brother and friend were as impressed by my wife's talent as I. Though I can think of no reason why they should not have been, nor why it should matter to me in the slightest.

"That is a splendid set of cufflinks, Doctor," Mycroft said. "The queen was well taken with you. She has spoken since about how her husband would have enjoyed your stories of my brother's exploits."

"Exploits!" I scoffed.

"You must forgive your husband, my dear sister," Mycroft said. "I fear he is still vexed that the queen honoured him and not you."

"Poor Sherlock," my wife said, laughing. "To have all the glory and none of the notoriety. But see what an exquisite ring he has given me." The gem sparked rainbow colours in the candlelight.

"I never before appreciated how vexing a thing it is to be a woman," I said. "Were you a man, you would have been given the honours that are properly yours."

"A wife is an extension of her husband, is she not?" she teased. "Therefore all honour that comes to you comes to me as well."

Oh how well she knows how to mock me.

Stevens brought around the carriage. While Watson and Mycroft waited, I said goodnight to my wife.

"I am thinking of going to Italy," I said. 'Now the last of that gang has faced the noose. A month wandering around the art galleries, attending the symphony, perhaps a visit with the pope… it is a splendid cure for these dark winter nights."

A BIASED JUDGEMENT

She said, "It sounds splendid. When will you go?"

"We," I said. "I thought you might come with me. A honeymoon, if you will. It is the custom, is it not? To take honeymoons."

"Well, not in the plural as a rule," she said. "But Italy… I've never been and I've always wanted to see it."

"I know. You told me once."

"Really? You don't mind there being just the two of us?"

"I realise such things are not in our contract," I said, smiling. "But perhaps we might…"

"Try something new?" She gently rested her fingers against my cheek. "I would like that, Sherlock."

I brought her hand to my lips and said, "To something new."

EPILOGUE

Jack closed the journal, stretched, and drew back the curtains. They blinked in the sharp daylight.

"Everyone still awake? Everyone still alive?"

"If that's a crack about my age, young man, you're not too old for a spanking," John said.

"It's incredible," Harry said. "What a find. Thank you, Lucy."

Jack coughed.

"Thank you too, son," Harry said, rolling his eyes.

"We have our work cut out for us, getting through those documents," John said. "There must be a hundred journals in there…"

"Not to mention letters, photographs and other memorabilia," Arthur said. "Mother's diaries are there, too. I spotted her handwriting."

"They're a national treasure," Lucy said. She yawned and eased herself up off the floor. "Can you imagine the reaction when people discover Sherlock Holmes really lived?"

"We've kept him, his notoriety, a secret all this time," Arthur said. "I'm inclined to let it stay that way."

"He was never a man to look for fame," John said. "But I think we should see what we have before we make any decisions. This is your legacy, Jack. Ultimately, it will be your decision."

"I'll go and make breakfast," Lucy said. With her hand on the door she stopped and said, "There's only one thing I really want to know. Were they happy?"

John and Arthur exchanged a look and smiled. They said, "Exquisitely."

A BIASED JUDGEMENT

Acknowledgements

This book would not exist without Sir Arthur Conan Doyle's extraordinary creation of Sherlock Holmes, nor without the readers, publishers, editors and filmmakers who keep him alive.

I would like to thank to my daughter Cara and her partner Chris for their unfailing support, and my family and friends for their encouragement.

A big thank you to the ladies on the IMDb discussion boards, many of whom were first readers of my manuscript. Also, to the loppies for their years of friendship, concerts, and far too much red wine. Assuming one can have too much red wine.

A special thank you to Jane and Sherrill who read endless drafts of the manuscript, gave tough feedback and encouragement as needed, and were unfailingly enthusiastic about the book.

Thanks to Alice for her great job editing my manuscript.

Finally, to Sherlock Holmes fans everywhere: I'll see you in the bookshop.

About The Author

Geri Schear has worked for the Dublin Theatre Festival, several Dublin theatres including the Olympia and the Gaiety, and in an operating theatre in London. She has been a nurse, a sales clerk, a hospital administrator and a teacher. Primarily, though, she is a novelist and short story writer.

She is passionate about Sherlock Holmes, Richard the Third, books, history, and musical theatre.

Ms Schear was born in Dublin but spent most of her early childhood in London. She has also lived in Jerusalem and in Ohio.

Her first novel Shakespeare's Tree was a winner of the Irish Writers' Novel Fair in 2012. Her short stories have appeared in a number of literary journals in the US and in Ireland.

A Biased Judgement is her first published novel and she is currently working on a sequel.

She lives in Kells, Co. Meath.

Also from MX Publishing

MX Publishing is the world's largest specialist Sherlock Holmes publisher, with over a hundred titles and fifty authors creating the latest in Sherlock Holmes fiction and non-fiction.

From traditional short stories and novels to travel guides and quiz books, MX Publishing cater for all Holmes fans.

The collection includes leading titles such as *Benedict Cumberbatch In Transition* and *The Norwood Author* which won the 2011 Howlett Award (Sherlock Holmes Book of the Year).

MX Publishing also has one of the largest communities of Holmes fans on Facebook with regular contributions from dozens of authors.

www.mxpublishing.com

A BIASED JUDGEMENT

Also from MX Publishing

Sherlock Holmes Short Story Collections

Sherlock Holmes and the Murder at the Savoy

Sherlock Holmes and the Skull of Kohada Koheiji

Look out for the new novel from Mike Hogan
– *The Scottish Question.*

www.mxpublishing.com

Also from MX Publishing

Our bestselling books are our short story collections;

'Lost Stories of Sherlock Holmes', 'The Outstanding Mysteries of Sherlock Holmes', The Papers of Sherlock Holmes Volume 1 and 2, 'Untold Adventures of Sherlock Holmes' (and the sequel 'Studies in Legacy) and 'Sherlock Holmes in Pursuit', 'The Cotswold Werewolf and Other Stories of Sherlock Holmes' – and many more……

www.mxpublishing.com

A BIASED JUDGEMENT

Also From MX Publishing

THE AMATEUR EXECUTIONER
DAN ANDRIACCO
KIERAN MCMULLEN

London, 1920: Boston-bred Enoch Hale, working as a reporter for the Central News Syndicate, arrives on the scene shortly after a music hall escape artist is found hanging from the ceiling in his dressing room. What at first appears to be a suicide turns out to be murder.

Also coming in 2014 the second in the Enoch Hale series – 'The Poisoned Penman'.

www.mxpublishing.com

Also from MX Publishing

"Phil Growick's, 'The Secret Journal of Dr Watson', is an adventure which takes place in the latter part of Holmes and Watson's lives. They are entrusted by HM Government (although not officially) and the King no less to undertake a rescue mission to save the Romanovs, Russia's Royal family from a grisly end at the hand of the Bolsheviks. There is a wealth of detail in the story but not so much as would detract us from the enjoyment of the story. Espionage, counter-espionage, the ace of spies himself, double-agents, double-crossers...all these flit across the pages in a realistic and exciting way. All the characters are extremely well-drawn and Mr Growick, most importantly, does not falter with a very good ear for Holmesian dialogue indeed. Highly recommended. A five-star effort."
The Baker Street Society

www.mxpublishing.com

Also from MX Publishing

Close To Holmes

A Look at the Connections Between Historical London, Sherlock Holmes and Sir Arthur Conan Doyle.

Eliminate The Impossible

An Examination of the World of Sherlock Holmes on Page and Screen.

The Norwood Author

Arthur Conan Doyle and the Norwood Years (1891 - 1894). Winner of the 2011 Howlett Literary Award – Sherlock Holmes book of the year.

Also From MX Publishing

Watsons Afghan Adventure

Fascinating biography of Watson's time in Afghanistan from US Army veteran Kieran McMullen.

Shadowfall

Sherlock Holmes, ancient relics and demons and mystic characters. A supernatural Holmes pastiche.

Official Papers of The Hound of The Baskervilles

Very unusual collection of the original police papers from The Hound case.

A BIASED JUDGEMENT

Also From MX Publishing

The Sign of Fear

The first adventure of the 'female Sherlock Holmes'. A delightful fun adventure with your favourite supporting Holmes characters.

A Study in Crimson

The second adventure of the 'female Sherlock Holmes' with a host of sub-plots and new characters joining Watson and Fanshaw

The Chronology of Arthur Conan Doyle

The definitive chronology used by historians and libraries worldwide.

Links

MX Publishing are proud to support the Save Undershaw campaign – the campaign to save and restore Sir Arthur Conan Doyle's former home. Undershaw is where he brought Sherlock Holmes back to life, and should be preserved for future generations of Holmes fans.

SaveUndershaw
www.saveundershaw.com

Sherlockology
www.sherlockology.com

MX Publishing
www.mxpublishing.com

You can read more about Sir Arthur Conan Doyle and Undershaw in Alistair Duncan's book (share of royalties to the Undershaw Preservation Trust) – *An Entirely New Country* and in the amazing compilations *Sherlock's Home – The Empty House* and the new book *Two, To One, Be* (all royalties to the Trust).